KU-850-334

THE BUTCHER'S
DAUGHTER

VICTORIA
GLENDINNING

DUCKWORTH

This edition first published in the United Kingdom by Duckworth in 2019

Duckworth, an imprint of Prelude Books Ltd
13 Carrington Road, Richmond TW10 5AA
United Kingdom
www.preludebooks.co.uk

For bulk and special sales please contact
info@preludebooks.co.uk

© 2018 Victoria Glendinning

All rights reserved. No part of this publication may be reproduced,
stored in a retrieval system, or transmitted, in any form or by
any means electronic, mechanical, photocopying, recording or
otherwise, without the prior permission of the publisher.

The right of Victoria Glendinning to be identified as the
Author of this Work has been asserted by him in accordance
with the Copyright, Designs and Patents Act 1988.

A catalogue record for this book is available from the British Library

Text design and typesetting by Tetragon
Printed and bound in Great Britain by Clays

9780715652923

For my three granddaughters
Teddy, Sasha, Ursula

'With the dissolution of the monasteries,
the nuns were cast adrift'

CATHOLIC ENCYCLOPEDIA,
1913 EDITION

I

BRUTON

The destroyers straggled in through the gatehouse of Shaftesbury Abbey around noon on Passion Sunday. About twenty-five of them, stocky, short-legged and short-armed, with heavy boots and leather gloves, their caps pulled down over their ears and eyes. I and those of us who still remained fluttered around, unable to keep away. The men did not look at us and I did not recognise any of them. They were not local.

Master Thomas Tregonwell was there to receive them. Of course he was, he would be. He directed them to the stacks of tools and equipment which had been dumped in the yard yesterday – ladders, axes, shovels, mallets, hammers, pickaxes, iron bars, coils of rope, pulleys, a treadmill.

'Start with the church, as usual,' he barked at the foreman, a thick-set oaf of a man. 'Not the first one you come to, forget that, go for the big one, the Abbey Church. Take the roof down. Preserve the lead. Same with the windows. If you can save some of the painted glass, so much the better. That will probably be enough for one day. Keep the men in order, no looting.'

After that, he said, they could start on the cloister.

Then came the first of the shoutings and thuds, the crashings and clangings which filled our ears for the next weeks. We were instructed by the foreman to keep our distance. Stones and timbers would be falling all over the place.

The simple-minded sister who scoured the pots, scuttling past on her way to the kitchens as she did every morning of her life, humming to herself, was struck on the head by a gargoyle and fell down dead. We crossed ourselves. Perhaps it was God's mercy. What would have become of her, otherwise? We could not help laughing, just a little. We laughed at anything we could, we laughed at all the wrong things.

Dorothy Clausey and I walked together round the cloister. It was the first perfect spring day after the extreme cold we had suffered up until now. The cloister garden was thick with primroses. The snowdrops were almost finished, except for those in the shade of the rose bushes. The snowdrops had been magnificent this year, their drooped white heads lolling. At the Abbess's command, I had been weeding the cracks between the flagstones. The cloister, in the eternal moments before its destruction, has looked as peaceful and as lovely as it can ever have looked in all its hundreds of years.

Afterwards, we two walked to the edge of the ridge and looked down over the Abbey Park. The low sun shone in our eyes. In the Park the whitethorn had sprung into bloom overnight, scattering snowflakes over bare branches. We watched spotted deer stepping between the copses. A loaded cart was struggling up the curving track from the village below. It was the cart with the wobbling wheel, so the going was hard. The wheelwright and his apprentice had already left. No one now would be mending that wheel.

I wanted to give Dorothy something to remember me by. Not my emerald dolphin, oh no. I pulled off my green hood and gave it to her. It was part of my girlhood. I like to think of her wearing it. She put it on over her headcloth, smiled at me and thanked me.

The destroyers quit their labours at daylight end. By then the precinct was littered with sawn-off roof beams, loose piles of hands and heads of saints. We picked our way among them as darkness fell. Some of the workmen left the Abbey, I suppose to lodgings in the town. Others slept in the open, rolled up in blankets close to the fires onto which they had thrown broken-up pews from the choir. They must have been cold, but I felt no pity.

And yet they have mothers, and maybe wives whom they love, and little children, and they had to earn a living. Who is to blame? Who is to blame?

I spoke to one of them, who was standing on the edge of the circle round the fire scratching his crotch. I could not help myself.

'Do you understand, just a little, that this is a holy place?'

'Fuck off,' he said.

When it was properly dark, I went alone into the Abbey Church. I saw jagged broken walls, the painted surfaces in shreds and fragments. I saw stars and a half-moon where the vaulted roof had been. I saw fallen stones and lumps of masonry everywhere, and was half-choked by dust. That heap of splintered woodwork in the nave was the rood-screen. The Virgin Mary still stood on her plinth, but her face and the Holy Child's were smashed in. I hoped the two ancient nuns who stood together, day after day, in mute adoration of her, had not seen this.

The bulky figure of Father Pomfret loomed beside me. I turned and saw that we were not alone. Half a dozen of my sisters were behind us, standing motionless and apart as if no one else were there, black figures between pillars which supported nothing.

The falling masonry had unseated and cracked most of the floor tiles in the nave. I picked up an unbroken one and carried it away. The fired earth of my tile is painted with a yellow lion, at least I believe him to be a lion, with his tufted tail curled high over his back. I still have my lion.

Later I lay on my back on my bed in the dorter. Tomorrow, or the day after, the dorter would have no roof. It was almost deserted, so many of my sisters had already gone.

I did not sleep. The unthinkable was happening. In the times to come this 'unthinkable' of ours will be unthinkable in a different way. Because it will be not much thought about at all. There will always be new horrors and new calamities, and new opportunities. For my great-grandchildren, should I have any, this will be history. That is, if they have any knowledge of why the land in which they live is as it is.

It might not have happened at all, There might have been a voice in some great chamber as darkness fell crying out 'No!', and all heads turning, and a candle lit, and wine poured, and a different outcome. Who is to blame? Spin the coin.

But in the eternal moment it was happening to us, it was the End of Days. History is now and England. And it will always be happening, over and over and over again for always and ever. For you to understand the enormity, the desecration, the grief, I have to go back, to before the bitter spring of 1539.

'Forgive me, Father, for I have sinned.'

'In what ways, my child?'

'I have been impure.'

'You have been impure.'

My eyes were closed. I did not want to look at Father Pomfret. I heard him shifting his rump in the chair. I pulled my veil across my face even though the light was dim in this corner of the Abbey Church. I knelt facing him and wished there were something, a desk or a prie-dieu, between us.

'Impure – in thought, word or deed?'

'In thought.'

'And what are your thoughts, my child?' His hot hoarse voice.

'I think about a young man I used to know at home.'

'And what exactly do you think?'

'I cannot explain, Father.'

How could I tell this priest, who was too interested, that I permitted myself no carnal thoughts about Peter Mompesson, but that I saw him in my mind's eye and imagined in the night when I could not sleep that we were running to meet one another with gladness and open arms. Just that, over and over and over, and the gladness made me weep. I thought about the child too. Sadness like a stone.

'You are aware that to obtain absolution, you must make a full confession.'

'Maybe I am mistaken, Father, and there is nothing to confess. It is but a scruple.'

To change the subject, I confessed that I had taken bread from the kitchen to give to the little boys, and that I entertained uncharitable thoughts about the Novice Mistress and one of my sisters, whom I did not name, but it was Eleanor Wilmer. Father Pomfret gave me absolution and a penance of multiple Hail Marys, disproportionate to the sins I confessed. I knelt in the chancel and said the Hail Marys, feeling angry with myself and with him. And afraid of God.

I will set down what happened to us after that calamitous Passion Sunday in Shaftesbury. The same horrors happened in all the abbeys and convents and priories and monasteries, all over England, and everything is recorded in formal words and in high places. But no one has understood what it felt like to be us, the ones cast adrift, or how we felt ashamed, even though we had no reason to be ashamed. My own shame, and the reason why I was a novice in Shaftesbury Abbey, came about earlier, when I was fifteen.

I wanted to be with him. I cannot pretend I did not. I had noticed him before. He had been in the town all that particular market day, up and down the High Street, poking at pigs and cattle with his stick, hanging about at the new market cross just down the road from our shop in the shambles. He was lounging around on the stone blocks and bits of carving which were waiting for the masons to top it out. The market cross was a gift to the town from Abbot Eley, for market-people to shelter from the weather. It was nearly finished. The base with steps was there, and the six arches, but no canopy. The steps, and the loose cut-stones lying around, were handy for sitting on.

Dark curly hair sprouting under his cap. Skinny legs. A cocky way of looking around him. I was serving customers with cuts of meat all day and was bloodied all over.

It was dusk before he came and stood in front of our shop. My father had put up the shutters and gone inside. I had cleaned myself. It was June, the light fading slowly. I listened to Bruton emptying out, men and boys hollering as they drove beasts out of the town, carts rumbling away up the hills.

'Agnes Peppin, will you walk with me?' he said.

We went down by the river. On the other side, St Mary's Church loomed huge and dark. The lantern on the gatehouse of the Abbey was already lit. The bell for Compline had rung two hours ago. The grass along the river bank was trampled and fouled by beasts coming down to drink during the day. When we came to a clean patch under the plum trees he put his arms round me and pushed me down on the ground. I have said I wanted to be with him, but truly I did not want what happened. He was quite rough.

Afterwards he was soft with me, and we whispered together in the dusk. He asked me to be his sweetheart and go only with him and I said yes. It felt natural to say yes. It was what I wanted, then.

Then he had to leave me. There was no moon and he might miss the path back to Brewham once the night came down. He ran off back towards the bridge. I rolled over and buried my face in the long grass. It was cool and smelled good. I didn't want to move. Which was just as well, because I heard voices, and people approaching. It was Abbot Eley and one of the canons, I could not tell who, taking an evening walk. They were deep in conversation and did not see me huddled under the trees.

'My dear, this has been going on since I was a young man, since the great Cardinal's time. There is nothing new. There was agitation about what they called a reformation of the Church back in King Stephen's day. Nowadays it is a faction, got up by heretics from Europe. And by our King's lust and avarice, though I would never say that in public, and neither for Christ's sake and ours must you.'

'So there is nothing to worry about?'

'There is always something to worry about. They tell me now that Stavordale Priory is to be placed under authority.'

'Stavordale – half a dozen sickly canons who do nothing.'

'Correct. But Stavordale is only a short hour's ride away. We are under scrutiny. It may become as dangerous to be prosperous as to be failing. His anointed Majesty has designs on what we have. However, I am perfectly confident that we will come through.'

When I could no longer hear their voices I sat up. I knew more or less what they were talking about, though I did not know who the great Cardinal was. It had been announced in St Mary's that King Henry, and not the Pope in Rome, was head of the Church in England. What difference did that make to ordinary people like my family? None.

If the Abbey had something to worry about, so now did I. The weight of worry is the same whatever the issue. I was sore and sticky between my legs, and wiped myself on dock leaves.

'Peter Mompesson,' said my mother, sitting on her stool, stiff as a rod. 'I've been watching him. An uppish lad. A difficult family. They have come down in the world. Over in Brewham. A pity it has to be him.'

'That young man's granddad did me wrong before you were born,' said my father. 'Landed me with a dozen diseased cattle. I had the stinking carcasses loaded on a wagon and drove up to his place in the night and tipped the lot on his yard. Then he slandered me over what he said was an ill-cured side of bacon, which I swear was as sweet as honey. He lost me custom. We don't do business with anyone in that family. We don't ever speak to them.'

'What are we going to do with you now?' said my mother. 'You have disgraced us.'

My mother does not help with the butchering, or wash clothes. Our shifts and shirts are scoured from time to time by a little maid from a big family who is glad enough to be paid with a dinner. My father sees to it that we eat well. When he works on the couple of strips he has up on the Borough Field for our peas and beans, he brings back a handful of green stuff and throws it all into the pottage to soften along with scraps of meat from the shop. It is much better than anything the little laundress would have at home.

My mother had not looked after me when I was little. I looked after myself. She is pale and fleshless, and beautiful. I can see that. There was something wrong with her, my father said.

'She is not like other people.'

That was all he would say. He cared for her as if she were a holy thing. I am their only child. I know some people in the town who have no children, but I know no other couple who have only one. She wound her headcloth round her nose and mouth. She could not endure the smell of blood.

Yet she had given me to myself by telling me what I was like. When I was younger, I asked her, 'What colour are my eyes?'

'Blue, like your father's.'

That pleased me.

'And you are well-made.'

I knew that. I did not have one leg shorter than the other, or a bent spine, or a birthmark or scabby skin, or one eye which did not open, like some girls in Bruton. I knew my hair was brown because it was long enough for me to pull forwards and chew the ends. My mother said that if I swallowed my hair it would wind itself into a ball round my heart and I would die.

'You have an agreeable appearance, more agreeable than your nature. You have a good intelligence but you are pert, wilful and impatient.'

So be it. That is what I am like.

The one important thing my mother does is to lay out the dead. They knock on our door at any hour of the day or night: 'Mistress Dorothy! Mistress Dorothy!' Ever since I was about ten years old she has taken me with her. I carry her basket. I watch her cleaning up whatever nastiness has to be cleaned up, and arranging the corpse, and stuffing sweet herbs in the mouth and nose and up the backside. We always have with us in the basket a needle and thread and a piece of new cloth for a shroud. My mother buys the cloth cheap in the market when there is some fault in the weave. If the family cannot pay her for the cloth, my mother stitches something together from their own raggy shirts. She is deft. While she prepares the bodies for their burial, she sings to them – and to herself – the birdy little songs she learned as a child, always same ones. She never sang them to me, never just for me. I learned them anyway.

Father always asks, as soon as she comes home, what old Mistress Mary or young Master Thomas or whoever it might be had died from. She just shrugs.

'People do die.'

Sometimes there is something she can tell him. A lump, she will say, indicating on her own body where the lump was. Or a fever. A chill. Fits. Apoplexy. A witch's spell. Bleeding after childbirth, and the child stillborn. A poisoned wound. Hunger, and the bloody flux. But mostly they just die. Who knows?

My father wants to know because his Granny Peppin, who lived to a great age, terrified him when he was a little boy with stories of the Plague which had been told to her long ago when she herself was young. Granny Peppin had remembered too much and all of it horrible. Yet if no one told the old stories, there would only be now, and everything would be happening as if for the first time. Not that it would make much difference, as it is always the first time, when you are young and it happens to you.

'No,' my mother always said to him, 'it is not the Plague. Do not distress yourself.'

That evening when I told them what had happened with Peter I sat on the ground and cried. I had never pleased my mother and now I was a disgrace. She hit me about the arms and legs with the broomstick. She sometimes does that. It is no good trying to run from the beatings, because where would I go?

When she had satisfied herself my father moved the rushlight so that he would not knock it over and opened his hairy arms to me. I scrambled on to his lap, breathing in his reek, and he rocked me in an absent-minded way. He gave me a piece of bread, unrolled my mattress, laid me upon it and put the blanket over me. Still in my soiled shift, my bruises paining me, I fell asleep.

I saw Peter Mompesson only once more, in November. He sent a message through my friend Jeanne that he would meet me the day after Martinmas, an hour before sunset. I was to follow the river upstream past Batt's Farm, and he would be waiting in the woods on the other side. I already knew that I was carrying a child. I had not bled since I was with him. My mother said it was not yet certain and that it any case many first pregnancies came to nothing. But blue veins were standing out in my breasts and there were other signs. I was fearful.

I decided to say nothing about this to Peter. My heart beat and my gut flickered at the thought of seeing him again. It was a fine evening. I put on my cloak and my green hood and slipped out without telling my mother or father. Because of slaughtering and hanging the Martinmas beef, everyone in our row was busy.

Dogs barked as I passed the farm, and then I saw him far off through the trees. He could not see me because the low sun was shining straight into his eyes. I ran towards him and he saw me and began running too, and we met in a flurry of outstretched arms, swinging round together, and slipping and falling.

We talked and loved until the sun had gone down and it was dark in the wood. It was the happiest hour – a little more than an hour – of all my life. I will not put our promises to one another into new words. We said what we said, and we meant it, and for ever. It was a marriage even if the only witnesses were the birds in the trees.

Mother looked at me with her mouth tight. 'You need to take pennyroyal. And tansy and rue.'

No such herbs grow in our yard. She obtained what she wanted from the old dame on the backway behind our premises. Mother stewed the leaves up into a black liquid to make me bleed away what was growing inside me. I loathe the smell of rue, it is like cat's piss. I had to drink a cup of this stuff every day for a week. Nothing happened except that I vomited each time. Perhaps that was why the herbs did not work. After that my mother kept me in. She made me stay around the house and sheds during the daytime.

My mother laid off our little maidservant and put me to work. I brought in water, I kept the fire alive. I peeled reeds and rendered down mutton fat for rushlights. I shovelled up shit. I salted and soaked and packed chunks of beef and pork until my hands were raw. I scrubbed my father's leather aprons. I boiled up pig's blood for the black puddings and set it by the fire to solidify. My father prided himself on his black puddings. On market days, he sold as many as he made. Thomas Peppin's famous black puddings – delicious. Only my mother did not think so, and tightened her headcloth round her mouth and nose. The cluster-flies on the carcasses and on the walls and rafters of our two rooms were terrible that autumn. When I took down the shutters in the mornings, my fingers met gross new hatchings seething round the edges.

I was forbidden to get in touch with Peter and did not risk it. I did not want another beating from my mother. I did not want to be struck down by the Hand of God either. There is a painting on the wall in St Mary's of the Hand coming out of a cloud, with the thumb and two fingers pointing straight downwards, and the middle two curled up. You can see part of God's sleeve, banded with gold.

I walked out for air when it was getting dark and there was no one much about. When I was younger, before I learned butchery, I used to help out at the clothmaker's yard off Quaperlake Street, stretching the pieces tightly on the tenters to get rid of the creases. Jeanne Vile worked there too. She, my true friend from that former time, would come and sit with me now in the dusk on the steps of the new market cross. Jeanne is clever and she has beautiful rippling hair but one of her feet is turned inwards and she cannot walk fast.

The masons finished the canopy, with balustrades on top, and jars called urns on the corners. Inside, there were stone benches all round. One evening I sat in there alone. Jeanne did not come. I watched a stranger picking his way down Coombe Hill, carrying a satchel on his back. There were always pilgrims coming through on their way to Glastonbury, and travellers, and many strangers were visiting Bruton too at that time, to see the Abbot. This man walked on past me, down Patwell Street and over the bridge to St Mary's Church and the Abbey gatehouse – and then ten minutes later was back, with a book like a ledger in his hand. He sat down near me and began to scribble in his book. He was lean and weather-beaten with a big nose under a bulky cap. Not unhandsome.

He looked at me and began to talk. He told me he was John Leland, and he was a travelling scholar and a poet. He had walked that day through the woods and down the hill from Evercreech.

'Your Bruton lies in a bowl,' he said. 'The Great Forest all around you. But the Great Forest could not keep you safe from the Danes in times gone by. They arrived by sea.'

'I do not know about that. We say, the Forest keeps us warm from the east wind. There are tracks through it going into Wiltshire, it is easy to lose your way. The tracks split. There are wild families living in the Forest, and ogres and bad spirits in Pensel Wood. We do not like going that way.'

'There will be many ghosts in Pensel Wood. If you are quiet, you may overhear from the long-ago the clashing of steel and the cries of the slain. It has been a place of battles, even before your people tried to fight off King Cnut. That was a terrible time of fighting.'

'I do not know about that King.'

'You should. He was a Norseman and King of England for nearly twenty years and died not far from here, in Shaftesbury. More than five hundred years ago, no one will remember. The wood certainly makes it difficult to find you. I am making a record of all the places through which I pass. Your fine stone bridge, now – three spans, that is wide for a small stream.'

I told him about what I did know – about Bow Bridge only a few steps downriver, joining the Abbey to the town, just wide enough for a string of packhorses, and Legge's Bridge at the other end of town. I told him how Bruton was criss-crossed with streams and leets and culverts, and fords and ponds and footbridges, and how the Brue river rose when the rain was heavy and flooded the town.

It was perhaps not wise, then, he said, to have built those little tenements on the bridge. They would be washed away.

'But you are fortunate to have in plenty the two commodities that made life possible – water, and wood for firing and building.'

Master Leland was interested in the Abbot. He was going to call upon him, and inspect the Abbey Library. He showed me lists in his ledger of what he said were the titles of books, with descriptions.

'My work is to examine the libraries of the religious houses of England, and to note down everything rare or valuable. I have a personal commission from the King.'

'Why does the King want to know that?'

'His Majesty is a cultivated man. He takes an interest in these things, as I do. But I rather fear...'

He did not finish the sentence. He said, 'Knowledge of the whereabouts of antiquities and valuables is a boon for scholars. The use to which such knowledge may be put in the times that are coming is another matter altogether.'

This was the first time that I glimpsed the significance of lists – and of inventories and inspections and valuations – and sensed that there was something to be feared from them.

He asked me what was the general opinion of the Abbot, in the town. I told him the Abbot was well-liked.

'And the monks too?'

'They are called canons.'

'Any misbehaviour among the canons?'

Not at all, I told him, the canons are gentle, scholarly men.

'How many?'

'About seventeen, maybe.'

'A small community then. It may not last long.'

Two of the younger canons taught me and Jeanne Vile to read and write, in a dark little room off the vestry of St Mary's. Their names are John Harrold and Hugh Backwell, and they are scholars of Oxford. My mother did not oppose the idea, and father was in favour. He himself can calculate numbers, and mark the figures down, but he cannot write words, or read words.

Our teachers also taught Jeanne and me how to speak our words so that they might be understood by people who are not from hereabouts. I was trying to put that into practice with Master Leland, but he sometimes had to ask me to repeat. He said he was born and raised in London, and that London people would not understand me, nor I them.

'I have studied at Cambridge where, in order to understand one another, men find a middle way, or speak to one another in Latin.'

'I know what Latin sounds and looks like, but I do not know many of the words, or the grammar. But I can write and I can read.'

Master Leland looked at me sharply. He was astonished, I think.

I directed him up the High Street to the tavern, and had no further talk with him. A few days later I spotted him in the distance loping off out of the town in the rain, back the way he had come.

I asked my father what he knew about King Cnut.

'Never heard of him,' he said.

'He came here. He was a Norseman, from over the sea. I think they use different words.'

I had not told Master Leland everything about the Abbey. It is true that Abbot Eley is generally well-liked. He has not been here long. Father says John Eley is a new broom. Soon after he arrived, when I was about thirteen, he acquired a licence for us to have a great three-day fair on the feast of St George, in April.

Bruton goes crazy on those days. People appear like eels slithering down the steep paths through the woods from the villages and farms, the men with hooks to swipe at the brambles growing across the narrow ways. There is music and singing and stalls selling food and garments and cloths and trinkets and tools and pots and poultry, you can hardly walk up the High Street for the stalls and wagons and carts and packhorses and oxen. The inns are crammed, the drains overflow all over the roadways, the din is unbelievable, and after dark torches are lit and young men full of ale pull down their hose and their breeks and show what they have and chase the girls. Some like to be caught. Not me. The old folk complain, but St George's Fair does bring a lot of trade into the town. For that everyone is grateful to Abbot Eley.

There is one man in Bruton who hates the Abbot. John White worked at the Abbey in Abbot Gilbert's time, and the old Abbot paid him £10 a year, I've no idea for what. Then Abbot Gilbert died, and Abbot Eley was elected, and he did not see why he should go on paying £10 a year to John White. There was a bad quarrel. John White has not given up.

Another trouble is the Abbot's injustice to Tom Legat. Tom killed a man, a halfwit from Batcombe who appeared on a wet afternoon all hung about with rabbits which he had trapped on Creech Hill. He hoped to sell them but no one wanted them. Bruton and Batcombe never do get on at the best of times. Tom Legat was finishing off the market cross. The Batcombe fellow sat down and they exchanged jokes. Then Tom remarked that blood from the coneys and mud from the man's person were spoiling the new-cut stone, and bade the man remove himself. The man from Batcombe, taking this amiss, slashed at Tom's face with his knife, the same that he had used to gut the rabbits. Tom swung his great mallet and brought it down on the Batcombe man's head, smashing his skull.

The dogs licked up the brains spattered on the road. The dead body was sent back to Batcombe on a cart. Tom Legat was arrested. He was tried at the Court House and cleared of the charge of murder since he acted in self-defence. In any case, the Batcombe man was a known idiot. There it might have ended. Abbot Eley would not let it lie. He always has his own views on any matter and he let it be known that Tom Legat was in the wrong and should be punished. This defiance of the Court's ruling, like the business of Master White's annuity, was reported to London by our landed gentlemen. They were turning against the Abbot.

Abbot Eley is a difficult, principled man and he does make enemies. Everyone knows that. John White swears he will get his money and his revenge. He is large man of around forty years old who struts around the town with a band of lesser fellows. You would want to keep out of their way, especially at night. I am surprised to see that our canon Hugh Backwell sometimes keeps company with him. I think it is political, to do with dissensions within the Abbey, and between the Abbey and London.

Nor did I tell Master Leland that my friends John Harrold and Hugh Backwell are as close as brothers, yet not like brothers. When they walk out at dusk by the river they hold hands. The Abbey wall on the town side has buttresses built against it to support the stables on the other side. It is always dark on the narrow roadway there, because of the high wall and the gatehouse of the Free School opposite. It is common knowledge that John and Hugh lean together for many minutes in an angle between wall and buttress. As if two people become one. Anyone who passes by keeps their heads bowed. It is unlawful for canons to lie together, but everyone speculates that they do. It was because our two canons never pester the girls of the town that my parents were unworried about the lessons in the room off the vestry.

Once I learned to read, I read everything in English that I could lay my hands on. Hugh brought me books out of the Abbey Library. I wrote down the words which I did not understand and learned their meanings. I learned to recognise from their forms which words were really Latin and which were really French, even though I know no French or Latin. Hugh said I did, but that I did not know I did, because the French and the Latin were all mixed up with our words. He can speak French, the French of France as he says, not the garble used in this country.

John showed us a printed book, the first we had ever seen, called a Book of Hours, and we learned to read the words in that black lettering. Another day he brought out from where he had hidden it under his scapular a printed book which was the Bible in English, not in Latin.

'This is a secret. It was brought to me by a brother who had been in...' – ah, he named some foreign town, I no longer remember. 'We have had parts of the Gospels in English before, but nothing like this.'

John was flushed and excited. Hugh was nervous. He took the key from the other side of the door into the room where we worked, and locked it from the inside.

'That is stupid, Brother Hugh, my dear,' said John. 'They will think, if we are discovered, that we are molesting the girls.'

Hugh sat with his head sunk on to his chest while John read to us from the Bible in English the story of Christ in the house of Martha and Mary. We already knew the story, because there is a picture of it painted on the wall of St Mary's. Jesus is seated, and Mary is at his feet, looking up into his face. Martha is away to the side, looking towards them with an angry face, with a pile of pots and bowls beside her.

I am drawn to this story, and copied it out when I was in Shaftesbury Abbey. We had an English Bible there. In our last year, it was ordered that every church in the kingdom must have an English Bible – even though the translator had his head cut off, and even though a great man in London, Sir Thomas More, said it was heretical, and he had his head cut off too – either for that or for something else. Perhaps it was because he would not agree that the King, not the Pope, was the head of the church in England.

'Keep up, Agnes!'

As Hugh would say.

It was hard to keep up. I thought then that the confusing rule-changes were a boring matter of nit-picking and pedantry, were it not for the beheadings and burnings alive. And I did like the Bible in English and the story of Martha and Mary. It begins like this:

'It fortuned as they went that he entered into a certain town. And a certain woman named Martha received him into her house. And this woman had a sister called Mary which sat at Jesus' feet and heard his preachings. And Martha was cumbered about much serving and stood and said: "Master dost thou not care that my sister hath left me to minister alone? Bid her therefore that she helps me."'

Fair enough. But Jesus told Martha she was wrong. He told her that she was bothered about many things, whereas 'Verily only one is needful. Mary hath chosen that good part which should not be taken away from her.'

Jesus was unjust. Someone always has to prepare the food, and serve it, and clear it away, even though there will always be something else more interesting and enjoyable that she would prefer to be doing. That is how life is. That is *what* life is. Mary was selfish, sitting with Jesus, drinking in his words, leaving everything that had to be done to her sister.

Hugh and John insisted that nothing was more important than attending on the words of Jesus. Still, someone has to get the dinner and wash the pots. At home, I was Martha and did not like it. Though even if I had the courage to be Mary, there was no Jesus in Bruton at whose feet I might sit. Hugh and John did not quite qualify.

When my birth-pains began it was night. No one saw Mistress Dempster the midwife coming to our house. Mistress Dempster is quite young, her mother was a midwife before her. She has dark and warty skin and a crooning way of speaking. My father fetched her from her bothy up in the woods and then absented himself till morning.

Mistress Dempster brought Our Lady's Girdle with her. It was our most solemn relic, kept in a gold box in the Abbey chapel. I had never seen it, though I knew that pilgrims to Bruton Abbey had to pay to kneel in veneration before the gold box and receive blessings from Our Lady. It used, in olden times, to be lent to women heavy with child who had to go on a journey.

'I begged it from the Sacristan,' she said, 'just for the one night.'

It is a little shocking that the Sacristan allowed this. A sign of the times. Or maybe, as Jeanne believed, Mistress Dempster is a witch.

'You may be the next one to be going on a journey,' she said, 'from what I feel in my bones.'

She unwrapped the Girdle in the firelight. It was just a broad ribbon of thin red silk fading to brown, transparent.

'The King's own mother, they say, wore it for her lying-in. And I have been shown pictures,' said Mistress Dempster, 'where Our Lady is wearing it. She favours red.'

I touched the Girdle. The roughness of my fingers snagged on the frail stuff. She hung the Girdle from the high shelf where we keep our cooking pots, securing it with the foot of a skillet, so that I could see it from my mattress.

My baby is a boy. He is perfect. He was born, for the record, just before dawn in mid-February 1535. He lies in the bed with me, and I feed him, and talk to him, and touch him everywhere on his little body, and he is mine and I am his. I call him Peter. Peterkin.

After a month my mother wrapped him up and took him away. I feared she would. I did not ask her what she was going to do with him. Some of the answers she might give were so terrible that

I would not want to hear the words. Perhaps she was going to lay him down in the woods and leave him there.

She turned at the door and said, 'He is going where he ought to be. It has been arranged.'

She was too angry with me to tell me what was going to happen to my child.

'Tell them his name is Peterkin.'

It was Mistress Dempster who let me know that Peter Mompesson's sister lost her husband in a flood, and then their newborn child died, and she had breasts full of milk and much sorrow. I know the sister by sight, she looks healthy. My child was to become her child. She was living now with Peter and their father up in Brewham. My baby would be growing up under the eye of his own father, who would be also his uncle. My father had gone up to Brewham to make his peace with his old enemy's grandson for the sake of my child.

A farmhouse, full of light and warmth, and the voices and bright looks of Peter and his sister. Peterkin in a cradle by the hearth.

I too had breasts full of milk and they ached and leaked. I hid my face under my blanket and the stony feeling came into my heart, which is still there always. I was shut outside everything that I wanted. I was forbidden to see Peter. Being at home was an exile.

When my father told me I was going to be a nun in Shaftesbury Abbey, it was a relief of a dark sort. A gateway opening on to — I knew not what. I had no religious vocation. But it would be a new life in a new world. Above all, there would be books.

'But how can I go there? A girl like me? They only take in the well-born. Not the daughters of common people.'

I felt ashamed for implying that Thomas Peppin, my dear good father, was lowly born.

'You are well-born. Through your mother.'

Then he told how my mother's father, my grandfather, was a FitzJames, cousin to Sir John FitzJames of Redlynch – a big man in our parish and a big man in the great world. This cousin had sired the child who became my mother with his own stepsister. The little girl was fostered out with a Redlynch tenant farmer.

'I was stockman then at Redlynch. I saw your mother when she was fifteen. I knew what she was and I said I would marry her.'

He paused, and then:

'Agnes, your mother was lovely as a flower.'

Her father agreed, and set my father up in the butchery in Bruton on a lease from the Abbey on condition that he was never approached for money or for anything at all, ever again.

My mother's mother, afterwards, married a Hibberd. The Hibberds, said my father, are numerous around Tisbury, on the other side of the Forest, in Wiltshire.

'I never met her at the time. She was not interested in her little bastard.'

But after my baby was born, my father went to Tisbury and called upon her, and she proved not so hard-hearted. She paid a visit on my behalf to the Abbess of Shaftesbury, Dame Elizabeth Zouche, who was her distant kinswoman. Apparently the Abbess is often in Tisbury because Shaftesbury Abbey owns a big property there, Place Farm.

'Can this girl read?' the Lady Abbess asked my grandmother Hibberd. 'Can she sing in tune? Is she healthy? Is she well-made, not deformed or ill-favoured or an idiot? We cannot take in any more unfortunates.'

My father did not explain any of this easily. Short, broken sentences. Pauses, while he passed his big red hands over his face. At the end, sitting on the stool with his elbows on his knees, clasping and unclasping his hands, he looked straight at me.

'Now you know.'

All this time my mother had been lying on her mattress with her face averted. So intent was I on what my father was telling me, I had forgotten she was there, though it is her story more than mine.

She said, 'Does Agnes have to know all this?'

'Agnes has the right.'

I said that it seemed to me like a tale one might be told, a fairy story.

My mother sat up.

'There are stories like this,' she said, 'in every family, down all the years all the way back to the beginning. The tales people tell are about what has always happened. Misbegotten children hidden or abandoned or done away with. Especially girl children. Like me. Or growing up fortunate and marrying well – the fairy-tale ending. With something horrid added, a witch, or a beast, or a spell or a curse. Storytellers only half-know what happens. Like children.'

I never heard her say so much at one time before. Whatever it was that made my mother not like other people, she was not witless.

'Fairy tales,' said my mother, 'teach children what to be afraid of.'

'I do not think I am afraid of much. Maybe of something or someone pouncing out at me in the dark.'

My father grew impatient.

'Give her the – thing – that you have.'

My mother, groaning, got up off her bed and rummaged in the chest where we keep cheeses and spare cloths, scrabbling right down to the bottom, and brought out a small black bag. She threw it to my father. He stretched out an arm to catch it, and missed.

It fell at my feet where I sat on the ground. I pulled the draw-string apart and in the bag was a curved stone on a silver chain. I held it to the firelight. It was carved into some sort of fish, with a turned-up snout and a frill down its back. When I turned it between my fingers I saw that the underside was polished, and glinted deep green.

It was an emerald, my father said. An emerald dolphin.

'Don't you remember them carting in the new bell for the church? No, you were too young. That bell has a dolphin scratched on it, the dolphin is the FitzJameses' – there's a word for it – it means that there's a dolphin on everything that has anything to do with the FitzJameses.'

Emblem. The word he wanted is emblem. Or crest.

If my mother had been married off to a gentleman, I would have been somebody else. I would have been a gentlewoman. But I cannot wish that my father should be any other than he is.

'Your grandfather gave it to your mother on the day she rode away with me, to be married.'

He may have had some fond feelings after all, and wanted his child to know who she was.

I wore the dolphin on its chain round my neck under my clothes from that day onwards, even in Shaftesbury Abbey, until my enemy in that place tore it off me.

Jeanne and I returned to our lessons with the two young canons, and so heard more about what was going on than most people did. Hugh and John were consumed by events, and could not stop talking about Abbey affairs, often over our heads. So we knew that Our Lady's Girdle was taken, a short while after my mother took Peterkin away. It was purloined by one of the King's Commissioners, whose name was Dr Richard Layton.

Poor Abbot Eley announced this grievous happening from the pulpit of St Mary's. I was not there, but no one for a while talked of anything else – that is, until there was something else to talk about, which was that the King was taking a new wife, a Lady Anne Boleyn, while his wife Queen Catherine still lived. When we prayed now for the health of the Queen, the Abbot said, we must think of the Lady Anne and not of Queen Catherine. I was in the church on that occasion. His voice had no expression at all.

I did see Dr Layton on the day he arrived. He rode with two other gentlemen down the High Street. They greeted no one as they crossed the bridge to the Abbey, as if Bruton people were animals and did not require a greeting. The ridiculous thing was that a second King's Commissioner turned up later the same day, equally eager to take inventories of the gold and silver and to persuade the Abbot to make it all over to the King. This second Commissioner was called Dr Leigh. He was young and haughty and rude.

'He foully abused the Abbot – a man of God and old enough to be his father,' said Hugh Backwell, 'for not being present in the gatehouse to welcome him when he arrived. But the Abbot had no warning that he was coming.'

Hugh also witnessed an encounter between the two Commissioners in the Abbey cloister, with Dr Leigh poking Dr Layton in the chest and accusing him of interfering.

But Dr Layton had arrived there first. 'Go and boil your head!' he said to the other.

They came to blows. One of them might have been killed had both not remembered how much was at stake to their own advantage in the share-out. 'Greed brought them to their senses,' said Hugh.

The Abbot was impatient with pushy Dr Leigh. 'That means more letters of complaint about our Abbot being sent to London, and we know what was written in them.' The Abbot of Bruton was obstinate and difficult, the Commissioners reported, almost as obstinate and difficult as the Abbot of Glastonbury.

Dr Layton, it appears, called the Girdle, our holy relic, 'a quaint curiosity'.

'He sent it up to London to Master Thomas Cromwell himself.'

Hugh and John exchanged long meaningful glances but said no more to Jeanne and me about Thomas Cromwell. I had never heard that name mentioned before. Later I heard it all the time, as if he and not the King were in charge of all that happened.

I never did, in all the time to come, set eyes on the fellow.

The London people, said John, probably put less value on the Girdle than on the gold box in which it lay, now doubtless on Master Cromwell's writing table.

I was, then, the last woman in childbirth to benefit from its power.

In June, the month in which I left home, Bruton was full of whispers. I have to say that it always is. Which tradesman's business is failing, who has acquired a better strip on the town field, who is pregnant and by whom, which tenement is about to become available, who owns that neglected piece of sloping pasture at the top of St Catherine's Hill, what exactly Mistress White said about Mistress Green which has caused the husband of one to assault the husband of the other behind the White Hart, leaving him so much bleeding meat.

These whispers were different. The reason we no longer see the Abbot around the town, they said, was because he had been forbidden by the Commissioners to leave the Abbey precinct. Could that be so? His enemy John White was in jubilant mood. I saw him one night on the street, surrounded by his cronies, shaking his fist at the Abbey and shouting up at its walls:

'I'm coming to get you, Eley!' and then, 'Don't think you can escape what is coming to you!'

They were throwing stones against the gatehouse, which nowadays is kept closed and barred most of the time. I felt shocked and ran away.

I myself entered the precinct of Bruton Abbey for the first and only time shortly before I went away. My mother was called in the middle of the night to lay out an old canon. We went in through the wicket gate between St Mary's Church and the Abbey, the one through which Hugh and John passed when they came to give us our lessons. We were admitted by a lanky canon with shreds of red hair around his tonsure whom I did not know. He introduced himself as Richard Halford. He led us straight to a high chamber lined with beds which was the Infirmary, and where by the light of two rushlights we began our work upon the corpse of a small and shrivelled man, a dead elf.

Canon Richard Halford remained in the chamber, prowling about, keeping an eye on us, all the time that my mother worked on the elf. I passed her what she needed and brushed the bluebottles away. Bluebottles sense death from great distances. Within half an hour of a last breath the first bluebottle arrives, blundering its way through closed doors and shutters. They go for the face. That is why we pull a cover over the head at once, and not for any reasons of respect or propriety as many believe.

Canons came and went in the room while we worked, crossing themselves in deference to the dead elf, and speaking to Richard Halford in quiet urgent voices. I pricked up my ears. I am such an eavesdropper.

'Our father in God, our Abbot, is not sound. He puts us all in danger. I have received enquiries. What can I say? What answers can I give, when I am asked if I have heard him speak against the new Queen?'

That was Richard Halford.

Another voice: 'Abbot Eley is a man of God and his own man. He follows his conscience.'

'We each have a conscience. They do not lead all in the same direction. John White has a conscience, and a grievance, a dangerous combination. He has made accusations. John White would be happy to see the Abbot's head parted from his shoulders. In the times we are living in, each man must look to himself.'

'I have no doubt that you will, Brother Richard, no doubt at all.'

*

I travelled to Shaftesbury with my bundle of spare clothing on a cart, squashed between bales of wool. Jeanne came with me for company, and would travel back with the carter. We left during the night. It was dark and misty when my mother and father stood in the street outside our shop and kissed me goodbye. It was the longest journey I ever made and I slept most of the way, having been anxious and wakeful the whole night before.

I awoke at dawn, before we reached the town, and heard larks. We must have been passing through open fields then. The carter dropped us off in the market place. I have been in some of the villages near Bruton, but never in another town. Shaftesbury is much bigger and noisier with wagon traffic and shouting and swearing and dogs barking and children howling, and the roads thronged, as if it were a Fair Day every day.

The carter set us down in the market place. We had to ask the way to the Abbey. We followed a high wall and the backs of buildings along a street they called Bimport and came to the gatehouse, its entrance wide enough for wagons. It is like a real house, with rooms above and to the sides. I hugged Jeanne and said goodbye, and knocked at the smaller door set into the gate. And so I entered Shaftesbury Abbey.

2

SHAFTESBURY ABBEY

Shaftesbury Abbey is a town within a town. In my first days there I frequently lost my bearings. If I try to gauge its extent in terms of the fields and closes I know around Bruton, I would guess it covers about four acres. There is more Abbey property in the town, beyond the walls – an orchard, a farm, a school for girls called the Magdalen and, on the Market Place, the Broad Hall where nuns from the Abbey serve soup and bread to the poor, like an inn except that no one has to pay. The town, up on its high hill, is one great crossroads, with ways running steeply downwards in every direction.

Our home in Bruton is two rooms – one of them the shop – with earth floors and the midden outside the back door. At the Abbey there is space and light and air, even though it is so ancient. It was founded by King Alfred for his daughter hundreds of years ago. Another King gave the Abbey the village of Tisbury in Wiltshire, and another gave the manor of Bradford, on the River Avon. That is only the beginning of the long list of the Abbey's lands and manors, mills, forests, fisheries, and God knows what else. There are special words for everything here, and these are the Abbey's 'temporalities'. They are managed for profit. Hugh and John told me some of this when I went to say goodbye. They were impressed that I was going to Shaftesbury Abbey: 'Rolling in money.'

What are called the Abbey's 'spiritualities' are the rights to collect tithes and appoint parish priests. These too bring income to the Abbey. So not very spiritual at all.

Once there were a hundred and twenty nuns living here. Including myself, there are now only fifty-seven. The special word for the senior nuns is 'Obedientiaries'. They hold named positions with particular responsibilities – the Cellaress, the Chambress, the Infirmaress, the Sacrist – and the Prioress, who is the most important nun after the Abbess. Since the Abbess is often away, and has so much business to see to, the day-to-day running of the place is overseen by the Prioress.

I was told all this as I was walked round the Abbey by Sister Mary Amor, who was kind to me in a brisk sort of way. I did not take it all in as I pattered after her. 'Keep up, Agnes!' as Hugh would say.

On each side of the gatehouse and its entrance court, she showed me stores, hay barn and granary, built up against the boundary of the precinct, with small gates out on to Bimport. Near the wall separating the Abbey from Magdalen Lane, she pointed out the brewhouse. There are thatched tenements, freestanding as in a village, and a network of courts and yards for workshops, smithy, malthouse, laundry, bakehouse, stables, the offices of the Obedientiaries, the Steward's house.

'The Steward is the most important man in the Abbey, he is the Abbess's right hand,' said Sister Mary Amor.

On the right of the gatehouse is the Treasury and what they call the Star Chamber, where cases concerning leases and tenancies are settled. The novices' quarters are on this side too, and guesthouses for church and government officials. Pilgrims and vagrants are herded in a timber shed.

'Unfortunately,' said Mary Amor, 'the novices' dorter and parlour are in a shocking state of disrepair. Everyone, nun or novice, has to sleep nowadays in the main dorter. It was built in times long gone by, when there were more sisters than we have now, so there is plenty of room.'

I had thought that this would be a world of women, but in and around the yards and courts there is continual noise and shouting from men making and mending, hammering and sawing, carting and unloading, and visitors on horseback clattering in through the gatehouse – and nuns flittering about trying to complete some chore before the bell rings yet again for the Holy Office.

When later I had reason to penetrate this hurly-burly on some errand, I saw one or other of my sisters stopped in her tracks, transfixed by the sight of sweat-gleaming half-clad young workmen wielding pickaxe or hammer. I saw the young men glance up and grin, alive to the gaze of a woman.

You must know that the life of the Abbey is shot through with dreams, fantasies and denial. And betrayal.

Mary Amor led me away from the din of the gatehouse area, towards the quiet parts not penetrated by casual visitors.

There are two churches within the Abbey. The first one you come to, with a pathway from a door on to the road, is for servants and people from the town. We walked on, through their graveyard, and then the nuns' burial ground.

'You and I will be laid to rest here when our time comes,' said Mary Amor cheerfully, making the grave sound as cosy as a feather-bed.

We went into the Abbey Church.

On that summer morning the interior was flooded with brightness from the windows. I had of course seen glass, and glass painted with little scenes within the panes, in the church in Bruton, but never such dazzling expanses as this. Colour leapt out from the paintings all over the walls, from the vaulting, and from the gilded figures on the screen straddling the nave, with the Holy Rood, Christ on His Cross, hanging over all. The red blood pours from His side, His feet, His hands. His face is full of pain. I always found it hard to look for long upon the Holy Rood.

The Abbey Church is transformed by another kind of magic after dark. When I first saw it by night, by candlelight, with the high shadowy roof pierced by glints of gold and scarlet and blue, I was dumbstruck.

On that first day, following Mary Amor up the nave between fat columns, I saw how the floor we walked upon was tiled all over in squares decorated with flowers and animals and shields and emblems, all different. I came to love looking at those tiles. I stole one, when the End Time came.

The air in the Abbey Church is heavy with whisperings and mutterings from the side aisles. That first day, I thought they were spirit voices. They are the voices of priests saying Mass for the souls of the dead, in the chantry chapels. That's what chantry priests do, day after day, for ever. They say Masses and pray for the souls in Purgatory of those who can afford to endow a chapel and its priest, and so ensure a place in Heaven. The chantry priests have lodgings in neat one-storey tenements along the far edge of the nuns' burial ground. Tedium apart, they do not have a difficult life.

Beyond the screen, with the Holy Rood hanging above it, is the choir and the high altar. This is the holy part of the church, and where the singing of the Holy Office is done. Nuns were filing in as we stood there, taking their places in ranks opposite one another across the chancel. It was time for Sext. Mary Amor made to join them.

'Wait for me,' she said.

I dropped back and listened. One pure voice, like a dawn bird-call, then many, rising and falling, the individual voices blurred by echoes from the vaulting. I have heard the chanting of canons in Bruton — deep, warm, rhythmic. The chanting of women is different. There is sadness and longing in it.

We left the church through the south transept, opening into a covered passage with stone benches down each side.

'This is the slype,' whispered Mary. 'It is a pleasant place to sit and read, if you like reading.'

'I do like reading.'

'I never seem to find the time, myself.'

Along the slype, out into the cloister. In the middle is a garden, with white and red roses and low grey-green bushes, some of which I recognised. There was a nun bent over these, working with a tool.

We walked all round in the shade of the arcades. Mary Amor pointed out how this door led into the kitchens, that one into the refectory, down that stair are the cellars for beer and wine, and the place where you wash your hands before eating, these stairs led up to the nuns' dormitory, the dorter; underneath it is the warming-room, through here is the Chapter House, there the Library, over there, look, look, on the other side of the cloister, that tall archway leads to the Abbess's lodging.

'King Cnut died here in the Abbey,' said Sister Mary Amor. 'He was a good Christian man in his own way, even though he was not so great as our own King Alfred.'

'King Cnut came from another country and ruled England for nearly twenty years,' I said, blessing Master John Leland in my heart.

Mary Amor shot me a sharp look. People who enjoy giving information prefer you not to know anything.

I became mightily confused as she showed me around, although I had already eaten in the refectory, seated at the very end of one of the long tables set against the walls. In the middle is a lectern for reading aloud during dinner and, at the far end, on a platform, the high table where the Abbess sits with guests or with the Obedientiaries. And I had already slept my first night in the dorter, a long chamber divided into many small ones with wooden partitions, each with its little window open to the winds. Even with the shutter pulled up, my cubicle is more airy than is comfortable. I have a bed, a little desk and a kneeler, a bench, and a shelf. It is a tight fit, but more space than I had for myself at home in Bruton.

We have our own reredorter through an arch at the end of the chamber – a passage with closets along both sides, emptying into a drain below. I do not know where the drain discharges itself. I expect, down under the Park. Beside the hole in each closet is a slot in which stands a stick with a sponge on it. There is a basin at the end of the chamber in which to rinse the sponges. I am impressed by these arrangements.

In spite of the warm outside air, the stone walls weep with damp. I do sometimes miss the smoky herb-tinged, dung-tinged fug of home. There is in fact too much space and air. Many of the buildings in the nuns' part of the Abbey, so grand and venerable with their carvings and inscriptions, are dirty and dilapidated. So much for 'rolling in money'. In our dorter, the wooden rafters are black with mould and tubs are set to catch the drips for when it rains.

Outside, the mud and filth underfoot after rain – and the rats – are naturally no less troublesome than anywhere else I have been. But the clean parts, and the perpetual cleansing of those parts, are such as I have never seen before. Turds are cleared away almost daily from the stairs and passages. The kitchens and the cooking pots are scoured by sisters who are capable of nothing else, and the refectory and dorter swept by women from the town. The nuns' linen is bleached and starched in the Laundry to a perfection I did not know was possible.

Mary Amor told me that this whiteness is achieved by steeping the linen in piss before boiling. She showed me a barrel outside the Laundry into which the chamber pots of the lay inhabitants of the Abbey are emptied, except in hard winters when the contents freeze solid. Everything in nature including urine, I suppose, has its uses.

Except fleas. I cannot see what benefit fleas bring to anyone or anything. Yet knowing something of the strange ingredients which go into the concoctions of apothecaries, who knows whether a paste of fleas might not have some medical application. It would be hard, however, to harvest them to make the experiment, as they jump so.

I said as much to Sister Mary Amor, thinking to make her laugh. But again she looked at me sharply.

'You are whimsical, Agnes Peppin.'

I said nothing. I am not whimsical, not in the least. It is just that one thought leads on to another.

Beyond the cloister I was shown the Infirmary, perched near the edge of a ridge beyond which the ground falls away, down and down and down. The first time you see this view, you cannot prevent yourself from exclaiming aloud. On the steeply sloping land beneath us I saw copses, enclosures, beehives, fishponds, and green spaces, all enclosed within high walls. This is the Abbey Park. Right at the bottom, way down in the valley, is a village with its church and cottages.

Sister Mary Amor and I stood at the fence on the edge and looked down on to the Park.

'You see we live up on a cliff,' said Mary Amor. 'On a clear day, you can see Glastonbury Tor from here.'

It was not a clear day. We were looking straight into a hazy sun. A string of horses hung about with bundles was labouring up through the Park, with a gaggle of young men urging them upward.

'Everything has to be brought up from the bottom,' said Mary Amor. 'Even our water. We do have a well up here, but it does not give enough for the laundry, the kitchen, the brewing. So we draw it from the spring down on the road towards Sherborne, and it is carried up in barrels by packhorse. It's a costly way to get water, but it does provide employment for people.'

Far away across the valley, forested land rises in curves like the backs of beasts.

'We have the same difficulty with firewood,' said Mary Amor. 'That has to be carried all the way from Gillingham Forest, which is a Royal Forest. That is in the other direction. King Harold gave St Mary's at Gillingham to our Abbey, and we have the right to take wood from the Forest. But this too requires heavy labour, and much to be paid out in wages. King Alfred was a great man but he was not practical, he did not think about the necessities of life when he founded our Abbey up on this high dry ridge.'

It is indeed strange to be in a town through which no river runs. She had said 'Gillingham'. I know the cart that brought me to Shaftesbury had passed through Gillingham. Somewhere far beyond the Royal Forest, and somewhat to the west, lies Bruton.

'The Lord knows there is enough wood and to spare,' said Mary Amor. 'They say that the trees in the Forest are so dense that a squirrel could leap from branch to branch all the way from Shaftesbury to Gillingham without touching the ground.'

I entered the Abbey as a postulant, but I did not remain one for long. There was no point in it, they told me. There were no other postulants, and I might as well join the novices in their instruction.

The day I became a novice I met with the Chambress in my cubicle to be clothed. That is the expression. To be clothed. She carried over her outstretched left arm an array of garments in black and white, hanging down to the ground. She laid them out on my bed. I stood shivering barefoot in my shift while she took up my own things and bundled them on the floor. I said or rather looked a sad goodbye to my green hood. I had hidden the emerald dolphin on its chain under my mattress beforehand. They were not going to take that from me.

Deceit was in me, from the beginning.

Everything of mine would be kept, she said, until I was professed as a nun, in case I apostatised – that means running away – or in case, before the two years of my novitiate were up, I was found unworthy of the habit of a Benedictine.

She cut off my hair. I sat on the stool and she chopped away, long pieces falling on the floor and wisps floating in the draught. I did not like this. In order not to feel what I felt, I became a block of wood. Badgers, when they are frightened, attack. Rabbits freeze. I am a rabbit. I know that. But I would like to be the best rabbit that can be.

She passed me the new garments in order, making the sign of the cross over each, and helped me to put them on. First, a black underskirt. Then my tunic – a black woollen gown. Then the scapular, a long piece of black cloth with a head-hole, hanging down before and behind.

'In olden times,' she said, 'it served as an apron, but we have separate aprons now with a loop round the neck for when we do dirty work like gardening, or in the Infirmary.'

She put an ordinary white cap over my head, covering my ears. Then the white wimple, like a headcloth but fitting close under the chin, concealing my throat.

'You have a long neck,' she said, tugging at the edge of the wimple so that it covered the opening of my tunic.

She spread out the white veil of a novice on her upturned hands, turned toward me, and placed it over my head. She came up close and pulled it forward so that it concealed my front hair and my forehead. I smelled her fishy breath.

'Only bold girls bare their foreheads,' she said.

One difference between the habit of a novice and the habit of a professed nun, apart from their black veils, is that they tie an extra broad white band across their foreheads. I am spared that. She secured the veil to the wimple with pins and left a packet of pins with me, for as she said, they are easily dropped and lost.

Then she put a broom in my hands, told me to sweep up my fallen hair, took up my own clothes, and bade me not to be late in choir today of all days.

The Novice Mistress was waiting for me at the great door of the Abbey Church to escort me to my place among my sisters. As we walked up the nave every head, the black veils and the white, turned to look at me – stiffly. I learned, in a single hour of wearing my habit, about the constriction around my head. I could not turn my neck freely or very far, I could not toss my head or scratch my scalp, and it was already itching. From now on I was walking as nuns walk, looking straight ahead.

The Novice Mistress's name is Dame Monica Slater. She has small black eyes and almost no teeth, which makes it hard to understand what she says. She calls us her 'little minchins'. We sit on benches in her office. She issues us each with a small book printed on paper, a Book of Hours, such as I saw in Bruton, which is called here a Primer. This is a costly item and we are to take care of it. It is to be our regular reading matter in our free time.

The Primer consists of a calendar of the saints' days and church festivals, short parts of the Gospels, the psalms, and prayers to God, to the Blessed Virgin, and to the saints. Dame Monica said we should each cultivate a special devotion to a particular saint, to whom we should pray, and who would protect us and intercede for us in Heaven.

'The saints in Heaven can do great things for us sinners down below. You, Agnes Peppin, could do worse than make your devotion to St Agnes the Martyr. Martyrs go straight to Heaven without spending time in Purgatory.'

She told me to read about St Agnes in the Lives of the Saints.

I am named for St Agnes because I was born on her feast day. When I read about her I was disconcerted. She was martyred for her faith at the age of thirteen for refusing to allow her purity to be stained by marriage to the Governor's son, insisting that Christ in Heaven was her only spouse and she could accept no mortal husband. She stood out against the anger of the Governor, against the offer of rich gifts, against imprisonment, and against being thrown into a house of sin, where an angel protected her virtue. Finally condemned to death, she laid her neck to the sword as happy as a bride on her wedding day.

A terrible story, from every point of view.

She is most unsuitable as a heavenly advocate for me. I read about other holy women and am attracted to Zita, who lived three hundred years ago in Italy and served the same family as a maidservant all her life. She finds lost keys for those who pray to her. That is really useful. From what I read about her, she is not officially a saint, though she is greatly venerated. She said: 'A servant is not holy if she is not busy.' I like her because she was a good Martha.

St Agnes, the saintly child of thirteen, would hardly have time for me, whose purity is already stained. She was a true Bride of Christ. Not only virgin martyrs but every professed nun is a Bride of Christ. Just imagine those thousands of Brides over the centuries. Their teeth fall out or become worn to stumps, they lose their eyelashes and become bent and stiff and grow hairs on their chins, and then die, still and always Brides. On entering into Heaven, is each restored to youthfulness? Will St Agnes be perpetually thirteen? And what, please, is meant by Original Sin?

When I raised these questions with the Novice Mistress she grew impatient. She explained to me yet again the doctrine of Original Sin. But was the sin Eve's, or Adam's? I am not even sure what Un-Original Sin is, beyond breaking the Ten Commandments. 'Meditate on the nature of faith,' said the Novice Mistress, 'and pray for your own faith to be strengthened.'

She told me that what she called my 'scruples' were unwhole-some and self-concerned, and that I should keep my thoughts under control.

'You will then be happy, my dear, in this school of God's Service. St Benedict, our founder, did not wish our lives to be harsh or burdensome. We are not called upon to do perpetual penance, nor to apply self-punishment. We avoid scruples and manifestations of extreme zeal. We do not encourage the transports and trances of which you may be reading in the lives of some saints. Such things smack of self-vaunting.'

'But what of Sister Onora?' asked another novice. 'She sees things that we cannot see. I have an aunt on Exmoor like that. It's not self-vaunting at all, with her. She just sees things, she cannot help it.'

Sister Onora saw an angel last week, floating over the Park. When we rushed out, there was nothing. But she had seen it and she is not a liar.

'Some people do have special sensitivities,' said Mother Monica. 'They are receptive to signs and omens. There can be holiness in them. It is thought that what they see, and others cannot, is a way granted by God's grace to convey what may not be perceived directly. They see in parables.'

She paused.

'Such powers can do harm, if abused,' said Mother Monica.

'Like witches,' I said.

We speculated that with witches, their special powers had been harnessed by the Devil. We agreed that Sister Onora was certainly not a witch.

Mother Monica steered us off the subject of Sister Onora. 'This is beyond your greenstick understandings. It is for priests and bishops to determine the nature of visions in any particular case.'

She brought us back to our duty. Each of us, she taught, will be leading with our sisters a life in common, under our Rule, in this place, for our whole lives.

'This is the Rule of Stability. No roaming about the town, no travelling, no visiting friends and family, no going on pilgrimages. You will be living until you die within this House.'

We might not leave the precinct, ever, without permission. This community was our family and Shaftesbury Abbey was our only home.

'The Abbess is your spiritual mother, and your authority under God. Like a wise mother, she consults with her family over all important matters. Like a wise mother, she meets with her family who are free to voice their inquietudes. Like a wise mother, she makes the final decisions.'

She explained about the Chapter House. Once a week the whole community meets 'in Chapter' with the Abbess or, when she is away, with the Prioress. She delivers herself of any items of news, and gives her views on them, and invites us to speak. Any sister can raise any matter to do with the community, or make complaints about the behaviour of others, or report injustices, or disagreements between individuals.

'But this should not be an occasion for unreasonable grumbling and tale-bearing.'

And the Abbess herself, Dame Elizabeth Zouche – she was away for some of that summer on Abbey business, and her sphere is a million miles from mine. Before I knew her I imagined a witch, or an angel, or sometimes a loving mother such as I never had.

When I saw her for the first time it was after nightfall. She was expected. There were cries and a crashing unlocking of bolts, and her coach rumbled in through the gatehouse. I had not seen a coach before. Carts, wagons covered or uncovered, yes. It must be strange to travel in a closed box, as if one were a wild animal. The Steward, Father Pomfret and the Obedientiaries hurried out to greet her. So did we all, at a distance.

The oxen were led away, and then I saw her in the light of the flaring torches. She was wearing a fur-lined coat with the fur turning outwards to make a collar, like a man's. Her veil was held far back and raised by a gable hood, showing her grey-fair hair. Behind her fluttered two nuns carrying bags in one hand, extending the other to help her over the rough ground.

As her coat swung open I saw a curving figure under a dark gown. Her face is pale-complexioned, with thin features, wide eyes. I could not in that unreliable light discern any lines on her face. She looked divine. Slowly she walked with her attendants, followed by men hefting boxes and baskets, down past Holy Trinity and the Abbey Church to the cloister and thence into her own house.

I heard her say to the Prioress, 'I am so very tired.'

She presided in the Chapter House the following day. Someone – I did not yet know the names of many of the nuns – complained that there had been maggots in her mutton at the previous night's supper. There was a silence.

I said, and not in a whisper, 'Blowflies.'

Everyone turned to look at me, black veils and white, old and young.

Wishing I had kept silent, I explained that blowflies lay eggs in a sheep's fleece at the rear end and the maggots hatch out within about three days, and a week later they have entered the flesh and begun to consume it, destroying the meat and the animal herself. 'She will die.'

I did not say how I knew. When my father was deciding whose sheep to buy in the market, he made me search through the fleeces in search of maggots and their eggs, my fingers being more nimble than his and my eyes sharper. I only had to do this with the sheep of strangers. It is only ill-kept sheep that become infected.

The Abbess thanked me without a smile.

'The mutton comes from one of our own farms, and the matter must be looked into at once. I will speak to the Steward. The Rule of St Benedict did not require us to submit to maggots in our meat.'

One of my fellow novices does not like me. Her name is Sister Eleanor Wilmer. I was an object of interest in the Abbey because I was a new person, the most recent arrival. Before I arrived, she had been the most recent arrival. Perhaps she is jealous. She does not like Sister Onora either. She may be jealous of her too, because of the visions. I am not sure that she really likes anyone. When I first joined the instruction classes with the Novice Mistress, I saw Sister Eleanor staring at my face, my hands, my body under my habit. When I met her eyes she looked away but was soon staring again. Whenever I speak to her, thinking to make friends, she puts her hand over her mouth when she answers, and does not meet my eyes.

Eleanor Wilmer is short and sallow-skinned. Her best feature is her large dark eyes, which are often upturned in prayer, because she is very pious. She is also educated. She is quicker than I at calculations and numbers. She is a fluent reader and writer. Really we should be friends. But she looked daggers at me in Chapter when I spoke up about blowflies. As we filed out, she whispered to me:

'You seem to have a high opinion of yourself, Agnes Peppin.'

I was nettled, and whispered back, 'And you? You imagine that you do not have a high opinion of yourself, Eleanor Wilmer? You and your precious holiness?'

This was very wrong and childish. But there is something infuriating about her public prayerfulness. She kneels in the slype so that one has to step around her. There she so frequently is, with her hands clasped at her breast and her great eyes upturned and often welling with tears. The Novice Mistress, Mother Monica, encourages us to speak about the progress we feel we are making in our inner lives. I talk about what I am reading, and what I conclude from what I read. Eleanor Wilmer talks about her spiritual development, which is all that she is interested in.

'You have no idea how I suffer,' she said, looking around her at the group of us, 'I suffer unbearably, night and day, when I think of my sins and of the sins of the world and the pain caused to Our Lord Jesus Christ. I share His agony, I feel His wounds. And then my love for Him overwhelms me. My only desire is to grow ever closer to Him.'

Eleanor Wilmer looked towards Mother Monica, seeking approval. Mother Monica sucked on her splintery teeth and contemplated Eleanor Wilmer.

'There are many ways of growing closer to Jesus Christ,' she finally said. 'We must remember that our love for God, and God's love for us, is also our source of peace and joy.'

'Perhaps I am not praying hard enough,' said Eleanor, sighing, casting her eyes down in humility.

Feigned humility, in my opinion. My lack of charity towards Eleanor knows no bounds. Just being with her is an occasion of sin, for me. I must avoid her company as much as possible. This will not be hard as she does not seek mine, though I still feel she watches me. May not 'suffering' as she experiences it be an indulgence, even an avoidance? Eleanor is never anywhere to be seen when there is some dull or unpleasant job to be done. She never offers to fetch or carry.

I am back in the conundrum of Martha and Mary. I myself probably do not suffer enough, spiritually or in any other way. I flow, I adapt.

'We have first and foremost our duty to God,' says Mother Monica, 'but also our duty to our fellow-men, and in our case, to the community.'

Yet we have little work here, not in the home sense. No nun searches sheep's fleeces for maggots. No nun flails spent vines to beat out the dry beans and peas. The essential duty of a Benedictine nun, says Dame Monica, is the communal daily saying and singing of the Holy Office at the proper and regular hours of the day and night, psalms and prayers in praise of Almighty God.

That is what we are here for. It is more important than anything else we can possibly imagine doing. It is the Work of God, *Opus Dei*. The Novice Mistress's voice trembled as she said those words. I was momentarily proud that I too would be playing my part. I can perhaps be Mary, not Martha. I cannot believe that Mary was anything like Eleanor Wilmer.

I knew already the order of the seven services – the Hours, as in the Books of Hours. The night Offices, Matins and Lauds, are sung together at two o'clock in the morning. Everyone finds this the hardest, though we don't have to go out into the cold to enter the church. There is a night-stair built into the walls, curling down from the dorter directly into the chancel. Then we creep back up to bed without speaking until Prime at six or seven in the morning.

There is a light burning all night in each quartile of the cloister, and one at the foot of the dorter stairs. They don't use rushlights, but blocks of stone with little hollows carved out and filled with tallow, with a wick. In the Abbey Church itself there is always one tall wax candle in the nave, one at the entrance to the choir, and one on the steps of the Sanctuary. This does not give enough light to read easily. We learn by heart from the Primer the words of the night Offices.

We have breakfast after Prime. Three more morning services – Tierce, Sext and None – and the daily hearing of the Mass, and then dinner, with reading aloud. Vespers are at five o'clock, which comes fast or slowly depending on the season. Supper is after Vespers.

An hour of the clock I think is just made up, as you might say 'a handful of hazelnuts'. We do not have clocks at home, and we don't speak much of hours. There is a modern thing, a mechanical clock, here in the Abbey. It is a pointless artifice, although I see it has its uses so far as discipline is concerned. It is adjusted to calculate time differently in winter and in summer. The clock's hour is longer in summer, because daylight end comes later. In summer, the hours between dinner and Compline are stretched to take advantage of the long evenings. We are meant to go to bed straight after Compline, and to get some sleep before the bell for Matins breaks into our dreams. As the days get shorter, the hours between services become shorter.

Outside the Holy Office, our occupations must be useful, quiet, and conducive to meditation. Serious study is not expected. 'We do not expect scholarship from you, few of you have been raised for that, but we like you to study the lives of the saints. We will all be helping one another to achieve self-discipline, and the eradication of self-will.'

After the acceptance of the Rule of Stability, our first work on ourselves must be what Mother Monica calls *conversio morum*, a conversion of our manners and habits towards regularity and detachment: poverty, chastity, obedience. On being professed, we will take a vow of poverty – personal poverty. All that we have will pass into the possession of the Abbey – our money, our clothes, the keys to our boxes and to the door of our old home, our jewellery. (I thought of the boxes, baskets, chests and crammed closets I've seen in the dorter but said nothing.) The Abbey provides us with all the necessities – including a little knife.

'We appear simple and frugal, but not like beggars. We do not wear our clothes until they are full of holes and in shreds, or they would be no good to the poor to whom we pass them on.'

We must avoid occasions of sin, and never give scandal. Particular friendships, and cliques of intimate friends, she said, are to be avoided, as offending against the family life of the Order.

'You may never go into the town on Abbey errands alone, but always with one of your sisters. Within the Abbey, we must never be alone with any man, not even one of the priests, except when making our confessions.'

I suspect that at that moment in all our minds, including Mother Monica's, was the face and figure of Father Robert Parker. He is one of the chantry priests. Most of these are either elderly, like snuffling Father Bucket, who smells of sheep's cheese, or raw youths with pustules on their necks. Father Louis Pomfret, the Abbey chaplain, is fat and crafty. But Father Robert Parker is well-shaped, and so pleasing to look at that it is hard to avoid resting one's eyes upon him. He wears his curling dark hair long. He looks rather like Peter Mompesson only taller.

There is a chasm between what must not happen, according to our Rule, and what actually does happen.

It is easy to slide into what Mother Monica calls 'laxity'. What is not put into words is not happening. Our Great Silence, usually observed, is between Compline and Prime. There is another silence, fragmented into little silences, composed of matters never spoken of.

No one mentions that one pair of sisters talk and walk always and intimately with each other and no one else. Everyone knows it. The Prioress and the Infirmaress, Dame Agatha Cracknell and Dame Alice Doble. Their saints' days fall on consecutive days. They celebrate together in the Prioress's house with strong ale and honey cakes and invite their favourites to join them. The two call their favourites their 'little family'. I am not of their number.

Their favourites come from a group of novices and young nuns whose families must be interconnected. They all seem to have known each other since childhood. They all look much alike. I call them the Fairheads because they are all blonde-haired. They are well-grown, with clear skin and strong teeth. This is how rich girls look and they are rich girls. Except in the Chapter House, where they are under the Abbess's eye, they wear their veils far back and raised in front, showing not only their foreheads but bands of shiny hair.

Unlike the rest of us, the Fairheads do not live in dream and fantasy. They are not in denial of anything. The Rule does not seem to apply to them. If they are reprimanded, they are contrite and lower their eyes and then go on as before. In the dorter they have cubicles close to one another at the far end of the chamber. Before they go to bed they clean their heads, combing out their hair from scalp to ends, over and over, with fine-toothed ivory combs. They rub salves into their hands to keep them smooth. They pare their fingernails into points. In their cubicles they keep overflowing baskets of bright ribbons, embroidered shifts and coloured gowns. I know, because I have looked, like a spy.

I have seen them reading letters brought in by messengers. I have seen them slip out into the town by side doors wearing their coloured garments. So many lay persons come and go freely in and out of the Abbey that it is not hard to escape notice. Two of their gentlemen friends actually found their way up to the dorter one autumn night while we were in Compline. Coming up to bed in the dark, the rest of us heard squeals and laughter and the whispering rumble of male voices, then a clattering of boots down the stairs and the downstairs door banging. The Great Silence took over. No one brought the matter up in the Chapter House.

I do not dislike the Fairheads. I would like to be one of them. They never talk to me. They chatter among themselves in light voices about their friends in the outside world. Conversation, the Novice Mistress taught, should be limited to essential communication. No idle gossip in the cloister or over domestic tasks. At mealtimes requests should be indicated wherever possible by gestures, or in whispers.

*

There is a woman about five years older than me who lingers on the edge of the cluster of Fairheads. They tolerate her. I think now that they must have known who she was. She wears the veil of a novice, but not always the full habit. She has a blue gown, and a grey one, and her eyes are greenish. She attends the Holy Office and has a sweet singing voice which holds the pure line. She eats with us. She does not sleep in the dorter but in one of the houses within the walls occupied by old retainers, boarders, widows, Court pensioners from London and Abbey dependents, both men and women, waited upon by servants. They are called 'Corrodians'. Most have paid a hefty sum down to secure shelter and subsistence for the rest of their lives. For the Abbey, it is a gamble. Some die off wonderfully quickly while others linger for years, eating and drinking their heads off.

Among them lives this young woman. She is called Dorothy, like my mother. Dorothy Clausey. I learned about her from Sister Anne Cathcart. Anne is a nun professed already for several years, but she had a London life when she was young and she knows everything. If one were uncharitable one would call her a nosey parker and a gossip. She is entertaining, and her ways are so warm and winning that any one sitting with her in the slype or walking with her in the orchard willingly reveals her private thoughts and secrets. She lives in and for the everyday world and is the complete opposite of Eleanor Wilmer.

Anne sought me out, baiting her hook by telling me something intimate about herself, apparently confidential but in fact quite inconsequent. Another day she shared with me a disobliging truth about the Novice Mistress. I became compelled, even desirous, to reciprocate with some revelation about myself. I told her about Peter and Peterkin. She is a sympathetic listener. Later, in my bed, I cursed myself for a fool. If she told me other people's secrets, she would surely tell other people mine. There is nothing exclusive about Anne Cathcart's friendship.

I even showed her my dolphin. In return she fished out from under her habit a ring which she wears on a ribbon round her neck. It is thick gold, set with what she said was a diamond. She told me it had been given to her by someone who loved her. Then she said no, that was not true.

'I stole it. But I have confessed the sin.'

'You confessed it to Father Pomfret?'

'He made me tell him where I had taken it from and why I could not return it. He gave me absolution.'

That is all she would say. Anne prefers asking to telling. She probed me about Peter. Did I think he would have made a good husband? I told her I did not know, only that he was the only man in the world for me.

'There is a certain kind of man,' said Anne, 'whose wife is as his mother was to him when he was an infant. He looks to none but her. His home-place is her body, its nooks and crannies, its odours and flavours. It matters not at all what she comes to look like or smell like as she grows old. He could no more think of bedding another woman than of bedding a peacock.'

Might Peter have been like that, with me? But Anne had just got into her stride.

'There is another kind of man who just needs a woman, often, and any woman. He will take his wife with a good heart because she is available, but he will not content himself with her however much he swears, at the beginning, that he loves only her. And he will mean it when he says it. But the passion for one woman does not last. Nor for that matter does the passion of any one woman for one man.'

'How long does the passion last?'

'Listen well, little Agnes. I have lived, and I have observed. Four years, at the most. A marriage is for a lifetime. It has its own serious purposes. Far better to farm out in other beds the itch of the flesh, without repining.'

'Can one then ever be happy?'

'You do not know when you are happy. You only know afterwards, looking back. You say to yourself, "I was happy, at that time." Even then, you may be deceiving yourself.'

I was always intrigued by what she said. It remained with me. But at that time I was more interested in what she could tell me about Dorothy Clausey, who became my friend.

Dorothy initiated the friendship: 'You are the first female I have met since I entered this place who has any intellect.'

'What about Eleanor Wilmer?'

'She is distorted.'

Dorothy told me she liked my voice and the way I spoke. She herself does not speak much. She holds back most of her opinions. She too is a reader, and we sit together in the Library in the afternoons. The heavy Library key is kept by us at the back of a niche in the cloister wall, behind the figure of St Catherine. Actually there are two keys on the one ring, the hinge of which is so rusted that the second, smaller one cannot be removed. This smaller one is the key to a wooden door across a hollowed-out cavity in the wall of the Library. That is where is kept the illuminated Psalter with a jewel-encrusted binding, the most precious object in all the Abbey's collection. We are allowed by the Prioress to take the ring with the two keys when we want, so long as we lock up when we leave the Library and put the keys back in their hiding place.

I have been reading anything in English that I can lay my hands on – our Rule of St Benedict, chronologies, annals, spiritual exercises, chronicles, accounts of other Benedictine Houses, sacred poetry ... There are little Books of Hours in Latin which I love for their coloured pictures.

I have come across some pleasing things, crushed behind heavy volumes at the back of shelves – recipes, sets of verses. The best is a delicious poem written on creased vellum about the first snowdrops of spring, which are likened to the drooping heads of novices. Dorothy calculates that it was written by a nun who lived in this House some two hundred years ago, because the English is not quite like our English and the script is not quite like ours either. It took me several afternoons to puzzle out and transcribe the poem. I wonder who the nun was, and what happened to her. Nothing and everything, I suppose. She grew old and died in the Abbey and went to Heaven.

Dorothy Clausey was taught Latin before she came to the Abbey, and has continued her study of it since. Father Robert Parker joins us and sits close beside her, helping her with difficult texts and correcting her own Latin writings. I envy them. If the truth were told, it is Dorothy whom I envy, both for knowing Latin and for having the attention of Robert. They are so absorbed and happy doing their Latin. When they raise their eyes from their books and smile at me, they are coming back from far away. Some of the Latin books and manuscripts are more interesting than what is available to read in English. She has been studying a big illuminated manuscript about medicinal plants, and another about animals and fishes.

They do not always exclude me. One late autumn afternoon of slanting sunlight and disturbing fragrances, we three left the Library and crossed the roadway to the orchard. The grass, uncut since midsummer, was lush and soft. The apple trees cast shadows, making the green seem black. We lay down on our backs in the long grass in a patch of sunlight between the trees, in a row like salted herrings – Dorothy in the middle, Robert and I on either side of her. No touching. We must have looked comical to anyone who chanced to see us. No one did see us, or so I wrongly thought.

Robert picked up a windfall, and the sound of his teeth biting into the crispness of it made my mouth fill with water, as if I were tasting the sweet sharpness myself. Apple-juice saliva. We lay there a long time. Was this an occasion of sin? It was certainly an occasion of happiness. I knew that I was happy that day, my happiness welling up from the grass and down from the sun and from the nearness of Dorothy and Robert. Anne Cathcart was wrong about happiness.

'I suppose you know who your great new friend Dorothy is?' said Anne Cathcart. And then, in a lower tone, with her knowing look and air of giving me a special gift:

'She is the Cardinal's daughter.'

She paused for effect. All I could say was: 'Oh?'

'Of course, cardinals cannot marry, but ... Dorothy arrived the same year as I did, in the old Abbess's time. She was only fourteen then, a pupil boarder.'

When the old Abbess died, and Dame Elizabeth Zouche was elected, letters were sent to her from London explaining who Dorothy was and asking Dame Elizabeth to keep her on in the community, as there was nowhere else suitable for her to go.

'Then, the year after that, as you know, her father the Cardinal died. If he had not died naturally, his head would have been cut off within the week.'

Another tale told to scare children, it seemed to me. I felt stupid telling Anne that I had no idea who the Cardinal was, although I had heard him spoken of.

So Anne settled herself more comfortably on the bench. Cardinal Thomas Wolsey was the son of a butcher (that endeared him to me) who rose to be what Master Thomas Cromwell now is – a wily government servant, ambitious, able, close to the King – also, as Master Cromwell is not, a Prince of the Church. He was the King's chief advisor and confidant, his fixer. He supported the King in his desire to procure from the Pope an annulment of his marriage with Queen Catherine. When the

Cardinal failed to bring this about he lost favour with the King and with the Lady Anne Boleyn who did everything she could to bring him down.

'The King always liked the Cardinal and piled honours on him. The Cardinal got above himself. He grew gorgeous, extravagant. Gross. Wealthy beyond imagining. He built himself an outrageous palace on the Thames at Hampton.'

Then the Cardinal mismanaged some political business with France and the King, 'egged on by Anne Boleyn', turned against him and issued a warrant for his arrest.

'The Cardinal died on his way back to London from the north to answer the charges. That is the end of the story of the Cardinal. The King grabbed for himself all his fine possessions and his palace too.'

'And Dorothy? Who is her mother?'

For once Anne Cathcart was at a loss. She shrugged.

'I do not know. Perhaps the Cardinal pleasured himself with a maidservant.'

3

TREGONWELL
AND ARUNDELL

When my father goes out in the long summer evenings he will always say, 'I have to see a man about a dog.' What man? What dog? I wondered when I was a child. He could not answer me. He does not have the words to explain that it is figurative or, as Hugh Backwell would say, a *façon de parler*. It is what men say when they intend to go off to do something and do not want to tell anyone where they are going. I expect my father wants solitude and just walks the roads for an hour or so. Or maybe he meets a woman? I do not think so, but what do I know.

We do have a real dog at home. He is called Ratter because ratting is his job. His domain is the yard and outhouses. He is not allowed into our living quarters and I have never been fond of him. When he is not gnawing a bone he is scratching himself or slobbering over his private parts.

There are dogs too here in the Abbey – guard dogs chained up outside the workshops and stores, to protect tools and materials from thieving townspeople at night. They growl and snarl when anyone comes within six feet of them. I steer clear of their yellow teeth, as do the Abbey cats. The Prioress has a comical white creature which she carries on the palm of her left hand, with its hind parts up her sleeve. It is a dog but it is more like a child's plaything. We are not permitted to keep pet animals, but then much is done that is not permitted.

I never felt affection for any animal, let alone a dog, until Finbarr came.

She belonged to the two little boys. I remember one morning, the boys laughing and laughing, they could not stay upright, they threw himself from side to side until they fell on their backs on the ground waving their legs in the air, still laughing.

'Finbarr has Sister's shoe! Finbarr has Sister's shoe!'

Finbarr ran round and round in circles, tossing Sister Catherine Hunt's sandal in the air and catching it again, while Catherine lunged around trying to retrieve it. Catherine is plump and not a quick mover. Finbarr settled down with the sandal between his front paws to chew at the straps. When Catherine came near, he danced away with the sandal, out of reach.

One of the boys, suddenly exhausted, began to cough. He lay there coughing. The dog abandoned the wrecked sandal and came to lick his face.

That boy's name is Weasel, or that's what he told us. He and the black boy, whom he calls Dick, had been found huddled together outside the Abbey gatehouse one chilly night. Weasel and Dick seemed to be about eight years old although it was hard to tell. They were taken in and fed, and questioned by the Prioress, but could give no account of themselves, other than that they had crept in among the bundles on a cart on the quay at Bridport – Weasel knew that much – and fallen asleep. When they awoke it was dark and they did not know where they were. The oxen had been taken out and there was no one around.

The Prioress looked at Dick and at his black face.

'Did you come off a ship?'

He could not say.

'He does not know the words,' said Weasel. 'He has other words.'

Dick was a quick learner. Quite soon he knew a lot of our

words. The boys stayed. No one said that they could, and no one said that they could not.

Dick and Weasel came and found me where I was reading about St Augustine in the slype. In their haste they almost tripped over the feet of Sister Eleanor Wilmer, kneeling in prayer with her elbows on the bench and her head for once buried in her hands.

'Sister Agnes, something bad,' whispered Dick.

'Very, very bad,' whispered Weasel. 'You have to come.'

They pulled at my tunic. I followed them out, stepping over Eleanor's feet, and up past the churches to the gatehouse. I had not asked permission to go to the town that afternoon. I had no sisterly companion with me, and so I hesitated.

'You have to come,' said Weasel.

They turned left on to Bimport and ran ahead of me. Past the backs of Abbey buildings there is a row of low dwellings with no windows and rotting thatch. Families from here come in through the side-gate and hang about the kitchen door for food. The boys stopped at one of these tenements, and Weasel took hold of the latch on the door.

'It is horrible,' he said, 'but you mustn't mind.'

Everything and everywhere and everyone smells of something, but I had never before smelled anything quite like that place. It was full of withy cages, and in the cages were animals lying in swamps of their own waste — cats, dogs, badgers, foxes, birds. Even with the door open it was hard to see, but all the creatures seemed dead, and some had been dead a long time and were coming apart. Flies crawled all over them and over each other. The flies all rose up in a filthy cloud when we came near and then settled back.

There was something — someone — on a mattress in the corner. The boys pulled me towards it.

'She dead,' said Dick.

He took my hand. I was glad of it. The woman's body was covered in sacks, but her face was upturned and still haunts me at bad times. She was just recognisable. It was Mistress Winterbourne, one of the women who came regularly to the Abbey to beg.

The room darkened. Two young men stood there.

'We didn't know what to do for the best. Thought we had better just leave everything as it was. Our mother, and – and everything.'

That was the taller one. John Winterbourne. His brother is called John Winterbourne too. He never speaks, he has never spoken in all his life. The brothers make baskets, and hurdles, and fish-traps and skeps for bees, and sell them in the market.

I took a deep breath.

'I will get help for you,' I said, and made for the open door, but Weasel tugged at my hand.

'The little dog,' he said, 'that one – ask them if we can have it.'

They dragged me over to a cage in which was an animal not dead. It crouched there in its mess and looked at us.

I could not stand another minute of being in that place. I am not over-delicate, everyone sees dead bodies, and I more than most. I accompanied my mother laying out corpses, I have seen vagrants frozen stiff against the Abbey wall in Bruton on January mornings, and children crushed and spilling out their little guts under the wheels of market wagons, and newborns washed downstream from God knows where, caught in the rocks of the Brue where it runs shallow at the back of the Free School. I have seen boys from the school poke a little corpse with sticks to set it off downstream again. I am a butcher's daughter and a dead person is no different from a dead animal. But the rats had been at Mistress Winterbourne's face. I went out and vomited in the roadway.

At first the dog was too weak to walk, and Dick and Weasel trundled it all over the Abbey grounds in a handcart. We grew used to the particular clatter of its wheels on the cobbled parts and the cries of the boys, 'Come out and see our little dog!'

She was starved and parched, she had lost most of her coat, she was covered in sores and would not have lasted another day had they not rescued her. The boys won the heart of the Cellaress, who allowed them to take stale bread and bones for the dog from the kitchen. They cuddled her between them at night. She was very young – less than a year old, we thought – and as she became well she became inquisitive and destructive, so the Prioress told the boys they must keep her on a leash. They made a slip knot in a rope and put it round her neck. No one had the heart to tell them the dog must go. So she stayed.

This newcomer had a sweet nature, she never barked, and clung to Dick and Weasel like their shared shadow. She arrived full of mange but as she recovered she grew a glossy black coat. Her ears were silken flaps. She had comical habits. If we gave her something that she especially liked – a pig's ear for example – she did not chew it up but carried it around in her mouth whimpering, suffering from an overwhelming desire to bury it. We had to stop her digging holes in the nun's graveyard. Then she discovered she could wriggle under a weakened section of paling behind the Infirmary, and raced with her treasure down the slope and far into the Abbey Park, out of sight. The pig's ear would not be seen again.

'What is her name?' I asked the boys.

They did not know that dogs have names. I told them that if they gave her a name, and she learned it, she would come when they called.

'She comes anyway. We say "Little Dog! Little Dog!"'

Then that was her name, I told them.

'*Sister* Little Dog,' said Dick, and the two found that funny, and Sister Little Dog jumped all over them.

In their first weeks at the Abbey the boys slept in the hay in one of the barns. Then on one of their perambulations round the

Abbey they came across the remains of a small structure – just two jutting sections of crumbling masonry, at right angles to the wall. The Abbey is littered with abandoned tenements and sheds and lean-tos. Nothing is wholly cleared away, though the best stones and timbers are carted off to be reused. When King Alfred built the original Abbey, the timbers of the buildings would have been fresh cut, clean and pale, and the reed thatches crisp and dense, like the new bakery and the best guesthouse are now. But even the new bakery is built on the footings of something old. Nothing in any place where people have been settled for a long time is ever all new, or all old, at the same time. It's just the same in Bruton.

The boys begged some old planking from the joiners' workshop. They nailed the warped pieces together to make a roof over the broken stone walls, and found a hurdle to use as a door. It served to keep the dog in at night.

Dame Onion gave the dog her name. Dame Onion is old and from Ireland, and she has other words, like Dick, and sometimes it is hard to understand her even when she speaks our words. Her name is not Onion, it is something in Irish that sounds like Onion, and no one could pronounce her family name the way she said it either, except that it too began with the 'O' sound, so she is just Dame Onion. She said the kennel-house the boys built was like the cell of St Finbarr near where she was born.

'Finbarr was a holy man and he lived with other holy men on an island on a lake.'

'Finbarr,' said Dick, and looked at Weasel.

'Finbarr,' said Weasel.

The dog became Finbarr.

But Finbarr in Irish means fair-haired, said Dame Onion, and besides that, Finbarr was a man, and this dog was female and as black as sin.

'That's why we call her Finbarr,' said Weasel, 'to fool people.'

*

Dame Elizabeth Zouche never left the Abbey alone on her coach journeys to inspect her properties, or to spend time at Place Farm in Tisbury. Apart from servants, at least two nuns always accompanied her. They were chosen from among the Nondescripts, as Anne Cathcart classed them, because they were meek and middle-aged and we could never bother to remember their names.

There was also one special nun who was her companion and assistant in her own house. When I first came, that position was held by Mary Amor, the sister who showed me around the Abbey when I arrived. Then the Chambress complained in Chapter that she had too much to do and asked for a special assistant to act as her deputy when necessary, and the Abbess gave her Mary Amor.

'The Abbess may be asking for you now,' said Anne Cathcart.

'Why do you think so?'

'You are clever and strong and in good health. There is not much competition.'

She gestured toward the scatter of nuns and novices who like ourselves were walking at that hour in pairs or on their own around the cloister, and I saw our sisters through Anne's critical eyes – too old, too young, or too silly, dull, or ugly, too weak in mind or body, or untutored, or witlessly devout. The able ones are busy already on Abbey matters, or too grand. The Fairheads could hardly be expected to spare the time. These were bad thoughts, of a kind to be owned up to in the confessional, though I did not do so except in the most general terms – 'uncharitable thoughts about my sisters'.

'Why would she not ask for you?'

'Dame Elizabeth Zouche does not favour me. She never has. I know too much about her.'

'Like what?'

I should never lead Anne on. She seduces me.

'For a start, the Zouches are lucky rascals. They always were. They have noses like hounds. Ever since they arrived from France long ago they have followed the scent of money. They are courtiers, office-holders, collectors of royal appointments. They have influence. When times change they fall, and lose all they have won, or if they are clever they change direction. And they marry well and carefully.'

She told me that there are two branches of the Zouche family, one with estates in a county far from here, and another, who are the lords of Cary. I became more interested. Cary is but a short distance from Bruton. Our Abbess, Anne said, is inward with the Lord Zouche of Cary.

'And yet, though the Zouches have many Elizabeths among their sisters and cousins, I have never to my satisfaction understood where our Dame Elizabeth fits in, or who her father is. Yet she is surely a Zouche, she has that Zouche hair, fair and frizzy, dry like hay. And those wide-spaced eyes. You can tell a Zouche at twenty paces. I have made enquiries about her background, believe me. And she knows it.'

'How could she know?'

'In another life I was acquainted with a Zouche who was lady-in-waiting to Mistress Anne Boleyn. When she was riding high, I wrote to her and asked her what she knew about our Abbess. She sent me a most disobliging reply. When Dame Elizabeth was in London and conferring with the great men of the town, I was – betrayed.'

For the first time, I saw Anne Cathcart blushing crimson, and discomfited.

'I and the Zouche girl,' she said, 'had what I prefer to call a disagreement. About something else. I should never have approached her. The Abbess knows about that disagreement, too. She never speaks to me. She affects not to see me at all.'

She changed the subject back to the next assistant to the Abbess:

'There is of course one other possible candidate. Sister Eleanor Wilmer.'

'How so?'

'She is well qualified for the post, and she has infinite capacity for devotion. If she were to devote herself to the Abbess, she might not spend quite so much time on her knees pestering Almighty God. And I know she is interested, because I saw her running after Sister Mary Amor and questioning her about her duties.'

I thought about what Anne said about the Abbess affecting not to see her. I know that the Abbess did see me, by which I mean she looked at me, ever since I spoke up about blowflies. She had never spoken privately with me, but I saw her watching me in Chapter, and if I looked towards her in choir – when she was in choir, which was by no means always – I would always meet her eyes. Her gaze was neutral, speculative.

Dame Monica told her I was good at reading and writing, and I was given pen and ink and a piece of vellum to copy out the Lord's Prayer to show her what I could do. The vellum had been written on before, and scraped down to use again, so it was not smooth and I was not best pleased with my work.

But I was sent for.

Her house is a mansion, with a stone-tiled roof. You approach it through an archway on the east side of the cloister. To me, it is a palace. When I knocked on the great door at the appointed time, a little maid in clean clothes told me that Dame Elizabeth would receive me in her bedchamber. I followed her through a hall room and another room and another room and up a wide staircase with carved banisters.

Her upstairs chamber is large and high, with dark chests and cupboards. Two doors opening into other rooms. Everything gleamed. A lot of red, and hangings on the walls. The two big windows were shuttered. There are polished tiles on her floor, new-made rush mats, and a table at the foot of the great bed with gold and silver boxes arranged upon it.

There the Abbess was, sitting up in the bed, supported by pillows, the bed-curtains open. With her right hand she was holding up what looked like a letter to the light of the tall candle that stood beside the bed, and with the other hand she clasped a crumpled paper to her bosom. Other documents, ledgers and rolls were scattered over her coverlet and piled on the small table beside the candle. Hooked over the carved bedhead was something I had never seen before, a string of red beads with a crucifix dangling from it. I thought it might be a necklace. Later she told me it was called a rosary, that the stones were garnets and that it had been sent to her from Rome. If you say a prayer for every bead, you acquire significant graces and indulgences.

She was wearing a nightgown and long sleeves. Her cap was tied under her chin, with her Zouche hair showing at the front.

'There is a stool,' she said, 'under that table. Bring it out and sit down. I will attend to you presently.'

Her mouth worked in and out as she strained to read the letter. I sat on the stool and while I waited I studied her bed-curtains, which were of a greyish background colour embroidered all over with wavy blue streaks signifying water, and swirls of curving dolphins in a darker blue. I could tell they were dolphins. I fingered through my tunic the emerald dolphin on its chain round my neck.

I read the letter aloud to her as she asked, and she nodded and told me to come back after dinner the next day.

News travels as fast as an infection in the Abbey. By daylight end it was common knowledge that I was the chosen one. It was unheard of for a novice to be the Abbess's assistant.

When I went to my cubicle that night there was a dead rat on my bed. I picked it up by the tail and dropped it down one of the holes in the reredorter, praying that the running drain below would carry it away. Sometimes in dry summer weather the water in the drain falls and ceases to run, and nothing is washed away at all. In winter it can freeze over. Modern contrivances have their disadvantages. Shovels and middens cannot go wrong.

I have no doubt about how the rat came to be on my bed. I imagined challenging Eleanor Wilmer, and imagined what she might say: 'You are that rat.'

Even though I would not challenge her, and even though she would not really have said those words, they remained in my mind as if she had indeed uttered them. From then on whenever we were thrown together I do believe that a dead rat was in the mind's eye of us both.

I spent so much time with the Abbess in the time that was left to us that my conversations with her become confused in my mind. The Abbess likes to talk. I found this difficult at first. The monastic way of speaking little except at certain times and in certain places suits me, though I do like talking to the little boys. I feel soiled after my conversations with Anne Cathcart but I cannot resist her. When I was a child, I would sometimes not speak for a whole day at a time.

'The cat has got your tongue,' my father would say, tickling me to make me laugh.

Spending most of the day in silence, thoughts bubble up in your mind which would never come if you were chattering freely. You have time to follow where they lead, or else dismiss them. Only if I am unwell, or low in spirits, does the silence seem an enemy, closing in on me, closing me down.

The Abbess said: 'So you are a FitzJames. Through your mother, I seem to remember. I have not met your father. A fine man, no doubt, but—'

'He is a fine man, Madam.'

'Do you understand what will be required of you from now on? You will be with me whenever I need you, as my witness. I shall be discussing grave matters with government servants and the King's Commissioners and what is said must be recorded. You will sit out of their sight and take notes. Can you do that?'

'Yes, Madam.'

'In the Greek language, the word "martyr" means "witness". A witness for Christ. You will be my witness. You will be my martyr.'

'Yes, Madam.'

'There is one more matter. My eyes are no longer good. They have grown dim. I can read easily in daylight, at a window, and preferably in sunlight. If the ink is pale, if the writing is small and cramped, I am lost. If I am passed a paper to be read by the light of candles I put it by and say I will read it later. I will need you to read letters and documents aloud to me, and to write letters at my dictation. Can you do that?'

'Yes, Madam.'

'I do not wish this weakness of mine to be generally known. I do not wish it to be known at all.'

'No, Madam.'

'You will be privy to the inventories, accounts, rolls and records, such as are kept by me here in my house. You will not be responsible for other records or the cartulary of the Abbey's temporalities, which are held in other offices. Everything here must be in order and up to date. The Commissioners and their clerks are hoping to discover irregularities.'

So I was to be busy. My hours in the Library became curtailed. One of the doors from the Abbess's bedroom leads into her private parlour, the other into a bare chamber. There, with a stool and trestle and writing materials, I began to sort out jumbled papers and documents, and to copy letters received, and to transcribe in my best writing the letters that the Abbess dictated to me and which she would sign, the 'Z' of 'Zouche' elaborate with trailing curlicues.

'We will be seeing much of Master John Tregonwell. He is one the King's Commissioners. Their job is to persuade monastic establishments to surrender their property to the King and vacate their Houses.'

'How can that possibly be, Madam?'

She flapped her hand at me. Irritated.

'This is nothing new.'

That was what I had heard the Abbot of Bruton say, down by the river.

'They have always said that surrender is entirely voluntary. Now they are saying that they are inviting surrender, and making it seem like a threat, though only to small, unprofitable Houses. In our case, of course, surrender is unthinkable, and indeed unthought of. We are a Royal foundation, and rich, and many hundreds of people depend upon us for their livings and their well-being.'

'Of course, Madam.'

'They used to say long ago that if the abbot of Glastonbury could marry the abbess of Shaftesbury, they would be richer than the King of England. You have probably heard that. Master Tregonwell, by the way, is from Cornwall.'

'I have seen Cornishmen in the market at Bruton, and tried to talk to them. They have different words,' I said.

'It is another country. The clever and rich ones have our words too. The younger sons who will not inherit property come upcountry to make their fortunes. Master Tregonwell is one such. He is inward with Master Thomas Cromwell. He is familiar with the King. He has decided to appoint himself my rent-collector.'

The Abbess sighed and made a face.

'I thought it wise to agree. It means he now pries into the accounts of all our temporalities.'

But he still had to come to her, she said, to have the mark of the Great Seal affixed to the foot of any legal document. Only the Seal transformed a piece of writing into a deed. The Abbess of Shaftesbury has custody of the Seal, and is the only person who could authorise its use.

'Master Tregonwell acted for the King in the matter of his divorce, and then in the proceedings against the Lady Anne Boleyn. Or the late Queen Anne as I should say. The wrong words at the wrong time get one into trouble. Now we must say, Queen Jane. The King needs a son.'

The Abbess knew about these upheavals as they happened, and so now did I, though I did not understand all the implications. She received letters from London and from the Abbots and Abbesses of other Houses. I read them out to her, and she puzzled over them again for herself, screwing up her eyes, folding and unfolding the papers, lips tight closed. Sometimes she passed news on to the community in Chapter. We knew when Queen Anne was beheaded, leaving a little daughter whose name is Elizabeth. It is curious that I learned more about what went on in the great world shut up in a nunnery than I ever did living free in a town.

'The Cornish people who came to our town,' I told her, 'did not go to Mass.'

'Cornwall is a godless country. Or they follow their own gods.'

'In my town, the Cornish people who come, they go out together into the woods, to the spring where our river starts from. They tie scraps of cloth to the trees round the spring. It is something holy for them.'

'Superstition. There are still country people who do that around here.'

I thought of Our Lady's Girdle. A scrap of cloth. But red silk, kept in a gold box, in God's House. Not just any piece of rag. Did that make the difference? Would its power fail, now that it had gone from Bruton Abbey and was no longer a sacred relic? I had heard from one of the sisters that there was another Our Lady's Girdle, at Westminster, and she believed that to be the real one.

I asked the Abbess about it.

'There is the True Thing,' said the Abbess, 'and then there are fakes. It need not signify. A portrait of a person is not the real person. A copy of that portrait is not the real portrait. What signifies is the meaning. Our own divine worship is but a simulacrum of the perfect worship of the saints in Heaven. In that humble spirit it is graciously received by God. The only truth is God Himself. While we are in this world we strive to be close to Him by whatever means.'

Perhaps, I thought, the new Queen Jane will wear the Westminster Girdle.

'Of course,' said the Abbess, 'all devotion is heartfelt. Nevertheless, ignorant people are pitifully deluded.'

She was still talking about country folk and the rags in the trees.

Our own most sacred relics at Shaftesbury Abbey are, as everyone knows, the bones of St Edward the Martyr. They are kept in a lead casket within a gold ossuary in a side-chapel in the north transept of the Abbey Church, and we have a constant stream of pilgrims from all over England coming to venerate them and acquire virtue and indulgences thereby. Miraculous cures have been recorded, but not I must say for some time. The pilgrims are lodged and fed, but they pay to venerate the relics.

We acquired a house at Bradford-upon-Avon centuries ago so that, if the Abbey were ever again in danger from attack by Norsemen, there would be a safe place to hide the relics. That house is still maintained, said the Abbess, with a few of our nuns and a priest. 'But it is no safer now than anywhere else.'

No one imagined that danger to the holy bones could ever come from within, and nor did we, not even now.

One day I ventured to say: 'Those are dolphins, Madam, on your bed curtains. A dolphin is the emblem of the FitzJames family.'

'Sister Philippa and Sister Joanna worked them for me when I was elected Abbess. Those two were great needlewomen in their time. They toiled together on my bed-curtains for upwards of three years.'

'And the dolphins?'

'That was the ladies' choice, and their design. Dolphins do not belong to the FitzJames family. Dolphins can mean many things. They are swift and agile in the water, representing a keen desire to seek after Christ. A dolphin guides souls across the waters of death. A dolphin can represent human love. A dolphin can represent Christ himself. Christ is the True Fish.'

Christ as a fish, however true the fish, is as far beyond my comprehension as rags in the trees. I will take my dolphin as a symbol of human love.

'Your friend Dorothy Clausey. You know that she is the daughter of the late great Cardinal Wolsey?'

'I do, Madam.'

'You do. And that her mother is Joan Larke. I used to know Joanie in London. She is a dear good woman, and has fallen on her feet I am happy to say.'

Ha! I know something that Anne Cathcart does not know. I said nothing for fear of interrupting the story.

'Joanie's brother was the Cardinal's chaplain, so it was all in the family so to speak. Joanie had another child, a little boy, before she had Dorothy. Then Wolsey became a great man. Even before he was Cardinal, once he was a bishop he could not have these unofficial children and this unofficial woman dangling about him. He found a husband for Joanie, and boarded their two children out, in different families. Dorothy was taken in by the Clauseys until she was old enough to come into the Abbey.'

'So Dorothy may not know her own brother?'

'Probably not. Their mother had more children with her husband. Then he died. And when the Cardinal lost favour, and died, that was when I had letters from London instructing me to continue caring for Dorothy. And Joanie, widowed as she was, has gone and married a marquess as her second husband.'

Some stories do have happy endings. It depends, however, on what manner of man the Marquess is. I think there must be many more kinds of men than just the two described by Anne Cathcart.

I have had very little experience of couples, except from a distance – lovers in the lanes, families harassed by squalling infants, pairs of ancients on sticks. I hardly count my parents, they are unlike other people. The married pair I observed at close quarters with Anne Cathcart hardly enlarged my understanding.

They were Master Piers Perceval and his wife Mistress Agnes – another Agnes, like myself, so I was curious to see her. The Percevals are friends of Anne's from her London days. Passing through Shaftesbury on their way to visit relatives in Cornwall, they sent a message inviting Anne to call upon them at the inn where they were spending the night. Having attained permissions from the Prioress for an hour's visit to her old acquaintances between Vespers and Compline, she took me with her as her companion, as was the rule.

The Percevals greeted Anne with cries of pleasure. The three of them sat around the table, and Master Perceval called for ale. I sat to one side, on a stool, to all intents and purposes invisible. That was only proper. I was only the chaperone.

Mistress Agnes was voluble. After desultory questions as to her dear Anne's health and spirits, she began to talk. She talked unceasingly throughout our visit. With many a merry laugh and toss of the head, she spewed information about her cousins and their marriages and their children, and those children's marriages and places of residence, about her servants and their foibles and short-comings, and the new gowns she was ordering from the new Queen's dressmaker. She recounted stories within her stories, returning to the main path before setting out to regale Anne with anecdotes of who said what to whom and when, and who had been unfaithful and with whom, and how the property was to be divided, veering off into the ill-health of some rich uncle and its probable cause.

She was neither wholly malicious nor wholly charitable. She was a market-woman setting out her wares. She was a female mounte-bank intent on inspiring wonderment.

There was no sieve between what passed through her head and what came out of her mouth, to hold back the dross. Even Anne was silenced, and it is hard to silence Anne. Her initial lively interruptions, her essays at inserting into the torrent of trivia some contributions of her own, were overridden.

Master Perceval meanwhile sat with his hand on his chin, and never took his eyes off his lady wife for one moment. Nothing she said can have been new to him, but he appeared to give her his whole attention. I do not know what was in his mind.

Perhaps he was thinking: 'She is the most fascinating creature. See how she moves her hands, see how expressive are her sweet feat-ures! How utterly charming she is. I am the most fortunate of men.'

Perhaps he was thinking: 'What have I done to be tied for life to this petty self-concerned creature, this small-minded little rattle. I wish she would die.'

I cannot know. But the encounter did have a purpose. When I scraped the legs of my stool on the flagstones to convey that our hour was nearly up, Mistress Agnes looked at her husband. He leaned forward and addressed Anne.

'May I enquire, Mistress Anne, what is your understanding of the future of Shaftesbury Abbey? Is it much spoken of, amongst yourselves?'

'We hear the rumours,' she said. 'But Shaftesbury is safe. Shaftesbury is unassailable.'

'Ah. But in the unlikely – the most unlikely – event of, shall we say, the ultimate catastrophe, what would be your own plans?'

'I have not even thought about it. I suppose I would go to London and throw myself upon the mercy of old friends. But it will not happen.'

'Of course not. But' – he glanced at me – 'may we perhaps speak alone, in confidence?'

'No,' said Anne. 'That is not allowed, under our Rule. Besides which, Sister Agnes is my friend.'

No one thought the coincidence of names worth commenting on. Master Perceval plunged on.

'If you were to return to London you would be in danger of arrest. What you did is known. You are safe so long as you are a nun, but as an unsupported woman you would suffer the full force of the law. The interested party lost her position at Court because of what you did, and the interested party may be hot for revenge.'

Anne blushed scarlet and said nothing.

'I knew your father,' said Master Perceval. 'That is the reason I am here. He was good to me when we were all young. I remember you as a little girl. A very pretty little girl too. Very pretty indeed. I would like to help you.'

His wife gave a laugh, the snort of a horse. She rose from her seat, as if to bring the interview to an end.

'I did not do it, what they say I did,' said Anne.

'So be it,' said Master Perceval. 'I have said what I wanted to say. You may call upon me if you are ever in need, at any time of the night or day.'

He finished what was left of his ale, and stood up.

*

Dame Elizabeth Zouche, I note, is becoming a politician, fostering alliances with influential men with whom she has some personal connection. One of those on whom she is relying for counsel is Sir Thomas Arundell.

'I am selling the leases of some lands to Sir Thomas Arundell. He is very pressing on the matter. Sometimes it is advantageous to concede in small things in order to gain greater things.'

We have had several visits from Sir Thomas Arundell. He and the Abbess sit at the table in her parlour. She sits at the head in her great carved chair. Another chair is carried in for him. I have a stool and small trestle in a corner behind him, taking notes on the conversation.

'As to the lands I am acquiring,' he said to the Abbess on the first occasion that I was on duty, 'I will need your Abbey Seal on the deeds to validate the sale, for afterwards.'

Afterwards? What afterwards?

'It will be advisable,' Sir Thomas continued, 'not to mention our arrangements to anyone outside these four walls. We do not wish to cause scandal or awaken jealousies. Oho, oho, the King himself might be jealous!'

Sir Thomas laughed a false laugh.

He is a persuasive young gentleman. Dame Elizabeth is beguiled by him. For his visits, she wears a high gable hood showing her front hair, and a silk veil. She smiles and uses her eyes. I never saw her coquettish like that with anyone else. He likes her too, though not half as much as he likes himself. He treats her as a woman of the world, leaning back in his chair, one leg in sleek black hose thrown across the other, giving her the news from London, who's in and who's out. A man can be riding high, honours and appointments piled into his lap. Then one false move, or one accusation of treachery, and he loses everything, sometimes his life.

'Sir Thomas Wyatt is one such,' said Sir Thomas Arundell. 'Did you ever hear of him, Madam, down here in your western fastness? A curious poet and a handsome fellow. He was intimate with the Lady Anne Boleyn. How intimate cannot be proven, and of course I would never enquire directly of him, but he has spent time in the Tower under suspicion of adultery. He was only released because his father is a good friend of Thomas Cromwell. That is how the world works.'

He drew a paper out of his shirt-folds and spread it on the table.

'I dined with him only last week, which may have been unwise on my part but he is good company. He gave me some verses which he is passing around among his friends. They have not been printed, they cannot possibly be printed. I will read to you only the beginning. The latter portion is of a nature to land him straight back in the Tower:

> "They flee from me that sometime did me seek
> With naked foot, stalking in my chamber.
> I have seen them gentle, tame and meek
> That now are wild, and do not remember
> That sometimes they put themselves in danger
> To take bread at my hand; and now they range,
> Busily seeking with continued change".'

He read with emphasis and in a dramatic whisper.

'Continued change, Madam,' he said, 'continued change. That is what we must expect.'

He threw the paper down on the table and left. I put it away. I read the rest later. I quite see how it could have resulted in the poet's rearrest.

This Sir Thomas Arundell is another Cornishman, like Master Tregonwell, and another second son. How they do get around, these men from Cornwall. I suspect he is ruthless, though charming when he chooses, as he chooses to charm Dame Elizabeth Zouche. He wears a long, curling blue feather on his hat. The blue of the feather is deeper than the blue of forget-me-nots or the blue of the sky, it is the most intense, drenched blue I ever saw. When he visits her, he lays his hat upon his knee and smooths the feather with his fingers. He has been informing her recently about an 'outrageous' uprising of both clerics and laity in Yorkshire and Lincolnshire against the closing of religious Houses.

'The small, failing Houses, of course?'

'Yes, Madam, of course. We have to put the ruffians down, and hard. Parliament is passing an Act giving the closure of small monastic Houses the full force of the law. Then there can be no misapprehensions.'

Sir Thomas is some kind of kinsman to the King himself. He lets that drop casually. He is close to Master Thomas Cromwell, and was knighted at the coronation of Queen Anne Boleyn. His wife is a first cousin of that unfortunate lady. He is frequently at Court and attends all state occasions. In our own part of the country he has a finger in every pie. His coach, as he brags, is continually on the road between London and the West Country.

'There are courtiers, and there are those that are courted,' said the Abbess to me after he left. 'Sir Thomas is on the cusp between the one and the other. He is a government servant who is looking to improve his position. I have to say that the Arundells are all good Catholics.'

'Why, Madam, did he say that the King might be jealous of the land purchase?'

'If the land sales were known, and we were ever investigated, which God forbid, both we and Sir Thomas could be charged with an exchange of property which should properly, in these strange times, be accruing to the King. If we retain Sir Thomas's support, it will save us any aggravation.'

So at their next meeting it fell to me to note down that she was taking Sir Thomas Arundell's advice and ceding to Master

Thomas Cromwell, as he requested of her, the next presentation to the patronage of a parish in Wiltshire, which would mean a loss of tithes to the Abbey. She dictated the formal letter to me afterwards: 'I am content to facilitate Master Cromwell in this matter and hope that it will give him pleasure.'

Lady Elizabeth puts faith in kinship. She reminded Sir Thomas that she was connected to him through John, Lord Zouche of Cary, whose first wife's mother was an Arundell.

'His first wife's mother, you say.'

He spoke the words laboriously, as if a first wife's mother was a concept so obscure that he had difficulty in apprehending it.

'Is that so, Madam?'

She did not elucidate her own connection to Lord Zouche. He was not interested.

She explained the land transaction with Arundell to the community in Chapter as part of her plan to secure the prosperity of Shaftesbury Abbey for another six hundred years.

'I have every confidence. You will pay no heed to rumours, or to stories about what may or may not be happening elsewhere.'

That autumn of 1536 the Abbess's confidence began to seem misplaced. She learned from her letters details of those uprisings in Yorkshire and Lincolnshire against the closing of monasteries.

The uprisings were put down with violence. Thousands of people had occupied Lincoln Cathedral and refused to disperse. It began as a protest against the closure of Louth Park Abbey – a once great Cistercian House, but with only ten monks remaining. The vicar of Louth was hung, drawn and quartered. Around two hundred others were hanged.

This horror is something quite new. It is hard to apprehend. But it is hundreds of miles away from Shaftesbury.

*

We had our own first experience of a closure soon after the Abbess received this horrid news – which she chose not to share with the community in Chapter.

The Novice Mistress, Mother Monica Slater, called us together and told us that three new sisters were expected, and that our help would be required in preparing places in the dorter and making them comfortable. These sisters and their Prioress were coming from Cannington Priory near Glastonbury, which was being closed down. We were taking them in.

She made it seem unremarkable, unthreatening. Small, failing Houses, she said, had been closing over many years, and Master Thomas Cromwell was simply speeding up the closure of those which could no longer manage their affairs and had no money and could hardly even feed themselves, let alone help the poor. 'It is just common sense.'

While she was speaking thus calmly, I was thinking of the new Act of Suppression to which Sir Thomas had referred, the text of which the Abbess had been sent from London. She required me to make several copies of it. I already had the notion that one day I might compose my own record of what happened – although it is turning out to be more about myself, like a journal – and so I made and kept my own copy:

Forasmuch as manifest sin, vicious, carnal and abominable living is daily used and committed among the little and small abbeys, priories, and other religious houses of monks, canons and nuns, where the congregation of such religious persons is under the number of twelve persons, whereby the governors of such religious houses, and their convent, spoil, destroy, consume, and utterly waste, as well as their churches, monasteries, priories, principal houses, farms, granges, lands, tenements, and hereditaments, as the ornaments of their churches, and their goods and chattels, to the high displeasure of Almighty God, slander of good religion, and to the great infamy of the King's highness and the realm, if redress be not had thereof...

And so on and on.

I said, after Mother Monica ceased speaking about the arrivals from Cannington, 'But what if in the end we too are ordered to close down?'

The words flew out of my mouth. There was a moment's silence. The Novice Mistress crossed herself.

'Do not make yourself ridiculous, Agnes Peppin. Cannington is a small, failed House. Shaftesbury Abbey is in a different category altogether.'

'What will happen to Cannington?' asked a Fairhead. 'I know that House, it is in the middle of the village, a good House.'

'I understand it is being acquired as a residence by a private gentleman. But that is none of our business.'

But all the precious things the Cannington nunnery possessed – and there had been Benedictine nuns in that village for three hundred years – in the way of books and manuscripts, silver and gold plate, pewter, vessels, embroidered vestments, altar cloths, manuscripts, tapestries, glassware, were packed into wagons and saddle bags and taken away after dark up the long road towards London, where the King's new Court of Augmentations would receive them into his coffers. The Commissioners did not go empty-handed, either.

The nuns from Cannington arrived after dark, in the rain. I watched them totter in through the gatehouse, drenched and bewildered. The man who brought their bundles in on a handcart dumped them down on the cobbles and left. We took the shivering sisters into the parlour and fed them soup. They were thin and hunched, their habits muddy at the hems, and no longer black but brownish with age. The Novice Mistress told us that the Cannington sisters were well-born, and had been 'naughty nuns'. In times past, there had been scandals. They did not look naughty now.

Their Prioress, Dame Cecilia de Verney, was old and weak and had no notion of where she was. She was led off to the Infirmary. I was allotted the task of tending her there. I thought to myself that this work might have been given to Eleanor Wilmer, since I already had so much to do. Not that Eleanor would have been any good at it. And the Novice Mistress said that I needed a lesson in humility. The work had its advantages. The Infirmary has fires burning, and is warm.

Dame Cecilia muttered sometimes in a tongue that they said was the French of France. Once she said to me politely, in English,

'Madam, may I go home?'

'Where is home?'

She looked at me with her pink-rimmed eyes and said, 'Away, away.'

'Back to Cannington?'

'No, no, no … Before.'

Once a week I washed her face and hands and feet, and wiped down her bald crotch and shrivelled shanks. Clean linen absorbed the smells. I would have liked to wash her whole body, but the Infirmaress told me that fatal infection from water enters through the skin. I said to myself, please God let me never grow old, I would rather be dead.

Dame Cecilia did die. It was the hour of Matins, the darkest hour, and we were all in choir. In the morning I laid her out, as my mother would have done. I filled the openings in her body with herbs. I sang for her the little songs my mother sang. Dame Cecilia was buried with no marker in the nuns' graveyard.

I prayed for her soul. Whatever my distaste, I know that my hands upon her body were kind, by the grace of God yes my hands were kind.

Not everyone in the Infirmary was kind. The women from the town who did most of the nursing were rough. I saw one of them slap a sick nun across the face because she was crying out loud for the pain in her belly. I saw another forcing lumps of hard bread between the lips of a nun whose mouth was covered in sores. She whimpered and turned her head away but the nurse yanked it back by the strings of her cap. I saw other disrespectful happenings which I prefer not to record. This was not good.

I did not say anything to Dame Alice Doble, the Infirmaress, because since she stalked up and down the ward a dozen times a day she must have seen everything I saw. I did not dare to bring it up in Chapter, which may after all have been the right thing to do. I told Dame Agatha Cracknell, the Prioress, who seemed to me to be the proper person to correct irregularities. I went to her office, where she was surrounded by business. Stupidly, it slipped my mind that she and the Infirmaress were particular friends.

Dame Agatha put her finger to her lips.

'Keep your voice down, Agnes Peppin.'

Later she walked round the cloister with me. We were living through difficult times, she said.

'The Abbess has enough to worry her without inflicting upon her the opinions of a petulant novice. And this is not a subject to be brought up in Chapter. The Infirmaress is doing her best, with more sick sisters than usual. Our older nuns seemed to be falling ill from nothing more than anxiety. If fever or the flux broke out in the Infirmary and spread through the Abbey there would be many deaths. We can only pray.'

If the helpers from the town were turned away, she said, it was unlikely that more would come forward, or that any who did would be of better quality. With increased traffic in the town from visiting officials and their retinues there was more and livelier work to be had in the taverns.

'What is more, Sister Agnes, the running of the Infirmary is not your affair. I would remind you of your duty of humility and your vow of obedience.'

Those Cannington nuns were winter cows. At home in Bruton, when the dark days come, the cattle are brought in from the meadows and woods and tethered in byres within the houses, or in barns on the backways. We bring our own cow, Blossom, into a stall in the room where we sleep.

The cows feed on hay and leaves which before the end of winter are sparse and sour. Their ribs and hipbones protrude from the loose and scabby skin. Some slump down and do not stand up again. The ones who die have to be dragged out with ropes and disposed of.

When the spring comes, the survivors are driven out to smell the air and taste new grass. Some have to be half-carried. Then they are reborn. They gambol, insofar as cattle can, and within a couple of weeks' grazing they are plump and well.

The Cannington winter cows looked as if they could never gambol. But they did settle down – and became quite demanding, as if we owed them something instead of the other way around. There were complaints about them in Chapter.

We all called them the Melancholies. They were not sick in their bodies, but something had gone wrong for them, and we tended to avoid them as if they carried some infection – except one, who fascinated me. I would come across her sitting alone in the slype, sometimes with her hands over her face, sometimes staring ahead. There was something familiar about her pale, thin face. I think that she looked like my mother.

I wanted to know her. When she saw me coming along she sat up straight and picked up the Primer on the bench beside her and pretended to read. I know that when I passed, she sank back into inertia. One day I took a piece of sewing – stitching up torn lace on the hem of a surplice for old Father Bucket – and sat on the bench directly opposite her, and looked at her over my work. She kept her eyes on her book but did not turn a page. I tried to imagine what it was like to be her. I thought about the time when I was waiting for my child to be born, when my life closed down. And of the time after they took him away. And again of my mother, who did – nothing. No meaning for her in anything, no colour, no pleasure.

'Are you missing Cannington?' I asked my Melancholy.

'No. There was nothing there.'

'Are you unhappy here? Would you rather be somewhere else?'

'It makes no difference to me where I am.'

She got up and walked away.

When I told my Abbess about her, she was neither surprised nor alarmed. This is what happens to some nuns, she told me. 'They fall into darkness. They lose touch with life, with God.'

'They lose their holy faith?'

'Perhaps not. Many in the religious life find their faith paling from time to time. If they are well-rooted, it hardly matters. The routine of the Rule carries them forward. The community contains and constrains us all. And apart from that, of course, private prayer...'

I have seen the Abbess kneeling in private prayer with her head high and her eyes open before the statue of the Blessed Virgin in the Abbey Church. Her face at such times shows no ecstasy, only stillness and hardness.

I could ask the Abbess about most things. Observing the amount of business she had on hand, and the enormous sums of money which came in and went out, I did wonder aloud to her about our vow of poverty. But we own nothing for ourselves, she said, looking at me sharply.

'We administer our wealth for the glory of God, and for the well-being of the people in our charge. A religious house that does not prosper is not fulfilling its obligations and responsibilities and cannot survive, especially in these disturbed times. We are exceptional of course, we are an ancient and Royal foundation.'

How many dozens of times have I heard her say that?

But there were some questions that arose in my mind that I could not ask. God is all-merciful and all-powerful. Why then do the chantry priests spend so many hours of their days and nights praying for the relief of the souls in Purgatory? He could admit them into Heaven whenever He willed. And why did He need our continuous praise? But the Holy Office was the point of our lives. Without that, what were we here for?

'It was easier for the sisters to find meaning in their lives in the olden days,' said the Abbess, 'when they made their own clothes, and cooked their own food, and worked in the fields and workshops and with the animals. It made for health and it gave variety. It is the lack of variety that drives some sisters into foolishness and misbehaviour, and others into petty bickering, and some into accidie. Manual labour used to be considered to be a means of salvation. No longer, not for a long time.'

She stretched out a hand and picked up her cup of wine, and took a morsel of the white wheat bread that only she and her important visitors ever tasted.

So in the olden days all nuns were Martha, as well as Mary. I begin to think that Martha and Mary are the same person. Spin the coin.

The Abbess had said 'accidie'. Never having heard the word, I thought she said 'accident'. I have learned from reading that it means spiritual sloth, apathy, a deadness of feeling. It was that from which the Melancholies suffered. They could not enjoy breaks in routine even when they occurred, as in the parlour after Compline – after which we should go straight to bed and observe the Grand Silence until after Prime the next morning.

But sometimes we sat up late and gossiped. It was an irresistible temptation, but the result was that it was painful to be woken when the bell rang for Matins and Lauds in the small hours. Occasionally one or two of the Fairheads missed Matins altogether. I was often among those who, half-asleep, fumbling with tapes and pins, and late, stumbled down the curling night-stair from the dorter into the Abbey Church. I have seen nuns sleepwalking down the night-stair and dozing all through the Office.

The three Melancholies, though they seemed loath to go to their beds, took no part in the parlour conversations, but looked from one face to another, as if they did not understand the words, and they were mute in choir. I myself am sometimes overwhelmed in choir by the sweetness of our chanting curling up out of the silence and dimness like the song of blackbirds. I like it when one voice flies up above the line of chant, making a harmony, or weaves in and out of the melody, making patterns. Such chanting really does bring peace to the soul. It is entirely unlike the jaunty modern airs which Father Robert Parker plays on his lute, or the eerie laments, starting and stopping, slipping between the notes, that Mother Onion sings in her own language.

Sometimes, though, I become disconnected. When we have choir practice, clustered around the great choir book, I imagine the black squares of the notes arranged up and down on the four lines of the stave to be rooks on a fence, perching or alighting or flying away. And none of us articulates the words of the psalms and prayers and canticles in choir properly because we have little idea what most of the Latin means, or even where one word begins and another ends, and it sometimes becomes just a slurry of sound. Then the Prioress, who is also the Choir Mistress, raps with her ivory baton on the ledge of her stall and makes us begin all over again.

So I did not always maintain my holy pride in taking part in the Work of God, and have sometimes felt it is an empty form.

That was my kind of accidie. It was not grave. Routine is the root of our Rule. Love and duty are not what you feel. Love and duty are what you do. I do believe to this day that it was enough that we did it, and that God heard it.

I restrain myself from dwelling on such questions. 'Scruples,' as the Novice Mistress would say.

Some of the Fairheads send messages to each other during the Holy Office, keeping the line of the plainsong intact:

'Shall we go out to the town later?'

'Yes, there is a handsome new ostler at the inn as I hear.'

They do it so cleverly, it makes us laugh behind our hands.

The Melancholies' lips move in choir, but no sounds come. They never smile or laugh, though when my own particular Melancholy chances to speak I see that she still has teeth. I suppose she is about thirty.

We happened, she and I, both to be in the cloister at dusk, waiting for the bell to ring for Compline, watching starlings wheeling above us in complicated skeins and circles. She was facing away from me, but I knew it was my Melancholy. Although the habit makes all of us the same, I recognise my sisters even from the back or at a distance from the shape and tilt of their heads under the veil, from the slant of their shoulders, from their height and girth and gait. Some few of them limp, or wave their hands about because they are half-witted.

There are two ancient nuns who are by no means half-witted, and who are recognisable from a great distance if only because they are always together. They were professed nuns already when Dame Elizabeth Zouche came to the Abbey as a novice. They knew the previous Abbess, and the one before. Our King was only a child of five when their second abbess was elected. They love to tell you that.

They are Dame Philippa and Dame Joanna, the ladies who embroidered the Abbess's bed-curtains. They do not do needlework

any more because their sight is weak, and Dame Joanna has a trem-
ble in her hands. They are inseparable. Because of their great age
they are excused the night Offices. Neither would be able to get
down the winding night-stair from the dorter without tumbling.
They both walk with a stick – Dame Philippa because she is large
and her swollen legs cannot carry the weight, and Dame Joanna
because her back is bent and she is in pain from her joints. Dame
Joanna's mouth has caved in for lack of teeth, and her nose and
chin nearly come together. Dame Philippa has a face as flat as a
full moon.

They totter round and round the cloister as if yoked, the high
bulky one and the low crooked one, reminiscing about the old
days. Sometimes they stop and look at one another in delight and
laugh their cracked laughs. They share their stories with anyone
who will listen. They came into the Abbey as young girls and had
dear friends, all gone now, buried in the Abbey graveyard, God rest
their souls. They speak the names of their lost friends, and recall
their foibles. Their first Abbess found the records and accounts,
and the vestments and the altar cloths, all in a terrible state of
muddle and neglect when she was elected. The two of them had
helped her sort everything out. Before their time, the Infirmary
nuns used to bring men in, and drink with them, lolling on the
patients' beds. The old ladies cackle at the very thought.

They have a special devotion to the Blessed Virgin and spend
long minutes standing side by side every day before her statue in
the Abbey Church, in veneration. They have their holy faith, they
have each other, they have their memories, they have spent all their
lives in the Abbey and the Abbey is the whole world. They are
the incarnation of the Rule of Stability. I have never known such
joyous women.

There is no Vow of Stability in the outside world, and in
Bruton people come and go. There are new families, squatting in
an abandoned hovel, arriving during the night from God knows

where. Young men – and sometimes young women – just disappear. They go to look for work on the coast, or down Exeter way, or have found a position in some gentleman's house. And yet there are men and women in Bruton who in all their lives only know the town, and the fields and forest where they graze their beasts, and maybe they have been to Batcombe or have relatives in Wincanton. My father is one such, and his father before him.

Rich people are different. Gentry who live in great houses visit other great houses many miles away, in other counties. Those who have fingerings in the great world know London. No one whom I knew in Bruton had been to London. When the Abbess asked Master Tregonwell what first drew him to London, he replied:

'The arrow of ambition.'

In Bruton, many a man's arrow of ambition falls no further than on a more favourable strip of the Borough Field. He may never speak in all his life with anyone whom he has not known since childhood. Rich men meet new people. To live among strangers – an impossible thought for my parents – holds no threat. The greatest men have business in countries over the sea, beyond London. I have never seen the sea and cannot imagine it.

My father's ideas, such as they are, are his own. I think he is more perfectly himself than is any aping courtier. I begin to think that the intensity of experience is the same for all, whatever one's range, and that few people lead more fulfilled lives than Dame Philippa and Dame Joanna.

My mind wanders easily because I live in my imaginings and silences. Thinking about the two old ladies, I forgot my Melancholy for an eternal moment.

Ravished anew by the starlings, I said to her – because she was the only one there, and the thought came:

'The birds of the air are free as no human beings are.'

'No,' she said, without turning towards me. That would have taken too much effort on her part. 'The starlings are not free. They must do what they always do, what they always have done since the Creation. They cannot help it. They have no decisions to make. They are of one mind, they share one mind. A bird with ideas of its own does not survive.'

I told her something that John Harrold had told me – that there are insects like big foreign grasshoppers which are born solitary and are all marked and coloured differently until they come together in a swarm. Then they change and all become of one and the same colour and pattern. I asked my Melancholy whether she thought that was some kind of enchantment, like with the starlings. She said:

'It is the alchemy of propinquity. Like the way that many of us bleed at the same time every month.'

When our monthly bleeding occurs we go to a bin in the Laundry and take a handful of rags. The bloodied rags are thrown in another bin to be washed. The first time, I was there alone and picked over the rags seeking the least noxious, for they are boiled up and used again and again. Then my bleedings became irregular, and had I not known that it was impossible I would have feared I was with child again. But after a few months I was never alone at the bin. We scavenge for rags together because many of us bleed in unison. What my Melancholy said was true. I am a starling, I am a foreign grasshopper, I am a woman in a community, I am a nun. If I have ideas of my own, I might not survive.

4

UNTHINKABLE

Master John Tregonwell is a pest. He lacks the urbane attraction of Sir Thomas Arundell. He is a squat creature, bundled up in mantles and furs whatever the weather, as if he were always cold. He has the run of the Abbey, and access to all documents, by virtue of his new position as the Abbess's rent-collector. He is constantly coming into my office and standing behind my stool, leaning over me as he affects to check what I am doing.

One day he put out a hand, grabbed my chin and jerked my head round towards him, his eyes bulging:

'Sweet Agnes Peppin...'

I told the Abbess.

'Is that all?' she asked.

'It is disagreeable, Madam. What should I do?'

The Abbess sighed and turned her head from me.

'When something goes wrong between a man and a woman, it is always the woman's fault.'

'Even when it is not?'

'Women are the daughters of Eve. We share in her shame. Offer it up. Pray to Our Lady for special grace. And keep out of Master Tregonwell's way.'

How can I?

✻

Dame Elizabeth Zouche had believed that her compliance to Master John Tregonwell, and her special relationship with Sir Thomas Arundell, would solve any future problems.

In private, with me, propped on her pillows she wondered whether she should adopt a different strategy and challenge the constant demands, as would a man — even though the Abbots, monks and canons were all being put under similar pressures and did not seem any more able to withstand them than did the convents.

'As the Abbess of Shaftesbury I have the statutory right to sit in Parliament. Did you know that? No Abbess has ever availed herself of that privilege. I have considered it. I could challenge the government's policies. I am not bashful. But it is not expected. My lords would not hear a woman's voice. They would just hear a twittering and wish it to cease. My words would not reach them, even though my understanding might outstrip theirs. You see how it is with Tregonwell and Arundell.'

I did see. She told me about Elizabeth Barton, a nun of our own Benedictine Order who had spiritual influence in the days of Cardinal Wolsey and was received by the King. When she condemned the King's attempts to annul his marriage to his first Queen and his annexation — as she saw it — of the English Church from the Pope, the King of course turned against her. She did not give up. So she was accused of sexual irregularities and of being insane.

'Elizabeth Barton made prophecies and saw visions. That was the only way she could get attention and make her woman's voice heard. She prophesied that the King would die if he cast off his first queen.'

'Madam, he did not die.'

'Indeed he did not. He flourishes like the green bay tree. Maybe Elizabeth Barton was in truth a little mad. But she had courage.'

'Where is she now?'

'She was arrested and condemned without trial. She is the only woman whose head has ever been boiled and stuck up on a spike on London Bridge. This was not so long ago. It was the year before you came to the Abbey.'

I remembered hearing how Dr Layton said to Dr Leigh, in Bruton, 'Go and boil your head,' and understood now the meaning beneath it. The severed heads are boiled so that they do not decompose so fast. Then they fix iron cages around them so that they do not fall to pieces.

'Yes, Madam, it is voluntary,' said Master Tregonwell, clutching his fur collar closer beneath his double chin. He has no neck to speak of. 'We are inviting surrender from all the smaller monastic Houses. But in the long run the government will be looking further afield, at the greater Houses. Nothing of course is on the statute book yet.'

'Unthinkable, impossible,' said the Abbess. 'Civil society would break down.'

'How so?'

'The great Abbeys look after the poor. We feed them, clothe them, give them shelter, tend them when they are sick. Many of our Houses give girls the only education available to them. Who would do that if not us?'

'Madam, private charity can do as much. The worst cases of poverty can be looked after in the wider community. Legislation is in process even as we speak to devolve the care of the impotent poor on to the parish.'

'But it is we, the great Abbeys, who have the means. You forget that we are rich.'

'I do not forget that for one single second, Madam. You are rich because you own too much land and property. You have appropriated over centuries great tracts of good land – and mills, and manors, fairs, markets, farms, churches with their tithes – in the form of dowries from your nuns, to be held in perpetuity. It is wealth that is thus stolen from the commonwealth. It is removed from the polity, it is dead to the nation. There is less and less for the King, and less for freemen to buy and to sell. There is no development, no innovation, no enterprise. Only stagnation and decline. Even your donors, perceiving the trap, would like their properties back. I have seen correspondences.'

'These are opportunists, who see the way the wind may be blowing.'

'Opportunity and the ability to profit from it are the drivers of prosperity for all.'

'We care for the land, Master Tregonwell. We pay for the maintenance of bridges and roads on our properties, which all men who travel must use. The great abbeys and monasteries provide employment for thousands of people up and down the whole country.'

'Whoever is lord of a manor provides employment. Ultimately all land belongs to the King. He desires to put the accumulated wealth of the monastic Houses to better use. Not just the land, which will be leased or sold, but the materials of your establishments and the silver and gold and costly items that are locked up in your coffers.'

'Put the wealth to better use? What possible better use?'

'Schools and colleges for the betterment of the general population. The well-being, security and defence of our country.'

'We already educate children who come into our charge. We already contribute to the Crown annually not only cattle and sheep on demand but the accoutrements of a settled number of the King's soldiers. I think it was six that this Abbey fitted out last year. It is expensive.'

'Six is nothing. I am talking about an army. We are threatened by war with France.'

'You cannot,' said the Abbess, 'overturn the great work of six hundred years in an afternoon, as you seem to believe. Shaftesbury

Abbey has stood where it stands since the days of our founder King Alfred.'

'That is just the trouble, Madam. Times have changed. Look at your buildings. Leaking and rotten and draughty. The mean, unglazed windows. As for your steps and stairs…'

'What of our steps and stairs?'

'They are hollowed out and worn, the treads are chipped and uneven.'

'Our steps and stairs are hallowed by the pious feet of generations of our sisters.'

'Quite so. They are a hazard.'

'We are continually repairing. We renew the thatches regularly.'

'Thatch is for peasants and villagers. Any building of note now is tiled.'

'We are restoring the damaged parts of the Abbey Church. The lead on the church roof is superb.'

'You are wasting your time. And you may be sure that the quality of the lead on the roof has not escaped my notice.'

'My house, this house in which you are sitting at your ease, Sir, is tiled with stone.'

'You always knew how to look after yourself, Madam.'

'It is not for me but for my sacred office as Abbess of Shaftesbury, and for my successors.'

'Quite so. Reflect upon the peculiar temptations to which an Abbess like yourself is prone – independent, comfortable, autocratic, and too many luxurious entertainments of those whom you are wooing as donors.'

'Entertainment is expected. Just as the entertainment of distinguished visitors and government servants like yourself is expected, sir. Will you take another cup of my good Rhenish wine?'

'Thank you, I will.'

There was on the table a pewter platter containing the Abbess's favourite dish, mushrooms dressed in cream, well-peppered, with a thick scattering of chopped parsley. Two silver spoons lay beside the platter. Dame Elizabeth raised a mushroom to her lips with one of the spoons and gestured to Tregonwell to take the other.

'This is royal fare,' he said, his mouth full of mushroom and cream, 'but distinguished visitors will in years to come be entertained equally royally by the gentlemen who build their mansions on land previously hogged – excuse the term – by the monastic houses.'

'I do not excuse the term. It is inexcusable.'

There was a pause. Tregonwell slurped his wine and burped. He wiped his mouth with the back of his hand. His face was becoming red.

'It is not just the material conditions, it is your ways of thought. You are incapable of thinking new thoughts.'

'I see no need to think new thoughts.'

'That again is the trouble, Madam. Europe is alive with new thoughts – not all of which the King agrees with, he is a good Catholic, but you cannot send time running backwards. The Church of England belongs to the people, as does the Word of God, to be heard and read in their own language. It does not belong to clerks and clerics muttering in a tongue which neither they nor their congregations understand. Nor to nuns and monks chanting psalms and prayers into the empty air seven times a day, nor to chantry priests under the illusion that they are saving the dead some years in Purgatory. Years have no meaning in the eye of eternity. Nor is intercession needed between the soul of a Christian and his God. Nor does the Church of England believe in monks and nuns taking money from credulous pilgrims in return for the chance to venerate painted effigies and a few old bones. Salvation cannot be bought and sold. Superstition, barbarism. I am sorry, Madam, but it is so.'

'You are mistaken, sir. All the art, craft, architecture, sculpture, music, the works of holy charity itself and everything in the known world that is not barbaric, came through religion and is upheld by religion, by the Church.'

'It did. And the Church has held on to its sole possession of these things quite long enough. The human spirit is on the move. Time has teeth, Madam, and the new men are inspired by holy zeal. Nothing is for ever. Nothing remains the same. Not even the same remains the same.'

At breakfast next morning, Sister Onora said that during the night she had seen from a window an enormous white cat on the roof of the Abbey Church when she was on her way to the reredorter. She was not normally compelled to visit the reredorter between Matins and Prime, but there had been something in the soup which did not agree with her.

There was a whispered discussion about the soup. There had been shreds of pig meat in it which were perhaps tainted. We had all felt queasy. Sitting next to Sister Onora as I was, I asked her in a low voice to say more about the enormous cat. Just how big was it?

'As big as a dog,' she said.

I said that if it was the same size as the dog which the Prioress carried in her sleeve it was a normal cat.

'It was as big as a big dog. As tall as a goat. It was a white goat with the head of a cat. It is an omen. I believe it was the Devil trying to find a way in.'

We wanted to know from which window she had seen the Devil, and she said it was from the last one before the archway into the reredorter.

'But you cannot see the roof of the Abbey Church from that window.'

'It does not signify. Sometimes it is possible to see something that cannot normally be seen.'

We could not gainsay that. Sister Onora was calm, as she always is when she tells what she has seen.

'Will you tell the Abbess?'

'The Abbess will already know, if the Devil is let loose in the Abbey.'

'We are not praying hard enough,' said Sister Eleanor Wilmer.

Under the circumstances, knowing what I knew, all this talk of omens left me uneasy.

Master Tregonwell came to us again, this time about money. The Abbess sought to impress him by reminding him yet again of the wealth of the Abbey, thinking to intimidate him. Money is power. She still could not see that the Abbey's wealth was precisely what most inflamed Master Tregonwell against us.

'Shaftesbury Abbey is rich – on paper – in rents, dues, taxes, tithes, and the ample produce your lands and farms afford you. But you are merely turning money over. Why are you so frequently in difficulties? Why is there never ready cash for emergencies such as a failed harvest? I have uncovered mismanagement, wastage and fraud. Your investment is so diffuse that even you cannot oversee it all.'

'I visit all our estates annually and go through the accounts everywhere and give instructions to my managers for any improvement necessary.'

'I have made a study of all the accounts. Your systems are antique and unreliable. There are too many middlemen and a tolerated vagueness that would be considered culpable in any other commercial enterprise.'

'Shaftesbury Abbey is not principally a commercial enterprise. It is a place of prayer and holiness.'

'It is indeed a veritable prayer factory. The question is, of what use are these incontinent prayers, sprayed into the air by night and by day?'

'If you do not recognise the power of prayer then I despair of your immortal soul. What you call the new thinking disregards the foundations of our holy faith. It is a pity that I gave you the position you now hold. I had looked to find in you a wise friend and an advisor.'

'That is what I seek to be. The position I now hold places me well to make an assessment, which happens also to be my duty as a Commissioner. I have noticed that many of the sisters here do not obey your Rule. I have seen and heard such things as would cause scandal to any decent Christian.'

'There are among us some young women who affect the modern manners. You accused us before of being mired in the old world. You cannot have it both ways, Master Tregonwell.'

'His Majesty the King can have it any way he wills. But let us return to the question of money. No one wishes monks and nuns to starve when their houses close. There will be pensions.'

I could tell that the Abbess was now paying him a keen attention.

'In the most unlikely event of this becoming necessary, how would the pensions be calculated?'

'By negotiation with the Head of each House, to be confirmed by the signature of Master Cromwell. A great Abbess such as yourself could naturally expect a generous allowance, and her nuns something less, by agreement. This of course would depend on compliance. Refusal to comply would result in nothing, and – as has already happened up north – something far, far worse than nothing.'

'You are threatening me.'

'I am setting out the facts.'

'And what do you get out of it all, Master Tregonwell?'

'Opportunity.'

He grinned his wolfish grin.

*

The King has given Gillingham and its castle to Queen Jane, who is expecting a child. Anne Cathcart tells me that Queen Jane has a mean little mouth. She also tells me that the late Queen Anne's sister Mary was much the prettier of the two, and that the King had her, as well. Anne knows from hearsay many things but few of them are important. Meanwhile Dame Elizabeth Zouche has been concerned that the Abbey's vital arrangements concerning wood-collecting in Gillingham Forest might be affected. Fortunately the Queen's agents seem to take no interest in the matter.

The next thing that Dame Elizabeth hears from London is that Queen Jane has died in childbirth. It is a boy, at last, and he lives. The King has a son. He is named Edward. He will be the next King of England. It is said that he looks just like his father. But I do not know what King Henry looks like.

During the autumn of 1538 we had a Visitation from the Bishop. There is meant to be such a Visitation every three years, and the present Bishop of Salisbury – we belong to the diocese of Salisbury – had not visited since his election.

The Cellaress had to bustle about getting in stocks of provisions for the entertainment of the Bishop and his retinue. Geese, carp, flour for the white bread, salads, fruits. The cost, she warned us in Chapter, was formidable. Next year we would be on short commons.

Carts loaded with produce rolled in from the Abbey's farms. Normal routine was overturned. The Bishop's clerks would be examining the books and accounts of every department of the Abbey, both temporalities and spiritualities. Everything had to be in good order, ready to be presented, as would an up-to-date inventory of all the House's material goods. The financial position must be made clear. Even the foundation's Charter, and the certificate confirming the election of the present Abbess, would have to be produced for inspection. The Bishop would also be examining every nun individually from the Abbess to the newest novice, who was myself.

Monasteries of men are also subject to scrutiny from their Bishops, but there is a subtle difference when it comes to nunneries. Dame Monica used the phrase 'the frailty of women' to explain why nuns are subjected to particularly rigorous Visitations. Women require supervision.

'It is unthinkable that women could be ordained in Holy Orders or administer the sacraments, let alone celebrate the Mass.'

I know that. These are matters that lie outside a woman's sphere.

'It is understood by the Church,' said Dame Monica, 'that women are constitutionally and morally the weaker sex and that women's communities are therefore more prone to irregularities and laxity. As all priests are our fathers in God, and the Bishop is God's representative, it behoves us to bow our heads, emulate Our Lady, and submit to the Church's rulings.'

We bowed our heads as she spoke. I was thinking of Father Pomfret, and of Father Robert Parker – and of John Tregonwell. For all these I do agree that 'frailty' is the wrong word. Yet I know many women both here and at home who are strong and self-disciplined, as men are meant to be, and some are. And many men who are moody and weak, as women are believed to be – and as some women indeed are also.

Authority belongs to men. Their authority cannot be denied because it is not an idea. It is fact. Yet I do not wish I were a man. So many men are like children, they cannot think beyond their own concerns and desires, and they tailor their opinions and allegiances to serve the same.

*

It was arranged that I should be professed as a nun during the Visitation of the Bishop. I would be exchanging my white veil for a black one. I would prostrate myself before the Bishop and the Abbess in the chancel and confirm my lifetime's vows on obedience, stability and humility. The Bishop would give a homily to mark the occasion. Mother Monica impressed upon me that it was an honour to be professed in the presence of the Bishop. I was looking forward to this. I wanted to be a full member of the family at this difficult time – for our community is a family, of a strange kind.

The Abbess announced the Visitation in Chapter. The Bishop's name was Nicholas Shaxton. He was, she said, one of the best known bishops in the realm, a distinguished man who had preached before the King himself.

'The elder of you among my daughters will have experienced a Visitation before. Many of you have not.'

So she told us what would happen. The Bishop and his entourage would arrive at the door of the Abbey Church, robe themselves in the vestry, and proceed to the altar of the Abbey Church for a High Mass. Then we all would go into the Chapter House to hear a sermon given by one of his chaplains, mercifully in English. After that would come a sequence of formalities which we would, said the Abbess, find tedious. So far as we were concerned, the important part came afterwards.

The Chapter House will be cleared, and each one of us will enter in turn, alone, to be cross-examined by the Bishop, our answers and comments noted down by his clerks. He will ask us not only about ourselves but about our sisters – what breaches in discipline we have observed, what departures from the Rule. We are obliged to give the name of any sister against whom we make an accusation. We will also be asked whether we had any complaints about the conditions under which we lived.

'Each of you,' said the Abbess, 'will speak according to your understanding of the truth. You may or may not consider that the trivialities which normally occupy us in Chapter may be overlooked – the quality of your food, the occasional breaking of the Great Silence, some particular weakness of one of your sisters.

'Or you may feel it your sacred duty to deliver yourself of such complaints. That is your right. There is no reason why even personal animosities should not be recorded. When it comes to any serious irregularities that you may have observed, only private prayer and meditation will enable you to reconcile charity, and the good of the community, with the duty of disclosure.'

Grave complaints about the behaviour of a sister, she said, would have grave repercussions. The sister in question would be recalled by the Bishop to hear the charge against her. If she denied the charge, she would be allowed two hours to bring forward four sisters able and willing to confirm her innocence.

'In my experience,' said the Abbess, 'it can be hard to find so quickly four sisters willing to involve themselves in such procedures. Grave accusations against a sister or sisters therefore should only be made under the strongest prickings of the individual conscience.'

The Abbess paused, smoothed down her gown over her knees, folded her hands in her lap, and raised her head, scanning the benches, looking at each one of us individually.

'If you feel you have no complaints, you only have to answer every question with the words "*Omnia bene*" – "All is well" – and he will enquire no further.'

The Abbess was speaking with double tongue. I cannot tell to what extent the less subtle of our sisters understood what she was saying. I was not even quite sure myself what she was saying.

'The Bishop will be exigent and critical. Everything, from the cleanliness and correctness of your habit, to the cleanliness and purity of your hearts and minds, and your adherence to our Rule, will be opened to him. After the examinations, both of the management of the Abbey and of each of us, he will deliver himself of what are called Injunctions, and administer penances, individually and collectively.'

Privately, the Abbess told me more about this Bishop Shaxton. He is not one of us. It was the patronage of Queen Anne Boleyn which set him on the path to a bishopric.

'He is known to have studied heretical books. He is known to have prayed at Mass that the clergy be relieved of their vow of celibacy. Bishop Shaxton is firmly in what is called the reformist camp.'

His continuing rise depends on the favour of Master Thomas Cromwell, who is well ahead of the King when it comes to matters of reform.

'Well, my child, they call it reform,' said the Abbess. 'I call it blasphemy and sacrilege. I do not expect any advantages to accrue to us from this Visitation. We must be on our guard. If he chooses to find irregularities, or if any sisters are impelled by conscience to make grave accusations, it is upon myself that the heaviest blame will fall. That is as it must be. But such an outcome would strengthen any the arguments for our dissolution. Although that is of course unthinkable, it will make the negotiations harder.'

Bishop Shaxton turned out to be a stunted man with a face like a pug. He wore for the High Mass the Abbey's richest cope, heavy with gold thread and green silk embroideries. It was made by our nuns long before the days of even Dame Philippa and Dame Joanna. I have seen it close up. It is worn out, the embroideries in shreds. From a distance it is still gorgeous, and it swamped the small Bishop.

Then came a surprise. He did not mutter the Mass under his breath as all priests do, as if in private communication with God with the congregation as distant spectators. This small Bishop has a large voice, which raised bellowing echoes in the vaulting. I was not predisposed to like him, but his celebration of the Mass stirred me. He was including us. We were sharing in the Mass. His voice will have reached far down the nave to where a few devout people from the town were standing. I have never forgotten that Mass. If that is an aspect of 'reform', I am in favour of it.

My interview with him two days later was the last, since I was the last novice to be admitted. As I went in, the Chapter House seemed vast. I had only known it filled with our rustling, whispering, sweat-scented community. He stood at a desk, and I stood before him. The clerks with their writing tablets sat on benches against the wall behind him. I was prickling with nervousness.

I had spent the two days trying to decide what to do. I could tell the Bishop about the Prioress's little white dog, which slept in her bed. Our Rule prohibits the keeping of any pet animals. I could tell him about Sister Catherine Hunt's greed. If a piece of bread, the merest crust, is left unattended at table, she puts her hand over it and it is down her throat in an instant. No wonder that she is fat. She is a kind soul but this slyness infuriates me. Anger is a deadly sin. Small annoyances fester, in a life as close-knit as ours. I had confessed my feelings about Sister Catherine's greed to Father Pomfret, but did not bring them to Chapter, as I might have done.

I could tell the Bishop about the evenings of chatter in the parlour after Compline, when we should have been observing the Great Silence. I could tell him my suspicions about Dorothy and Father Robert Parker. I could complain about Master Tregonwell, though I knew that would not do me any good at all. I could tell him all about the Fairheads and what they got up to. I could tell him that Sister Eleanor Wilmer put a dead rat on my bed.

As I waited for my turn to go into the Chapter House, my heart thumping, I became certain that I did not want to tell the

Bishop any of it. Partly because our frailties and shortcomings are our own, between ourselves and God, and between ourselves and our sisters. If that is heretical, then I am heretical. Also because I wanted to protect Dame Elizabeth Zouche, and to protect the Abbey itself against any possible catastrophe. She was so confident. But every time these days that she used that word 'unthinkable', I had a sinking feeling.

So as I stood there before him, whatever Bishop Shaxton asked me, I answered '*Omnia bene*'. He looked exasperated. Before he dismissed me he asked me where I was from. When I told him, he said: 'Ah, Abbot Eley. An interesting man.'

And then: 'Do you not have anything at all that you feel you should tell me?'

I said: 'I know we are all uneasy here about what the future will bring.'

He shuffled the papers on his desk.

'We are all uneasy, daughter. Change rocks the foundations. What will be will be.'

After Compline, thinking that the Abbess might need me, I made my way to her house, was let in by her maid, went up the stairs, and approached her door. I heard her voice winding on and on, and did not like to interrupt by entering. Then I heard the Bishop's deep voice, raised to a roar: 'MADAM, BE MUTE!'

I did not stay.

The next day we assembled with trepidation in the Chapter House once more to hear his conclusions and Injunctions. We waited and waited. No one came. Bishop Shaxton and his entourage had left Shaftesbury at dawn.

The Abbess swept in and announced without comment that the Bishop had been recalled urgently to London in order to lend his voice to an important conference at Lambeth Palace. Then she dismissed us and told us to return to our normal occupations. The ceremony of my profession as a nun was due to take place that day after Vespers, and that never happened either. It was 'postponed', I was informed. I felt rejected, realising that I was of no importance in the scheme of things. My profession was never mentioned again. I remained a novice. That caused me to suspect that the Abbess had, maybe unknown even to herself, begun to give up hope.

She did tell me that Bishop Shaxton had been summoned to a conference with German theologians who had travelled from their country with the intention of formulating an agreement with the English bishops on Christian belief and practice. Some English bishops were concerned that the German Protestants sought to push them further than they, or certainly the King, would wish to go.

'The Germans,' said the Abbess, 'are not only against the celibacy of the priesthood, but against holy images, against private masses, against the veneration of angels. And much else. Bishop Shaxton would be supporting the Germans.'

In the event the King dissolved the conference. Everything I have ever heard about the King convinces me that although he defied the Pope for his own reasons, and was excommunicated, he retains his Catholic faith.

'Bishop Shaxton,' said the Abbess, 'is trying to keep in with both the King and Master Cromwell. That is not easy in these days. They seem to speak with one voice but they do not. Cromwell will surely overstep the mark and fall, but not soon enough.'

She could not bring herself to say, 'Not soon enough for us.'

Shortly after the Visitation she saw Sir Thomas Arundell again. He stroked his blue feathers and told her about a further and more violent uprising in the north against the suppressions, this time in Cumberland and Westmoreland. The rebels called it the Pilgrimage of Grace.

'I,' he said, 'call it the Pilgrimage of Disgrace.'

Two hundred people were hanged and many slaughtered.

'My dear Dame Elizabeth, I speak to you now as a friend. I do advise you to surrender your Abbey now. Most are doing so. Follow the moo, my dear, follow the moo.'

'What do you mean, follow the moo? I am not a cow.'

'Quite right, indeed you are not. It is London street talk, it means to follow the majority.'

'Shaftesbury Abbey is no part of the majority.'

'There are to be no exceptions, Madam. It is not only the smaller religious Houses that are being dissolved now, but all. Including the great Abbeys. Including Glastonbury, and Shaftesbury. Surrender is no longer voluntary. It only ever was in theory. It will be less painful, and more advantageous, to follow the moo. Refusal to sign the deed of surrender would have extremely unpleasant repercussions, and endanger your nuns' pensions, not to mention your own. Another Act is being prepared in Parliament, to give a general suppression the full force of the law.'

'All of them? All of them to go? Do you realise how many there are? Nuns and monks in their thousands will become homeless. It is quite impossible.'

'There are something more than five hundred religious Houses remaining, as I understand. It is a vast undertaking indeed. Master Thomas Cromwell plans to have them all closed, vacated and demolished by the end of next year.'

'Demolished?'

'To prevent any attempt at return. Unless, of course ... Do you by chance know of a Sir John Horsey?'

'I know the family,' said the Abbess. 'There is a Horsey house at Clifton Maybank, a parish in our county of Dorset.'

'Correct. This Sir John of Clifton Maybank is a man of a certain age, with four children to place in the world. He is a close friend of Sir Thomas Wyatt, of whom you have heard me speak.

Sir John Horsey rolls in money. Rolls in money, Madam, do you hear? Money talks. And he is one of the King's knights.'

'It is well for Sir John. So?'

'Sir John Horsey desires the possession of Sherborne Abbey and its demesnes. Intact.'

He paused, and then: 'I do not want to use a harsh word which if bandied abroad could do damage. I can perhaps without offence use the word inducement, or the word enticement. Sir John Horsey, a few years back, when he saw which way the wind was blowing, induced or enticed Master Cromwell to forcibly appoint as the Abbot of Sherborne a right-minded man who could be relied upon to surrender, with his sixteen or so monks, without causing trouble.'

'John Barnstable. I heard of his appointment. But I did not know—'

'How should you know, Madam? It was not intended that you should know. Sir John Horsey will of course have to compensate the King, that is, to pay the King for the Abbey, upwards of a thousand pounds as I hear. My only purpose in telling you this is to demonstrate what can, in extreme situations, be brought about.'

I had become momentarily distracted, finding the name Horsey comical, and trying to recall one of my mother's songs about a little horsey, but failing to retrieve more than the sweet silly air of it. So I may have missed something. I picked up my quill in time to hear Dame Elizabeth Zouche saying with solemnity, as if making a great concession:

'I am prepared to offer His Majesty the King five hundred marks and Master Cromwell personally one hundred marks in return for the survival of Shaftesbury Abbey.'

A silver mark is worth less than a pound, only about thirteen shillings and four pence. I think Dame Elizabeth may have been offering her own personal money. So paltry a sum, when they were poised to benefit from the incalculable wealth coming from the Abbey, would hardly tempt either the King or Master Thomas

Cromwell. And her speaking of marks, instead of pounds, was — what? — countrified. I wished for her sake that she had not made the attempt.

There was an awkward silence. Sir Thomas said, 'If you will take my advice, Madam, you will do no such thing. That could not change your situation except for the worse. In any case the survival of Shaftesbury Abbey as a monastic House is not negotiable, any more than it is at Sherborne. This is not the point in question.'

'Nevertheless, I would ask you to do as I say and pass on my offer.'

Sir Thomas bowed. The customary dish of mushrooms was at her elbow. In the silence that followed she spiked one mushroom after another with her knife in quick succession and brought it to her mouth. She did not offer the dish to Sir Thomas.

Before he left he said, almost pleading:

'Madam, think. These changes may be the most important things ever to have happened in England. These changes mean freedom from Rome. England is becoming her sovereign self. All our people will benefit.'

Well, he and men like him are certainly poised to benefit. Whether Sir Thomas relayed the Abbess's proposal or not, she received no response. I do not imagine that her offer ever reached the King. As for Master Cromwell, over-stretched in his many undertakings, he was content to have set the dissolutions and demolitions in train and to leave the rest to the Commissioners. According to Arundell, he was much occupied in negotiating the King's next marriage, his fourth, to a German princess.

I have never heard of a man so given to marrying as our King of England. I cannot think why he does not just take concubines, it would save so much trouble. But he is obsessed with male issue, and there are always foreign politics involved too. He has never seen this German princess, whose name is Anne, but he has com-missioned a portrait of her. As the Abbess said, seeing a portrait is not the same as seeing the real person. I would wager that it will be a flattering likeness, even if she has a face like a lump of dough.

'My dear Dame Elizabeth,' said Sir Thomas Arundell, standing up, ready to leave, stroking his blue feathers, 'Do not think that I do not feel for you. We have always been friends, have we not? We have always understood one another, have we not, in a quite particular way?'

'I have thought so, Sir Thomas.'

There was a sad vestige, as she said this, of her former manner towards him.

'You are fortunate,' he said, 'and I must take some credit for this, that your surrender will be taken by Master John Tregonwell, and not by Dr Leigh or Dr Layton, who are perhaps over-assiduous and inclined to violence and insult in the execution of their duties, which to my mind is not appropriate. Master Tregonwell is a reasonable man.'

The Abbess raised her eyebrows.

'In comparison to others,' said Sir Thomas.

'The Abbey of Shaftesbury will never surrender,' said the Abbess. 'And Master Tregonwell is a blowfly.'

She met my eyes over Sir Thomas's shoulder.

That Christmas season of 1538, there was something desperate about the festivities. Nothing took place that year which did not take place in the Abbey every Christmas and throughout the twelve days. In the daytime everyone behaved relatively normally. Only we avoided one another's eyes, knowing and not-knowing what the next night would bring.

Again as usual, loads of extra firewood were brought up from Gillingham. As usual, geese and ducks and fishes were roasted, mountains of loaves were baked. When darkness fell half a dozen fires were lit in different places on the cobbles and flagstones of the Abbey precinct, singeing the branches of trees. Up against the brewery were butts of ale, freely available to anyone sober enough to set a tankard under a tap. Bands of musicians from the town swilled in through the gatehouse, creating discord as the rhythms and melodies of flutes and fiddles and whistles and lutes mingled.

People came out from their lodgings, shrieking and whooping, most of them unrecognisable. Our labourers, porters, tradesmen, craftsmen, stable boys, apprentices, clerks, chantry priests, maid-servants, cooks, are transformed every year into flocks of crazed nuns of all shapes and sizes, lifting their makeshift habits as they stomp and stamp in their dance round the fires. Some of them blacken their faces with charcoal. This is a truly comical sight.

By the end of the twelve days people are exhausted and ready for normality. Many of our sisters have neither the courage nor the humour to join in. They cling together, giggling behind their hands, affecting outrage, jigging just a little to the music. But I do remember Mother Onion, in her normal black habit, dancing as if transported, her feet describing a jumping pattern as if her knees were on springs, with her head erect and her body still as a statue.

The Fairheads did not so much disguise themselves that Christmas as appear in their true guises. They wore their bright-est clothes, they curled their hair and brought ringlets forward on to their cheeks, and fixed their veils at the crowns of their heads, all hung about with coloured ribbons. The youngest novice, who always represents the Abbess, was this year a Fairhead. She put cushions under her tunic to simulate the Abbess's bust. She chalked her face white and drew wrinkles on it with a dirty stick. She probably saw the Abbess as a crone.

This year the travesties were more extreme than usual. I shan't forget the antics of the Infirmaress, wearing a cloak over nothing but a shift. She threw off the cloak, raised her shift at the back, and ran around a bonfire with her rear end exposed, pursued by Mother Catherine Hunt in outsize hose with a switch in her hand, screeching like an owl. Men disguised as nuns, very drunk, with their tunics pulled up to expose hairy legs, lolled around playing cards. Against the Abbey wall, half-concealed by the brewery buildings, a row of couples – I could not tell which were men and which were women – were fumbling and humping. I remember a tall figure in a floating green gown and veil, with long dark hair, being roughly handled by the head carpenter, his red beard defying any attempt at disguise. The figure in green shimmered into the firelight, her arms outstretched as she dipped and swayed, singing in a high voice. It was Father Robert Parker.

I saw Sister Eleanor Wilmer run to him, grasping his gown: 'Dance with me!' she said.

He shook her off.

And I? I was not myself either. I hardly then knew Gregory, the Steward's assistant, but I noted that we were much of a size. Gregory lent me a pair of tight mulberry-coloured hose, a short jerkin with sleeves, and a little wool cap. So that Christmas, after dark, I was a boy and I drank and swaggered like a boy. The little cap did not disguise me enough. I drew out from among charred twigs a brimless object so dirty and misshapen that it was no longer recognisable as a hat unless it was on a head. I pulled it down over my brow. I don't think many people recognised me. Certainly the Steward did not. He slumped down at my side.

'I have a riddle for you, lad. What's the difference between a nunnery and a bawdy-house?'

He gave me the answer, rocked with laughter and punched me on the shoulder.

'Pass it on! By Our Lady, living in a house of women is not all beer and skittles, my lad. It's the smell. The female reek. It's like living in a basket of toadstools or' – a couple of Fairheads skittered by – 'a bowl of figs.'

He lumbered off to find a livelier audience and more ale.

That final night would normally have been the least rampageous, the tensions and desires diminishing into quietude. But there were disturbances. Weasel and Dick, with Finbarr at their heels, came to me in distress, wearing little skirts and red paper crowns, their faces and hands smudged with wood smoke. They had no trouble recognising me.

'Father Pomfret,' Dick said. 'Father Pomfret.'

'Dick does not have the words to tell you,' said Weasel.

Weasel could not find did the words to tell me either. We sat down on the ground all three, with Finbarr, in the nuns' burial ground, the quietest place I could find, and I teased it out of them. Father Pomfret, in his normal clerical clothing, but drunk, had sought them out where they were playing and told them to come to his chamber. He wanted, he said, to train them to serve the Mass at the altar. When they entered his chamber, Father Pomfret was naked. He smiled and told them what he wanted them to do for him, or to him, and that they were to take their clothes off as well.

'So what did you do?'

'We just laughed. We could not help it. Father Pomfret naked! Only think of it, Sister Agnes.'

Father Pomfret became angry. He tried to catch hold of them but he was too drunk and they were too nimble and ran away out of the door and came to find me.

'We do not want to have to go and see Father Pomfret.'

'You do not have to go and see Father Pomfret again. I think he will not ask you. It was just tonight. Do not think about it any more.'

It was a lesson for them, I thought, in what the real world was like, and perhaps salutary. They had not been harmed and they had learned something.

*

The twelve days of Christmas turn the world upside down. The excesses may seem risky, but they are fun and serve as a release. We tolerate one another's peculiarities better afterwards. Like a blood-letting.

But this year there was no joy in the naughtiness and rule-breaking. I think transgression is transgression only when it is a temporary escape from a willed submission to grace and order. Otherwise it becomes something quite other. There was dread, maybe despair, in the rampages this year. The world turned upside down in a bad way.

A few days afterwards Master Tregonwell sent a message asking me to wait upon him in his office beside the gatehouse. I imagined there was some detail of Abbey business on which he wished me to inform him. I had Finbarr with me because the little boys were being taught their letters that morning by Sister Catherine Hunt. She can barely read and write herself but no matter. She loves the boys.

Master Tregonwell locked the door of his office and pocketed the key. He lost no time on civilities.

'It is all over, little Sister Agnes. You understand that, don't you? When your Abbess signs my Deed of Surrender, you will be cast adrift.'

'The Abbess will never sign.'

'She will. She must.'

'No.'

He picked me up as if I were a child and laid me out across his knees in his chair. Taken by surprise, I froze. He pulled up my tunic and my shift and gazed upon my private parts. He held me down with his left hand while he explored me with his right hand, and began to talk in a husky, hurried voice, as if he had long been planning what he was going to say.

'I will thread red ribbons through this bush of yours, and wind Spanish lace round your belly, I will stuff your hole with apricots and eat them out of you. I have a sensitive nose, my dear. You will rub yourself with rosemary and lavender, for me. You will be my sweetheart.'

'I will not marry you. I am a nun, I am the Bride of Christ.'

'You are not a full nun, you are a minchin. Christ has a sufficiency of Brides. And excuse me, who said anything about marrying?'

I have always disliked this man. I struggled to sit upright. I found my tongue.

'What do you suppose that there is about you, John Tregonwell, which would incline me or any woman to go with you as your concubine?'

He was taken aback, a spoilt child. I was taken aback too, by what I had said. Then he grinned his scheming grin.

'You do not understand. I shall soon be rich. Very rich.'

There was no arguing with that.

His heaving lust was disagreeable and his breath smelled of meat but his hand was skilled. The body is witless and mine was melting, even as my mind did not for one instant stop working.

What good outcome might there be, for me? Four years at the most, Anne Cathcart had said. Then what? Spoiled, ruined, older, I would be abandoned.

'No,' I said.

'I will give you a fine dwelling, and a horse to ride. You shall have fruits, and wine, and silken gowns. Did I mention already that I shall be rich? And you shall have flowers to put between your little titties.'

Oh poor, sad idiot. But still...

'And books, will you buy me all the books I want?'

'Why books? What books? What would a pretty creature like you want with books?'

'Then again no.'

'You are stupid, my dear. You have been this way before, I can tell. I am not a fool. You are not a maid. You are a slut. What better chance do you have?'

Finbarr had all this while been sitting upright beside us in her heraldic pose, front paws together, head held high, watching. She suddenly moved, sinking her teeth into his sleeve and ripping the fabric. Master Tregonwell kicked out at her, catching her in the chest. This hitherto silent dog stood on her four feet and barked. Her bark became a hound's howl, her head and throat raised towards the roof. Her floppy ears rose up like wings. They must have muscles in them, I never knew. For an instant I was more interested in that than in anything.

Master Tregonwell tipped me off his lap, roaring. I scrambled to my feet and got hold of Finbarr's rope.

'Get rid of that filthy dog!'

He was bellowing above Finbarr's howls. If there had not been much shouting going on outside, the pair of them would have been heard all over the Abbey.

'No.'

He stood up and brushed himself down, adjusting the tapes of his hose, shaking out his wrecked velvet sleeve.

'I give you until noon tomorrow. Send me a message. If we can agree, you ride away with me after the signing, whenever that is. Without the dog. If not...'

He unlocked the door and bowed in an exaggerated manner. I fled with Finbarr.

In February a man turned up at the gatehouse, a man of the roads, grizzled and bearded, seeking shelter. He was taken in, given bean soup and a place to sleep. He had travelled on foot from the north of England over many weeks, he said. He had seen terrible things. It was a miracle of God when he came to Shaftesbury and he found the Abbey still standing. The Abbess's maid, overhearing, pricked up her ears and told the Abbess who ordered the man to be brought to her. She asked me to take notes.

He stood before Dame Elizabeth in her parlour in his muddied clothes, his cap in his hands. She, sitting upright in her great carved chair, asked him what he had seen. He found it hard to speak.

All the way that he came, he managed to say, he had found abbeys deserted and half-demolished.

'Small ones?' she asked.

'No, Madam. The great ones. Fountains Abbey has gone. Jervaulx Abbey has gone. Many more. Dozens. Scores. I cannot tell how many. I heard tales of monks and priests beheaded, hanged, burned. Of nuns turned out and cast adrift.'

Never taking her eyes off him, she bade him say more.

As he came south, he said, where the weather was less cruel, the abbey churches already had young nettles springing up between broken floor tiles, under naves open to the sky. He saw holes of badgers and foxes in what had been cloisters. In one place he shared his bread with women squatting in the ruins. They were nuns with nowhere to go, and half-crazed. They prayed each night that in the morning everything would be as it was before. When they woke among the fallen stones, they knew that they had not prayed hard enough. They would try again. He saw people with barrows picking over fallen stones and broken carvings and taking them away.

'Madam,' he said, 'you must understand. Our land is strewn with ruins.'

He began to sob and could not stop.

The Abbess motioned to me to give the man a coin from her purse. She blessed him and let him go. She told me to go too. The day was darkening but she waved me away when I went to light her candle. I left her in the dusk in her great chair. The next morning I saw that she too had been weeping. That made me frightened for the first time, and I remained frightened.

I am not sure how much our sisters knew. Most of them received letters. Travellers, pilgrims, vagrants, carters, market-men brought garbled news to anyone who went out into the town and stayed to hear it.

'Our land is strewn with ruins,' the weeping man had said. I could not forget it.

After his visit the Abbess held a meeting with the senior nuns and the Obedientiaries, to which I was not privy. I believe she took them fully into her confidence. I believe they agreed that the community must not be disturbed.

The routine of our lives went on unbroken. The complaints from my sisters in Chapter were as they always were. Too many bones in the fish. The beer was weaker than normal, was it not? Was there something wrong with our hops? Since it was so cold, might we not have extra bed-coverings? Those two boys with the dog were a nuisance, they did no work, why were they here? Anne Cathcart complained that the spoons were not scoured properly. She did not care to eat from a dirty spoon. Upon which the Cellaress suggested that Sister Anne might care to clean the spoons herself.

Dame Elizabeth Zouche dealt with everything in her dry manner, and deflected further hostilities between Anne and the Cellaress by commending the general concern to uphold the high standards of the refectory. It would be a good idea to have the refectory freshly whitewashed when the spring came. She would speak to the Steward. As for the two boys, the Prioress had been thinking of apprenticing them to the blacksmith, and would set this in train immediately. That would keep them out of mischief.

I had a worry more immediate than anything from the outside world. Something was amiss with Dorothy Clausey. She looked sickly, and in the Library she sat picking at the skin of her face with a fingernail, on and on at the same spot until she drew blood, upon which she gave a sigh, wiped away the blood with the palm of her hand, and returned to her book. Sometimes she picked at the little scabs and made them bleed again. It seemed to make her feel calmer. I did not understand it and did not like to speak to her about it. We all have to find ways to endure what we cannot endure.

It entered my head, I know not why, that she might be carrying a child, though she did not show. Anne Cathcart, whom I consulted, cast her sharp eyes upon Dorothy and said she certainly was.

'There is a look. She has the look.'

Before Christmas Dorothy disappeared. She did not come to those last festivities, she did not come to the Library, she did not come to the Refectory. That need not mean she was not eating. As a Corrodian, she could order food from the kitchen in her apartment.

I had not seen her for weeks when on a dark winter afternoon in late February I glimpsed her leaving the Abbey Church. She had probably been making her confession to Father Pomfret, it was his day for it. I ran after her and called her name. She looked towards me. I asked her if all was well.

'I can't,' she said. 'I can't.'

'You can't what?'

She turned and walked fast away from me in the direction of the house where she lodged.

I worried during the night, sleeping not at all between Matins and Prime. The next afternoon when the light was fading I gathered my courage and knocked at the door of her apartment.

She must have been sitting in the dark doing nothing – except, maybe, praying? She was always thin, but she was skeletal. When she lit her candle, I saw that her face was white, with dark circles under her eyes, and more of those little scabs on her cheeks and brow. I made to embrace her, but she was as unresponsive as a stick.

'Dear Dorothy, is there an infant? You have a child?'

She pointed to a low door at the back of her room.

'Is he asleep?'

'She. I don't know.'

'May I go and see her?'

I made for the little door, Dorothy following me. It opened into a chamber as small as a closet, icy cold. I waited for her on the threshold, where she stopped.

'I left the window shutter open,' she said. 'I thought she would be too hot.'

I went back for the candle and tiptoed into the chamber. I saw a cradle, but there was no baby in it. There was a bundle on a bench under the window. I looked at Dorothy.

'I thought the high sides of the cradle might frighten her. Like being in a prison.'

'When did you last feed her and change her?'

'I cannot remember.'

'Pick her up. Bring her through into the other room.'

'I cannot.'

I went to the bench and picked up the bundle.

'She's soaking wet, she's freezing. Why in God's name did you not—'

'I could not.'

'What do you mean?'

'The longer I left her, the more I could not. I kept thinking that she might be ... and I just couldn't go in there in case she ... and then it was getting dark. Please do not be angry with me, Agnes. I could not bear it. I was thinking all the time about her all alone and cold, and not knowing.'

I carried the wet bundle back into the other room and Dorothy followed. I set the bundle on my knee and unwrapped it.

The infant's eyes were closed. Her hands and feet were cold. Her lips were creased. She had no colour. She looked like a very old person, and as if dried out. I wrapped her up again in the damp shawl.

'Hold her, warm her,' I said. 'Just wait. I'm coming straight back.'

I ran to the kitchens where they were preparing the Refectory dinner. Avoiding the Cellaress, who was counting out dried herrings, I begged from the servants a ewer of warm water, and a corked bottle of boiled water, and snatched up the very smallest spoon I saw — a sliver of pewter, a salt-spoon. It was an emergency, I said. I hurried back with the spoon in my pocket and the bottle floating in the big bowl, water slopping all over the cobbles.

I suppose this took ten minutes. Dorothy had not moved, and was still holding the child.

She had in the room a basket of linens and towelling and pieces of fine woollen. I took the child on my knee, removed the shawl and the wet interior wrappings, and wrapped a piece of the woollen stuff around her. I tried to make her take the boiled water from the spoon, but she would not open her mouth.

'Let me do it,' said Dorothy. 'You don't know her. You don't know how.'

I transferred the child from my lap to hers. She held her in the crook of her left arm and teased and pushed the spoon between the dried-out lips. The infant twisted her head away — the first movement she had made — put out the tip of her tongue, felt the water, and began to suck at the spoon. Dorothy rocked her a little.

I took a deep breath. In a few minutes I said, 'I think we should bathe her in the warm water now. She is chilled. Will you do it?'

Dorothy shook her head.

'I cannot.'

I laid the naked infant in the bowl, my left arm under her head and shoulders, and splashed warm water over her. After a short while she flailed with her arms and kicked with her legs. I was ready to laugh with relief. We dried her together, on Dorothy's knees, and wrapped her in clean cloths. She began to cry.

'Why is she crying?' said Dorothy, stiffening.

'I think she is hungry. Water is not food. Do you have milk?'

She pulled up her tunic and showed me her shift, damp and stained at the top and a bit smelly. She had milk all right, and she fed the child, who sucked with her grey-blue eyes locked on to her mother's.

Dorothy began to talk. She was more herself.

'An infant is either all right or not all right, there is not much of a middle way.'

'That is so,' I said.

She began to sing to her child:

'"Greensleeves is my delight, Greensleeves is all my joy, Greensleeves is my heart of gold..." My father used to sing that when I was young. I can't remember. Just his voice, and his big ring with a ruby. He let me play with it.'

The Cardinal's ring. I would have liked to hear her to say more, but thought it better not to press her.

'Tell me what went wrong. Why do you leave the little one alone, why do you not attend to her?'

'It is something that happened. To me and to her.'

'What if I had not come? What would you have done, all night?'

'Nothing. She was not in pain. She was closing down. She did get cold, and she was hungry, and I did hear her crying, before.'

'How could you not go to her?'

'She was not remembering being warm or the milk or me or anything, not what we mean by remembering. She's always now. She does not know about hoping that I will come. She does not know she is cold or what cold is. She just is it.'

'What is the "it" that she is?'

'Terror, that is a word I could use. But that is not right because she does not know that word or what it means, and she does not remember not-terror. She does not have a before and an after, or not that she can get hold of. I can't explain.'

'You live too much in your head. How can you possibly know what she feels anyway, when you leave her in there alone in the cold?'

'This does not come from inside my head. I know because she is me and I am she.'

I remembered how I had been with Peterkin. Dorothy had taken a strange turning. But for a split second, I did understand.

'Her name is Esther,' said Dorothy.

'We will find somebody to help you to look after Esther.'

'I cannot,' said Dorothy. 'I cannot look after Esther.'

For a few days I went in to her whenever I could spare the time and helped her with Esther.

'Was it Robert Parker?' I asked.

She shot me a look and lowered her eyes to Esther on her lap.

'It was only the once. It was – an error.'

'Did he force you?'

'He did and then he did not. You could say it was a rape, and then you could say it was not a rape. He never came to see me again. He has not spoken to me since then. I would like to kill him.'

She meant it. There was nothing to say.

I spoke next morning to Sister Mary Amor, as the most sensible and able woman around, about what might be done. I told her the story so far as I understood it. She made no judgement.

'You could do worse,' she said, 'than to ask the Winterbournes to take the child in. The money would be a help to them.'

I could not believe my ears. The only time I was in the Winterbournes' hovel was the day I went there with Weasel and Dick and we rescued Finbarr.

'It is different now. There is a young woman there, with an infant. She is a country girl from Devonshire. Emilia. I do not know whether her child's father is the dumb John or the speaking John. It may be that they do not know either. Let us go and see them.'

We went out through the small door in the gatehouse and made our way to the row of tenements. We knocked on the

Winterbournes' half-open door and went in, leaving the door open.

There stood a plump, smiling young woman, with fair curls tumbling from her headcloth, wearing a man's shirt and a brown kirtle, neither of them clean but not filthy either. The same could be said of the floor. The room was ordered, with trenchers on a shelf, and an iron pot on the fire. There were three stools, and pallets stacked against one wall, and stacks of willow wands, and baskets hanging from the rafters. It looked like a home. Emilia was holding in her arms an infant of about five months old, as plump as herself.

Unalarmed, assuming we had come on some Abbey business, she sat us down on stools and took the third for herself and her child. It began to grizzle. She pulled down the opening of the shirt and put the child to a breast. Her Devonshire way of speaking was such that I could not catch her every word. Her Johns were out, by chance in the Abbey, repairing wattle fencing round the dwellings of chantry priests beside the graveyard. The foxes had been at it.

I let Mary Amor do the talking. When she had finished, Emilia cocked her head on one side, smiled, and simply said, 'Yes.'

This little one, she said, was a boy. She called him Little John. It would be pleasant for him to have a sister. She had milk enough for two. And if more came along – well, they would be a proper family.

I asked, 'But what will the Johns say?'

Emilia laughed.

'They are happy if I am happy.'

Emilia was no fool. She questioned Mary Amor about how and when the money for Esther would be paid. Monthly, said Mary. Emilia would apply to the Treasurer's office at the Abbey on a set day every month.

*

I know the Abbey is full of secrets. I had not realised how the secrets leak as from a cracked bowl. I do not know how Sister Eleanor Wilmer found everything out, but she did.

'Your Dorothy Clausey,' she muttered to me, behind her hand, stopping beside my stool in the parlour and bending over me. 'I knew a woman who murdered her newborn baby. There is a word for it. Infanticide.'

'Dorothy has not done that. Dorothy would never do that.'

Even as I whispered the words I was not so sure.

But that danger has now passed.

'She will not do that,' I said.

Eleanor pursed her lips and looked skyward.

'It happens. I shall pray for her.'

I locked my hands together in my lap so as not to slap her about the chops.

'As do I, Sister Eleanor. As do I.'

Mary Amor and Emilia went together to take Esther from Dorothy's apartment. I had no part in it. I would have found it painful. I felt deep sympathy for Dorothy. But under the sympathy was tamped-down anger. I struggled with it. She had this beautiful little daughter whom she could not, would not, care for. My Peterkin, whom I still loved with all my heart, had been taken from me.

I went to see Dorothy after Compline when I knew the deed was done. Crossing the precinct, I came upon a pair of foxes trotting along towards the kitchens. They changed their plan when they saw me and loped away across the graveyard towards the chantry priests' tenements, beyond which are hen coops.

I found Dorothy calm, and working at a translation by the light of a candle. I think she had no regrets. She had herself back to herself. She said she was well but tired and a little chilled. It was a frosty night.

'Stay with me,' she said.

She spread out her bed and we lay entwined together in the dark all through the early part of the night until the bell rang for Matins and I had to run from her to be in time.

Tenderness, acceptance, abandon – and amazement, afterwards, just thinking about it. My anger was assuaged by that night. We never lay together again, nor I think wanted to, and we never spoke of how or what it had been.

Dorothy resumed her visits to the Library, though Father Robert Parker no longer came and helped her with her Latin. She did not pick at her skin any more, or not so much.

During the first week of April, the Abbess greeted me with a grim face.

'Master Tregonwell has bad news – for you, in particular.'

'For me?'

'Bruton Abbey has gone.'

'Gone?'

'Fallen. Surrendered. Master Tregonwell is delighted with himself.'

There was no time to hear more because suddenly Tregonwell was in the room, stamping his feet, rubbing his hands at the fire, complaining about the cold outside, spouting platitudes. I retreated to my corner.

In my mind's eye I was home again, seeing St Mary's Church, and hard against it the Abbey gatehouse and the high Abbey wall running the length of the roadway, curling round at the end of the town, around the Abbey Park with its fishponds, bordering Dropping Lane, winding all the way back to enclose the church and the Abbey buildings. The Abbey is Bruton. Everything in Bruton belongs to the Abbey. How can Bruton continue to be, without the Abbey? I was finding it hard to breathe, but I pulled myself together. I must listen.

'And Abbot Eley?' the Abbess was asking.

'Ho ho,' said Master Tregonwell. 'He signed the surrender all right. Along with fourteen of his canons. But Abbot Eley still presents a problem. Possibly disloyal. Possibly not. He is taken to the Tower to be examined.'

I was too distressed to take notes but I do remember that this is what he said.

Sir Thomas Arundell, who came to the Abbess later in the day, told more. Bruton Abbey was not to be demolished, or not right away. Sir Thomas had official permission to grant possession of it to a good friend of his, a merchant from Bristol. No doubt he had good pecuniary reason for effecting this. But then Master Cromwell commanded him to dispossess the Bristol merchant and replace him with one Master Maurice Berkeley, to whom the Abbey was already promised.

'But who is Maurice Berkeley?'

'A youth in Cromwell's household,' said Sir Thomas. 'A young man on his way up. His step-father is Sir John FitzJames of Redlynch in the parish of Bruton. Cromwell himself wrote to Sir John FitzJames requesting – which meant demanding – local support for Maurice Berkeley in the matter of Bruton Abbey. His pretty mother also played a part. She wants her son living close to her.'

I pricked up my ears at the mention of the FitzJames family of Redlynch. However, my own connection had no relevance at all to the matter under discussion. I kept quiet.

Since Master Cromwell had chosen to further this young man's interests, there could be no argument.

'I complied. What else could I do?'

Arundell was agitated and in a bad humour. He had never appeared before us so stripped of confidence and urbanity.

'Master Cromwell is getting above himself. He goes too far. He believes himself to be above the law, he believes he *is* the law. He thinks that he can do no wrong in the eyes of God or of the King and that he can trample all over the rest of us.'

It was a measure of his anger and humiliation that he was so candid with the Abbess. He could not contain himself. He was ruining his hat as he talked, brushing the blue feathers the wrong way and smoothing them out again, over and over, until they would no longer lie smooth at all. The shafts of the feathers were bent and broken.

'Master Cromwell should remember the fall of the Cardinal, a greater man even than he. Already there are rumours.'

The Abbess smiled her thin smile.

'I would wager all I hope to gain,' said Sir Thomas, 'that two years from now Master Cromwell's head will no longer be on his shoulders.'

The Abbess said, still smiling: 'Nothing is for ever, as I have so often been reminded. That must apply to all who rise in the world, and even to you yourself, Sir Thomas.'

From my corner, I quoted the first line of the Wyatt poem. The words hung in the air:

'They fly from me that sometime did me seek.'

I was out of order. He turned and glared at me. A look of fury passed over his face. He spat in my direction, the gob of phlegm falling at my feet, and turned back to the Abbess.

'Of course, Madam, of course. God's will be done. But meanwhile...'

'Indeed. Meanwhile. You will find the spittoon beside the door, Sir Thomas.'

5

THE END OF DAYS

The week before Easter, 1539. The Abbess, wearing the simple habit, broke it to the community in Chapter that we were doomed. The night before, I had seen a piece of paper in the Abbess's bedroom on which she had written in a spidery hand:

'We are torn apart by the teeth of time and (which is more dangerous) mistaken zeal.' And her signature.

All fifty-odd of us attended Chapter. We knew already and at the same time we did not know. The wall between 'before' and 'after' is higher than any Abbey wall. But when the disaster does happen, the wall collapses like a rotten hurdle. As Tregonwell had said to the Abbess, you cannot send time running backwards. It seems to me that 'now' has very little meaning.

But it was 'now' when the Abbess sat very straight in the Chapter House and spoke to us in a calm voice.

'I have sad news.'

We were after all to be treated no differently, the Abbess said, in an even tone, from all the other monasteries and convents, the priories and abbeys, of whose dissolution and destruction we had been hearing over many months. The unthinkable was going to happen. To us. We stared at her.

'As your Mother in God, I must command you to join me in a willing and voluntary surrender of our Abbey to his anointed Majesty the King.'

If I had not been present, I would have imagined how my sisters must rise from their benches, cry out, tear their garments. Instead, there was dead silence. No one made a sound or moved except to scratch their flea bites, and except that Dame Philippa and Dame Joanna clutched at one another's hands, and Sister Mary Amor's face was white.

'We will be leaving the Abbey. All of us. Not today nor yet tomorrow, but soon. We will not be permitted to re-establish our community elsewhere. Each of us, perhaps in companionship with a sister, must make her own way. Some of you have families to whom you may return, or relatives who will give you shelter and a home. Those with the strength of spirit and body to travel may seek out Houses of our Order in France, Spain, Italy. The Chambress will return to those of you who are not yet professed the clothes in which you arrived at this place. I will help you so far as it is in my power to do so. You will not be destitute.'

Silence, again.

'In the coming few days, I shall be much occupied. After the departure of the Commissioners, I will meet in private with any of you who may require my counsel and advice.'

She stood up. Her voice was cracking.

'My daughters. My dear daughters. I have fought for more than two years to avoid this outcome. I always believed by the grace of God that I, your Abbess, and the ancient power and dignity of Shaftesbury Abbey, would prevail. But now I must ask you to understand that any further attempt at an alternative course, any refusal on our part to comply, would result in punishments and misfortunes more dreadful than anything that might have befallen any of us had we remained living in the cruel outside world. Meanwhile we shall perform our Holy Office, and observe our Rule, for as long as we can.'

With that she left, the Prioress and the other Obedientiaries hurrying after her, hands hidden in their sleeves, heads bowed.

I felt sorry for the Abbess. Yet it did enter my devilish head that if she did not sign the Deed of Surrender, any 'punishments' would fall on her personally, rather than on the lowly nuns for whom no one in the great world cared one way or another. She knew, and I knew, what happened to those Heads of Houses who did not comply. She was saving herself. The others she could not save, from whatever fates awaited us.

The solemn signing, the pitiful signing, took place in the Chapter House. I saw and heard it all, sitting in my corner of the bench against the wall. Tregonwell brought with him as his witnesses two officials, two young crows in black from head to foot, named by Tregonwell as William Peters and John Smyth. They sat to one side, at desks with stools, and did not look at us. I do not know which was which. One of them jiggled his foot continuously. The other picked his nose. They had been through all this before in other places. They were bored.

The whole previous day, Tregonwell and the two crows sat with the Abbess in her house, finalising the list of pensions for the sisters. Tregonwell left the Deed of Surrender with the Abbess for her to peruse overnight. It is an unworthy document. Shameful. The entirety is written on a mean piece of parchment, I would guess only about eleven inches by seven. There is no dignity in it, only an insulting parsimony.

There are a lot of ceremonious words on that parchment, the lines cramped, the words abbreviated, the writing minuscule. The Abbess with her dim eyes could not begin to read it, even by the light of three candles. I read it aloud to her.

Apart from the necessary particularities as to names and places, I surmise that it was copied from a template, the same legal formula for the surrender of every monastic House. I made two copies that night, in a clear large hand, sitting up late in the little chamber off Dame Elizabeth's bedroom, one for her and an extra one which I retained:

'To all Christ's faithful people to whom our present writing may come, Elizabeth Souch' – Tregonwell's scribe did not even know how to write her name correctly – 'Abbess of the Monastery of the Blessed Mary, the Virgin, and St Edward, King and Martyr, of Shaftesbury on the County of Dorset, and the Convent there, greeting in the Lord. Know ye that we the afore said Abbess and Convent, with one consent and assent considered in our minds, by our sure knowledge and mere motion of various good and reasonable causes specially moving our hearts and minds, more-over willingly and voluntarily have given and granted and by these presents to give and grant, surrender deliver and confirm to the most Illustrious and Victorious Prince and Lord in Christ, the Lord Henry the eighth, by the Grace of God, King of England and France, Defender of the Faith, Lord of Ireland and Supreme Head on earth of the Church in England, all our monasteries...'

'Willingly and voluntarily' – oh no. But there was no question of the Abbess being able to alter the wording.

There follows the catalogue of all that we are surrendering – our lands, manors, mills, ferries, courts, leets, hundreds, fairs, markets, parks, warrens, stew-ponds, waters, fisheries, rights of way, nominations, presentations, donations of churches, vicarages, chantries, hospitals – and a deal more. All our temporalities and spiritualities. All our charters and records, all our deeds and leases, and the Seal itself.

We are surrendering it all, 'to have, hold and enjoy by our Lord the King and to his heirs and assigns, for ever, to whom we surrender and submit the said Monastery and all rights; with all authority and power to dispose of ourselves and the said Monastery.

'And we the said Abbess and Convent and our successors will warrant our said Monastery, the precincts, site, dwelling house and church to our Lord the King and his heirs and assigns against all men in perpetuity.'

In perpetuity. The Abbey of Shaftesbury has been destroyed by the teeth of time and the hands of mistaken zeal. Our Easter Mass was joyless, our voices in choir tremulous, the early flowers on the altar a mockery. But then life went on. No choice.

Master Thomas Cromwell, we hear, is still much occupied with negotiations for the King's marriage to that Anne, who speaks only German. I do not know what German sounds like. Cromwell is greatly in favour of the match. The King is less sure.

They say too that the King has regrets and doubts about the excesses of the destruction and dissolution of the monastic Houses all over the country. But what do we care now about His Majesty's finer feelings? The Commissioners are acting autonomously and without supervision. They have got the bit between their teeth.

A strange occurrence. I discover that Father Louis Pomfret is not altogether a monster. He is an unhappy man.

Since we are still trying to maintain our customary routines, and it was my day for doling out the soup at noon at the Broad Hall in the town, I made my way there with Sister Eleanor Wilmer. She was, unfortunately for us both, my allotted companion. She did not throw me a word or a glance.

It was bean soup, made on a mutton-bone stock. There are never enough spoons so the old men and women – they are mostly old, the people who come to be fed at the Broad Hall – raise their bowls to their mouths and suck in the soup, raking up the solid bits at the bottom with their fingers. The bowls are so ancient that the wood has cracked, and they leak. We rinse the woodware afterwards under the pump, but it does not become properly clean. I would speak up in Chapter about the need to replace the bowls, but there is no future. Yet we go on behaving as if there were, as if the momentum of continuity might in itself prevent catastrophe.

Old men piss in the corners of the Hall. Clearing up after the midday soup is an arduous and messy business. We go down on our knees with a pail of water and handfuls of rags and wipe the floor clean of dirt and spillages. The stones are irregular and filth is embedded in the cracks. I do my best, telling myself that such labour teaches me the true meaning of holy charity – which is principally, if you are female, concerned with the bodily needs of others. I am destined to be a Martha whether I like it or not. Eleanor Wilmer has as much holy charity in her as a dead rat. She was on her knees as I was, but praying, and beckoning to those old biddies who had not stumbled away or fallen asleep on the benches to join her in prayer.

I struggled to my feet to tip the pail of dirty water out of the door. Just outside, on a bench, sat Father Pomfret. He came often to the Broad Hall to hear the confession of anyone who had a mind to make one. There was an anteroom set aside for the purpose. It was not frequently put to use. What he really enjoyed was playing with the town children. Today half a dozen little ones, barefoot and runny-nosed boys and girls, in little more than raggy shirts in spite of the winter cold, were clambering all over him, climbing on to his knees and up on to his shoulders, pulling at his clothes and his ears and his nose like puppies, shrieking and laughing. He was growling like a bear, grabbing the wriggling little creatures by the leg, or round the middle, tickling them, nuzzling them, pretending to eat them. They were overexcited. One little girl of about three years old fell off, hitting her head on the ground, and began to howl. I picked her up and tried to calm her but she fought her way out of my arms still snivelling and stumbled back to join the game.

Eleanor and I walked back to the Abbey in silence. I stopped in the gatehouse and she went on into the Abbey precinct. I sat on the bench in the gatehouse in order to clean the mud from the road off the soles of my shoes with a stick. Father Pomfret appeared. It was obvious from his appearance and demeanour that he had stopped on the way from the Broad Hall to fill or refill himself with ale. Ale loosened his tongue. He slumped down beside me.

'May I speak with you, Sister Agnes?'

'Of course, Father.'

'I think perhaps you understand human nature and its frailties.'

'I hope I do, Father.'

And then he began to speak about himself, with a great pressure of talk. He told me that his late father was an under-steward in Salisbury, in the palace of the Bishop.

'Not this one, not Shaxton, but the one before the one before.'

His father worked all hours and at the whim of his superiors and of the Bishop. He had not liked to see his father so craven and so obligated.

'I was enamoured – enamoured, you must understand, when I was a boy, by the liturgy and the ritual and the music. Salisbury Cathedral. The candles and the colours and the incense and gold. The unspeakable beauty of God. Only in the Cathedral did I see beauty. Everything outside its great doors was squalor. I wanted to serve God Himself, directly. I did not want to serve like my father some human acolyte of God. So I studied, and was ordained a priest. And have ended up here, in a house of women, hearing their petty confessions. It is not what I intended for myself. It is not. It is not.'

He spoke as if he were making his confession to me, instead of me making my usual dishonest confession to him. And he had not finished.

'Because you see, Sister Agnes, I have weaknesses. Urges. I am riddled with what I fear is sinfulness. But I do not harm those little ones. I swear to you. Christ says in the gospels, "Suffer the little children to come unto Me." And they do come unto me.'

He pulled a bottle out from somewhere within his garments and took a swallow. He began to ramble, and I understood but slowly that he was talking about his desire for boys.

'Some of them do not mind. They come for the penny and the sweets. And maybe they love me too, a little. Am I deceiving myself? I think not. The ones who find no love at home, or who have no home. I can give them love.'

'And the ones who do mind? Who run away?'

I was thinking of Dick and Weasel.

'They are just silly boys. They do not understand.'

Oh God, he took another draught from his bottle. This could only get worse.

'My only true and honest life lies in what men may say is my sin, or is it just a weakness? I made a vow of celibacy and indeed I have violated no woman. But I am a dead man, outside the joy that my desires brings me. Is it a sin, Sister?'

I thought perhaps it was not but remained silent because I wished him to refrain from unburdening himself further. It was unseemly.

'Whence comes this love, this joy, this rapture, if not from Christ Himself, who is all love?'

I did not know what to say to him. Looking back, it seems to me that Christ cannot be greatly concerned about whom or what or how we love, so long as we do love.

I said: 'So long as we do no harm.'

'Sometimes I let into my lodging older boys, young men, rough types from the town. After dark. There is danger in it. They could do me harm. The danger is – delicious.'

He seemed unwell, fetching his breath with difficulty, his chest rasping.

'But enough, enough. What does it all matter, now.'

'But then what does matter now, Father?'

I really wanted to know.

'Nothing matters. And everything matters. It's the same thing. It depends on your point of view. Look to yourself, Agnes Peppin.'

He lurched to his feet and shambled away into the precinct. I sat there, bewildered, wishing I had given him some comfort, unsavoury though he was. I do think that he was a little crazy that day. But was there not a logic and even a wisdom in all that he said, and what do I know?

We had until the end of April to make our arrangements. That month was bitterly cold, colder than February, though there were more and larger snowdrops in the cloister garden than ever before. I saw them as a good omen. Something surely would happen to bring us redemption.

The icy wind tore at our garments and scoured our faces and hands. We wore our cloaks and hoods all day, indoors and out. Our clothes were always damp, and our outer garments stiff with frost when we put them on after being in bed. Wetness seeped up through the flagstones even within doors, and froze overnight. The older sisters were always slipping and falling. My feet and hands were never warm. The earth outside was rock-hard, with a scattering of snow which did not melt.

Dick was ill. Weasel wheeled him round in the handcart with Finbarr prancing alongside. Many of the sisters fell ill too and the infirmary was overwhelmed.

'My chest hurts,' said Dick. 'When I breathe.'

I found him an extra blanket and told him to lie down in the kennel-house. After that he slept. Weasel and Finbarr sat beside him. Weasel was not well either. He shivered and coughed. I brought them bread, but Dick remained asleep and Weasel gave both their shares to Finbarr.

When I went to see them the next morning Weasel was lying down and could barely speak for coughing. Dick was dead. I said nothing to Weasel, and went to tell the Steward. When they came to take Dick away, Finbarr growled and bared her teeth. Weasel did not even notice. He died that evening alone while we were at Vespers.

The labourers buried the boys after dark in the lay churchyard – shallowly, the ground was so hard. They died unshriven. But they had committed no mortal sins and I prayed to St Nicholas, the patron saint of children, to intercede for them. Old Father Bucket unwillingly muttered a few prayers over their shared grave, then scuttled back out of the wind, his hood up and hands tucked into his sleeves. I was the only other person there to hear him speak the words. Afterwards I cried and cried, in my cubicle in the dorter. I loved Dick and Weasel.

Finbarr would not leave the place where the boys were buried. No one could approach her. She snarled, she became savage. After a couple of days the Steward sent orders that she should be killed. When I saw a workman approaching her with an iron bar, I could not endure it and pleaded with him to spare her. I was so distressed that he lumbered off, swearing at me and throwing down the bar. I sat down on the ground beside Finbarr and talked to her and stroked her, and slipped her rope collar over her head, and she came away with me.

She has become my dog. She lives in the kennel-house and I bring her food, and I exercise her on the rope. Sometimes I tether her to the old handcart and she will sit in it bolt upright and front paws together, her nose to the wind, waiting for the boys to come back.

Perhaps they have been spared Limbo and are running and laughing together in Paradise, waiting for Finbarr to join them.

I imagine Paradise to be a green sunlit garden, with a river running through it and kingfishers and dragonflies. Perhaps I would have done better to let her go to them there straight away, and not saved her life. Mother Onion says there is no Heaven for animals because they have no souls. I do not know how anyone can be certain about that.

After the momentous meeting in the Chapter House, Mother Onion became an old woman overnight. She all but lost the use of her legs and could only move about with the help of two sticks. As for our greedy Sister Catherine Hunt, she lost her wits. She scampered around brandishing an ale-bottle filled with what she said was holy water, cackling with laughter and sprinkling the water on anyone who did not get out of her way quickly enough. The bedridden creatures in the Infirmary, who could not evade her, were soaked.

'Sister Catherine is away with the fairies,' said Mother Onion.

At the next meeting in the Chapter House the sisters broke out of their silence and wailed out their woe. A discordant choir of fear and grief. The Fairheads did not weep, they stared around them, aghast, frightened like children by such misrule even though they themselves had never embraced any Rule.

I wept, not for myself only but for injustice and cruelty so smoothly accomplished. I wish I had stabbed Tregonwell in the nape of his thick neck with the small sharp knife in my belt on the day of the signing. Yes, I could have done it. That was a sinful thought and I pushed it away.

Only my Melancholy did not weep or cry out. She sat upright, like Finbarr, with her hands folded in her lap.

Mother Onion staggered to her feet and howled through her sobs how she could never return to Ireland, she did not know the way.

'My family will not know me now. There is no place for me at all in this world, I will die among strangers.'

Sister Mary Amor went over to Mother Onion and made her sit, stroking her face while the wailing of the sisters rose and fell. That weak wailing will echo among the stars until the Day of Judgement. Faith, fortitude, dignity, lost and gone with everything else.

The Abbess finally raised her hand for silence. There was no reassurance she could give and she attempted none.

'Before each of you leave, you should collect your pension for this coming year from the Treasurer's office. The amount each one of us receives is a private matter. There will, I implore you, be no resentful comparisons. Sisters who have been here the longest or who have served the Abbey in an official capacity as an Obedientiary will naturally receive more than some others. But you must believe that I have striven to ensure that each one of you receives her due and that no one will be without the makings of a new life outside the Abbey.'

She took a deep breath and made the sign of the Cross over us all.

'All shall be well and all shall be well and all manner of things shall be well. That is not my saying, it is the saying of a holy nun who died more than a hundred years ago. I want you to carry her words in your heart always, wherever you are. God bless and keep us all.'

Then she left the Chapter House.

Afterwards we clustered in the cloister. We needed to be together, as if of one mind though we were not. This last Chapter broke the community into fragments. That was our actual dissolution. We were all afraid of being left alone. Sister Catherine, her bottle empty, but still frenzied, came up close to me and whispered in my ear:

'There will be changes. I am to be Bishop now. It will soon be announced. I have had intimations. You will be my chaplain.'

I put my arms round her and rocked her back and forth.

We moved into the parlour, drawn by music. Father Robert Parker was in there alone, playing a melody on his lute, idly, with stops and starts. We sat and stood around him and listened to the music. No one spoke. He changed key and began to sing to us in his clear light voice:

> *'I had a little nut tree*
> *Nothing would it bear,*
> *But a silver nutmeg*
> *And a golden pear.*
> *The King of Spain's daughter*
> *Came to visit me,*
> *And all for the sake*
> *Of my little nut tree.'*

It is a sweet air, one of the old songs that my mother used to sing to the dead. So the words cannot be about our King and his first Queen, who did come from Spain. Maybe it is about another King. I suspect there is a lewdness in the words, if one knew. Just then the bell rang for Holy Office. We did not expect this. Tregonwell had ordered the clock to be stopped. A few old dames rose and moved off towards the church, as dogs called by a whistle. The rest of us stayed where we were.

'It does not matter now,' said Anne Cathcart.

If it does not matter now, why was it important only yesterday, and the day before, and for hundreds of years before that? The farmers report to the Abbess that crops are failing, animals are dying, lands are flooded, the winters are more cruel – I can certainly vouch for that. It is the Hand of God, punishing His children. But God is just, so it is we who are at fault. How can we atone? The Abbess says there will always be nuns and monks praying somewhere, if only in other lands. But there are thunderstorms, lightning strikes, sicknesses. Not just the end of Shaftesbury Abbey but the End of Days may be at hand. That's what Sister Onora says.

My Melancholy stood up. We all looked at her. She raised her arms high and wide, dropped her head sideways, and began to dip and turn, slowly, and then quicker and quicker, her habit whirling.

I could not believe my eyes. Melancholy was dancing! Robert adjusted his playing to her dance, following her steps, leading her on.

I stood up and began to dance too, and one by one so did almost all of us. We wheeled round and round the parlour table each in her own way, touching fingers as we passed, jigging and kicking our legs, veils all awry, until – soon, and suddenly – Robert clamped his hand over the lute strings, the music stopped and we fell back against the walls and on to the stools round the table, gasping. Robert had seen, as we had not, the Abbess standing in the doorway.

Only my Melancholy continued to dance, slow and stately now, to a music in her head, finishing what she had begun. If she saw the Abbess it made no difference to her, and the Abbess, white-faced in the half-light, did not stay.

My Melancholy stopped dancing and stood stock-still, tears pouring down her face. She wept and wept, dragging sobs from deep within. It was frightening. I was nearest to her, and went to embrace her. She is taller than I, it was like embracing a tree. I drew her over to the table and made her sit down. She looked round at our flushed faces, one by one, and for the first time I believe since she came to the Abbey, she smiled. Her face, still wet with tears, was shining.

'Forgive me, sisters. I do not know what possessed me.'

'Was it the Devil?' asked the littlest Fairhead. 'I saw a raven fly over when we passed through the cloister just now.'

She took the gold pin from the top of her veil, put it in her mouth, adjusted the folds of the veil and repositioned the pin, all without taking her eyes off Melancholy.

'It was not the Devil. It was not grief. It was not fear. It was not joy. It was – it is...'

She shook her head. 'I do not have the words.' She took deep calm breaths and smiled again.

Was it freedom? My Melancholy could fly free? But not I think only from the Abbey and its routines and the Rule. It was more than that, although until that moment I could not have conceived that anything could be more than that.

We were like a community again because the tension was broken and we had one vast problem in common. We who were not yet old began to talk fast between ourselves. What might we do? Where might we go? What is London like? How hard is it to take a ship to the Continent? Do you have a father, a brother who would take you in? Would the pension run to leasing a tenement and an orchard?

Castles in the air. And it was an illusion, we were not really a community any more, because every one of us was, in her heart, keeping secret the paltry possibilities of her own future.

The gales of uncertainty blew us apart and blew us together, back and forth. The more isolated each of us felt, the more we sought to cleave together. How can 'cleave' mean both to separate, and to cling? Spin the coin. And after the strange dancing, something even more strange happened.

The following afternoon the sisters began to laugh. They gathered in the cloister and looked at one another and could not stop laughing. In a mindless way they were utterly of one mind. They laughed until the tears poured down their cheeks and their noses ran and they choked. They laughed themselves to a halt, gasping and clutching their stomachs, then caught another's eye, and set off laughing again, and set all the others off again. It was an infection. They were having fits. Fits of laughing. They were laughing at nothing. They were laughing because all the others were laughing. They did not really look as if it was giving them pleasure. They just could not stop laughing. Anne was among them, and all the Fairheads, and Mother Onion and Catherine Hunt and the Novice Mistress and even Eleanor. All laughing. Drawn by the noise, and watching from the archway to the slype, I felt the twitch and the itch of it and for two pins I would have stepped among them and joined in. But the Prioress came up beside me and thanks be to God the moment passed.

'Shall I fetch the Infirmaress?' I asked. 'Or the Abbess? Or the Steward? Our sisters have all gone quite mad.'

'No,' she said. She held tight on to my sleeve, which was just as well.

'I have seen this before. In a convent in France. It is something that happens to women and girls. The worst thing you can do is try and stop them, or reprimand them. Any intervention sends them off again. They must be left. It will blow over. They will exhaust themselves and the devil-spirit will go from them.'

She was right. At supper it was as if nothing had happened. We talk and think so much in the religious life about suppressing the self and being of one mind. It can lead, I now see, down some peculiar paths.

My own cleaving was other. I walked slowly with Dorothy Clausey round and round the precinct in the chill of the wind. We were lost in our own thoughts and did not speak much, but it was comforting to be together. I was going to miss her. I had an impulse to give her something of mine. No, not my emerald dolphin, not that. As we went round the cloister for the second time, I pulled off my green hood, which I had retrieved with my other belongings from the Chambress.

'Would you like to have this? To wear, to remember me by?'

She flushed and smiled and put it on and looked at me.

'It becomes you, it brings out the green in your eyes.'

'Thank you. Thank you, Agnes Peppin.'

'What are you going to do? Have you decided?'

We sat down on a bench under cover and out of the wind.

'Did Dame Elizabeth not tell you? I thought she told you everything.'

No, Dame Elizabeth had told me nothing. Dorothy grimaced. Dame Elizabeth, she said, had received a visitor from London, from one of Master Cromwell's people on his way to inspect Glastonbury Abbey, requesting that arrangements should be made somehow for Dorothy to remain in Shaftesbury.

'It would be inconvenient for me to appear in London. That was the word: inconvenient. But it was an order.'

'Because of your father?'

'Yes. I am the Cardinal's – I will not say the word. I am an inconvenience, an embarrassment. Dame Elizabeth sent for me to tell me this, and she was kind enough, but I was stiff with her, I was mortified. I told her that I would comply, and remain in Shaftesbury, but that I would make my own arrangements.'

'But where will you go? How will you live?'

She looked me in the eye and said, 'I am going to live with the Winterbournes.'

I was aghast. My scholarly, nervous Dorothy, in that cabin with no windows, day and night, shut in there with the two Johns, and Emilia and Little John, and – and then, then I understood.

'You will be with Esther!'

'I will be with Esther.'

She smiled, her eyes brimming with tears.

Of course. She can never look after Esther on her own. Do not ask me why, but she cannot. With Emilia in charge, and the two Johns to provide for them, Dorothy can learn to be content. Her tears were tears of hope. I had a flash of seeing how it might be. There may be more children for Dorothy and Emilia. Maybe no one will ever know which John fathered which? I laughed inwardly at this thought, though the idea of such mixings in such close and foetid quarters is disagreeable.

But in the long summer evenings the fields and woods down the steep lanes outside the town are above all things agreeable. Dorothy's father may have been the Cardinal, but the Cardinal's father was a butcher, like my father. There is common blood in her veins. Such an arrangement as she envisaged will not be unprecedented, life being what it is and love being wherever you can find it.

I cannot tell whether Dorothy's imagination ran quite so far ahead as mine did. I rather think not.

'I shall teach Esther and Little John to read and write. I shall teach Esther to understand Latin. I might have a little school, just for girls.'

Truly her face, framed by my green hood, was radiant.

'What will you do?' I asked Anne Cathcart.

We were walking down into the Park, away from everyone. She linked her arm in mine, leaning into me. I shall miss her easy, fleshly affection.

'I shall go back to London. It is where I belong. The Percevals will take me in, for my father's sake of course, until I establish myself.'

'But they said you might be in danger. I did not really understand.'

Anne stopped, I stopped, and she pulled out the ring, on its string, from the top of her tunic. She turned it in her hand.

'You are a little obtuse sometimes, Agnes. But I will tell you.'

So she confessed to me at last the whole story. She had told me before that she was a good acquaintance of Mary Zouche, who was lady-in-waiting to Anne Boleyn before the King married her. She used to visit Mary Zouche in Anne Boleyn's apartments when the lady herself was absent.

'Did you see Anne Boleyn?'

'No, I never did. So, one day, while Mary Zouche was in a closet off the bedchamber, folding laundered nightgowns and laying them in a chest, I picked up a diamond ring from an open box on the table. I put it in my pocket.'

'Why that one?'

'I knew about it. We used to go through all Anne Boleyn's belongings, trying things on. That was normal, anyone in such a situation does that. How would one not, why would one not?'

She had not particularly coveted the ring. It was not showy. The thick gold band was good, but the diamond was uncut and unpolished. Yet she knew it was the most valuable one of all, because lady Zouche had told her so.

'I did not decide to take it. My hand did it.'

I can well imagine how that might be.

The loss of the valuable ring was swiftly noticed.

'Mary Zouche was dismissed and to save her skin she named me as the only possible thief. I had to run away. I had to leave London, or I would have been arrested.'

So, having nowhere to go, and being of good family, she applied to enter Shaftesbury Abbey.

'Piers Perceval spoke for me to the Abbess and provided my dowry – a good one, a mill in Dorchester.'

'But why should he do that? What was his interest?'

'You are being obtuse again. Let's just say he had, still has, a long-standing interest. In, ahem, me.'

I still found it puzzling.

'And then you contacted Mary Zouche again? To find out about the Abbess?'

'I was so very curious, when I first came here. I do like to know things. Knowing things always comes in useful.'

'Did Mary tell you what relation she was to our Dame Elizabeth?'

'She told me nothing at all, and worse still she let it be known that I had been making disobliging enquiries about our Abbess, and it was reported to her. The Abbess looks just as they all look, but no one knows which one fathered her or who her mother was. The Zouche men are incontinent and not fastidious as to the beds they lie in at night as they ride around the country. There are lads and girls in all the villages calling themselves Zouche who work as day-labourers and servants. Our Abbess was a fortunate one.'

'Perhaps she had a Piers Perceval of her own.'

'I think we'll never know.'

We had reached the bottom of the Park and were walking beside the fishponds.

'You could throw the ring into the water, now. Then you would be safe.'

'Are you quite mad? Listen, Agnes. Anne Boleyn is dead. God only knows where Mary Zouche is now. She is probably married off to some halfwit gentleman and living in a crumbling castle at the back of beyond. Or she may be dead. Dead would be best. I shall sell the ring in London. No diamond merchant in Hatton Garden will think to enquire how I come to have it. He will look at it through his glass and all he will recognise is its quality. He will think about how little he dare offer for it and how much he dare ask for it afterwards. I shall drive a hard bargain. Then I shall hire with the proceeds a house in a good street, and rent out apartments, and give entertainments. Piers Perceval will introduce me to all his friends – Sir Thomas Wyatt I hear is back in favour – and to ladies who desire to widen their social circle.'

We did not speak as we walked back, because Anne carries much soft flesh and finds it hard to get her breath when walking uphill. I had time to think over what she said. It seemed to me that Anne meant to become a fashionable kind of brothel-keeper. She will surely thrive, for a while anyway. She is handsome and generous and ruthless. Her judgment is not always sound, however, so when we reached the top, I said:

'You might have to watch out for Mistress Agnes Perceval. She seems like a jealous woman who could do you harm.'

'Do not speak of what you do not understand, Agnes Peppin. You are impertinent and know nothing of the great world.'

That is true.

Anne was angry. She walked away from me and called back over her shoulder:

'Go back to the butcher's shop where you belong, Agnes Peppin!'

But when we met outside the church next morning after Mass she laughed and opened her arms to me and we embraced. She bore no grudge and honest to God neither did I. Anne is Anne.

I came upon Dame Philippa and Dame Joanna sitting on the ground in a sheltered corner of the bakehouse court, their walking sticks at their feet. They turned their faces towards me when they heard my footsteps on the stones, and I greeted them.

'Is that you, Sister Agnes? The light hurts my eyes and I cannot tell.' That was Dame Joanna. They shifted closer together and Dame Philippa patted the ground, indicating that I might sit with them.

'What will you do? Where will you go?' I asked them, with trepidation, because I could not think what they could possibly do, or anywhere they could possibly go.

They beamed at me. Dame Joanna leant forward, straining across Dame Philippa's amplitude:

'We will go nowhere. We are going to remain here!'

And they nodded in unison, still beaming.

Had they lost their senses? I explained with a heavy heart that none of us could stay here. Our community was dissolved. Our Abbey will be destroyed. We have to leave. It is over, for us.

'No. We have heard,' said Dame Joanna, 'that the chantry priests' tenements are not being demolished. Or not straight away. We heard the workmen talking. There is nothing of value there for the robbers, you see.'

'We have decided,' said Dame Philippa, 'that we will move by night into Father Robert's house as soon as he leaves. It is not so large as Father Bucket's or some of the others, but it will smell less foul. No one will know we are there. When the robbers have departed, we shall venture out.'

'But how will you live, what will you eat?'

'We will beg for bread in the town. And we know where the barrels of last year's onions and roots are hidden. The Steward has shown us. His boy Gregory is going to help us to carry some in baskets to our new home when the time comes. We shall make pottage.'

'Will we have no peas or beans for the pottage?' said Dame Joanna. 'I do love beans, I need beans, I would miss beans.'

'The Lord will provide, sister. We may find beans. Later, there will be blackberries, and apples from the orchard.'

'Yes, yes.' Dame Joanna rocked back and forth, hugging herself. 'We shall have plenty.'

I was not convinced.

'What if they destroy the wellhead and block up the well?'

'What if, what if, little Sister Agnes? We shall find water. All shall be well and all shall be well and all manner of things shall be well.'

They were looking forward. I stood up and kissed each old face in turn. No one had been caring for them in these recent days. The creases in their faces were inlaid with dirt. Their habits were so worn and soiled, their wimples so creased and askew, that it would take little to transform them into the kind of poor old women one saw on every street corner. And if the citizens of Shaftesbury recognised them for what they were, they would surely take pity.

'What we shall pray for,' said Dame Philippa, holding tightly on to my hand, 'is that God in his mercy when he takes one of us, will take the other at the same time. So that we may enter into Heaven together and stand before God's Holy Mother together. We have always been together. If you pray for us, in the days to come, will you pray that this may come to pass?'

I have so prayed, many times.

As I walked away, I heard them calling after me: 'Sister Agnes, do you know what is to happen to the Abbess's bed-curtains? Which we worked for her with our own hands? Will she carry them with her when she leaves? Will the robbers take them?'

This was too painful. I knew they had already been torn down. I pretended not to have heard.

I was worried about what I would do about Finbarr when I left the Abbey. My plans were vague. I might have to walk the roads for many days. How would I find food for her? I might wish to call upon the Zouches at Cockhill, or on my grandmother Hibberd in Tisbury, in the event that I had the courage or the wit or the means to reach either place. Even though I had my emerald dolphin to prove who I was, a shabby young woman leading an exhausted dog on a string would appear a vagrant, and might be turned away. But I was unwilling to part with Finbarr.

I had also suspected for some time that Finbarr was in pup. I always tried to keep an eye on her when she came into season, but she was a little stouter, and her tits were standing out on her belly. So I was not altogether surprised when I found her in the kennel with five tiny creatures, brown and white and flat-nosed and as ugly as sin. I do not care to think to which of the foul chained-up curs she had crept up one dark night in her need. The pups scrabbled all over each other to get at their mother, who looked up at me trustingly.

'Oh Finbarr! What are we going to do?'

I fetched Dorothy, who sat beside Finbarr and stroked her head. We looked at one another in despair. I did not intend or plan to say what I did:

'When I leave the Abbey, will you keep Finbarr?'

I began to cry as a child cries, unstoppably, my hands covering my face. A hard stony something crumbled in my heart and the crying came, and not only for Finbarr. Dorothy did not try to comfort me. She sat there on the ground stroking Finbarr and looking at me.

'But would she stay with me? Would she be happy with me?'

I stopped crying. We had to think.

'She knows you almost as well as she knows me.'

'But first we have to dispose of the pups.'

I went to fetch Gregory, and he came with a sack and took four of the pups away. He left one with its mother until the following day, so that the shock of separation would be lessened for her. I do not know whether he drowned them, or gave them away, or sold them. I did not really care.

Finbarr recovered fast. We devised a plan to decide her future. It seems so mad, to think of it now. Like an ordeal, as if we were trying witches, or as of we were witches ourselves. Or like jousting, without lances. It was Dorothy's idea. She is a strange woman. 'Not like other people.' That is what my father said about my mother. Perhaps Dorothy is indeed a witch, or could be. Perhaps my mother is a witch, or could be. Yet no one is 'like other people' once you really know them. If any one of us is a witch, then we are all witches.

This is what we did. We walked Finbarr to a flat place near the top of the Park. I told her:

'Sit. Stay.'

Finbarr is good about that. She can be relied upon to do that.

Dorothy and I moved away twenty paces in opposite directions, and turned. As agreed, I counted to three, raised my hand, and Dorothy and I both called in unison: 'Finbarr come!'

Finbarr looked at me, looked at Dorothy, put her nose to the ground and sniffed, ran to Dorothy and sat at her feet looking up into her face.

So that was that. It was not inevitable, it could have turned out otherwise. If my voice were louder. If the wind were blowing from the other direction, if some scent in the grass between Finbarr and Dorothy were less alluring. Who knows?

Finbarr would live with Dorothy and the two children and the two Johns in the hovel on Bimport.

'When the time comes,' I said. 'When the time comes. And – afterwards – I will come back and visit you.'

'Of course,' said Dorothy.

'Meanwhile, she will stay with me.'

'Of course,' said Dorothy, adjusting the green hood. There was a strong west wind every day in that last week.

Relief and heartbreak. Opposite sides of the same coin.

I need now to consult with someone wiser than myself about my own future. Not Anne Cathcart, not Dorothy, not my Melancholy. Not the Abbess either.

I need someone not too close, and someone discreet, who might address my difficulties without being excessively intrigued or self-concerned. I really do need help.

I thought of Sister Mary Amor. She is sensible and reasonable. I think she is comfortable with daily life and its challenges, and does not torture herself with scruples or with what might have been. She agreed to meet me in the slype. It was going to be a cold night with no moon, and so unlikely that anyone else would be there.

It was indeed cold and dark in the slype. Pale illumination filtered in from the cressets in the cloister. We drew our cloaks around us and raised our hoods and sat close together. It is easier to speak freely when neither can see the other's face. I did not want to be searching Mary's expression for contempt or boredom.

'What will you do?' I asked her.

'There is nothing that I can do. My whole life is in this place. Do not give it another thought.'

'There is a world elsewhere. There are new places to go, new thoughts to think.'

'I know all that, but I do not want any of it. I shall make my arrangements. But you, Agnes – it is different for you, what will you do?'

I told her how I was torn between possibilities, none of them promising. I could try and remain within the Order, and seek another House abroad, as the Abbess had suggested to us in Chapter. Or I could go back to my parents in Bruton and be a help to them in their old age. Then, my heart in my mouth, I confessed to her about Peterkin. Because my third possibility was to seek out Peter Mompesson and fulfil the vows I made to him (and he to me) before we parted for the last time. Peterkin would not know me. But I am his mother still. Then I stopped speaking, because I was fighting back tears.

Mary did not say anything for a while. Then she asked:

'Does the life of a nun suit you? Would you be content?'

'I believe so. I like the complication of it. The complexity.'

'Most people on the outside believe it to be constricting and limited.'

'Such people perhaps do not understand the way of life. I have come to think that constriction and freedom both come from within.'

'Then you have learned the most important lesson of all.'

'And if I were professed as a nun in another country, I could learn new words, another language, and that would be an adventure.'

'I am beginning to see you, in years to come, as a lively Abbess ruling over a French convent.'

She laughed a little.

'Have you spent time with Sister Isobel?'

Sister Isobel – that nonentity, as Anne would say? Sister Isobel is small and plain. She keeps apart. She sits always very still and straight-backed. I have never in all my time here spoken with her. I shook my head.

'I am sorry for that. Of all our sisters, she is the one who best knows why we are here. She walks with God. Her life is within, with Him. She exists in a state of grace. To talk to Sister Isobel even for a few minutes is to open a shutter into sunlight. She says nothing profound but everything becomes simple and true – and accepted, inevitable, even glorious. I am so sorry that you do not know her.'

Sister Mary Amor fell silent. She was somewhere far away. She came back to me.

'And how would it be if you went back to your parents?'

This was difficult. I told her it was perhaps the most dutiful course of action. The life at home was familiar, I could slip back into it as if I had never been away. I told her that I loved my father dearly.

'But I would need more,' I said. 'I would need to read and to study, somehow. Otherwise I would go out of my mind.'

I did not say to her that I have relatives in Tisbury who do not know me. A grandmother, if she still lives. I could seek her out, but she might not receive me. I did not say, I could show my grandmother my emerald dolphin. Perhaps in my innermost heart I already did not believe that it was a real possibility.

'And if you were to seek out your son, and his father?'

'That is the unknowable thing, like walking out from home with no idea of where you are going.'

Silence again.

She gave me no advice. She said:

'You tell me that you have three choices. We say that accidents happen in threes. There are three degrees of light – Lux, Lumen and Illumination. Everything comes in threes. That is why the mystery of the Holy Trinity – Father, Son and Holy Ghost – has such potency. Everywhere, even here in the Abbey, there are three kinds of people – the powerful ones, and the unfortunates, and the self-sacrificing helpers. Christ is the son of Almighty God, and at the same time He is the Suffering Servant, the victim – have you read the Book of Isaiah? – and He is also our help in time of trouble. We too are all three, in turn and often at the same time – a punishing Jehovah, a victim, and a helper. This is not comfortable. The Holy Trinity is the redemptive resolution of a natural dissonance. Look into your own heart.'

I found this triangulation theory too far-fetched. Mary Amor was more eccentric than I realised. But maybe there was something in it. I asked her, 'Is Martha in the Bible a victim, or a helper, or a punisher?'

'She is all three. When a helper, a Martha, begins to see herself as a victim, she becomes as angry and as punishing as Jehovah. Then she feels guilt and shame and the wheel turns again.'

'And her sister Mary?'

'Ah ... That is an interesting question. Perhaps she is that within us which stands outside the daily round, intent upon wholeness and holiness. Martha and Mary struggle for survival within one soul.'

'I too have thought that. And – sin? What about sin?'

'If men and women were not sinners, there would be no need for redemption. We would be innocent as the animals are, as Adam and Eve were before they ate the apple. If we were without sin then the mercy and forgiveness and love of God, and Christ's death upon the Cross, would have no meaning. There would be no need for us to pray to God and to worship Him.'

Sister Mary Amor rose. She turned to me and I saw her face, ravaged.

'Either one is capable of change, or one is not. I am not like Sister Isobel, but I committed myself to the life of a nun in Shaftesbury Abbey long ago with the certitude that I would lie when I die in the graveyard beside my sisters who have gone before. My path was plain before me. I have no longer any choice. But you ... God bless and help you, Agnes Peppin.'

She made the sign of the cross with her thumb on my forehead.

I was left in the blackness and the cold. I saw in my mind's eye the track out of Bruton which leads towards Wincanton, though I never got so far. Over the hill, it splits three ways. I walked that track with my father once towards daylight end, and when we came to the splitting, he said:

'Home now. We don't want to lose ourselves in the dark.'

Poor Father Louis Pomfret broke down in an unpleasant manner. I do believe that he was possessed by the Devil. But there was a desperate honesty in him. If it were not absurd, let alone heretical, I could believe that God and the Devil too were opposite sides of the same coin, like Martha and Mary. He began to spill out the secrets of the confessional, which are beyond anything private and sacred. He was drunk, as he was drunk all day and every day now.

He stood purple-faced outside the Abbey Church, where everyone passed – and where everyone stopped, to hear him

shouting out his foul betrayals like an itinerant friar preaching dam-
nation to attract a crowd. Father Pomfret did attract a crowd, not
only of us nuns but of workmen, tradesmen, servants, apprentice
boys and even Tregonwell's clerks and the destroyers. I was in that
crowd. Most of what he was shouting was gobbledygook, half of it
in Latin, with obscenities thrown in, and meaningless. Every now
and then he paused, drew breath, and uttered a single sentence:

'The Cardinal's daughter is a whore!'

Off he went again into his rigmarole and then:

'Your Lady Abbess is a bastard!'

He had to be stopped.

'Robert Parker is a fornicator and a sodomite! Eleanor Wilmer
is a deluded nincompoop who fingers Christ in her filthy dreams!'

Mother Onion, beside me, put her hands over her ears.

'Sweet Jesus, this fellow gives my arse a pain.'

Father Pomfret, a weighty man and out of his senses, could have
knocked any woman to the ground with a single swipe. We sisters
should have overcome him in unison like small birds mobbing a
predator. I wish we had. But we were not of one mind and the men
in the crowd just could not get enough of the show and were not
going to make a move.

I saw Sister Mary Amor running off towards the Steward's
house, just as Father Pomfret, after more mumbo-jumbo, was
starting in again, out of control.

'The Cathcart bitch is a thief, she stole a diamond. Eleanor
Wilmer, I haven't finished with her yet, is an infanti—'

Up strode the Steward. He grasped Father Pomfret by the
shoulders, looked him in the eyes, spoke to him in the way
that a stableman speaks to a frightened horse, and led him
away stumbling and needing support. I have never had any
personal dealings with this Steward apart from our encounter
round the bonfire at Christmastime. He was for all his crudity a
sound man.

We drifted away to wherever we should have been and did not speak of what had occurred. There had always, in the Abbey, been matters which were not spoken of. Now there was less and less of which we could safely speak at all.

In the morning the Melancholies had disappeared.

Sister Onora told us that the previous night she saw three nuns high in the air flying across the face of the moon. The night had been clouded. There was no moon to see. But Sister Onora sees what others cannot see. I am a little afraid, however, that when we all have to leave the Abbey, the outside world will not understand this about Sister Onora, and that she will be condemned as a witch. I am worried for her because she lacks common sense.

The last time that Sir Thomas Arundell visited the Abbess in her house he asked her where she would go.

'I would like to retain Place Farm in Tisbury.'

'Unfortunately you are not permitted to retain anything that belongs to the Abbey, that is to say, that did belong to the Abbey, and now belongs to the King. Tisbury will be sold.'

The desolation in Dame Elizabeth's face was pitiful. She turned her head away, unable to look at him.

'But perhaps,' said Sir Thomas, leaning forward, 'we can come to an arrangement.'

She motioned to me to put down my writing things. This was not a conversation that would be recorded.

He told her that he himself was negotiating to buy the manor of Tisbury from the Crown. He did not tell her what we afterwards learned, that he was also negotiating to buy the Abbey site. He had a courtier's tact. He said he was prepared to lease Place Farm to Dame Elizabeth for her lifetime at the market rate. She could easily afford this out of her pension. In return, he would expect recompense after her death for the loss of amenity to himself.

'And since you will live long and well, the time of waiting for me will not be short.'

She said, 'I will make a Will. I will make you my heir.'

He bowed in acquiescence.

'You will make your Will, and your man of law and mine will also draw up an agreement.'

She bowed her head.

'And the Seal, Madam? You have not yet handed over the Seal. The Crown requires it.'

The Abbess motioned to me to leave the chamber. The handing over of the Seal of the Abbey was so terrible for her and so final that she could not endure to have it witnessed. I cannot bear to think of her shame and her pain.

Late that night, when I was getting ready for bed, a maid came from the Abbess requiring me to go to her in her house. I was exhausted and so was she.

'Where will you go, Agnes Peppin? I need to know.'

'Home, Madam,' I said, 'probably home to Bruton, just at first. After that, I know not.'

What Dame Elizabeth had to say astonished me.

'I am entrusting to you the holy relics of St Edward. I removed them myself from the casket inside the ossuary. The ossuary, which has great monetary value, is to be taken tomorrow by the Commissioners. The lead casket is heavy and no one will suspect that it is empty. The holy relics must not fall into impious hands. When you leave, you will take them with you. You will tell nobody.'

'But what will I do with them, Madam?'

'I will send word to you as to where you will bring them when all has quietened down.'

She went to her cupboard and took out a black silk bundle. She placed it on the table and unwrapped it in the light of the candles.

I saw a pile of bleached bones, one large one and half a dozen splinters. The Abbess crossed herself and I did the same. Neither of us spoke. The Abbess wrapped the bones up again in the silk. She double-wrapped the holy relics in a piece of cloth, and put the whole thing in a canvas bag.

'I also want to tell you that I have loved you, Agnes, my martyr. More than you know.' She touched my cheek and took my hand. Her hand trembled and her touch was not maternal. There was carnality in it. The ashes of carnality. I wanted to unlace my fingers from hers. The moment seemed to go on for ever. I almost stopped breathing. But I loved her too, I still do. It hurts me now that I did not tell her so. It was a sin of omission.

'Send to me, where you are,' she said. 'Send to Tisbury, to Place Farm, even if I am not there the people will know where to find me. I will send to you, as I will to all our sisters, when I can, and we may be together again if only for a short while.'

'Where is Tisbury?'

'It is not far from here. Over the border into Wiltshire.'

'I have family in Tisbury whom I have never seen. My grandmother's name is Hibberd. I believe she paid you a visit to arrange my coming to this place.'

I longed for her to say that she remembered the visit well, that my grandmother was a fine woman and her own kin, and I should surely attempt to seek her out. She said nothing of the sort.

'You may be right.' She passed her hand over her face. 'I do believe someone did come to see me about you. I cannot remember. So much has befallen us since then that there is much that I forget. My mind is not so sharp as it was. Tisbury is full of Hibberds.'

She let my hand go and stood up. I too stood up.

'I will be requiring your services again, but I will not be speaking with you in this way again.'

She embraced me, holding me close to her bulky body, and made the sign of the Cross on my forehead. She pushed the canvas bag into my arms and turned away.

Then she called me back:

'The cloister is a disgrace. There are weeds growing up between the flagstones. Kindly, Sister Agnes, clean it up.'

'Yes, Madam.'

She sounded unhinged. Her mind has become weak. Why would we be weeding the cloister now? And why me? Perhaps it was to remind me of my duty of humility. I was shaking as I walked through the cloister and crept up the stairs to the dorter in the dark. Her demeanour unnerved me.

But there is worse. I am a butcher's daughter. I know bones. Those bones I was carrying away, the holy relics of St Edward the Martyr, were not human bones. I knew at a glance what animal they came from. I will not name that animal. I will not betray the thousands of pilgrims who travelled long miles to pray on their knees to the holy relics of a saint, and who paid money, and who went away strengthened and sometimes cured of their ills.

In the morning, between one ill-attended Holy Office and the next, I procured a blunt knife and a basket and, on my knees, began to scrape away the grass and weeds growing between the paving-stones of the cloister, which was destined to be in a state of perfection for an eternal moment only hours before it was destroyed. There was a great growth of parsley in one corner of the garth. Last year the parsley had not germinated well. This past summer the conditions had been right and in spite of the cold the stems were still strong, topped by clusters of dark green leaflets. I broke off some and chewed it as I worked, thinking how this parsley would self-seed, so that next year there would be even more. No one would come to cut it for the Abbess's mushroom dish, because she would not be here, nor would any of us. Only ruins where once had been the whole fine world we made.

Finbarr was playing around me, nosing at the gaps between the flagstones where weeds and grass had been, scenting worms. I had been at it for an hour when Master Tregonwell appeared. He walked heavily round and round the cloister, stepping past me as I worked, and then sat down near me on a ledge beneath the arcade. I could feel his eyes on my backside.

'Are you interested in architecture?' he asked me.

'I could be,' I said. I sat up.

'I have an idea,' he said. 'I am much struck by the notion, the idea, of a cloister. It is a form known only in monastic Houses. It permits access from a covered way into separate chambers.'

Of course it does. I did not know what was so special about that. He was going to tell me, anyway.

'In great houses, one is compelled to pass through one chamber after another to reach where one desires to be. Have you ever been in such a house, Agnes Peppin?'

'No, sir, except that it is surely normal to pass from one chamber into another, even if there are only two. What else should one do?'

'The passing from one chamber to another through high door-ways, in great houses, is a matter of glory and ostentation – a great vista. They call it *en enfilade*. That is French.'

'I thought it was French. I know what French sounds like.'

'Of course you do. The *enfilade* of rooms is inconvenient, especially at night, when people are sleeping all over the place, or not exactly sleeping, which is even worse, ha ha. My idea is to build a great house with a long covered way, a passage, within the building itself, so that one could walk along and enter only the chamber where one wished to be.'

'How would one know into which chamber each door opened?'

I went back to my weeding.

He lumbered off, shouting at me:

'That is how I am going to build my great house! It is revolutionary! They all will copy me! You are stupid not to see it. In the coming time there will be a building and a rebuilding such as England has never seen. And why do you not rid yourself of that filthy dog?'

Finbarr was still with me, or so I thought. But she had distanced herself when Tregonwell was talking to me.

Because I did not know where to stow away safely the relics of St Edward, and was unwilling to let them out of my sight, I had brought them with me in their canvas bag and wedged the bag in a niche in the cloister wall. I chanced to look up at the very moment when Finbarr placed her front paws up on the shelf of the niche, sniffed, and grabbed the canvas bag between her teeth.

'Finbarr!' I yelled. 'No! Drop that! Drop it! Drop it!'

She pranced off, the bag in her mouth, and was away out of the cloister before I had even got to my feet.

I chased that dog past the Infirmary and had nearly caught up with her – because she dropped the bag, and took a moment to retrieve it – when she reached the fence on the edge of the ridge, and was under it, with the bag, racing down the slope of the Abbey Park and disappearing into a copse. I saw her wagging tail on the far side, then she was gone.

There was no point in my attempting to go after her. When the Devil is in her, Finbarr is not to be caught. She did not reappear until daylight end, and then only because she was hungry. I gave her some bread in broth. There was no purpose in being angry with her. She would have no notion of why she was being punished. I watched her as she gobbled her food. I knew exactly what she would have done down in the Park. She would have buried the bag as she buries all her stolen treasures.

What she buried has no value. It is possible that the true remains of St Edward were lost or stolen, and substitutions quietly made, and nothing said. It is equally possible that St Edward was saintly. Because I never did understand his story. He became King when he was thirteen years old and was murdered by relatives who wished his half-brother to be King. I do not see why that makes him a saint and a martyr. He was the grandson of our first Abbess. Maybe it was a family matter and he was made a saint in compensation for the wrong done to him.

For it seems there is no spiritual advantage to souls after death that cannot be bought or sold or bargained for. Meanwhile, what was I going to do?

I decided to do nothing at all. If I told my story there would be wailing and outcry. The Abbess would be furious, and mortified, and maybe punished, for having her ruse for the rescue of the relics known. Finbarr would be arraigned as the Devil's tool and killed, and a search of the Park would be called for.

The Park is vast, and the ground, even where it is not covered by trees and bushes, is much grubbed up by rabbits, deer, foxes, badgers. The bag would never be found.

I persuaded myself that the Abbess in her wisdom, or what remained of it, would approve of my decision to keep silent, and also that it would be kinder in me not to lay this burden of knowledge upon her. Again, what is not put into words has not happened. If in the future I have to account for the bones I shall tell some monstrous lie.

Finbarr curled up beside me where I sat on the ground and went to sleep. I stroked her silky ears. I still sometimes, even now, think about that bag of pig's bones. There, I have named the animal. The bundle will not have lasted long. The canvas and the silk wrapping will have rotted away, and the bones themselves been chewed or scattered by the animals.

I can give no coherent account of the final few weeks. The destroyers move in. The roof of the Abbey Church is brought down. The precinct has always been alive with noise, but it was the noise of repairing and making, not of destroying. Walking in the precinct, we pick our way through rubble and around smouldering fires and piles of wood and lead. Fragments of stone carving, grotesque heads, the hands and the feet of holy images lie scattered around. A charnel house. It was on one of the first days that the old nun I mentioned before was struck on the head by a gargoyle on her way to the kitchen, and died instantly. I have also told how I went into the church after the destroyers had stopped work for the day, and saw my sisters standing apart and aghast in the roofless nave, and encountered Father Pomfret. I did not tell it all. Not the worst sacrilege.

The beautiful Holy Rood, the great crucifix with the gaunt figure of the dead Christ hanging from it, lay awkwardly across the top of the nave. An arm of the cross was broken off, and Christ Himself lay face down on the ground, torn away.

The back of the figure was not shaped or coloured at all, except for streaks of paint round the edges. It was just a piece of splintery old timber, scarred by marks of tools and nails.

Someone came up behind me and stood close. I knew from the odour that it was Father Pomfret. He was no longer insane, but he was not totally sane either. I moved a little distance away. He stood there staring at the meaningless lumber at our feet.

'It is all mummery. Cheap mummery. It always was.'

'No,' I said. 'No.'

I could not engage with him about the Holy Rood only ever being a representation. Its crudity was shocking. But I would not comfort him. Because of what is happening I am becoming less kind. I have little tolerance.

'It is sad,' I said. 'It is just very sad.'

That was when I stooped and picked up the lion tile from among the dislodged floor-tiles beside the broken Cross and went away from him.

The next evening we sang our last Vespers in the ruined choir under the dark sky. We never ever knew, until a moment before, who would be called upon by the Prioress to give out, alone, the first phrases of the Magnificat. She would point her baton, and the chosen one would take a deep breath and begin. I was never chosen. My voice does not carry. Dorothy Clausey was not there. The Prioress pointed at Eleanor Wilmer. Her voice has depth.

Our open-air singing that evening had little resonance, but I think the chanting was more carefully done than ever before. It was perfect. Before we finished a small rain began to fall. Our veils were damp as we moved afterwards into the body of the church — the headless body of the church — carrying tapers. Owls called above our heads, and there was a scuttering in the dimness of the nave from some animal or animals whom we were disturbing with our footfalls.

We saw then why animals were in the nave, and what had lured them in. There was a dark mass on the floor which did not seem to be just another pile of masonry or timber. We gathered around it with our tapers. It was the corpse of a man. It was the corpse of Father Louis Pomfret. There were stab wounds in the back of his neck. Congealing blood lay in a sticky pool around his head, which lay downwards. I could not help thinking of black pudding. I wondered if anyone had ever made black pudding with human blood. I expect so, because there is nothing that could happen which has not happened, somewhere, at some time. The Prioress bent and turned him with her foot, and we saw his face. There were more stab wounds all around his throat, the gashes livid now, the blood having ceased to flow. The deed must have been done some time ago.

The Prioress sent someone for the Steward. The rest of us remained, keeping watch, motionless. The Steward and Gregory came with lanterns and a handcart.

'It would be for the best, ladies, if you left us now,' said the Steward, and we did. I do not know if the blood was ever cleaned away. What does it matter? I did not go into the church ever again, not once.

If anyone, other than the perpetrator, knows who murdered Father Louis Pomfret, they have not yet told me. We talk about it, but guardedly, and do not speculate. It is too dangerous, and perhaps better not to know. Every single man and woman in the Abbey carries a knife for the needs of daily life, and everyone takes pride in keeping them sharp. We sisters call them our 'little sharpies'. The killer or killers could have been from among the rough young men of the town whom poor Father Pomfret found so dangerous and delectable. It would be impossible to interrogate the hundred or so souls who came and went from the Abbey in those last days. The machinery of the Abbey's law and enforcement was no longer in operation in any case.

During the night I did wonder if Anne Cathcart had done it, to shut his mouth about her theft of the ring. But next day she was the same as ever. Surely one could not do such a thing and remain so calm. But perhaps one could? A mission successfully accomplished? I even wondered whether the murder had been ordered by the Abbess, because of what he might have known about her antecedents. She kept within her house and did not appear at the burial, clumsily conducted by Father Bucket.

I did not regret Father Pomfret's death. No one could. He will not be missed. But I did find consolation for such horror in the thought that our last and lovely Vespers served as his requiem.

The murder of Father Pomfret was like a disturbing dream. It might as well not have happened, because a new horror obliterated it. The death of our unloved priest was petty compared with what happened at Glastonbury Abbey. We could think and speak of nothing else.

Our Abbess and her friend Abbot Richard Whiting of Glastonbury were always on good though not confidential terms. I saw the letters which passed between them, as they kept one another abreast of the state of the country and the fate of different religious Houses. I would read his aloud to her, and transcribe her replies. Their letters were circumspect. Letters could be intercepted.

I recall their discussing the fates of the surrendered abbeys in our West Country, and the fates of the heads of these Houses. He thought to amaze her by telling her about Sherborne Abbey. Its new Abbot Barnstable and his sixteen remaining monks had just surrendered to the Commissioners. But Sherborne Abbey would not be destroyed. Sir John Horsey, wrote Abbot Whiting, was negotiating with the Crown – for which read Master Thomas Cromwell – to buy the Abbey and its properties for himself.

Well, the Abbess was not amazed, we knew all about that already, from Sir Thomas Arundell. For once we were ahead of the news. We knew too that Sir John Horsey was selling the great Abbey Church to the parishioners of Sherborne, cheaply, thus healing more than a hundred years of bad feeling in the town and securing its survival. So Sir John Horsey was not a bad or avaricious creature, and not all the opportunities grasped by the new men are selfish ones.

Dame Elizabeth Zouche's response to the Sherborne story was that she wished heartily that someone such as Sir John Arundell had negotiated for Shaftesbury Abbey in time to save it from demolition. But Arundell unfortunately had no desire to prevent the destruction. Abbot Whiting's latest letter, I remember, contained the words:

'I will not go quietly. Glastonbury Abbey will never surrender.'

That was more than a month ago.

*

And now came this, the news that made Father Pomfret's death pale into insignificance. I saw through an open door the young messenger ride in through the gatehouse in the evening. He and his horse were both sweating and panting; he must have come as fast as he could and Glastonbury is a good distance off, about twenty-five miles I do believe. He threw the reins to Gregory and shouted that he must see the Abbess at once.

I went on with what I was doing, which was helping the Chambress to sort through chests of gowns and tunics belonging to nuns before they took the habit – nuns who were mostly now dead. Normally, we give some away every year to poor women in the town. Now we were picking out the best to distribute among those professed sisters who do not wish to leave the Abbey and face the world wearing religious dress. Not that religious dress is so different from normal clothes – mainly a matter of colour, or lack of it, and of a severity around the head and in the wimple.

Something happens to garments which are folded away for a long time. They die, they lose their spirit, the moths and the damp get in. It was a dispiriting exercise. There we sat on the ground, making piles of possibles and impossibles, when Dame Elizabeth's little maid appeared at the door saying that Madam required me immediately.

In her parlour, stripped now of all grace and all ornament, all tapestries, holy pictures, cushions, furniture, the Abbess sat on a stool like any other woman. Standing before her in the empty space was the young messenger.

'Write,' she said to me. 'Make notes of what he has to say. This gentleman is – he was – the body servant of the Abbot of Glastonbury.'

It was uncomfortable because I had to squat on the floor with paper and ink and quill beside me, propped on one elbow, since there was no trestle, and no stool other than the Abbess's.

I could have stood, but then there would have been only my hand to support the paper. I have never written so badly or so illegibly.

The young man was unstrung. He was haranguing Dame Elizabeth, he was unstoppable.

'Do you know, Madam, what this means? Hung, drawn and quartered? Our dear Abbot with Brother Ambrose and Brother William, two of his most loving monks, were tied to hurdles and the hurdles were fixed to the backs of horses, he was dragged from the Abbey to the Tor and all the way up to the top where they'd put up gibbets. I followed. I couldn't keep up with the horses. They hanged him. Half-naked. He has a sore place on his chest, an insect-bite, I treated it with ointment just the night before, in his bed. I could see it.'

He put his hands over his face. The Abbess waited, immobile. He raised his head and went on.

'The hanging did not kill him. They did not intend it to. They cut him down and he fell and they took their knives and cut off his privates and stuck their knives into his belly and pulled out his guts with their hands. I was there and I could do nothing at all to help him. I could not tell the moment when his soul flew free from his body but I pray it was fast.'

He paused again. I looked around for water or wine to offer him, but there was nothing. He went on.

'Then they chopped him into four pieces and threw the bloody bits into a basket. The same with Ambrose and William, George, whom I love well. I could bear it no longer and ran away down the hill. Now the Abbot's head is fixed on the west door of the Abbey Church, I have seen it. I have seen it, Madam. Parts of him have been carried away to be exposed in other places. The Abbey is deserted. The town is silent, everyone is stunned. Our Glastonbury today is Hell on earth. Hell, I say ... And these things are done in God's name.'

With that, he gave a cry like that of a despairing child, and slumped down on his haunches against the wall, his head in his hands, shaking. I have never seen a young man so undone, so distressed, and I do not wonder at it. We were in shock ourselves, speechless.

When he had calmed himself a little, the Abbess thanked him formally for his visit.

'What will you do now?' she asked.

He was on his way to his father's house in Warminster.

'I regret that I have little to give you at this moment, but what I have here is yours.'

She gave him some coins from the pocket of her gown, and thanked him again. He struggled to his feet, saluted us, and stumbled out.

She had preserved her composure throughout, although as pale as death. That is only a *façon de parler*, how fond I am of that French phrase, for death is only pale for a short time before stagnant blood collects in black-blue puddles under the skin. As was the case with Father Pomfret.

After the young man left, she put her hand to her throat: 'I am ill.'

The Abbess of Shaftesbury staggered across to the spittoon and vomited. When that was over I helped her into her bedchamber. To my relief her great bed was still there, for which I felt gratitude – gratitude! – to the Commissioners. But it was without curtains or pillows. A blanket lay on the mattress. She lay down and closed her eyes. She was shivering. I sent her maid to fetch the Infirmaress.

Before I left, she opened her eyes and said to me, 'He was an old man. He was a good man. He was a brave man. Braver than I. He was my friend. God rest his soul.'

I remember my own discomfort, trying to take notes for the Abbess without any trestle or stool. It is a sorry fact that pettiness proliferates in proportion to great events, or so it has seemed to me in these days.

The matter of the Library keys, for example. One of Master Tregonwell's clerkly assistants, the nose-picker, was in charge of stripping the Library and supervising the packing of the books, scrolls and ledgers, including the precious Psalter locked in its cupboard. Again I was called for, and found the clerk fuming outside the locked Library door, with half a dozen workmen hanging around, and a stack of wooden cases.

'The door is locked!' he snarled at me. 'Kindly hand me the key. I am informed that it is in your charge.'

'I know where it should be, sir,' I replied. 'I will go and see.'

Since the destroyers are happy to break down any door which they find locked anywhere in the Abbey, it was hard to see why he had such scruples. He was one of those minor people who assert themselves by insisting on some random point. You find them everywhere, women as well as men.

I picked my way around the ruined cloister to the niche where stood the figure of St Catherine. Dorothy and I always stowed the keys there, behind her. Neither of us had used them for a long time. Quiet afternoons in the Library were a thing of the past.

St Catherine was no longer in her niche. She was on the ground, her face broken and bashed. The destroyers applied their hammers to the faces of our saints, even when they left the figures intact. I do not know why they did that. I had to clamber over wreckage to get my hands into the niche. Its base was covered in fragments. There were no keys there. I ran my hands through the fragments again and again. The ground at my feet was a jumble of broken stone. St Catherine lay across the top, too heavy for me to shift.

Then I remembered the Blessed Zita, the servant, the perfect Martha, whose special gift is the finding of lost keys. I closed my eyes. I prayed to Zita. *Please, Zita. Please. I will never ask you for anything again. Please.* When we pray properly, part of us closes down. The breath slows. Everyone knows this. I am not special. When I opened my eyes, I looked again at the rubble at my feet, inch by inch. I saw rusty metal protruding and pulled at it, and there was the ring with the two keys. Thank you, Zita.

I took them back to the nose-picker. I followed him into the Library.

'And the great Psalter?' he asked. 'His Majesty the King knows of it and is anxious to have it brought to him.'

I indicated the little door high in the wall. 'The smaller key.'

The key had rusted and the door would not open, however much he twisted and turned it. Then the shaft snapped. He swore and went away and came back with a man with a heavy hammer. Half a dozen thwacks from the hammer and the oak of the door splintered and fell apart.

The nose-picker thrust in his arm and from the cavity in the wall's thickness he withdrew the Psalter, and held it in his unwashed hands. I saw its stout cover, and the jewels set into it, but no more. I would have given anything to have him unloose the silver clasps and open the Psalter so that I might glimpse the pages. Never so long as I live shall I have such a chance to see such a glory of illumination. The nose-picker turned his back on me, hiding the Psalter from my sight.

'You may leave now.'

His workmen were clumping in and dumping their boxes on the Library floor. I stayed long enough to see them pulling volumes and rolls from their shelves and tipping them into the boxes. The poem I found on a loose sheet will be scuffed underfoot and lost and gone. When I go, and Dorothy, no one will know it ever existed. That is just one poem. How much that is precious, over centuries, is lost and gone?

*

Sisters disappear. The Prioress and the Infirmaress, transformed by bright coloured gowns and high gable hoods into Mistress Agatha Cracknell and Mistress Alice Doble, ladies of consequence, have gone off together in a coach and high fettle, full of talk. Two practical women with a pampered little dog, departing without repining from their sacred duties, from their companions, from their home, from the life of prayer. They plan to establish some commercial enterprise to do with cheeses from Cornwall. Master Tregonwell has given them some helpful contacts. The Fairheads too have all gone, picked up in clusters by brothers and fathers and admirers, carried away in wagons and coaches with all their ribbons and laces – some to marry and multiply, no doubt, some to decline into querulous dependent spinsterhood. But they will be all right. They will have enough to eat, and soft beds.

Sister Mary Amor has hanged herself.

I had thought, after our conversation in the slype, how selfish I was. She addressed my problems, and when she could say no more she had gone from me. I never either thanked her or thought to ask her enough about herself, and what she herself would do. I did not feel that it was my place to press her. I should have had a better understanding. Wishing to remedy my shortcomings, I asked her after dinner in the Refectory if I could come and see her in her office.

'No,' she said. 'Not today.'

'Tomorrow?'

'Not tomorrow.'

And then I said, as if I knew something that I absolutely did not know, could not possibly have known:

'But how shall we manage without you?'

She did not reply.

'Forgive me,' I said, 'that is of course not your concern.'

'No.'

When she did not appear in the Refectory the next day, and questions were asked – had Sister Mary Amor already left the Abbey, without bidding farewell to anyone? – I went to her office.

I saw her feet first, and then the rest of her, hanging from a rope attached to the central rafter. She was wearing her habit but had removed her wimple and veil. She had curling brown hair, I never knew. Her head fell crookedly from the rope. I am not going to write about her face. If you have seen, as so many in these days will have seen, a hanged woman or man, you will know. If you have not, you would rather not be told.

I closed the door and slumped down on the floor. I shuddered as if stricken by chill. The office was impeccable – files and ledgers aligned on shelves, the floor swept. Only a fallen stool. I rose, and saw that on the table was a packet with my name on it, and a white paper on which she had written in majuscule in black ink in her firm hand: 'I CAN DO NO OTHER.'

She was a reasonable woman. Killing oneself may be one of the most rational acts possible. Though it is a mortal sin.

So I thought afterwards. At the time, I simply fled, down the precinct and through the cloister and straight to the Abbess's house, and banged on the great door. Pushing past her maid, I ran through the house until I found the Abbess, puzzling over documents by the light of a candle.

I told her.

'Who else knows?'

'No one.'

'Nor shall they. Father Bucket does not have the strength for this. I will call for Father Robert Parker. Go now, and return to me at daylight end.'

She rose, summoned the manservant, and gave him certain orders. There seemed now to be nothing at all wrong with her mind.

*

The Steward and Gregory cut down Mary Amor from the rafter, wrapped her in a blanket, laid her on the ground, carried away the paper upon which she had written and the packet with my name upon it, and locked the door of her office. I watched them do it.

When I returned to the Abbess, Father Robert Parker was with her. On her table was the paper with Mary's big black writing on it, and the package with my name on it.

I always thought of Robert Parker as young, almost a boy, or even – remembering Christmas – a boy-girl. This evening, he was a grown man and a priest. The Abbess had found two more stools from somewhere.

'In the eyes of the Church,' Robert was saying to the Abbess, 'violence against the self is a crime. An atrocious crime, a mortal sin.'

'What about the holy martyrs, who rushed upon their deaths for the love of Christ?'

'That has been a subject for discussion and dispute. It is unresolved.'

'It is nevertheless possible, is it not, that Sister Mary Amor died a martyr's death?'

'A martyr and a witness,' I suggested. 'She was perhaps bearing witness to a great wrong.'

Robert passed his hands over his eyes. There was wine tonight and Dame Elizabeth Zouche poured for each of us. Robert drained his cup immediately and she refilled it. There was a pause.

'Our lives are not our own,' he said. 'We are God's property.'

A fly fell in my wine.

Property. That heavy, worldly word.

'A hard doctrine,' said the Abbess. And then, as if changing the subject: 'Well, we must think what to do.'

'We cannot bury her in the nuns' graveyard, nor in any consecrated ground,' said Robert.

'Then she shall be buried with every respect and solemnity in the orchard, late tonight, after Compline, when the sisters should be in bed. I shall instruct the Steward. The grave must be dug immediately. Will you speak with him now, and officiate at the burial, Father Robert? I shall not attend.'

'Of course, Madam.'

Neither Robert nor I chose to remind her that there was no Compline, not any more. He rose to leave, and kissed the Abbess's ring. When our eyes met I know that he was thinking of our time in the orchard with Dorothy. Perhaps Mary Amor's grave would be in the spot where we had rested. I hoped so. The peace and happiness of that time might also, by God's grace, become hers.

I also perceived that there was unfinished business between Robert Parker and myself, and that he knew it too.

After the door banged behind him, the Abbess took hold of the package with my name on it.

'Open it.'

Inside, beneath a further wrapping, was a length of bronze-coloured silk, transparent, crusted with gold embroideries of flying birds, and with gold fringes at its ends. Beautiful. As I let it fall upon the Abbess's lap a small paper floated out. The Abbess retrieved it and tried to read it, screwing up her eyes and then opening them as wide as they would go. She just could not, and passed it to me. I held it to the candle and read it out:

'This is my only possession from another time and place and it will be yours now. I pray that you will find your right path.'

'May I keep it?' I asked the Abbess.

'You may keep it.'

I went from her, leaving my wine-cup with the dead fly. Mary Amor's piece of silk, and the tile with the lion painted on it, are treasures that I shall be taking with me when I leave.

I did not attend her burial in the orchard. I encountered Father Robert Parker at dawn the next day. He was pale, and looked unhappy.

'I was thinking,' he said, 'of saying a Mass for Mary Amor in the Abbey Church. But there are no vessels, no vestments, and the altar is cracked. Just the wind blowing through. Will you come and sit with me a while?'

We walked to his house, in the row of chantry priests' houses on the far side of the graveyard. Dame Philippa and Dame Joanna were right, the destroyers had ignored them, at least so far. Robert's room was as ordered and as simple as a nun's — a stool, a desk, a mattress, a crucifix, garments hanging from nails, a little chest with his lute propped against it. I sat on the stool, he paced up and down.

I asked, 'What will you do?'

That was the question we all asked one another all the time.

'I am still in love with God.'

He told me he would go to Salisbury, to call upon Bishop Shaxton. There might be a position for him in the cathedral, or in one of the nearby parishes. It was easier for men, he said. I knew that. They could become teachers in schools. Vicars and rectors would still and always be needed.

'One only has to conform to the new dispensation, which has much in its favour. It is perhaps an opportunity,' Robert said. 'The life of a chantry priest, in a house of women, is hardly illustrious, and of a tedium — God forgive me — that is quite unimaginable.'

'I begin to hate this word "opportunity",' I told him.

'You are mistaken. Change brings opportunity for every one, including you and me. Just for now, we are as free as birds.'

My Melancholy had said that birds were not free. Neither was I. I allowed myself to be led by him to the mattress, and he lifted my tunic, and I welcomed a man's body into mine for the first time since I lay with Peter Mompesson in the woods so long ago. It was an act of tenderness, not passion, and no less true a connection for that. And he was clean and sweet. I thought of Dorothy, and perhaps he did too although we did not speak of her.

As I was preparing to leave, Robert said:

'In God's name, I had all but forgotten! I have a letter for you, a drover brought it to the gatehouse this morning and I promised I would deliver it into your hand.'

The letter was from my dear Jeanne Vile in Bruton, she had inscribed her name on the back of the cover. I snatched it from Robert and ran towards the slype. On my way down through the precinct I saw the Abbess's bundled-up bed-curtains being thrown on to a fire. I felt nothing. When everything is being lost, each further, single loss loses the power to hurt. The slype was filthy with stone-dust and mud from the destroyers' boots. I sat on the bench and ripped the cover paper apart and read what she had to tell me.

Jeanne's letter, in the hand which is identical to mine because we had the same teachers, was guarded, as all letters now must be.

Hugh Backwell and John Harrold had gone from the Abbey, she knew not where. No one knew where Abbot Eley was either. The Abbey was empty, stripped of everything that had been in it — furnishings, plate, treasures, vestments, books, everything — but no one had yet come to demolish the buildings. The Abbey belonged to Master Maurice Berkeley now. He was much in evidence in the town, and it was said that he slept in the Abbot's bedchamber. Richard Halford — this was the lean red-haired canon I had heard talking when my mother and I laid out the elf — was much in evidence as Master Berkeley's chaplain. John White was in attendance upon Master Berkeley, and his people were measuring and surveying. Master Berkeley planned to bring the Abbey down and build a great house for himself from the ruins. His steward was already collecting the rents from the town. He had guards on the gatehouse, but there was that place on Dropping Lane near the fishponds where the wall was easily climbed. Boys from the town went in by night and reported what they saw.

And then, at the end:

'P.M. is still in Brewham. His sister has died and his father too a year past and he has the farm now. Your father is not well, he has lost his strength.'

She said nothing about my mother and nothing about Peterkin. I read her last sentences, the only ones that mattered, over and over. I crushed the letter in my hands and then let it fall among the debris on the floor of the slype.

My sisters are leaving silently, in twos and threes and singly, clutching their bundles, their heads bowed. They do not bid one another farewell, or embrace. We all, I know, feel ashamed. We have somehow failed, and we are unwanted. We are trained to humility and submission. *Mea culpa, mea culpa, mea maxima culpa.*

I make my preparations. I go to the apple store and collect as many of last year's apples as I can easily carry. On my way out I see Dame Monica Slater, the Novice Mistress, in company with Father Bucket. Mother Monica is clinging on to his arm, though Father Bucket is unsteady on his feet at the best of times. Both have sacks slung over their shoulders. Mother Monica is in tears. They have both been drinking.

'We are expelled from Paradise!' moans Mother Monica. 'Cast out from the Garden of Eden.'

I want to say, do not be so foolish. Instead, I say:

'Why not have an apple?'

Mother Monica wails louder, her mouth a toothless O, and the two of them totter out of the gate, turning towards the square, merging in the dusk with people and cart traffic until I see them no more. God only knows what will become of them. I go and knock on Robert Parker's door.

*

We did not lie down together again. The desire that flickered between us was extinguished. It had served its kindly purpose. Robert took a silver knife from the pouch at his waist. He pared an apple for me and another for himself. He told me he had filched the knife when the Abbey silver was piled up in the Refectory, waiting to be packed into boxes by the destroyers. Because he was a priest, he was allowed in by the guards on the door.

That had been a bad day. We had all peered in to see the tapestries, cushions, velvets, vestments, altar-cloths, chalices, ciboria, censors, piles of linens and lace, stacks of pewter plates and silverware, goblets, ewers, glassware, copper pans, gold boxes, candlesticks ... all jumbled together as if in some goblin market, waiting to be carried away in a train of covered wagons to London. Which way that was, and how long the journey would take, I did not know.

I told Robert about Dame Monica and what she had said.

'If she thinks the Abbey was the ante-room to Paradise, she is mistaken,' he said. 'It was not intended to be, that was never the idea.'

I seemed to have lost the power of speech – the cat had got my tongue – and was too tired to enquire what he believed 'the idea' to have been.

'Remember, Agnes,' he said, 'the really important things will always go on just as before. Beans will sprout. Children will be born. There will be butterflies.'

The next day his House was empty, the door hanging open. I was glad for the two old ladies, who would be moving in. I hope I will see Robert again one day.

'There will be butterflies.'

I have often recalled that, at odd times and out of the blue. It is comforting because it is true.

*

I stand under the arch of the gatehouse. Dorothy is there, with Esther in a sling across her breast. She has come to say goodbye. She is wearing my green hood. Esther is now quite the most beautiful little baby girl I have ever seen, and I have seen a good many babies. I say this to Dorothy and she tells me that Sister Isobel had been to see her at the Winterbournes' house. Esther was in her crib, and Isobel looked at her and said:

'Eternal peace is lying in the hay.'

'Were those her own words? Was she repeating something written down?'

Dorothy does not know.

'Sister Isobel, I think, was speaking about the Christ Child.'

'Obviously she was.'

'Although Esther is a girl. It doesn't really make any difference.'

'So is Finbarr a girl. And so are you and so am I. Maybe.'

We laugh, both knowing what is meant but unable to pursue the thought, there is no time. We embrace, taking care not to wake Esther, and I give her Finbarr's rope to hold.

Mother Onion is there too, sitting within the gatehouse on the stone bench, her sticks propped beside her. She is breathing with difficulty, or uncontrollably sighing, I know not which.

'I have a thought,' she says, 'to go and spend some time in the orchard over the road. It is a fine soft day. God know there is no need for hurry. I am no longer myself. I am away with the fairies now like poor Sister Catherine.'

Dorothy sits beside her and takes her hand. Dorothy has become kind. Unlike me.

John Winterbourne, the one that does not speak, is there too, standing on one leg and then on the other, waiting for Dorothy to be ready to leave. It is strange saying goodbye to her and to Finbarr, even though it may not be for ever. Nothing is for ever. Is that still true? As I watch them depart, it's as if I am departing from myself. From my old self.

Turning away, I hear the rumble of men's voices in the chamber above the gatehouse. I recognise them. Master John Tregonwell and Sir Thomas Arundell.

I creep halfway up the curling stair, stopping where there is a landing and a slit window looking on to the roadway. The door to the upstairs chamber is open. They must be standing at the window, seeing what I see, watching the sisters leave.

'They look ashamed,' says Tregonwell. 'Guilty.'

'All those dried-up Brides of Christ.'

'They are not all of them dried up. There are some tasty morsels among them.'

'I had my way with one of them, a plump one, no country girl, she knew her way about. They aren't allowed to marry, you know, even though they've been turned off.'

'Who said anything about marrying?' says Tregonwell.

I have heard him say that before.

'I have been told,' says Arundell, 'by a Frenchman at court, how the Mohammedan lords keep quantities of women shut away for their use in enclosed houses. Just like nuns. Only not.'

I hear the clink of bottle against wine-cups.

'A forebear of mine went on a crusade to Alexandria' – Arundell is relaxed, half-tipsy – 'and they broke open the harem and turned the women out on to the streets, fitted for nothing but whoredom. These Brides of Christ will become whores. Christ has not turned out to be so great a husband. He never was.'

'Many of these women,' said Tregonwell, 'are too old or sick to make their living that way. Look at that one, with the two sticks, crossing the road. She can hardly walk.'

'She will not last long. Have some more wine. Dame Elizabeth kept a good cellar.'

Clink, clink.

'I am impatient,' says Tregonwell, 'for the demolition to end. I fear one will have to move fast to salvage the best before everything is burned or carried away. I plan to build a house in the town from the stones. I particularly desire the great lintels, to set over my doors and windows. I have my site already.'

'Me too,' says Arundell. 'Mine is the best site in town, just along the way, on the corner of Bimport and Tout Hill.'

'Then we are in competition for the spoils.'

Arundell made a snorting noise.

'Perhaps. But this is all provisional, for me. Great men do not live in towns, they build their residences in the countryside, surrounded by hundreds of acres. I am acquiring as much of the Abbey as I can, and will develop the sites for profit, and live in the town for a while as lord of the borough. But I have my eye on Wardour Castle.'

'And I have my eye,' said Tregonwell, 'on the manor of Milton. I may have to pay the Crown a thousand pounds for it. And I intend to buy in some of the Abbey plate, and some furniture, if it is not all spoken for in London before I can arrange matters. I do rather fancy the Abbess's chair.'

'I,' said Arundell, 'am acquiring the manor of Tisbury, the greatest prize, with a lesser manor which I will sell on. I am not interested in the baubles, I leave those to you. Our great rebuilding will be all about light. You will see, the walls of my house will not just have openings set into them, the walls will be the supports and settings for great windows flooding my high chambers with sunlight, moonlight...'

They are watching, as I am, a young woman in a green hood with a bundle on her back and leading a black dog on a rope, accompanied by a commonplace man.

'That is the one who assisted the Abbess,' said Arundell. 'I saw her a while ago wearing that green hood. Pretty woman.'

'That one is no maid. And she is a little fool,' said Tregonwell.

Arundell was not sufficiently interested in Tregonwell, or in the woman in the green hood, to enquire further.

'I must tell you I have an idea for the great rebuilding,' said Tregonwell, 'about the function of a cloister. It could be adapted to a great house...'

'I think,' said Arundell, interrupting him, uncaring, 'that I will seek out a workman and take a wander down to the Abbey Church. I want to check how much of the painted glass has been salvaged without damage. I gave full instructions, but I fear they may have smashed a good deal of it. That old painted glass would look well in a hall. Some of the plain yellowish glass might be useful too. Will you walk with me?'

'I have to see a man about a dog,' said Tregonwell.

I hear boots on floorboards and slip back down the stairs, out of the gatehouse, and hide. Tregonwell emerges, shouts for his horse, throws his legs across its back, and rides off in the direction taken by Dorothy and John Winterbourne, with Finbarr. He will not catch them up.

The destroyers have now taken half the roof of the dorter. The chamber is filthy and strewn with stones and timbers. It is time to go. But not quite yet.

I sit on the ground outside the gatehouse with Gregory, his bundle beside him. He is chewing on a pudding. He is lucky, he is going with the Abbess to Place Farm in Tisbury. He is concerned for me. He gives me advice on how to walk the roads safely:

'If you get lost, follow a river and it will bring you to some place with people. Keep your eyes peeled for bridges, which are there for a reason, and church towers. Do not travel after daylight end. Avoid hollow ways where the trees meet over the path. Bad spirits.'

And then he jumps up, picks up his bundle and runs from me, because the Abbess's coach is there at the gatehouse. Her boxes and bags are being loaded.

Then I see her, Dame Elizabeth Zouche, the last Abbess of Shaftesbury, in her fur-lined cloak and high gable hood, with her little maid and Sister Isobel, and the Steward – and, now, Gregory. She passes within three feet of where I stand but she does not look at me. She looks straight ahead. I do not move towards her, I do not raise my hand in farewell. After a while I hear the coach rumbling on the cobbles, and then, nothing. She has gone.

It is time for me to go too.

It is tempting to sleep my first night away from the Abbey curled up with Dorothy and Esther and Little John and Emilia and the two Winterbournes in their cabin. Finbarr would jump all over me and lick my face in the old way. But that would only put off the evil hour. To avoid fresh heartbreak it is better to go. I see in the late afternoon light the precinct overrun by destroyers and looters. I hear hammering and the harsh rasp of saws.

But still I did not go. When it grew dark, I climbed the stair back up to the dorter. The roof over my cubicle and the next was still there, but just beyond was open sky, and a half-moon, and stars. There was a drip-drip-drip from some leaking eave.

I had retained my novice's habit, hoping thereby to avoid the groping hands of the destroyers, who tend to waylay any unwary female after dark. Now I unrolled my old brown gown from the bundle of my home clothes and put it on. I put my knife in my pocket. No more veil, no more wimple. No more tightness and restriction. Just a headcloth, loosely, round my head and neck.

With the dropping of the novice's habit, everything else fell away. I was somebody else now. Who is that person? I was emptied out. I had my own clothes, I had my emerald dolphin. What else, from my previous life?

Did I still care about Peter Mompesson? Dare to be truthful. No, I did not still care about Peter Mompesson. I shall always remember our coupling as something unutterably sweet from long ago. That is a sober way of saying that he gave me pleasure and the taste of what love is. I would like to taste love again.

But what about my son, my Peterkin?

Dare to be truthful. This one is harder. Our time together, his mouth at my breast, was short. It would only confuse the little boy were I were to erupt into his life and attempt to reclaim him. Perhaps much later I might come to know him again. At the very least I would like him to know, one day, who his mother is.

In truth, the loss of Finbarr meant more to me right now.

The change had taken place without my realising it. I had been carting around old thoughts like so much baggage, without examining them. More than once I have had a dream about a house that in the dream I know well (although in my waking mind I do not know it at all), with one chamber leading into another and, at the end of the suite of rooms, the *enfilade* as Master Tregonwell would say, a locked door.

I sat on in my cubicle for a long time, having no new thoughts but venturing into a new space. As if my mind were a chamber swept of dust by an invisible hand, an angel, or the Blessed Zita, leaving this clear void. Maybe this is something like what my Melancholy experienced when she danced, and wept, and smiled, and could not explain why.

I do not know what is behind the locked door. Maybe it is only a store room. Unwanted baggage has to be deposited somewhere. Well, I shall discover.

I was just thinking, I should try and sleep, in my damp bed under the damp blanket, when I heard footsteps coming along the dorter in my direction. My first thought was that it was a destroyer on the prowl. I fingered the little sharpie in the pocket of my gown and sat still, planning how to kill him if I needed to. This was not a new thought. I would have killed Master Tregonwell, had I the courage. My heart beating, I stepped out of my cubicle, shivering, and looked into the darkness down the length of the chamber.

By the light of the half-moon I made out a figure coming towards me. The footsteps were too light and quick to be a man's. It was not one of the destroyers, nor any man, it was a short woman in a cloak and hood carrying a bundle.

'Agnes Peppin? I know you are there. I saw you mounting the stairs. Is that you?'

It was Eleanor Wilmer.

I am relieved to see her, or rather to see that it is she and no other.

'Come,' I say, 'come and sit on my bed, I will take the stool.'

She sits on my bed. Even in the quarter-light I see how she narrows those great eyes of hers and purses her mouth.

'Before we part, I wanted to tell you that I do not like you. Ever since you came to the Abbey you have been consumed by jealousy of me as if I were a poison.'

'Why on earth would I be jealous of you? Is this your notion of a joke?'

'You knew I wanted to be the Abbess's assistant and you inveigled yourself into her favour. You stole that from me. On purpose.'

'No.'

'I saw you lying in the orchard with Robert and Dorothy. I saw you go to Robert's lodging the other day, I saw you come out again. I wanted Robert. I could have had him. You stole him from me.'

'No.'

'You were jealous of my closeness to Our Lord Jesus Christ. So you mocked my love for Him. I know it.'

Water outside my cubicle drips from above.

She leans forward and snatches at the chain round my neck. It breaks and she grabs it with the emerald dolphin dangling. She runs off towards the reredorter stumbling over fallen stones and before I can reach her she has thrown the dolphin down one of the holes into the sewer beneath. I catch up with her and peer down into the hole. It is black dark. I put my whole arm down and scour the foul water but it is useless. The dolphin is small, the sludge at the bottom is deep and disgusting, the water is running fast. My emerald dolphin has gone.

The dolphin was my passport to a possible future life. It had been given to my mother. It was proof of who we were, she and I.

Besides which, it had monetary value.

Besides which, I loved it. The dolphin was my most precious possession.

I do not scream, or attack Eleanor, or scratch her face, pull out her hair or stab her with my knife. I am numb and dumb. She too. We face each other in the dim light.

'How did you know?' I ask eventually.

'How did I know what?'

'What I had, the dolphin – which you have just...'

I cannot put into words what she has just done.

'Anne Cathcart told me about it.'

'Yes.'

We go back into my cubicle. My right hand and arm are filthy and stinking. I use my white veil to wipe myself and throw the veil into a corner.

Eleanor had said that I was jealous of her closeness to Jesus Christ. That annoys me. I say to her:

'It is true that I believe Christ loves everyone equally and that one cannot buy his greater love by excessive manifestations.'

'You understand nothing. You do not know anything about love.'

'How can you be so sure of that?'

But indeed, how can I be sure that I understand anything about love?

Eleanor reaches inside her clothes and brings out a bottle of wine. It is Holy Communion wine, I can tell by the shape of the bottle.

'Do not distress yourself,' she says. 'It is unconsecrated. It is just cheap red wine. I stole it from the sacristy.'

'How will we open it?'

She smashes the neck of the bottle on the stone floor and snaps off the spikes from the neck of the bottle with a loose stone. Oh, Eleanor!

'Do you have a cloth?'

I pull off my headcloth and hand it to her. She wraps it round the jagged neck of the bottle and takes a long swallow and then passes it to me. She begins to talk, and continues to talk as we pass the bottle between us.

I talk too. We talk all night.

This is what she told me.

Her father was assistant to the Treasurer at Sherborne Abbey. He was kind, but busy, and he has died.

'When I was little I sometimes could not eat, I do not know why, and my mother used to put my food on a shelf and serve it back to me next day. In summer it was speckled with flies' eggs and mouse dirt, in winter it was frozen. When I tried to eat it I was sick, and then my mother would shut me in the cellar and tell me I could not come out until I had eaten the food and also the vomit that was upon it. I knew I could not do that. I thought I would be in the cellar for ever.'

In the end someone always came and let her out, her younger brother or her father. Her mother behaved as if nothing untoward had happened. Other times, she shut Eleanor up in the fowl coop, where she could neither stand nor sit.

I always knew my mother did not like me. But what were a few beatings with a broomstick, compared with what Eleanor suffered?

'Why were our mothers as they were? Why could they not love us?' I ask her.

'I think they were sad and angry, but not really with us. And no one's mother ever loves them enough.'

The bottle passes between us.

'I would be a loving mother,' I say.

And then think of Peterkin, who had been given away. I correct myself.

'I am not a good mother. I have a son whom I may never see again.'

I explain. We drink more wine.

'And I had a daughter,' says Eleanor. 'No one knew. I was quite a stout girl, and it did not show. When I thought it must be my time because I was hurting I went out into the fields by the old castle and birthed her there under the trees. I thought I would die. She was scarcely bigger than a squirrel. I bit through the cord. I looked at her and she was dead. I lay there holding her in my hands, dead. I pulled on the cord connected to something inside me and pulled out the mess. I do not really know what that is. I threw that and the sticky dead little thing into the river, and rinsed my hands. And then I went back home. I was bleeding, but my mother thought that was my normal courses. I told no one.'

'Poor Eleanor. That is very hard.'

A word is clanging in my memory.

'But then why did Father Pomfret start to say "infanticide" just before he was stopped?'

'Because I confessed to him that I killed my newborn child.'

'But you had not.'

'No.'

I roll my eyes and take more wine.

'I will tell you.'

＊

Her explanation was repetitive and contradictory. It took a long time. She is such an extreme person. She was all too ready to lavish her love on the father of her child, but he ran from her. She was young then and he was younger still, sixteen years old, a church musician with all his life before him. So great a hunger for love and attention as Eleanor has may be a heavier burden than most people can carry. I remember her asking Robert to dance with her and how he pushed her away. Eleanor exudes desperation.

No one in the world can love Eleanor enough. God is love so He would love her as no one on earth ever would or could. She unloaded all her love on to God and on to his son Jesus Christ. To receive His ineffable love and forgiveness, and to achieve unity with Him, it was necessary for her to be a great sinner because there is more joy in Heaven, the Gospel teaches, over one sinner that repents than over any number of the observant faithful.

I think that's what her reasoning was. It is hard to be sure.

Her great sin, which would elicit Christ's unconditional love, was that she had killed her child.

Except she hadn't.

When she confessed this to Father Pomfret she was not telling a lie. She believed it to be so when she said it. She had to believe it. It was part of the bargain she was making with Christ. Perhaps because she is a Treasurer's daughter she thinks in terms of contracts, bargains, profit and loss.

'But Eleanor, God who knows everything would know that you did not kill your child.'

'God understands everything and He understood my necessity.'

I never heard anything so convoluted, yet there is a mad kind of logic in her thinking. Mary Amor had said: 'If men and women were not sinners, there would be no need for redemption.'

'What did Father Pomfret say to you?'

'He said I had committed a mortal sin for which I would do penance for the rest of my life unless and until I achieved perfect contrition.'

'And did you achieve perfect contrition? Did he give you absolution?'

'After a long time, many months, he did.'

I was more confused than ever.

'But Eleanor, you had committed no mortal sin at all.'

'I have now. It was I who killed Father Pomfret. I could not have him shouting out that word about me when it was not true.'

'You killed him with what, with your little sharpie?'

I see it hanging from her belt in its leather sheath. Her hand moves to touch it.

'It was easy. You would be surprised. I came up behind him in the nave and thought, if not now, when? He turned towards me before he fell and then I stabbed him again, from the front.'

'What did you feel at that last Vespers when you gave out the Magnificat, with his body lying only few yards away?'

'As if I had leapt from a high place and had not yet hit the ground.'

'And now?'

'I still have not hit the ground.'

I cannot remember whether Eleanor had another bottle of communion wine about her person or if the first bottle was miraculously inexhaustible. I do remember telling her that I had wished to kill Master Tregonwell, and had done so in my mind many times.

'Anyone can kill,' said Eleanor.

'I know it. I would have killed whoever came upon me here this night, had it not been you.'

'And when I had killed Father Pomfret, I no longer needed to think that I had killed my child. He gave me absolution, after all.

Listen, Agnes — I am wondering now if the absolution of mortal sin is transferable, like a credit note. May I perhaps believe that he absolved me of a crime that had not yet taken place?'

'You mean your murder of him?'

I laughed a good deal at that, my hands covering my face, and she laughed too. I said before that in the End Time we laughed at all the wrong things. This may have been the most wrong thing we laughed at.

'God rest his soul.'

'Amen,' said Eleanor.

She unpinned her veil, pulled off her grubby wimple and her cap, and I saw her black hair. Even cut short, it waved and turned up at the ends. Crisp hair that would fall gracefully however wild the weather. She saw that I was admiring her. She turned her head, her eyes slanting.

'Why did you dislike me so?' she asked.

'Because you disliked me so. And you infuriated me. You woke the Devil in me.'

'Because of my holy religion? I was...'

'Distorted?' I suggested.

That is the word that Anne Cathcart used to describe Eleanor.

'Yes. I was distorted. But that is over now. Though I will still and always pray.'

'As will I. I would be a feather in the wind if I did not.'

Away from the Abbey we will have no discipline in our lives. Just one day after another.

Where will we be? What will we do? It will not be so frightening now there are two of us, looking out for each other. What can I do, what can Eleanor do? I do not suggest that we should earn our livings by laying out the dead, which I would find easy. We do not have to do that. We can cook and clean for rich people. She grimaces. She does not want to do that. Very well. We have our pensions. She raises the stakes. We can start an enterprise. We can do anything. For the first time the word 'opportunity' sounds sweetly in my ears.

And what if we fall out? Neither of us has an easy character. Eleanor's entrepreneurial instincts make me uneasy. She is more forceful than I. She is labile. She is unpredictable. You could say, I smell a rat, an old dead rat.

But then, so am I labile and unpredictable. I might want a contemplative life of reading and writing. In a convent abroad, I say to her, I might, as a lay sister, sit at a desk with a bunch of quills and copy old manuscripts. It would be peaceful.

Eleanor mocks me:

'Keep up, Agnes. Everything will be printed now, in hundreds of copies. And perfect. Copying and recopying by hand is a thing of the past.'

Ah. She is right. New thoughts, I must think new thoughts. Nothing remains the same, not even the same remains the same.

But what if we do discover that we want different ways of life?

Then we will part without recrimination, she says:

'Better to part than for one to become a log tied to the leg of the other.'

We may have slept a little.

A silvery sky, and antiphonal birdsong. So many, many birds. If there were still a roof over the dorter, we would not be hearing them in this way. And there are hundreds of thousands more birds beyond our hearing, in the Abbey orchard and down in the Abbey Park and in all the gardens of Shaftesbury and out in the fields and woods and forests outside and beyond the town and, far away, the larks soaring high with their songs over the Borough Field in Bruton.

Not all birdsong is so beautiful. Some of it is raucous.

The swallows and swifts and house martins will soon be back. They will make new nests in the abandoned Abbey in the crevices of fallen walls, as they will in all the wrecked remains of cloisters and chancels and naves in our West Country and throughout our England. It is the hour for Prime though no bell rings. The birds are singing the Holy Office for us.

No, they are not, they are staking out their territories and seeking mates. Spring is on the way.

There will be butterflies.

We had talked ourselves into sobriety.

I pick up my bundle. I am taking the roll of my writings, tied with a string, the lion tile, Mary Amor's piece of silk which rolls up into a sliver, a spare shift, a grey gown even shabbier than my brown one, a spare pair of sandals, and the apples. And my knife, my little sharpie. I am wearing my novice's cloak because it is made of thick felted wool and has a hood. I draw it around myself.

Eleanor pulls up her hood too and picks up her bundle. She stands for a moment and looks at me.

'I am sorry about the dolphin.'

I have nothing to say. It happened. I nod my head.

We turn towards the stairs. We leave the ruined dorter.

Already our life in the Abbey belongs to the past. We are going now. There is no one about. It is chilly. Puffs of smoke rise from the embers of yesterday's fires as we pick our way through the desolation and reach the unguarded gatehouse.

We are going.

We have gone.

6

SHERBORNE

I was persuaded by Eleanor to go with her to Sherborne where she said she had family. When we arrived she asked everywhere after her mother, but was told that she had left the town. So we were on our own now.

Those first days were desperate. We slept in the fields — not in the open fields, but in hedged closes, which gave some shelter. By asking around, we found an attic room at the top of that house which stands on the corner of Trendle Street and Acreman Street, a stone's throw from the Abbey. We had it free, on condition that we kept an eye on the old gentleman on the ground floor.

His name was Master Anthony Palmer. I never learned what he had done to earn his living, because he himself did not remember. Maybe he never did anything, there are such people and they get by.

I was impressed by Sherborne. It is at least three times larger than Bruton, and there are always people sitting about, and walking about, in between the houses and up and down the roads. I do not know where they are going or what they are doing but they are friendly and ready to talk, which is how we found out what was going on. In Bruton, if it were not a market, or a fair day, there was often no one out of doors at all. Just, at daylight end, the men coming home from the fields and boys let out from the Abbey school behaving as schoolboys do.

*

The deserted Abbey squats in the centre of the town like a great holy toad. It is built of dark golden stone. The bells of the Abbey Church still ring and punctuate our days and nights. One bell was a gift from Cardinal Wolsey; I would like his daughter Dorothy to know that. Sir John Horsey did a great service in transferring the church – for a reasonable sum – to the people of Sherborne. The townspeople do not seem exactly grateful. They believe it is their right. As a mere parish church, it is of an extraordinary size and magnificence. The roof is criss-crossed with stone patterning of a delicacy to take the sight out of your eyes. (That is an expression I learnt from Mother Onion.)

I attempted to convey my impressions to Master Palmer as we sat with him slurping our soup, he propped up on his pallet, Eleanor and I cross-legged on the floor.

'Rubble,' he said.

'Ah,' I said.

'Sherborne is built of rubble. Most of it just faced with stone. Rubble. Just like myself. Rubble.'

'Even the Abbey?'

'Even the Abbey. Rubble.'

Master Palmer was long and bony and unable to look after himself, in that he had lost the use of his legs and his mind wandered. One day when Eleanor and I came home, he looked at us in wonderment and asked:

'Do you two know one another?'

'Yes and no,' I said.

'We do and we do not,' said Eleanor.

Another day, he asked us:

'Are you angels?'

'We do not believe that we are,' said Eleanor, 'but you never can tell. We may be. Or we may be devils.'

He sprawled all day on his pallet, only rising to relieve himself into the bucket. We emptied his slops into the culvert. We went every day to the woods beneath the old castle to pick up firewood. We found a sharp little axe propped behind a tree, forgotten, and took it away with us. Eleanor, because I asked her, showed me the spot where she had given birth, and the place in the river where she had disposed of her dead baby. When she first told me this story, that last night in Shaftesbury Abbey, I had believed her.

This time I was not so sure. What she had told me did not quite tally with the place where we were. Eleanor was a such story-teller. I understood her because there is a twitch of fabulation in me too. Perhaps the tale of her harsh treatment at the hands of her mother was not true either. Just true for her. To deceive other people you must first deceive yourself. Or is it the other way around?

I knew in my heart that Eleanor was not to be relied upon, for anything.

Master Palmer's widowed sister, almost as decrepit as he, sells old clothes from her tenement in Cheap Street. She would appear at day's end bringing roots and cabbage for the soup, for him and for us. The vegetables were as weary as she, left over from the previous season and discarded by whoever grew them. And goodness knows where she picked up the shreds of rabbit-flesh which she brought us, wrapped in screws of dirty paper. Better not to know. Our old Vow of Poverty was not hard to keep. We were not too proud to pick out of the gutter a carrot or a fowl's carcass or a heel of rock-hard bread to throw into the pot.

Looking back I can see that those were hard times. Harder times than I have known before or since.

But the cold spring of 1539 became a delicious summer. We harvested fresh leaves from the meadows. There were butterflies.

We had to make a plan. How were we to live?

Eleanor Wilmer and I had interesting times. We shared a bed. After our first sleep each night we awoke, and played and pleasured like the young creatures we were. These were the best times, because the shocking delight of what we could do to each other made us laugh and we fell asleep again smiling. With men, laughing at such things is not always acceptable.

Yet when she wound her arms tightly around my neck in the darkness and whispered, 'You will never escape me,' a whiff of fear made me recoil. I remembered at those moments that she had killed a man and thought rather little of it. If indeed she had killed a man. Maybe that too was a story she told to herself, and to me. I cannot be sure.

Thinking of Eleanor, I would be the first to say that women are women's best supporters, for few men will help a young woman when she is down unless they wish to shove their hands up under her gown. I have met men who are sincere in their kindness, but it is the sincerity of a cat playing with a mouse. If you do not fancy taking the risk for a short period of pleasure and maybe some material advantage, it is wiser to run away before they pounce. Woman with woman on the other hand is self with self and we are each of us our best friends and our worst enemies.

Eleanor and I went to Mass on Sundays but no longer made any attempt to observe the hours of Holy Office, or even to be aware of them. Sometimes I went into the Abbey Church by myself. There is a side-chapel off the south transept, entered through a narrow low door, easy to miss, and it is always deserted. It must have been a chantry chapel when the monks were still here. I would sit alone there for half a morning. I did not pray. I just remained perfectly still, shutting out my worries, and just before I left the chapel I would pray for grace.

For I was missing something, I was uneasy. I saw a dog running wild, thither and up and down Cheap Street, out of its mind. It had a chain round its neck, dragging in the dust. It had lost its master.

I was a dog on a leash with no one holding the leash.

I knew what would happen to that dog. Before daylight end the chain would become trapped between two stones, or tangled in the branches of a thorn bush, and the dog would be unable to move. It could not bite through the chain. The dog would remain until someone found it, and if no one passed that way it would within a few days be dead.

Mustn't let that happen to me.

Sometimes I sang a snatch of a psalm, the familiar words and line of chant creeping into my head unsought, and Eleanor would pick it up, and twine harmonies with her voice around my voice, transforming the rhythms into ditties. She said:

'The psalms were our love songs to God. We need to learn new love songs.'

So we lingered around the market and listened to the travelling musicians, memorising the airs and the words, and then singing them for ourselves. Some days the music maker was one solitary man in a leather hat with his tuneless piping instrument, singing, if that is the word, for small coins to buy bread. Other days there would be a troupe passing through, working the markets from town to town. They sang about lost love, or lost home-places, and sometimes jaunty melodies for dancing, with saucy verses. We learnt all those, too, and at the end of the day snatched up the broadsheets and printed ballads fallen on the ground and took them home.

That way, we learnt news of events in the great world. By far the most momentous, in the late summer, was the arrest and execution of Master Thomas Cromwell, the Chief Minister, the author of all our woes and the reason why Eleanor and I were vagabonding in Sherborne market to no particular purpose.

We heard it from a London tailor travelling in the West Country to buy cloth. He was gathering a crowd. We pushed our way to the front to hear what he was saying. The tailor was a dwarfish man and he was lifted up on a cart so that everyone could see him. We could hardly believe our ears. The tailor had been present among hundreds of others on Tower Hill.

Cromwell, he said, spoke soberly from the scaffold. A crazed nobleman, who was to be executed after him, kept up a frenzied wailing and railing throughout, a macabre accompaniment.

'Cromwell spoke directly to certain gentlemen in the crowd whom he knew, telling them to take his plight as a warning. I cannot remember all his words. He said that he had been a poor man who had risen in the King's service to be a great gentleman. He told how he had never been content with all he had gained, but presumed to rise higher and ever higher. "My pride has brought its punishment."'

Those few words the tailor did remember and he repeated them. 'My pride has brought its punishment.'

The tailor said: 'All his properties and belongings were stripped from him when he was in the Tower. He had enriched himself, my friends, beyond our imagining. Thousands of pounds in cash in his house, they say, and chestfuls of gold and silver plate and church vessels set with precious jewels, stolen from the monks and nuns and withheld from the royal coffers by his Commissioners on his orders. The King has got it all back now. Or almost all. Sticky fingers.'

I thought of the gold box from Bruton Abbey containing Our Lady's Girdle. An item hardly to be noticed among the phantasmagorical jumble of pilfered treasure.

The market place buzzed with questions. For what was Cromwell arraigned? What was the crime that brought him down?

'Treason,' said the tailor. 'That covers anything and everything these days. He had enemies. Princes of the Church and certain great lords who resented a scheming low-born cur being preferred above them all. The King was persuaded by the plotters that Cromwell was too far gone in his passion for what he calls reform, that he was a follower of Luther, a filthy black Protestant. And Cromwell had urged the German princess on him, too. That's what they are saying in London, anyway.'

We waited. Was there no more?

'I could tell you good people about the execution,' said the tailor, 'but I have a terrible thirst upon me.'

Someone passed him up a jug of ale. He drank it all down, wiped his lips, and began again. What he said is burned into my mind. I feel as if I too had been there so that is how I will tell it.

Cromwell knelt in the straw on the flooring of the scaffold and prayed. He looked up at the executioner and begged him to cut off his head with a single blow, to spare his suffering. But the executioner was no master of his trade, a 'butcherly' man, said the tailor.

I bristled at that. A butcher would well know where and how to let the axe fall.

This man's first stroke missed the neck altogether and gashed the back of Cromwell's head. His second attempt did not sever the head, nor did his third. An assistant came to his aid. They slashed and chopped, between them taking many minutes – it seemed like an eternity, said the tailor – to achieve what should have been accomplished in seconds.

The crazed nobleman was then dispatched with no trouble at all. The two bodies were taken back to the Tower and buried in the church within its walls. The heads were boiled and stuck up on pikes on London Bridge. Cromwell's head was unrecognisable, being so horribly mangled.

The tailor was helped down from the cart. Night was falling. Most people straggled away home, heads bowed, muttering to one another. Others, in a state of excitement, trailed behind the tailor and his cronies all the way up Cheap Street to the George Inn, and Eleanor and I went along too. I should be ashamed that we did, but I am not. Curiosity is not a sin.

The inn was hot. The tailor downed more ale. His face was flushed and he was all too ready to tell more. Now he was talking about the marriage of the King and the German Princess Anne.

'She was nothing like her portrait. She was coarse and ugly and pockmarked and the King took against her the moment he saw her. This is no secret,' said the tailor.

The King confides in his gentlemen and the gentlemen confide in their friends. The tailor makes coats for several of these friends.

'Everyone prattles to his tailor,' he said, waving his hands, drunk on his own little self as well as on the ale.

So. The King let it be known that he did not tamper with the woman, even though for some months they shared a bed – a special, high-built, new-made bridal bed.

'She smelt foul. The King touched her fat breasts and belly and could not bring himself to perform.'

He made the non-consummation known because he wanted the marriage annulled, and it already has been. The King no longer has to bother with the Pope's permission. He annuls his own marriages through his own courts of law.

'There are,' said the tailor, pulling at his nose, 'those who say the King has become incapable of sexual congress. He is near fifty years old, and corpulent, with ulcers on his legs. He is now infatuated with a young girl, fifteen years old, placed in his path by her ambitious family. Her uncle is the Duke of Norfolk. The King thinks with her to recover his manhood and sire a second son. He married her on the very day of Cromwell's execution.'

By my reckoning this is his fifth wife.

'The King', said the tailor, 'still believes in true love.'

Ha ha ha! I could not help laughing.

The young girl's name is Catherine Howard.

'She may be high-born but she is no maid,' said the tailor, 'she has long been abused and huffed and puffed over by gentlemen thrice her age.'

I stop laughing, feeling pity for this distracted girl, suddenly the Queen of England and sharing a bed with an old monster. She should have behaved like St Agnes, and refused. St Agnes was put to death as a result. The same thing will probably happen to Catherine Howard even though she complied. Because this marriage will not last, said the tailor. His customers, in the know, were giving it two years at most, gossiping as they vacillated over the depth of a pocket or the turn-back of a cuff.

Well, well, well. Thus the bemused inhabitants of a small town in Dorset become privy to the bedchamber antics of the King of England. If, of course, what he said was true.

The tailor was passing his hat around the company, exacting his 'expenses', as he put it. Eleanor and I, standing near the door, slipped out fast. As we scampered away down Cheap Street, Eleanor said that the tailor was probably telling the same tales, with variations, in every town through which he passed, and making good money out of it. I expect she was right. Everyone makes their money in whatever way they can. Some ways are more noxious than others. But I would not have missed the tailor's performance for all the world.

Some ways of making money are wholly innocent. One day after that summer's end, when the nights were drawing in, I was coming home along Long Street and heard from a half-open door women's voices singing psalms in the same way that Eleanor and I did, only better. I looked inside and saw about a dozen women sitting on the ground in a circle, working with their hands. In the middle of the circle was a pile of coloured stuffs. Standing at their door I was blocking what remained of the light. They stopped singing, looked towards me, judged I suppose that I was harmless, and beckoned me in.

I sat down outside their circle. They went on talking and laughing among themselves, their hands busy. Then with one accord, as if it was time for a break, they put down their work and turned to me.

One of them said, 'Welcome. What brings you here?'

'My name is Agnes Peppin and I am a stranger here.'

'We are all strangers here. We are strangers everywhere. Except in this chamber, where we are – sisters.'

They were all wearing cowl hoods in different colours and plain darkish gowns. Their feet were bare. There was a pile of sandals in a corner. They turned upon me a calm accepting gaze. I suddenly was sure what they were.

'You are, you were, in the religious life? You were nuns?'

They beamed and nodded.

'You too?'

So I told them my story and one by one they picked up their work again, still listening. They told me scraps of their own stories. Some were as young as me, some old enough to be our mothers. They were nuns cast off from abbeys and convents near and far, who had landed up in this place for different reasons, who knows why. They were from Kent, Sussex, Gloucester, Lincoln, I cannot remember the rest. They had never met anyone from Shaftesbury Abbey before.

'But we knew,' said one smiling woman of my own age, 'as soon as you came in the door and sat down, that you were one of us.'

They told me what they did. They begged snippets of woven stuff from tailors and seamstresses, and unsaleable remnants from peddlers. They acquired ragged old garments in the market and, it turned out, from our Master Palmer's sister.

They took anything, from sacking to satin, and made shifts, shirts, frocks and trews for children, patchworked fantastically. They fashioned clothes for wooden playdolls, and teased out shreds of silk for tassels and braiding and fringes. They unravelled old knitted garments and knitted up the twisty yarn into something else. They used sheep's wool picked from hedges to stuff shoulder-pads. They collected round pebbles and covered them with fabric to make buttons. From the shortest off-cuts of bright ribbon, and with birds' feathers from the fields, they contrived artificial flowers to embellish a gown.

They showed me a basket-load of their work. It is not the kind of merchandise that attracts me, but it is ingenious. Not art, but artful.

They call themselves the Winter Sisters.

At Eastertime the Winter Sisters hold a sale. The lady wives of Sherborne's prosperous tradesmen squeeze in to find what they would find nowhere else. Gentlemen buy trifles for their wives and sweethearts. In so short a time the Winter Sisters have become known, and sell everything that they make. For some, their connection with the old ways and the old religion forges a bond. Only the most fierce Protestants stayed away, the sisters told me.

In the summer each of the sisters goes her own way – finding work at hirings, harvesting, fruit-picking, working in hospitals and taverns, nursing the aged wealthy in their homes, caring for the children of the rich. After Michaelmas the Winter Sisters return to this abandoned tenement, to each other, and to their work.

'Sometimes we sing the Holy Office.' And out of the dimness, a sister gave out the first line of the Nunc Dimittis. It was a chant that I knew well. It was heart-wrenching to hear it. I was back in the Abbey Church in my place among the rows of black and of white veils. The other Winter Sisters took up the chant and played with it, jiggling the rhythm, some voices rising high and staccato, some swooping low, and all in harmony.

Two young boys stopped at the open door to listen. When the chanting came to an end the boys laughed and clapped their hands and went on their way.

'You could sing like that at fairs,' I said, 'and make a lot more money for less work.'

No, no, no, they said, a flurry of fowls flustering their feathers. It would be a blasphemy. They sang to make God smile, not to amuse ignorant loons.

'Forgive me,' I said. 'Of course you could not do that. It is beautiful.'

I did not tell Eleanor about the Winter Sisters. I cringed at the notion of her running straight off to them in Long Street, and talking too loud, and telling them what to do, like a fox in a henhouse.

Eleanor said to me, as we sat on a bench outside the Abbey eating apples in the autumn sun, 'Since we left Shaftesbury, and the religious life, it has been and will always be just one thing after another. No one to tell us what to do. We are free.'

Most of the population, I told her, live under these conditions, even though one may think that our freedom is limited by the demands of landlords, lack of funds or friends or family or oppor- tunity, or the general difficulty of being an unsupported female.

'We are a particular case because we were nuns,' said Eleanor. 'Nobody wants a cast-adrift nun with no wealthy family to fall back on. That's why I say that for us, it is going to be just one thing after another, with no reason for any of it. We have to go the way the wind blows us.'

'I am not a leaf,' I said.

'Neither am I,' said Eleanor. 'In which case we have to think hard about what we want.'

Eleanor and I, as it turned out, wanted different things. Her love for Jesus Christ and her belief in his particular love for her had seemingly waned. But she was the same Eleanor, desperate for some passionate attachment.

*

I think it was the following autumn, or maybe the one after, that Sherborne was again exposed to goings-on in the great world.

One October morning there was a great pressure of people making for the Abbey precinct, in the wake of a procession of armed soldiery and horsemen and fine coaches and one great covered vehicle painted black and with black plumes and hangings. Eleanor and I followed along. We love a spectacle. A funeral, and of someone important. The catafalque stopped at the Abbey door, and a big coffin with brass all over it was carried by eight hefty gentlemen into the Abbey Church. The gentry filed in after it, in black fur-edged robes. The rest of us were kept out by guards with halberds.

Grooms and pages held the bridles of steaming horses, loosening their girths, walking them around, bringing them water from the pump. Eleanor and I picked our way through horse-droppings, accosted a young fellow who looked approachable, and asked whose funeral this was.

'It's Sir Thomas Wyatt's.'

'The poet?'

The groom could not say whether he was a poet, but from what he did say I knew it was the same one. A great man, said the groom. He had been in prison. He had been in the Tower. A bit of a brawler. A ladies' man.

'Don't ask me about his poor wife, you don't want to know.'

He had carried on with Anne Boleyn, some said. Sometimes he was in favour with the King and sometimes he was not. But he served the King in high places, he was what they call an ambassador, said the groom. He had been ambassador to the court of the Holy Roman Emperor.

How did he die? Why is his body brought here?

Eleanor and I now found ourselves at the centre of a congregation of bored grooms happy to while away the time by gossiping. Between them, they told us what happened. Sir Thomas Wyatt and a grand entourage were on their way to Falmouth on the coast of Cornwall to greet the Emperor's ambassador who had sailed all the way from Spain, and to escort him back to London. Sir Thomas was a good acquaintance of this important personage, and feared to keep him waiting on shipboard. It is many, many miles from London to Falmouth and Sir Thomas, on horseback, rode as if the devil were on his tail; it was hard for the rest to keep up with him. He was no longer a young man, he was nearly forty years old.

Perhaps he exhausted himself, or else the sickness was already upon him. However it was, when they stopped for the night he collapsed on dismounting. He was running a high fever and could barely speak. By dawn he seemed a dying man. His gentlemen decided to carry him back some distance to his friend Sir John Horsey's house at Clifton Maybank.

I knew of course who Sir Thomas Wyatt was, because of Arundell's talk with the Abbess, way back. And we knew of course who Sir John Horsey was. Clifton Maybank is a nowhere kind of place a few miles downriver from here. It was there that Sir Thomas Wyatt died. A sad story.

The church doors were opened and as the gentlemen attendants and mourners poured out I caught sight of someone I had seen somewhere before. He was a crow among the grandees, not dressed in velvet and silk and fur, nor wearing a sword. I recognised his high black woollen hat, his long nose, his creased dark face, and the satchel slung from his shoulder.

I ran from the grooms and the horses and from Eleanor and placed myself in his way.

'Master Leland! Master John Leland!'

He looked hard at me, grasped my arm and drew me away from the procession.

'Do I know you?'

I reminded him of the day in Bruton, when we sat together on the stones beside the market cross.

'You are the little maid who can read?'

I said I was she — although I had been no maid. I was pregnant with Peterkin at the time.

We stood together. He swayed on his feet. He was in an emotional state because of the death of Sir Thomas Wyatt.

'He was my friend. I am, like he, a poet. I had no notion — it is pure chance that I happen to be here, and I was myself at Sir John Horsey's place quite recently. He has a fine library although the books are damaged by damp. I am still cataloguing, you know, though for my own interest now. Tell me, if you live in this place, what do you know about the Missal? The Sherborne Missal?'

I had never even heard of it.

'That is why I came back. It is the most important and the most beautiful missal in all these islands. Very large. It is the work of a single monk's hand, aided by one other. The paintings of birds alone are *sans pareil*, I have seen nothing like them anywhere. I held the Missal in my hands when I was here ten years ago and I marvelled. It is old, very old, and in perfect condition. The colours and the gilding, pristine. But no one knows where it is. It seems to be lost.'

'The Commissioners?'

'I would surely know if that were so. The acquisition of so great a treasure would be documented. I suspect it is in private hands.'

'Sir John Horsey?'

He sighed and shrugged. 'That is why I paid him a visit. He denies all knowledge. But who can say? One can only pray that whoever holds it, whoever sells, it, whoever buys it, will care for it. It will no doubt reappear, but alas not in my lifetime.'

Leland was not really talking to me. I could have been anybody, I was anybody.

'Have you not heard? Now that there is printing, vellum manuscripts are cut up and pasted inside the covers of books to stiffen them and then concealed by plain paper. What is written upon them is lost for ever. Histories, legal documents, letters. No one cares. There is no respect for the old ways.'

He turned to face me again and fixed his eyes on mine.

'You are, did you say, the little maid who can read?'

Yet again, I said that yes, yes, I was. He unbuckled his satchel and fumbled inside it and brought out a small fat printed book.

'Take this. It is in English but not quite in our English of today, nor quite in the way we write it, it was written down about one hundred and fifty years ago, but if you read the words aloud to yourself the meaning will be quite clear. This is a modern rendering, and the printing is somewhat cramped. Persevere. With Chaucer, you will never be alone.'

I took the book and thanked him and turned away to release him from my company. When I was ten steps away he called out to me:

'I shall now compose an elegy to my friend and fellow poet Sir Thomas Wyatt! A long one! In Latin!'

I think perhaps he has become a little unhinged. Like so many in these days.

The book he gave me is *The Canterbury Tales* by Geoffrey Chaucer. I have never before read a book that was not devotional or in someway religious. Ballads, yes, broadsheets, yes, but not a proper book.

It is a book made up of stories. A group of pilgrims are setting forth together on horseback from an inn called the Tabard in Southwark – that is a part of London – to visit the shrine of St Thomas Becket in Canterbury. They agree to tell one another stories to while away the time on the roads.

It is written as poetry, but not poetry as I have known it. Once you get used to the spellings you realise that Chaucer writes as we talk, in our ordinary way. That is what is astonishing about the book. One can do that? Write about how real people speak and behave? Well, Chaucer did, all those years ago, and his book is popular and respected, so anyone might do that. Even me.

The book accompanied me every day, weighing down the pocket-bag beneath my gown. I mostly read it in the open air, because the light was dim in our attic chamber. I read the words aloud, quietly, as Leland had instructed me. I did not read it from beginning to end. I read in it, here and there. Before I started in on the stories the pilgrims tell, I read the Prologue over and over, in which Chaucer describes all the people on the pilgrimage. I came to see them in my mind's eye. One of them is an Abbess travelling with a nun and three priests. Thinking of Dame Elizabeth Zouche, I read about her first.

Chaucer's Abbess is called Madam Eglantine. He writes that she has immaculate table manners. Her lips leave no mark on the cup. She drops no morsels from the platter on to her person. She speaks French with a London-French accent, not a Paris-French accent. I do not know the significance of that and have no one to ask, but I think the implication is that she is not truly cultured. She is kindly and tender-hearted. She has with her a number of little dogs whom she feeds with bits of roast meat. She is well-dressed, tall and grey-eyed with a wide fair forehead – nearly a span broad, Chaucer said.

In Shaftesbury Abbey it was considered most immodest to bare one's forehead. I do not understand the significance. There is a sort of nakedness perhaps in that smooth expanse. And also maybe a mark of breeding. Low people have low foreheads, the hair sprouting close above the eyebrows. I think Chaucer finds his Abbess amusing and attractive, and that he is mocking her as well. She is too genteel and womanish for me, and not at all like the last Abbess of Shaftesbury.

Master Leland was right. After *The Canterbury Tales* became mine I never did feel alone. But reading does not make any money and we needed to supplement our pensions. Eleanor was adamant that we should make a plan – together. My immersion in the book shut her out. Thus my reading became more secret. It was as if I were stealing away to meet a lover.

The plan which Eleanor and I evolved was not so unlike that of the Winter Sisters – that is, to make something out of almost nothing. Our idea was to buy wares cheaply and sell them on for a small profit, going from door to door. There are many old and infirm persons in Sherborne, as well as mothers with infants, all of whom find it hard to get to the market.

Over weeks, we observed the pedlars and chapmen and traders who came regularly to the market in Sherborne, taking note of what they set out on the roadside, and of what sold most and most quickly, and of their style of salesmanship. We decided that we would have nothing to do with foodstuffs, which we had nowhere to store and soon rotted.

We chose our trading partner. He was not there on every market day, but when he was, he made an impression. His name was Jack, that was all we knew, and we called him Jack Chapman. He was from Scotland and spoke in a way new to us which at first was hard to understand. A rowdy young fellow, as befits a huckster, with a yellowish beard and a round red face. We befriended him, and drank with him in the alehouse after market time, and we made an arrangement with him. That was not hard. It pleased him to have female company. That is, Eleanor pleased him. I think I made little impression.

The arrangement was that before he packed up his wares at daylight end on market days, we would buy from him, on favourable terms, as much stock as he had not sold and did not care to retain. He travelled all over the country and liked to travel light, in order not to tire his oxen. He was a lazy, hard-drinking man and roved the countryside as his fancy took him. He restocked before the next market he went to – which could be in Cornwall, or Wiltshire, or anywhere at all. But he always came back to Sherborne. The lassies here, he said, looking at Eleanor, were the bonniest south of the border. Eleanor flashed her great eyes at him.

She did the business amid rude jokes from him and shrieks of mock horror from her. I stood by clutching our purse and worrying whether we could afford to buy, or could ever sell, that short length of green ribbon, that roll of tape, that stained piece of velvet, those off-cuts of coarse linen, those wooden spoons, those tawdry shoe-buckles, or quite so many packets of needles and pins ... But Eleanor knew what she was doing, and we always sold almost everything.

I went from door to door, street to street, every day, rain or shine, with my basket of merchandise. I knew the sad story of the old lady whose husband had been caught in a millwheel and lost two limbs and his senses. I knew which child had been ailing, which wife had been wandering from home, which family had the lease on their tenement foreclosing. I came to understand better about the circumstances of people's lives. Sister Mary Amor, God rest her soul, said to me once that nothing is wasted, however trivial the task. There is always something to be learned which will turn out to be of use at some other time and in another situation. I believe this. My experience may seem to me sometimes so haphazard as to be meaningless. But nothing is wasted.

Jack did not work the markets alone. He had with him a partner or employed man, I know not which, who did the loading and unloading, the fetching and carrying, and arranged the display of goods. Meanwhile Jack cajoled the passers-by and attracted a crowd.

This other man's name was Colin. He was quiet, brown-skinned and black-bearded. He wore a blue cap. His dark eyes often fell on mine. Sometimes we exchanged smiles, complicit in amusement at the antics of Jack and Eleanor. Or so I imagined.

Jack began to stay the night in Sherborne on market days, instead of trundling off in his wagon God knows where. I do not know what Colin did. Eleanor, unlike myself with my book, really did steal away to meet a lover. She would leave our apartment to find Jack in the darkness, returning around dawn. Fortunately Master Palmer, the old man downstairs, was a heavy sleeper and was never woken by Eleanor thudding past his mattress and up the ladder-stair to our room. She had never been slender, and had somehow put on flesh since we left the Abbey.

I became unhappy. I liked her company less. We had little in common except our work, and even there the division of labour contrived to separate us. Around our third midsummer I told Eleanor that I was planning to leave Sherborne, and find another place to be.

I thought we would have a rational discussion about our futures. I was wrong. She gasped and flew into a rage.

'What? What? What are you saying? You cannot abandon me! You cannot go! We belong together for ever!'

And more of the same, on and on, pacing our small chamber up and down, back and forth, arms upraised, eyes flaring, hair standing on end – an animal.

I was horrified at what I had unleashed. I cowered on the floor, wrapping my arms around myself. I thought she was going to attack me.

'I am sorry,' I said. 'I am sorry. I am so sorry. I will not go. Of course I will not go. I will not leave you.'

Eleanor snatched up our little axe. I waited for her to bring it down upon my head. I was inert, a piece of wood, stock-still, beyond fear as a freezing person is beyond cold.

She placed her left hand on the stool and brought down the axe upon it. She screamed and cast the axe aside. I leapt to my feet to see what she had done to herself. I grasped her left wrist and held it upwards. She had chopped off the tips of her two longest fingers, the middle finger and the ring finger.

She was crying now, breathing badly. She was frightened. Her fingers began to pour blood. I laid her upon our bed and found cloths and bound up the fingers tightly. One of her fingertips lay on the stool, the other on the floor. Knobs of flesh. I picked them up and threw them out of the window. I went down to the pump in the yard, brought up water and cleaned up the blood on the stool and the floor.

In the morning we did not refer to what had happened, or rather we did not refer to why it had happened. It was as if she had suffered a misfortune which had nothing to do with anything or anyone. We cleansed and re-wrapped her fingers every day as the stubs healed, forming crusts and scabs.

'Don't pick at your scabs,' I told her.

When the scabs came off the new skin on the stumpy finger-ends was red and shiny. It hardened.

It was not I who left Eleanor. It was Eleanor who left me.

One night after that summer's end, she made an announcement. We were as usual in our attic chamber. She was sitting on our stool with pen and paper on her knee, the inkpot on the floor, and a rushlight close by. She was doing our accounts for the month. I stood at the mansard window, looking out into darkness, into nothing, and thinking of nothing.

'I am going from here tomorrow,' she said.

I turned back from the window and stared at her.

'Whatever do you mean? Where are you going?'

'I am going with Jack, wherever he is going.'

I still stared. She explained. She spoke as if she had planned exactly what she would say to me. Jack loved her, Jack was 'the answer'.

'What does that mean, Jack is the answer? The answer to what? What is the question?'

If I did not know, then I did not know, she said. She would leave with me half our profits for the month. Then she rose and put her arms around me.

'You and I,' she said, 'are something else. There is no one like me for you and no one like you for me. Wherever you are, I shall always find you.'

A promise, or a threat.

I went to our bed before she did. She was shambling around in the dark, putting together her belongings. I was bewildered. I never loved or trusted Eleanor but I was in thrall to her for good and for ill and together we had made a living and a life. And what was I to do now? When at last she came to the bed and lay down close to me and put her hand on me, stroking, I did not respond.

I was not tempted to beg her to stay. And so we lay like figures on a tomb, saying nothing. She turned the other way and was soon asleep. I was a welter of confused feelings – relief to be rid of her, and fear of the future, and the pain of rejection, which is sharp. It is a vanity, and ignominious. Rejection from whatever quarter triggers some old, unhealed misery.

Do not pick your scabs.

I was wakeful for a long time, so that I was fast asleep in that time before dawn when Eleanor left. I found in the morning a heap of coins on the top of the stool, my share of our marketing.

I had no desire or reason to remain in Sherborne. I threw out Master Palmer's slops and spoke to him kindly. I was never unkind to that old man. I gave him some milk, and walked round to his sister on Cheap Street, and told her that we were leaving. She must look after her brother herself now, or find other tenants. She shrugged her shoulders, barely looking up from a heap of old coats that she was sorting. They were men's coats. I wish that I had bought one. I am often cold.

I went to say goodbye to the Winter Sisters. They had reconvened in Long Street after their summer scatterings. It was early November.

'Stay with us,' they said. 'Why not? You are one of us.'

But I could not, and I was not.

I admire the Winter Sisters, they are good, but there is something about them that almost disgusts me. A complacency? Something visceral. Their workroom is heavy with that sweetish odour which permeated the dorter, the refectory, the parlour at Shaftesbury Abbey. The smell of women. I am a woman as the Winter Sisters are. Though – this is how I explain it to myself – I am female, strongly so, but not feminine. There is a difference. Further than this I cannot say because it is beyond my understanding and power of expression.

Sister Isobel would probably allow and then disallow in herself the thoughts I had about the Winter Sisters. The pool at the bottom of my mind is murky. I never know when vicious fish will leap, nor what they will cause me to think or say. I am myself superficial, an insect on the pool's surface. A crane fly, a water boatman. What do I know? I did know that I did not want to cast in my lot with the Winter Sisters and become one of them, 'one of us'. No.

I decided to go home at last to Bruton.

I was in a hurry so as not to miss my place on the timber-cart which would take me as far as Wincanton. I unlatched the house door and there, almost colliding with me on the threshold, was Colin, smiling.

'I was about to knock,' he said, taking breath to say more and still smiling. I did not let him finish.

'You must excuse me, I cannot stay, or I will miss my chance of getting away today.'

I kissed him on the cheek, I think to soften my brusqueness as I attempted to push past him with my bundle.

Colin stepped back, swept off his blue cap, bowed, and gestured me to pass with a flourish of his hand and the grace of a gentleman. The smile on his face twisted into a mask of disappointment.

I just ran, and thought nothing more of it at the time. I did not give Colin another thought as I took my place – I should say, my perch, and very uncomfortable it was – on the long timbers destined, I would guess, to be trusses and roof-beams, on the flat six-wheeled cart. The driver, sitting at a distance in front, nodded and did not speak. Off we went. A bumpy ride.

The timber merchant put me down beside the church in Wincanton. Go left at the crossing, he told me, take the road north, over the river. When you have a choice of tracks, take the left-hand one, it is not far to Bruton, maybe eight miles. If you become confused, ask at a farm.

So I started to walk. My bundle seemed heavy. I have more clothes than I used to have, and still the lion tile, and Mary Amor's piece of silk (which admittedly is weightless). Also my rolls of writings and copies of documents and letters which I brought away from Shaftesbury Abbey, and my books. One is entitled *The Birth of Mankind* about how babies are gotten and born, very enlightening. I bought it in Sherborne market. I also have the Bible in English, and the Chaucer. Books weigh one down but I could not leave them behind.

I found myself as I walked re-living the encounter with Colin. What had he intended to say? What was he about to ask? To take a stroll with him? To go with him, as Jack was going with Eleanor, and to be his sweetheart? I saw again his eloquent dark eyes and his smile and remembered our wordless sympathy.

I had behaved thoughtlessly. A path not taken. I could not go back, what is done is done. Yet if a person is ceaselessly moving along it is better to have an end in view and I did not. Colin and I could have leased a piece of land, and made a good life.

I hardly know the man. Such regrets were ridiculous.

But I felt lonely. No one on this earth, that day, knew or cared who I was or where I was of what would become of me. I call it 'the loneliness', not just 'loneliness', because it is a sickness that sometimes comes upon me, as on that journey.

The loneliness came upon me sometimes during those nights in Sherborne when Eleanor was out with Jack. Within the loneliness comes a flash of terror – an absolute terror of something just beyond my vision, too dreadful to confront. Perhaps it is a glimpse of Hell.

I imagined putting an end to my life. I have heard of women drowning themselves. But the river at Sherborne, running in the valley a short walk down the track from our lodging, is shallow. I knew I could not do that. I did sometimes think of seeking out a wise woman and acquiring a poison. On bad nights I had it all planned out. I would take twice or thrice as much as the wise woman told me, so as to make sure.

But then, on other nights, Eleanor's absence seemed a blessed respite. I am not sad by nature. I am sad in circumstances in which any normal person might be sad.

When I need to cheer myself up I read about the Wife of Bath in the *Canterbury Tales*. This makes me laugh aloud. She is like Mistress Agnes Perceval in that she talks a lot, the words streaming out of her. Her words, however, are very naughty and entertaining. It is all about marriage and sex. She has had five husbands – three good and two bad – and would marry for a sixth time if she found another good one. Jesus Christ himself, she says, did not speak against serial marriages, 'not bigamy nor yet octogamy'. What are men's sexual organs put there for, other than urinating? Chastity is a virtue that cannot be practised by all, or there would be no more children born, and chastity is not for her. She rattles on merrily about the private parts, about men's 'instrument', a woman's 'equipment', her 'belle chose'. That is French. I wonder whether Chaucer knew women like the Wife of Bath, or whether he was just delivering himself of his own opinions.

And so I walked from Wincanton to Bruton with my books, sad and then not sad, lonely and then not lonely, as the sun was obscured and then, low in the sky now, shone once more. I walked in deep dark hollow ways with branches meeting over my head and fallen leaves squashy beneath my feet, then up and out across open fields.

I met drovers with sheep, and a woman. I saw her from afar, a tiny figure coming towards me. As the distance between us lessened I saw she was wrapped in tattered cloths, her head covered, her back bent, walking slowly. This was somewhere near the village called Shepton Montague. You do not pass another traveller on the road with no greeting. I asked her if I was on the right road for Bruton. She told me I would have to bear right at the next division of the track. That would bring me down into Pitcombe, and up again, and then down again, into Bruton. I was reassured, though I did stop at a kind of tavern in Shepton to check again, and accepted some small beer from the landlord.

I never asked that woman where she was going, walking the roads like myself. But not altogether like myself. She had whiskers on her face. She spoke as if she were unused to speaking, the words like obstacles in her mouth. I do not think she was a nun, not 'one of us' as the Winter Sisters would say. Some people just walk the roads, going from nowhere to nowhere, homeless vagrants, filling the time before death.

I reached Bruton, my home town, late on that November day. Low grey light, no whisper of wind, and the scent of decay. In the lane down into the town I trudged through sodden mats of beech leaves. Unseasonably warm. A few leaves, ovals of rose and gold, clung to branches overhanging the hollow ways. One gale would carry all away.

I crossed the river at Legge's Bridge. It was already shutting-in time. I walked on round into the high street. I kept my hood up, wishing neither to be recognised nor not to be recognised. The few people that I encountered, scuttling home before the light failed, all mumbled a greeting but they did not know me and I did not know them. There were changes. Some dwellings I remembered as make-shift hovels were rebuilt with stone-framed windows and long lintels above their doors. One or two had fragments of stone carving set into the walls. All this adornment must come from the Abbey, I thought, and I was right. It gave some dignity to the dingy street.

When I came down to the end towards the market cross and turned my eyes to my parents' place, I saw desolation. Garbage was piled high up against the warped and splintering shutter. It cannot have been opened for a long time.

As I hesitated outside the door at the side, I was greeted. It was Mistress Joan Dempster, who had delivered Peterkin. She looked older, but then I suppose so did I.

'Agnes Peppin – is it you?'

She laid a hand on my arm.

'Wait. Do not go in just yet.'

And she told me that my father was no more. He had died around Michaelmas. Died of what, I asked, my armpits prickling, my blood draining away.

He had no disease, she said, that one could tell. His wits were astray. His father and grandfather had gone the same way. I had not known that. He lost the will to live, said Joan Dempster, when he was told that Master Berkeley was calling in the lease of his butcher's shop. Everything that belonged to the Abbey now belonged to Master Berkeley. His intention was to demolish the shambles and rebuild the row as workshops – masons' yards, a wheelwright, a forge, a paint shop – to serve the needs of the construction of his new mansion on the Abbey site.

'Your father's understanding was gone. He fell into unreasoning rages. He threw pots and knives around and banged his fists on the walls and growled and shouted. It was hard on your mother. She would sometimes run out into the street to escape him. In between times he sat silent.'

All I could think was, I shall never see my kind father again. He was lying under the earth in the churchyard.

She told me that she was bringing bread and onions and apples to my mother, as she did whenever she could. My mother did not eat well, she said.

'And she?'

'She has not long to live. She has given up trying.'

She put out her hand and stroked my cheek.

'Come and see me,' she said, 'tomorrow. I am still where I was, up the hill.'

I took the bag of food from her and pushed open the side door into my old home. I saw in the smoky shadows the familiar place, unchanged, a feeble fire burning in the middle. The air was sour. I saw the high shelf with our same utensils upon it, and the chest, the three stools, and sitting on one of them my dear father, his back bowed, leaning forward, arms folded on his knees. He looked smaller, shrunken, sunken.

No I did not. That was in my imagination. He was not there at all. But I saw him all the same. His leather jerkin hung on its nail.

In a wooden box beside his stool were as always his butcher's knives and cleavers, piled up higgledy-piggledy. They were real enough.

I saw against the wall a mattress, and lying upon it my mother, under a fleece. By this time of year, Blossom our cow would have been rustling and stamping beyond the partition. But silence – no cow, and no dog to bark at my arrival. So quiet. Old Ratter would have died long ago.

'Mother. It is I, Agnes, your daughter. I have come home.'

She stared, she stretched out her arms. I ran to her and embraced her and kissed her hands. She did not speak. In desperation I busied myself, and looked about me, and found in the store in the yard some tired roots to add to Mistress Dempster's onions. I made up the fire, and hooked the pot over it, and made soup as the night came down. I found bowls and served the soup to my mother and myself with chunks of the bread.

'So much,' my mother said. 'Too much for me.'

I ate and she did not.

'This bread is too hard,' she said. 'Take it away.'

She asked no questions about the end of Shaftesbury Abbey – did she even know, or had she forgotten? – nor about where I had been since then, nor what I had done, nor what my plans were.

I did not sleep much that night, as I lay on a pallet close to my mother. I had been living all this time as if I were alone in the world. That night I suffered fresh pain from my torn-up exposed roots. My father, my mother – my son.

The next morning, another damp, mild day, I walked back over Legge's Bridge and up the steep track to Joan Dempster's hut. It is cosy and clean. I took off my muddy shoes at the door. She was ever a gossip, on account of her trade. What I now wanted to know from her, and with urgency, was what had happened to Peterkin, whether he still lived or did not, and whether his father Peter Mompesson thrived or did not. And also, about Jeanne Vile. I did not confront Joan with any of this straight away. I knew we must become comfortable together before she would speak as freely to me as I wished.

The Abbey Church, she told me, was now the parish church. She told me where in the churchyard I would find my father's grave. We talked for a while about Maurice Berkeley's plans for his great house, and the employment he was giving to tradesmen and labourers in the town. She showed me a copper bowl with an intricate design round its rim. She had picked it up in the Abbey precinct, half-buried in the mud, and carried it away under her cloak.

'Something the greedy Commissioners must have missed,' I said.

She laughed. 'There is hardly a household in Bruton that does not have something rescued from the ruination of the Abbey. We were permitted to go in there with barrows to take away stones. Not that I have any use for stones. But the Abbey will live on for ever in our saved fragments.'

They had taken the lead from the chapel roof, she said, to melt it down. Lead is so valuable.

After an hour I could contain myself no longer and asked her what I needed to know. And she told me.

Peter Mompesson is well and farming still at Brewham, his father and sister both having died. He is bringing up Peterkin more or less on his own. Peterkin is a fine lad, and very like me in appearance, said Mistress Dempster. The same colour of hair, and slight and agile.

This made my heart leap and I felt my face flushing. To conceal my agitation I asked about Jeanne Vile.

Oh. This seemed problematic. Joan Dempster paused and lowered her gaze and scraped the copper bowl about on her trestle before she spoke.

'Jeanne and Peter Mompesson were close after the sister died and Peter needed help with his son. Jeanne has a daughter, but I do not know if she is Peter's. She married a farmer much older than herself soon after the birth, over on the Hardway, I just do not know. Whatever way it was, there is nothing between Peter and Jeanne now, They are friends.'

'Does Peter have any other woman?'

'How would I know? He is a man like any other. But there is no woman living with him and Peterkin up at the farm.'

She gave me a piece of sheep's cheese in a cloth. 'You will be looking after your mother from now on. You will need to melt the cheese, and soak her bread in milk or broth. That's the only way she can eat it.'

Joan Dempster gave me much to think about. Too much, as my mother said about the food I gave her. I walked back down the town and past our house with her words ringing in my ears: 'You will be looking after your mother from now on.' Not much choice there. I made a silent Act of Contrition for my selfish thoughts.

I crossed the church bridge, and saw the grey Abbey Church standing as it always had and, winding away to the right, the path beside the Abbey wall with its tall buttresses. Some of the school buildings on the river side of the path were in bad repair, probably no longer in use. Venturing through the open Abbey gatehouse, I saw what I expected to see.

The destruction was almost total. The Abbey buildings were demolished, with masonry and stacks of roof timbers lying around. No walls stood to their former height except a range furthest from me, where I think the Abbot's house had been. Perhaps Master Berkeley planned to incorporate it into his new mansion. But no cloister, no chapel, no dorter or infirmary or anything else. A wasteland. Grass and thistles and ash and alder were taking over the site – except where all was reduced to oozy mud by boots and wheels.

A dozen workmen with barrows were bringing stones from the random heaps and arranging them in piles according to size all along the boundary wall where the stables had been. Another set of workmen turned over the stones and hammered off the old mortar.

And then I saw him, in the name of God, of course it was he, Master Maurice Berkeley. A youngish gentleman – even then I knew a gentleman when I saw one. He was wearing long over-boots to protect his no doubt dainty shoes and hose. Stomping at one side of him was a bulky older man, a sheaf of papers in his hand, speaking urgently, prodding his papers with a finger, with the young gentleman nodding and throwing in his pennyworth.

I recognised that man. It was John White, Abbot Eley's enemy. He had landed on his feet. Undeservedly. I expect it was he who informed my poor father in person that his lease was terminated. On Master Berkeley's other side was a tall, thin, red-haired creature, fawning. I knew him too. It was Richard Halford, whom I had also heard speak against Abbot Eley, the night when my mother and I were laying out the elf-canon.

I could, maybe should, have approached Maurice Berkeley, and pleaded for my mother's shelter and support, and explained to him our family connection through his FitzJames stepfather. I did not have the stomach for it nor the resilience, at that moment, to bear his cold stare and John White's officious dismissal. If I still wore the emerald dolphin round my neck, I just might have had the confidence. I thought of my dolphin embedded in filth in a sewer and I cursed Eleanor Wilmer in my heart.

7

CHANCE AND CHOICE

I walked off and began to make my way through the fields and woods uphill towards Brewham. I had no plan.

There was no bright slanting sunlight as on the day when I ran to meet Peter in these woods at the same season so long ago. I walked that same way, and saw the long, low Mompesson farmhouse and its outhouses beyond the trees on the further side. The thatch looked to be in good repair. The half-door was swinging open at the top, so Peter could not be far away. There were a dozen or so sheep in a hurdle enclosure and fowls scratching on the track and in the yard.

I heard voices, not from the farmhouse but from behind me, and scrambled into the wet brambles to the side of the track to hide.

I watched them pass, talking and laughing. A thickset man, and a limping woman in a blue smock with wild hair escaping from her headcloth. She held the hand of a little girl, skipping along at her side, chirruping to herself as little girls do. Behind them trailed a skinny little boy with bright brown hair, hitting the stones of the track with a stick and sending them spinning, detaching himself from the family group as young lads do.

For they looked like a family. I struggled halfway out of the hedge and watched the four of them go into the farmhouse. I saw Jeanne looking out of the half-door. There was light behind her. They must have lit the rushlights, or a candle. She could not possibly have seen me. Dusk was falling, and the overgrown track would have been in darkness to her eyes. She stretched out an arm to find the catch on the half-door, and closed it with a bang.

So what did I do? I knocked on the door of the farmhouse. Peter opened the door, a lantern in his hand, and held it up to my face.

'Agnes! Is it really you! Come in, come in!'

I entered the firelit room, and Peterkin met my eyes. I opened my arms to him.

Peter drew me to a place by the fire and Peterkin followed, unable to stay away from my side. We gazed upon one. I smiled up at his father, Peter, and felt no whit of the old passion, only a loyalty to the past and an affinity. Jeanne was wrapping herself in her cloak. She came to embrace me.

'My first and best friend! Come and see us soon. I must go now, we have to walk all the back to the Hardway and to my old man. He will be wondering what has become of us.'

We – the little family, the first and forever little family – were left together to tell our stories and make our peace and plan our future.

That is not what happened. No, not at all. That is just what I have imagined. So what really did happen?

What did I do? I knocked on the door of the farmhouse. Peter opened the door, a lantern in his hand, and held it up to my face.

'Yes?' he said. 'Can I help you?'

He did not recognise me.

'It is I, Agnes Peppin,' I said.

He looked back over his shoulder.

'You had better come in,' he said.

I entered the room. Jeanne was bent over, attending to the food she was cooking over the fire. She jumped up and stared at me startled:

'Agnes! Is it really you! What in God's name are you doing here?'

I did not know how to answer her. Peterkin, my son, looked up briefly and then returned to what was occupying him. He was sitting on a stool in the corner, chipping away at a piece of wood with a knife. He was a boy who did not know me and whom I did not know. He was not interested. Peter said:

'I am sorry about the death of your father. If there is anything I can do to help you and your mother...'

I saw in his eyes just a confusion — regret, shame, pity, fear. I do not know what he saw in mine.

'Thank you, we do not need help. I came to see our son.'

I spoke softly. Peterkin, absorbed in what he was doing, could not have heard me. Peter glanced at the boy, his boy and mine. He rubbed his hand over his chin and sighed.

'Perhaps it would be better not to disturb his peace of mind. He is a good boy. He will have the farm when I go. Is there any need for — this?'

'He will become a man. I think a man should know who his mother was.'

'Come outside.'

We went out into the yard, closing the door behind us. I was alone in the dusk with Peter as in the old days, but he was as a stranger to me.

'Agnes, I promise you I will tell him when the time is right that his mother was a good woman. And that he can be proud of his heritage. I will tell him your name. Can you live with that?'

'Perhaps when you tell him he will want to know me.'

'Perhaps. I would put nothing in his way. But not now, not yet.'

We stood in silence.

'Then I should go away now,' I said.

'Perhaps' – and I heard the relief in his voice. 'Will you find your way? The moon is up, look, the sky is clear.'

I turned away towards the track. I looked back and saw him standing at the door, and raised my hand. He raised his hand. I walked away into the dark.

That is not what happened either. No, not at all.

But those scenes, played out in my mind over and over when I am walking, and during the nightly void between first sleep and second sleep, remain as real to me as if they really had happened. Sometimes my mind fabricates variations.

The pain does recede though the stories in my head do not. Telling them to myself has become a habit. A weakness of the mind. Peterkin may come to find me one day or he may not. Sometimes I feel as if it is of no consequence one way or the other. There is but the thinnest of veils between what happens and what does not. Sometimes I can no longer distinguish between what was and is, and what was not and is not. I know myself to be a little mad at those times. A little like Eleanor perhaps.

What I actually did that night, after I saw Jeanne closing the half-door, was to turn around and stumble the three miles or so back through the woods and along the river into Bruton by the light of a paltry half-moon, and collapse beside my half-sleeping mumbling mother.

*

I had few conversations with my mother which meant anything to either of us. Joan Dempster was right. My mother, never securely attached to her life, had given up trying and was waiting for the end. She said as much, in her dry way, raising herself upon her bed.

'The priest brings me the Host. They do not say priest here now, they say curate. A fellow put in by the new man. I have told him that I want to die, I am ready to meet my Maker. He said that unfortunately one has to wait for an invitation. The grave-digger, do you remember, is Mole. Master Mole. He will bury me in a mole-hole.'

I laughed at all that and she made to laugh too but the laugh became coughing and breathlessness.

'I am trapped in an old body. It's not mine. I want to fight my way out of it, kick and punch my way out.'

'And then, when you get out?'

'Then I will run away very fast and climb to the top of a tree.'

On what turned out to be her last day, though neither of us knew that, I sat upon the floor beside her and took her hand.

'So how is it with you, daughter?' she asked me.

I was moved, knowing the effort for her of any engagement, but did not know where to begin.

'It is well with me,' I said. 'I have been in Sherborne, and I am going next back to Shaftesbury and then to London.'

I do not know why I said I would go to London. It had not been in my mind until it suddenly was.

She looked aghast. 'But if you go away from here, your own place, you will not know where you are.'

'I shall find out,' I said. 'I shall discover.'

'But to live among strangers. No one will know you, or who your parents are. No one can live like that.'

It was for her completely unimaginable.

She died that night. I awoke in the small hours to hear her breathing change to a hoarse gurgling. The death rattle. I held her hand and thought, if she cannot get away by morning, I will help her to go. I will stifle her. Not for my sake, but for hers. No, for my sake too. I did not have to do it. Shortly before dawn the sound ceased. It was all over. I did nothing for a long while, to allow her spirit to fly free. I opened the back door as wide as it would go. I sat beside her. I prayed for her soul.

I washed her and laid her out as I had seen her lay out countless others. I sang to her the lullaby songs she used to sing. I whisper-sang to her, 'Luly, lulay' and 'Balulalo, balulalo', weeping from an empty heart, consuming my own substance. Had she ever, in all my childhood, filled my hungry heart with love, I would now be repaying that debt with joy and from an abundance. She extracted from me in her death what she had never invested in me.

I found in the chest a cleanish linen shift and a length of faded green wool. I also found a box of money, which I stowed in my bundle. Before her body stiffened I managed to put the shift on her and then wrapped her in the green wool. I went up the street to the carpenter's shop. I knew him of old. He makes coffins. He always used four iron nails on each side to secure the coffin lid. Bang-bang-bang with his hammer, then a pause while he positioned the next nail, then bang-bang-bang again, and so on. He is a respectful man and does not speak much.

He dragged a ready-made coffin from the stack in his yard on to a handcart and followed me back to our house. It was still early, no one about. The coffin seemed to fill all the space in the room. Together we lifted my mother into it. I arranged the green wool around her. I turned away when he pulled the hammer and nails from his pouch.

Bang-bang-bang, then a pause while he positioned the next nail. Four each side, as always.

I walked over the bridge to the church. Inside, it was not much changed. The Holy Rood still hung over the screen. The paint

on the stonework was chipped and fading, the gold on the cuff
of the Hand of God was dulled, but the statues of saints and the
tombs of long-ago priests had not been defaced and the old font
stood in the nave.

I found the curate doing nothing much in the vestry. I looked
at the closed door to the little chamber where Jeanne and I had
learned to read and write. The curate's name was William Wilton.
I asked him if he knew what had become of John Harrold or Hugh
Backwell, formerly canons in the Abbey.

'Never heard of them,' he said. 'The only one still around is
Richard Halford, poking his nose into everything.'

'I have observed him,' I said.

I made arrangements with Father Wilton for my mother's burial
next to my father.

We buried her in her mole-hole by lantern-light after dark. Just
the curate, Master Mole, Joan Dempster and myself. We prayed
for the departed souls of my mother and father.

With sorrow, and relief, I made my own departure – not, thanks
be to God, from life, but from Bruton. I took nothing from our
room except a grey headcloth of my mother's, which carried the
sharp scent of her, and a narrow-bladed knife in a worn leather
sheath from my father's box of tools. I have seen him use it a hundred times. The bone handle is polished by his hand. The knife
has lasted longer than he did. It will last longer than me. Someone
who knew neither of us will in the end throw it away. It will not
rot down as mortal remains do, fallen leaves. The blade will rust
but it will still be there, to be turned up by spade or plough God
knows when.

I would guess that by now our tenement and those on each
side will have been demolished and rebuilt by Master Berkeley's
men. If Father Wilton kept his promise to me and had their

names cut on a headstone – I gave him most of the money from my mother's box for this purpose – their names may be read. When all those who knew of them have long gone, someone will wonder:

'And who may they have been, Thomas and Dorothy Peppin?'

When I went to say goodbye to the curate, he remembered that he had a letter addressed to me. It had been brought to him from London. Some time ago, he said. He had put it by. He would go and look for it. I was exasperated. People are always forgetting to give me my letters. I waited impatiently until he returned with a crumpled folded paper. I snatched it from him. Mice had been at it.

I read it by the light of the dying fire in my empty home. It was from Anne Cathcart. I did not make it all out that night. I was weary and the light dim, but I took in the gist, which was that she had established herself in a house close to the city of London and had an occupation that brought in money and provided her with much amusement. 'Come and join me.'

There was a hint of danger and of naughtiness in what she wrote, but that was ever Anne's manner. So yes, I would go to London. But first, back to Shaftesbury. It was on the way, more or less.

I came up into Shaftesbury by Tout Hill. The carrier let me off at the hill's foot, having business out of the town. He told me that his cousin Jacob, a cheese man, would be leaving Shaftesbury for London the next day, soon after noon. He would be seeing his cousin in the tavern later, and would alert him. He told me where I would find his cousin's cart in the morning.

'How will I know him?'

'You will see the cheeses. And Jacob wears a red cap.'

It was near day's end, but not yet dark. I saw a big stone house under construction, with towers in the corners. Workmen were still scrambling on the scaffolding in spite of the lateness of the hour, carrying up stacks of stone roof-tiles held together with straps as if they were books. They must have been appallingly heavy. This must be Sir John Arundell's new mansion. I was standing there watching, hoping he was paying those men generously, when one of them shouted down to me:

'Fancy a shag, Mistress Pretty?'

I moved away fast and in the wrong direction. I finally found myself walking along Bimport towards the Winterbournes' house, sweating with nervousness. The way I came, I had perforce to pass the Abbey gatehouse.

I saw that the window-glass was gone from the chamber above it, and that the great timber doors had gone too. I averted my eyes. I was not ready for this yet. I walked on. The Winterbournes' low dwelling, to my relief, still stood unchanged. I hesitated before the door, as I had hesitated with Dick and Weasel on my first visit, not knowing what I would find.

I knocked, and heard a dog barking. I recognised that bark. The door was opened, I saw not by whom, because Finbarr – after standing stock-still for a second, her ears raised, was upon me – leaping, licking, scrabbling at my gown, and ripping a hole in it, her tail wagging so violently it seemed her rear end would fall off, whining and yelping, beside herself. I was beside myself too. Only when she and I calmed down and she was back on her four feet could I look around me.

There is much always said about unhappiness and misery, and little about calm and contentment. There they were, in that one dark chamber cluttered with withies and baskets, and with the playthings of children and, on the shelf with the pots, a pile of books. Emilia had a baby in her arms, her little John was banging with a wooden spoon, and Dorothy's Esther was up on her legs, running around, as pretty as a flower.

And there, there, was my Dorothy Clausey, plumper and rosier than I had ever seen her, and pregnant. We hugged one another, and wept and laughed, and I marvelled at the children and held Emilia's baby, a girl. We told each other scraps of our histories since we parted. Dorothy was using the abandoned Magdalen house to teach children to read. The two Johns have expanded their business, selling their basketry as far away as Salisbury market.

Then the Johns came, filling the place as if two trees had entered the room. The silent John took a pitcher and ran to the alehouse to have it filled. We drank it all down, and the jug went back to the alehouse a second time. Did we eat? I cannot remember. I do not know how far the night had advanced before the fired died, the mattresses were laid out in all remaining space, and we lay down, children and mothers and fathers and myself all together.

I have no way of telling whether one John belonged to Dorothy and the other to Emilia, but I rather think not. Who can say? Emilia held her baby close. She would have to feed her during the night. Finbarr curled up against me and did not stir till dawn. I slept more soundly than I had for months. Compared with the doings any one night among gentlemen and ladies of the great world, this was nothing at all. We would seem to them so much human vermin. Yet this was a whole world, the whole fine world that they made for each other.

But it was theirs and I could not have remained among them. I did not really want to.

Early next morning, Dorothy walked with me round the remains of the Abbey. We did not take Finbarr. Holy Trinity, the townspeople's church, still stood, isolated. Plants, even trees, were sprouting from the tops of the Abbey ruins. We stood in the roofless space that had been the nave, among stumps of pillars. The shock of being there once more was not so great. In truth, I felt almost nothing. The life and the lives that those buildings had contained, and the pains and passions of generations of sisters, had all been wiped away. Nothing is for ever.

'We will remember, though,' said Dorothy.

'So much as we need to,' said I, thinking of the bad times – Dorothy with baby Esther in those first dreadful days, for example. I did not dare to ask her if she heard anything of Father Robert Parker, though I would have liked to know.

'I think all the time,' she said, 'about what happened here and to all the other monastic houses. Have you ever thought, Agnes, just sometimes, that it was perhaps – perhaps – necessary? That it had to happen? That it was correct, a correction?'

No, I had never thought that for one moment. I was startled. But there was some thread of a thought beneath what she said which I could not trace or pursue. Her question was not the right question, or not for me at that time. My old question came back to me: 'Who was to blame?'

We were standing side by side, wrapped in our cloaks, in the sisters' graveyard, littered with loose stones and overgrown with weeds and scrubby bushes. I looked across to piles of rotting lathes where chantry priests' dwellings had stood, and asked, 'What happened to Dame Joanna and Dame Philippa?'

She said they survived the first summer and died the following winter.

'I used to go and see them sometimes, and take them food. They ate like birds, handfuls of grain and scraps of crust. They shrank, they were like ancient children. I blame myself for not visiting them more often.'

She stood silent for a moment, and then:

'I am ashamed. I failed in charity.' She put her hands over her face.

She raised her head and told me, her face turned away, 'It was I who found them dead.'

It was a hard winter, with weeks of freezing temperatures and hard frost.

'There was much sickness in the town and many infants and old people died.'

In former days, people looked to the Abbey for everything and found it – shelter, medicines, food, fuel. How could Dorothy possibly think that the catastrophe had been 'necessary'? She was not thinking such thoughts now. She was making a kind of confession to me.

'I postponed going to see the old dames, and the longer I left it the harder it became. I was afraid of what I would find. I made the excuse to myself that my first duty was to our own little household. Life outside a community makes us selfish.'

She was distressing herself, which was not good in her condition. To reassure her, I said, 'I think it is not selfishness. It is a matter of survival. The survival of the little unit for which each is responsible.'

'Selfish.'

She put a hand on her belly.

'The babe is leaping and I cannot stand now for very long, I need to piss all the time and I need to sit down.'

She raised her skirts and pissed. Then, walking slowly now, back along Bimport, she told me how she at last made her way over to the old ladies' dwelling. The door was open. Frost had crept in over the threshold. The two wizened forms lay together on a single pallet, the thin blanket covering them also speckled with frost, and stiff.

'Their bodies were frozen hard.'

'They had to die,' I assured her. 'They were together, as they wanted. It is all right.'

I told her what my mother once said, that dying from cold is not hard. It is just a closing down, from the extremities inwards, until the cold reaches the heart. Towards the end there is no awareness of cold, or of anything at all. There is no pain as the soul takes flight.

Back in the Winterbournes' house with Emilia and the children, everything was warm and normal. I asked when Dorothy's baby would be born, and she and Emilia discussed the matter in a desultory way, holding one another's gaze, knowing what they knew, whatever it was that they knew.

'If it is a girl,' said Dorothy, 'I shall call her Agnes.'

I was pleased.

It was hard to leave, but at noon I bade them farewell and with difficulty crossed the road to make my way towards the spot where I was to meet the cheese merchant. It was market day and it was raining. The roadway was filthy with slush and ordure, crammed solid with herded beasts and handcarts and wheeled vehicles and strings of packhorses, the droves cursing.

I gained the other side and chanced to look back. I saw Finbarr standing in the Winterbournes' open doorway, and she saw me. She sprang forward, wriggling through the traffic. She ran straight into the path of a growling, grinding eight-wheeled wagon piled high with stones. It was moving slowly but was so heavy that it could not have stopped in time even had the driver thought to stop, which he would not, not for a dog, and even had he seen her, which he had not.

No one was to blame.

The wagon lurched on leaving Finbarr a bloody mash in the mud, to be run over no doubt again and again until at day's end her remains were cleared away with a shovel.

There was nothing I could do. I went on my way to find the cheese-merchant.

She was only a dog, I said to myself over and over, on the long journey east towards London. She was only a dog. If I had not chosen to return to Shaftesbury I would never have seen her again anyway. And she was doubtless not the only dog who was run over in Shaftesbury that day. She was only a dog.

She was Finbarr. We had known each other since she was a starved and flea-ridden pup. We had been together with Dick and Weasel, who loved her. We had known each other better than I knew any human being. I fingered the gash her claw had made in my old brown gown and I have never mended it. I still remembered her trusting body against mine at night.

Finbarr, good dog, good dog, Finbarr. Of course dogs have souls. If Finbarr does not, neither do I.

Jacob the cheese man with the red cap was pleasant and comely, even though he had about his person a pungent odour of his cheese, great rounds of which were stacked behind us, wrapped in greasy grey cloths. Business in Shaftesbury, he said, had improved greatly since the new men began building fine houses on Abbey property. I did not ask whether he provided Sir Thomas Arundell, and I did not tell him that I had been a nun in the Abbey, at least not then.

The bulk of his wares were destined for the markets, taverns and great houses of London. He told me about the village of Cheddar, where he comes from, and how his cheeses ripen in caves in the rocks all around. Caves are good because caves are damp and the cheese does not dry out, and caves maintain the same temperature all the year round. There was more, much more. He could and did discourse for hours on end about cheese. One learns a great deal of useful general knowledge on the road. Cheddar is in Somerset, and he knew of Bruton.

It was all perfectly companionable, and the rain ceased, and the cheese man took my mind off Finbarr. We trundled on until after day's end, then found stabling and adjoining straw mattresses in a drovers' hostel. We made our supper of bread from a bakehouse and hunks of his strong cheese. As a result I slept well.

Before I slept I gave in to the cheese man's desire. Why not? I too have desire. He was guileless, like a grown-up child. After our first sleep we talked for a while, and I told him my name – 'I am Agnes Peppin' – and that I had been a nun, or rather a novice, in Shaftesbury Abbey. That ignited him all over again. Then we fell asleep again until dawn.

I smelled of cheese that morning. My crotch and armpits reeked. I washed myself under the pump in the yard. I helped him to fit his oxen into the shafts, and off we went on our way.

Jacob put me down on a broad highway at a crossroads well outside the city of London itself, although there were people on the road, and coaches and carts and strings of horses going in both directions. We joined the road from a track from the south-west. I told Jacob I was making for Hay Hill, which is where Anne Cathcart has her establishment. Hay Hill meant nothing to me. It might as well have been on the moon. He halted the wagon and sat there with the reins drooping and his red-capped head also.

He asked me if I would change my mind and remain with him, and continue with him into the city, and be his companion in life. He had the cottage in Cheddar, he said, where he was born and raised. There was a pear tree, and a pond. And the cheeses and the caves. He had aunts and uncles and cousin who would welcome me.

'It will be a good life.'

He raised his handsome head and looked hopefully into my face.

Without hesitation I said no, I could not do that, and I thanked him. I did not as an excuse say that I was still the Bride of Christ because I might have laughed, and he might have been bewildered. I just said no.

He nodded, stayed a moment, nodded again, stayed some more, then helped me down from the wagon and handed me my bundle.

I think Jacob was a person who did not ask much of life, other than making his cheese and selling his cheese. I think he did not really expect me to go with him. It was a long shot. I hope by now he has found a woman to love him. He is worth loving.

'That,' he said, pointing with his switch, 'is the King's new deer park. It was always, before, the park of Hyde manor. It belonged to the monks at Westminster Abbey. Anyone could walk through there. I used to stop off and graze the oxen. When it happened, the same as to you ladies at Shaftesbury, the King took the park from the monks and stocked it with game and put that fence around the whole of it. But people still call it Hyde Park.'

'Last time,' he said, 'when I came this way, I saw the King and his gentlemen on their horses hunting with their hounds. I am sure it was the King.'

That was a big moment for him. A glimpse of the great world. I feel bad that I turned him off so abruptly. He was a decent man. Though truth to tell, I was much relieved when my bleeding appeared at the proper time. It would not have been convenient to bear the cheese man's brat. It would have been a boy, and he would have smelled of cheese.

'You need to take the right-hand turn here,' he said, 'down that lane, keeping the park always on your right. If you kept on and on that way you would get to Westminster and the river. I'll be keeping on the old highway eastwards, into the city. I could take you on further, you could maybe find Hay Hill that way more quickly but – I prefer to say farewell to you now.'

He had his pride.

'So we are not yet in London? This is not London?'

'No, but it is not altogether the countryside any more either. They are building along the sides of the roads all the way into the city. You'll want to turn off for Hay Hill before the next big crossing of the ways. It'll still be open fields to the north, with tracks up to farms. You'll need to ask.'

I walked on, with the park palings on my right. Every now and then I asked passers-by for Hay Hill, and always it was a little further, and a little further, and night was beginning to fall. When at last I identified the turning, the track was flat, not a hill at all, and I still did not know how to find Anne Cathcart's house.

I encountered a gentleman on horseback. I called out to him and he reined in his mare.

He looked blank. The name Cathcart meant nothing to him. I told him, recalling her letter to me, that it was perhaps a kind of lodging house, or place of entertainment?

'Aha! You'll be meaning Mistress Arundell's establishment.'

Mistress Arundell? What was the meaning of that? Maybe I had been misdirected. Maybe this was all a terrible mistake.

I could not miss it, he said.

'A long, low farm place on the left of the rising track just where it becomes steep, with flambeaux lit on each side of the entrance. Big timber doors with a wicket and a bell-pull.'

He gave me a quizzical look, doffed his hat and trotted off down the lane.

It was as he said. Ten minutes later I was in Anne's welcoming arms. That night I slept in what was to be my own chamber, a loft up a crooked wooden stair, under the thatch, with a window looking out on to farmland. There were birds and bats and other creatures in the thatch. They were active in the night but I never minded their scrabblings and scutterings. Room for us all. There was a door from the lobby at the foot of my stair to the back of the house, so that I could come and go without notice. This turned out to be a godsend.

8

HAY HILL

The noise and bustle of Anne's house came as a shock.

Her hall room was long and low-ceilinged, the floor flagged with stone. A dresser was piled high with pewter plates and wine cups, and rows of tankards on hooks. There were half a dozen long trestles with benches, and small tables for private encounters. Candlesticks stood in clusters on the trestles and tables. After dark the room was a cavern of flickering lights. It was not luxurious but it was peculiarly seductive. And there was a routine which was not hard to pick up. This place became my home from home, even before I met my Thomas.

The guests, or clients, or customers, or whatever they were, would begin to arrive immediately after daytime end. Many were regulars, greeting one another and settling into ongoing discussions which seemingly had no beginning and no end. The food was not elaborate. The speciality of the house was mutton pies. As the night advanced the trestles became overloaded with platters, fragments of pie crust, with tankards and goblets, with ale-jugs and wine-bottles. There were always more men than women. The women did not sit apart. They talked and laughed and argued with the men, and were free and open in the way they laid their hands upon a gentleman's sleeve, or on the nape of his neck, or on his thigh, as they sat wedged close together on the benches.

At first I recognised no one among the guests except Master Piers Perceval. There was no reason why he should remember me and he did not. He seemed to have a special position in the house, strutting about in a hostly manner. He was proprietorial in his attitude to Anne.

She had her eye on everything, chivvying the serving girls, sitting momentarily at this table or another, drawing some shy young man or woman into the conversation by making them laugh at something she said. Anne looked confident and comfortable. Anne was in her element.

This much I took in within twenty-four hours of my arrival. On my first morning the place looked different. Empty, quiet, waiting. I wandered around. Behind the hall room was the kitchen, where Anne's man Luke was chopping mutton into collops for the next batch of pies. He turned startlingly blue eyes on me for a moment and returned to his chopping. Stacks of wood stood against the walls to feed the fires in the two brick ovens. A servant was rinsing the trenchers and the drinking vessels at a pump in the back yard. Another was sweeping out the hall room.

Anne had a parlour of her own, into which no one ventured without an invitation. She beckoned me in. Two cushioned chairs, a heavy oak table on which stood ledgers and account books and a money box. Anne patted her waist to show me where she kept the key to the money box, beneath her gown. There were cupboards and presses, a chest and a pair of silver candlesticks. Beyond, a curtained arch opened into an alcove where stood her bed with a carved tester and red curtains.

She and I gazed upon one another in wonderment and laughed, remembering whence we came.

'The Abbess of Hay Hill, no less,' I said. 'But why do they call you Mistress Arundell?'

She grimaced.

'The person who leased this house before – and for the same purposes as I – was a Mistress Arundell. I do not know whether it was her true name. So from the beginning I called myself Mistress Arundell. It made for continuity. And I am happy to mortify Sir Thomas Arundell, if ever he was to learn who I really am ... Did you not know? Sir Thomas abused me in those last days at the Abbey. I was such a fool. This way I have a revenge. I like to imagine him teased by enquiries about his connection with this house.'

Rippling with laughter at her own malice, she looked well, contented and prosperous. In the course of that first morning I gathered – Anne says little directly – that Master Perceval facilitated the renovation of the establishment and maintained his support.

'I never even had to sell the diamond ring.'

In return he made certain assumptions and asserted certain rights. I was often to see him sneaking from the hall room into Anne's parlour and remaining there with her for some time.

I find Master Perceval unattractive. He is a slithery man with too-small hands. There were newts in the Bruton ponds which revolted me when I was a child. Newts have spotted bellies. It would not surprise me if Master Perceval did too.

'And his lady wife?'

Anne threw up her hands. 'She knows nothing about it, nothing at all. She thinks he goes out to political meetings or to his dining-clubs in the city taverns.'

'If she knew, she could destroy you.'

'Why should she ever know?'

I explored the rest of the place, and learned its customs and unspoken rules. Anne – or Master Perceval – had built on to this ancient farmhouse a large barn with stables, where carts too were kept, and fodder. Visiting gentlemen left their horses there under the care of blue-eyed Luke. Anne had her own horse, a bay gelding called Minstrel. Luke loved Minstrel and treated him like a prince. Gentlemen whose inclinations lay that way came under the care of

Luke as well, slipping out through the hall door and into the barn to lie with him in the hay.

There was another new-thatched wing on the opposite side, divided up into small chambers, each with a pallet bed piled with coverings of patterned silk and fine wool. The kind of stuffs that it is a pleasure to finger. There was a doorway from the hall room into this part of the house, through which a gentleman with a lady could pass for an hour's privacy. These transactions were not covert, but they were discreet. Money changed hands – from gentlemen's hands to Anne's – as they paid for their food and drink. It was a rule of the house that nothing said or done at Mistress Arundell's ever went any further than her hall door.

I have to say it was a very harmonious little society.

Anne and I came to an arrangement. She urged me to remain for as long as I wished – 'I am in want of a confidential female friend' – in return for some help in the kitchen and in serving, not as a menial but in the role of her deputy, sitting with the customers, keeping the mood light and tempers sweet. She herself could not always be overseeing everything.

'I am to be your Prioress, then.'

Anne was generous. She had grown stouter, and took from her closet an armful of light gowns which no longer fitted her – yellow, green, tawny, her favoured colours. They were better than anything I had, and I liked wearing them. I let my hair grow long. I enjoyed myself, by which I mean that I enjoyed the experience of being myself, and finding myself gracious and graceful and admired. This was new to me.

After a morning's tuition, I found I had a light hand with making the crust for the mutton pies, and this became a regular duty. The vagaries of the ovens were too hard for me to master, so Luke retained charge of the baking.

*

I can no longer tell how many summers and winters I spent in Sherborne with Eleanor, nor how many summers and winters I spent on Hay Hill with Anne. I kept no tally. I know I was still in Sherborne in the January when the King died. He had been the King for longer than Eleanor and I had been alive. It seemed to everyone in the town to be momentous, as if the world would never be the same again, and indeed it was not, although as a matter of fact nothing had been 'the same' for years. Certainly not for the monks and nuns. The new King, Edward, was only nine years old – about the age my Peterkin would have been.

I do not know how or where all that time has gone. I was at Hay Hill Farm for some years before I met Thomas, my Tom. I met him soon after I saw Dame Elizabeth Zouche for the last time.

I have been reading over all that I wrote before I left Shaftesbury Abbey and am dismayed. How green I was then. How little I understood about anything at all. I think that I am at least thirty years old now. Many women die at my age. Our Abbess lived on.

I guess it was in 1552 or 1553 that she sent to every one of us who had been in the Abbey in those last days, requiring us to attend her at Place Farm in Tisbury. She addressed her messages, not written in her own hand but signed by her, to the parish church of our home towns or villages. Mine had gone to Bruton, I presume, long after I left for the last time. Another undelivered letter shredded by vestry mice. I only knew about the general summons at all because Anne Cathcart received hers. Anne did not care to go.

There had been much respectful talk of Place Farm in the old days and I was curious to see it. I found a carrier to take me as far as Salisbury, and continued on foot. That was like my former life – the solitary walking, the unease about the direction, the barking dogs in the farms that I passed.

Place Farm was, as I expected, spacious, and outside the encircling wall a massive barn. I entered through the open gatehouse and a second, smaller gatehouse. There was no one about. I crossed the yard to what must be the dwelling-house, walked straight in, and found myself in a large hall of the old-fashioned kind. The rush mats were frayed and whiskery. The shutters were splintery, their edges ragged, darkened by damp. I climbed the stair, feeling like an intruder and, too suddenly, came upon the Abbess herself – only I must no longer think of her as the Abbess – seated in the farthest corner of a long upper room. The light was dim, the air stale and cold.

'Madam,' I said, 'I have come to see you, as you desired.'

She had aged greatly in appearance. She was shrunken. Her front hair had lost all trace of the Zouche blondeness, and was thin and dry. Her face was a mass of wrinkles. There was no dish of mushrooms in cream on her table, no white manchet bread. A stick was propped against the arm of her chair.

She peered in my direction.

'Are you one of my daughters in God? Which one of you is this? I have a list here somewhere of those who have come, and those who have not yet come.'

I said, 'I am Agnes Peppin, Madam.'

She seemed not to hear.

'Maybe they are all no longer living. Where is the list, where is it?' She fluttered her hand over a mess of papers on the table.

'Maybe it was too far for some of the sisters to come, Madam. Maybe some moved away from their home places and never received your message. Has Mother Catherine come? Has Mother Onion come? Perhaps she managed to get home to Ireland, over the sea.'

'The Prioress and the Infirmaress came. Agatha Cracknell and Alice Doble.'

Those names from the past.

'They were overfed and noisy,' said Dame Elizabeth, 'and thought no doubt to raise my spirits with their prattle. They came with a pack of yapping little dogs which soiled my floor and they came only in order to collect what I will give to each of you. Mother Onion has not come. Sister Catherine has not come. Nor Dame Philippa and Dame Joanna. And what happened to my bed-curtains? I demand – demand – that they be returned to me.'

She banged her fists on the table.

'I cannot say, Madam.'

I repressed the memory of the dolphin bed-curtains smouldering in the dirt.

'Sister Philippa and Sister Joanna have died, Madam. They were old already. They are in Heaven now.'

'It is well for them. I have heard that some of our oldest sisters, from the very day that they left the Abbey, lost their wits and became as children or animals. And yet up until then they had been in possession of all their faculties.'

'Perhaps, Madam, it was the Rule that preserved their minds. They were like climbing plants which collapse when their support fails. They will be in Heaven by now.'

'Would that I too were in Heaven. And when I go, this house and the farm and all its lands will belong to Sir Thomas Arundell, as I promised. He has already taken out of it everything that made it beautiful. I live in the shell of a house that was once everything to me. You never saw it in the old days. I have been a fool.'

'But perhaps, Madam, it is better to be here in the house you have known for so long, than...'

I could not frame an alternative. She had entreated Sir Thomas to let her retain Place Farm. I well remembered Sir Thomas negotiating the agreement. I had thought even at the time that it was a mixture of ruthlessness and sentiment on his part, characteristic of that unsatisfactory gentleman.

'Arundell is a spider, waiting. He put in a bailiff and he sends in his man of business twice a year to make sure the property is well maintained. Arundell has got Wardour Castle now, yet another of his rich pickings. He rides over to see me from there and tells me all his plans for this house, once I am gone.'

'But he has built himself a fine house in Shaftesbury, Madam.'

'He will not live there for long and he will never make his home here, either. Place Farm is for him a speculation. It will not answer. It is not a gentleman's residence, it is the home of the Abbess of Shaftesbury and when I die no one will ever be able breathe life into my Place Farm ... And which one are you? Did you say? Did I know you?'

'I think you knew us all, Madam.' I told her again:

'I am Agnes Peppin.'

I seemed, ever since I left Shaftesbury Abbey, to be continually telling my name. I began to think it might not be my name; it became strange to me from much repeating.

She sighed and coughed and held out a ringless hand, and I kissed it.

'Of course. Agnes. My Agnes. You are alive and you have come. I can see your shape but not your face. There is darkness where your face is. Move into the light and let me look at you, my child.'

I went to stand at the window.

'Not like that, with your back to the light. Useless. Come closer.'

I did so. She made no comment. Perhaps she still could not see my face.

'And Sister Onora?' she asked. 'Have you heard anything of Sister Onora?'

'The last I heard was that she had joined the gypsies and was telling fortunes and selling charms outside the cathedral at Exeter.'

This was true. Eleanor's Jack Chapman told us.

'Ah.'

'Do you remember, Madam, that one of those last nights Sister Onora saw the three nuns from Cannington flying away? The ones I called the Melancholies?'

Dame Elizabeth raised her head and turned her eyes upwards, smiling, ageless, transfigured.

'Of course she did! Of course she did!'

And the three Melancholies fly and again and for ever, arms outstretched like swimmers across the face of the moon on that night of no moon, their veils streaming behind them.

'Of course she did,' I said.

Dame Elizabeth lowered her head, a defeated old woman.

'I see with an inner eye. I find my garments and open and close my bags and boxes by touch. I can no longer read at all. I cannot write because I cannot see what I am writing. I sign my name, if it is pointed out to me where I should write it. I am dependent on others. I become ill-tempered. There is no one in whom I can trust. There are only servants now, and they are never here when I require them. I need assistance.'

'Your family, Madam?'

'I have no one of my own. My family do not know me.'

She grasped the stick propped against her chair and banged it on the floor, one, two, thee times.

'The worst thing that can happen to parents is the loss of a child. The worst thing that can happen to a child is the loss of parents. An unwanted child is a terrible thing.' She banged her stick again, one, two, three.

'Yes, Madam.'

I thought of Peterkin, who seemingly was doing well enough without me. People do manage to make their way in the world in spite of Dame Elizabeth's tragic simplicities.

She turned away from me, brooding on I know not what, and said no more about family, or her family. The mystery of her birth remains, to me at least, a mystery. Elizabeth Zouche, so patently a

Zouche and as Abbess of Shaftesbury the richest and most powerful woman in the kingdom, ends up unacknowledged and alone, her history unshared.

She turned back to me and told how Sister Isobel had remained with her, from when they first fled to Place Farm until her death the previous summer from a wasting illness. 'It is an irreplaceable loss.'

'I have always wished that I had known Sister Isobel better.'

'It would have been well for you had you known Sister Isobel better. But it is not too late for you to understand the something beyond everything, which she knew. I have missed you, Agnes. By the way, what happened to your black dog?'

'She was run over by a wagon.'

'Just as well. I could not endure having a dog around my feet now.'

At that instant I apprehended that Dame Elizabeth Zouche had it in mind to ask me to be to her what Sister Isobel had been, and to remain at Place Farm with her.

It was a possible path for me to take. In the space of a few seconds I foresaw how it would be. I would be her scribe and companion and nurse until she died. I would be fed and housed. I would be safe in this world, and my pathway to Heaven unobstructed.

It was not what I wanted. I said nothing. The Abbess attended closely to my silence. I would say, she attended humbly to my silence, were that not presumptuous on my part.

The silence between us went on and on. Finally she said, 'Very well.'

Then, gesturing towards an oak chest against the wall:

'Open it.'

I lifted the lid and thought at first the chest was empty. But at the bottom lay some round dark objects. Dead mice? They were small leather bags.

'Take one of the bags,' she said, turning her head away, overcome by a fit of coughing, covering her mouth with a rag.

I stretched down my arm to take one up, and stood before her again. She said that the money inside the bags was her personal legacy to each one of us who came to her. 'Each bag contains the same amount.'

That amount was generous enough to make all the difference to me. I could go on my way and I could pay my way.

'You are one that never did consent,' said Dame Elizabeth.

'Consent, Madam? To the Rule, do you mean? I do believe that I did.'

'Not just to the Rule. That is not so hard. You did not give your soul's consent to what lies beyond the Rule. Not like Sister Isobel.'

'I was young, Madam. I did not understand in those days that such a consent was necessary. Nor did I understand to what one might consent.'

'And now?'

'I was never fitted for the religious life. I want to be outside, not inside. I suppose I have wanted the world.'

'I knew the world. But the position as Abbess is – difficult. And much good the world has done to me. I failed.'

'It was not you that failed, Madam. It was the times...'

'Shaftesbury Abbey. That great and ancient – thing. Arundell made me a little chapel here. It is the only kind act he has made, though it is cold in there. I spend much time in the chapel, repenting my failure. I should have fought harder. Longer. I should have saved the Abbey. All over, all gone. All gone. All gone.'

I kissed her hand. As I left her, I heard her saying to herself, 'I am so tired.'

That was the last thing I ever heard her say. It was also the first thing I ever heard her say, the night I first set eyes upon her, in her prime, when she returned from Place Farm wearing her fur-lined cloak, supported by solicitous sisters. Who now were her attendants?

I opened a door out of the hall into a passage and called out. No one came. I opened another and there was a great kitchen, with a wide fireplace set in the wall, littered with cold wood-ash. An elderly woman stood at a window scouring a pot. I greeted her uncertainly and explained my presence.

'Is it you, if I may ask, who cares for Dame Elizabeth now?'

'You could say that. I make her soup, I empty her slops, I wash her linen. She has not long to go now.'

The woman turned back to her pot.

I breathed the fresh air on the track outside Place Farm with relief. Only then did I realise that Dame Elizabeth never asked me about the bones of St Edward the Martyr, our holy relics, entrusted to my care. Perhaps she had forgotten all about them.

I think that she cannot not have lived much longer, although I never heard any report of her death and do not know where she is buried. That is shameful, shameful. I pray for her soul.

London, for me, spells Thomas Wyatt, my love, my Tom, the son of the poet-statesman whom Sir Thomas Arundell told us about in the days when I knew nothing and no one.

I heard the poet's son spoken of long before I met him. It was shortly after a visit to Hay Hill from someone from my Shaftesbury past, and from Anne's. When I came into the room that particular evening to make myself pleasant and to see to the needs of the customers, a gentleman at Master Piers Perceval's crowded table was playing country airs on a lute. He was long-haired, in a green suit with a lace collar. My heart jumped. It was Father Robert Parker.

I squeezed myself in on the bench at his side. For once I did not have to say my name. He put down his instrument, refilled his wine cup and mine, picked up a bottle, and we removed ourselves to one of the small tables. He sat with his hands supporting his face, and we talked. He looked older, naturally. But he was still a lithe and lovely man. He was the same and not the same. He told me he had, as he planned, taken a position in Salisbury Cathedral but had not stayed.

'Once a priest, always a priest,' I said.

'Yes, but...'

He was now, he said, a companion to gentlemen and ladies who required just that – a companion.

'The upper classes must have people always around them, as if they feared they might cease to exist if their every moment were not witnessed by admiring inferiors. The inferiors must not be too inferior or their witness and their admiration would not be worth having.'

We laughed together over the wine. I recognised the truth of what he said.

So Robert provides music, Latin tuition for children, and his social presence when needed, in return for hospitality in great houses for a month or two in the country in the summer and in London in the winter. I have no doubt he provides more intimate services too, to gentlemen or to ladies or both, but he did not say and I did not enquire. Sometimes he is required to say a Mass in a private chapel, though private Masses are strictly speaking disallowed now.

'For the moment, I am living with the Percevals. Lady Agnes Perceval has time on her hands and likes to have conversation and company.'

'Is that kind of life enough for you?' I asked. 'Will it do?'

He shrugged.

'The alternatives are drearier.'

'Are there butterflies?'

'Sometimes there are.'

We were wonderfully comfortable together because we remembered the same things – and because of our once-only coupling, if he recalled that. He was self-absorbed and probably always had been. He asked me nothing about myself, nor why I was where I was. I wanted to tell him about my visit to Dame Elizabeth Zouche, and about Dorothy Clausey and her new life, but there was no opportunity. He told me that he had seen Eleanor Wilmer.

'How? Where?'

'Late one night, outside The Cock in Fleet Street. I had been drinking with Master Perceval. There she was. She must have seen me going in.'

'She always wanted you, do you remember? Maybe she had been following you?'

'How would I know? She accosted me, I thought she was a whore. All she wanted was to know where you were.'

'What did you say?'

He shrugged.

'I told her what I knew which was not much.'

Then they were peremptorily calling him back to the big table, wanting more music. He jumped to his feet, kissed my hand and left me.

I was glad to have met him again. I tried to put the Eleanor story out of my mind. Poor dear dreadful Eleanor.

Anne remained in her parlour for most of that evening, but she emerged to greet Master Perceval before he and his party left and I noted that she exchanged friendly words with Robert Parker. Even if he had not recognised her, he would have known from Piers Perceval precisely who 'Mistress Arundell' was. I did not at the time realise how dangerous this could be for Anne.

The gentlemen who frequented Hay Hill talked about money, horses, women, land and property, faction, party and politics – not necessarily in that order. They brought in printed papers to share and discuss, and those with friends at Court pulled from their pockets private letters and read them aloud. Those in high positions were more circumspect, and every word that dropped from their narrow lips was received with the attention that one might accord to Holy Gospel.

The floor was scattered, after the pre-dawn departures, with discarded papers. Anne and I both had a curiosity about the affairs of the great world and it was good for business if we were sufficiently well-informed to engage intelligently with the customers. That much was expected of 'Mistress Arundell' and of myself. So we knew immediately of the death of young King Edward. Some, not the ones with inside knowledge, swore he had been poisoned. More likely, it was a disease of the lungs. He was only fifteen.

The great question was: Who will succeed Edward? Rightfully, his elder half-sister, the Princess Mary. But she is half-Spanish and a Catholic, 'the Pope's pawn', as Master Perceval said. Edward had named as his successor the young Lady Jane Grey, some sort of a cousin and newly married to a son of his Chief Minister, the Duke of Northumberland.

'Brazen coercion of the poor dying lad on the part of the noble Duke,' according to Master Perceval. 'There will be trouble. Bloodshed. You mark my words.'

There was silence at the table.

The talk picked up. That was when I first heard the name of Sir Thomas Wyatt spoken at Hay Hill. He was said to be raising a militia in Kent. But in whose interest? The Princess Mary's, or the Lady Jane's?

'Sir Thomas Wyatt is dead,' I said.

A dozen pairs of eyes turned towards me, swivelling and bloodshot on account of much drink taken.

'No, no, you silly little woman. This is the son.'

Keep up, Agnes. The slurred voices multiplied, vying in counterpoint to know better than the next man.

Young Thomas Wyatt was unpredictable, irresponsible. He was arrested for drunken street rioting and served time in the Tower.

As a mere boy he was a regular at this very house when it belonged to the previous Mistress Arundell, and she spoke up for him at his trial. He was a good lad, she told the court. He was led astray.

'Pity that poor little wife of his, down in the country. The only talents Tom Wyatt has are for begetting children and soldiering.'

He hardly minded whom he fought for. He was with an English regiment serving the King of Spain, though he disliked the Spanish. He went with a volunteer brigade to France. He was commander of the fortress in Boulogne in the cause of England and was knighted for his services.

'A poor follower but a good leader. A soldier to the soles of his boots, he can't handle peace. He's bound to make some rogue intervention now, God knows on which side. He needs watching.'

'But keep your distance, Mistress Agnes,' said Master Perceval. 'Thomas Wyatt is bad news.'

And he winked, and refilled my wine cup.

No wonder I was curious.

I first saw him when he came in with a band of armed followers. Anne did not allow pikes and muskets in her house. They were carried out to the barn. He ordered wine and took command of a long table.

I was serving that evening, hot and bothered. I was sweating, and my thin gown was clinging to me. I was barely respectable. I was fetching food and drink for the visitors from the kitchen, a perfect Martha.

He smiled but his eyes raked the room warily. His dark hair was cut short. He was clean-shaven. He wore a black tunic with no collar or lace, from which his neck rose like the trunk of a tree, sun-browned and muscular. When I brought more bottles to his table he held a candle up to my face and turned his back on the company.

'You are no London-born woman.'

'How would you know?'

'Your skin is fresh. You have not grown sallow and you are clean.'
He held the candle closer, lowering it to shed light on my body.
'You are not a maid. You are a woman. Where are you from?'

'I was born in Bruton, but am come lately from Sherborne.'

'My father is buried at Sherborne.'

'I know, sir, I saw his coffin taken into the Abbey for the funeral
Mass.'

'I was there. We should have met then.'

'I hardly think so, sir. I was one of a crowd.'

'You are a country mouse.'

'I am no mouse.'

'What is your name?'

So I told him. Yet again, yet again, I said my name.

'I am Agnes Peppin.'

I folded my arms across my breasts to deflect his gaze and told
him how Mistress Arundell and I had been in Shaftesbury Abbey
together. He laughed at that, throwing his head back, exposing that
long, strong throat. He asked me to sit with him, gesturing to his
companions to make room.

He said his father wrote a ballad about the country mouse and
the town mouse.

'He made me and my sister learn it by heart, as children, on
one of his rare visits to us at Allington.'

I wanted to know about Allington but he did not tell me, not
then.

The country mouse, he said, who knows well how to feed and
look after herself in her native fields, goes to the city to be with
her sister, 'to live a lady while her life doth last'.

'It is an old fable. The point was that men "seek the best and
find the worst by error as they stray", by abandoning everything
they know and understand.'

'My mother would agree with that.'

'Agnes — you did say Agnes? — I do not need to know about your mother right now, please listen. When the awful cat appears from beneath a stool, and think how terrible a cat must look to a mouse, with its "two steaming eyes in a round head with sharp ears" in my father's poem, the town mouse runs away fast and knows just where to hide. The country mouse has no notion of what to do. She just wishes she were at home. She makes for the door, slips, and is caught by the cat.'

'Did the cat kill the country mouse?'

'The poem does not say. I think Mistress Arundell is your town-mouse sister. She will always be able to look after herself. And maybe, maybe, I might look after you. For a little while, anyway. To speak honestly, I can barely look after myself.'

'I know one of your father's verses. I have a copy of it. In my chamber upstairs. The one that begins, "They flee from me that one time did me seek".'

His eyes widened. He was amazed.

'How is that possible? Shall we go and look at it? Shall we go upstairs?'

I told him how I came to have it, and he was amazed again, and we went upstairs, and so it began.

I am wearing the cloak as I write. It was the first thing he gave to me. He had it made up by the seamstress who makes clothes for his lady wife and his little daughters. It is shabby now, the rich blue colour faded and stained, the fur rubbed away to pale skin at the edge of the hood. I cannot throw it out. I should like to be buried in it.

When he first brought it up to me in my chamber in the Hay Hill house, and unwrapped it by the light of the candle, he seemed as excited as a child.

'Feel the softness of the wool. And what a colour! This cloth comes from Spain.'

He picked at the hem, breaking a few stitches, to show me the layer of fine whitish wool beneath the grey fur lining.

'It is warm enough for you to wear outside in the cold weather and light enough for you to wear indoors too.'

We turned it over and over, stroking its rich softness and each other's hands.

I put the cloak on and paraded about my chamber, scarcely more than seven steps one way and seven steps the other, looking at him over my shoulder. Then he took it from me and put it aside, and laid me on the bed. That was the night that he raised his head and looked up into my eyes and said:

'Pleasure! Pleasure! Pleasure!'

In that husky love-laden voice of his.

Later he gave me five shifts, cut from linen so fine that to wear one felt like having warm air between my skin and my outer garments. Those shifts have long gone. As the stuff of each one deteriorated beyond mending, I tore it into strips and used it to wipe up household messes. When they were soiled beyond further use I threw the strips on the fire.

In the times that we had together we talked and talked, leaning out of my unshuttered window, our elbows pressed together on the sill, looking out into the night.

He talked about Thomas Cromwell, now a black legend, whom I thought was the King's Chief Minister. That was not all he was, said Thomas. He held multiple offices. I don't now remember them all, but he was an adviser to the great Cardinal. And then Lord Privy Seal, Master of the Rolls, Principal Secretary, Chancellor of the Exchequer...

'Only three months before his arrest the King made him Earl of Essex and Great Lord Chamberlain. He could not have risen higher nor fallen further or more rapidly.'

'So why did he fall?'

Thomas shrugged. 'It is in the past now. He had enemies. The Duke of Norfolk, and then the fiasco of the marriage to the German. They say the King came to regret Cromwell's disgrace and execution. My father was there on that day, not to crow but out of respect. They were both risk-takers. Me too.'

The little tailor who came to Sherborne had got it mostly right.

I ventured to say, 'I have heard that Cromwell addressed personal words to certain friends from the scaffold.'

'You have heard much, and correctly. My father was one of those to whom he spoke. I do not know what Cromwell said to him, but they tell me that my father wept.'

He talked to me about his family, which he said was full of irregularities – like all families in my experience, as I pertly said to him.

Yet his life was so different from mine that it seems a miracle that we could know and love each other. There is the old castle in Kent, at Allington. Tom was born there, as was his father. Allington was, he said, 'a beautiful, intractable, terrible old place'.

'The summer before he died my father put in a long gallery, new panelling, a new kitchen, fireplaces. Everything that is modish, he just had to be part of the great rebuilding.'

This was not for his wife's benefit. Thomas's parents separated early. Thomas and his sister rarely saw their father, who accused the mother of adultery – with King Henry, no less:

'The King certainly had a soft spot for her.'

'What happened to her?'

'My mother has always been looked after. Not by my father, he gave her not a penny, but by her brother. And others. She has remarried, and well.'

When Tom told me his father grew up as a child with Anne Boleyn and her brother George, because they were cousins and because Allington was close to the Boleyns' place, I ceased my questions and interruptions. No more pert comments from me. I know that Peppins and Wyatts are the same in the sight of God, but nevertheless ... The King and Anne Boleyn came to dinner at Allington. Thomas's Aunt Margaret was one of Anne Boleyn's ladies, and accompanied her to the scaffold.

What is more, my Thomas saw the late King Henry naked.

That is because when he was fifteen he spent time at Court as an Esquire to the Body. The Body in question was the King's.

'I was a wild boy and my father arranged it, because he was anxious about me. In some ways he was a good father. He wrote me long letters about how to conduct myself, who was important and who was not, and how the Court worked. I cannot for the life of me say where those letters are now.'

There were, he said, half a dozen Esquires to the Body, well-born youths like himself who, for a few weeks at a time, in turn, helped the King to put on his underclothes in the morning and to take them off at night. Other young men helped him off and on with his outer garments. The topmost office was that of the Groom of the Stool who oversaw His Majesty's excremental functions and the washing of his body, behind closed doors.

'I have dealt with a lot of excrement in my time and no one ever suggested it was the topmost office.'

'Ah, but a King's excrement is divine.' He laughed. 'A King is never alone and never does anything for or by himself. That is what it is to be a King. Or a Queen.'

I could not restrain myself.

'What in God's name was all this like?'

The King was not then, Thomas said, as fleshy as he later became. He was a fine man.

'He liked to have a musician playing an instrument in his

chamber. He liked to sing. He quizzed me about which Court ladies I fancied. And sometimes he was in a black humour. He could not bear to be contradicted.'

What else?

'His face was ruddy but his skin under his garments was chalky white. His body hair was sandy-coloured. He had a strong personal odour. His private closet stank like a badger's sett.'

At home at Allington there was in his boyhood often no mother, and a mostly absent father, but there was always Elizabeth Darrell.

'My father loved many women, but Elizabeth Darrell saw them all off. She gave birth to three sons at Allington and the two elder ones bore the Wyatt name. The youngest was known as Darrell. Lovely boys, as dear to me as full brothers, and maybe one or two of them are my father's.'

He looked at me sideways. I held my tongue. He proceeded.

His father's mistress was eight years older than Thomas. She and he liked one another too well.

'At the time when I was coming and going from Court, she took me into her bed. It is possible that my two youngest half-brothers are my own sons. No one ever referred to this, it was not spoken of. But I am sure it is why my father made me marry once I was sixteen.'

'How could your father make you marry?'

'He was a hard man. Not what you imagine a poet or statesman to be like. He was violent, he had killed a man. He was not someone who could be crossed. He over-persuaded me, shall we say, into marrying. He himself had married at seventeen. What could I do? Though she was, she is, very sweet. My Jane. Would you like to hazard a guess at how many children I have sired with her?'

'Five?'

'Ten. Over fifteen years or so. I only have to breathe upon Jane for her to be in pup. I come and go, and am often away for months on end. I have to admit that I become confused over the children's names and ages. Though the newest little one has wormed his way into my heart.'

So be it. There was no point in my being jealous. I had what I had with Thomas and it was, to start with, enough.

On my own, I thought about that cousinage of landed and ennobled families. Thomas is a spoke in a wheel spinning above the rest of us, spanning every shire, connecting down the generations through bloodline or marriage, through inherited titles and property, through privilege and influence, with the Court at the hub. New men may rise and rise, and through advantageous marriage or high office join the gyre, but even a Thomas Cromwell is crushed by the wheel in the end. There are feuds and enmities, wheels within the wheel. There is so much to gain and so much to lose. The cousinage fixes places and positions for its kith and kin. Anyone Thomas meets at Court, or in great houses in the country, knows who he is and where he fits in on the wheel. From his earliest youth he knew who they all were, too, and their fathers, and the names of their home places and estates.

In that last respect, much like Bruton. I speak of 'the great world', but with rather less awe since one of Thomas's toenails, on the great toe of the right foot, curled inwards into the flesh and caused him pain. He could hardly get his boot on. I crushed herbs, mixed the green mash into lard, applied the paste to the toe and wrapped it. He had let his toenails grow too long. Even a Wyatt must pare his toenails.

When his father died, Thomas looked after Elizabeth Darrell. He could afford to. He sold some Allington lands to the King for four thousand pounds, which went to her, and made over to her other

Wyatt properties. She is presently living at Tintinhull in my own county of Somerset, and she has married.

Thomas let drop that his own mother's new husband, Edward Warner, made his fortune by buying and selling former monastic houses. I had a flare-up of black rage against the raptors, the well-connected land-grabbers, the parasites, the opportunists. I did not feel angry with Thomas Wyatt. I was enamoured, obsessed.

I told him about my own life, partially and rapidly, not wishing to weary him with what must seem petty beyond belief. Yet he listened, and asked questions. Often he laughed. He found my life a comedy. He found Eleanor Wilmer very comical.

I told him about the butcher's shop, and learning to read, and meeting John Leland, and Peter Mompesson and the baby. I told him about my emerald dolphin, why I had it and how I lost it. I did not say much about Shaftesbury Abbey – not the devotional aspect – but I told him about Dorothy Clausey and who she was, and about Father Robert Parker, and what happened to Father Pomfret, and about my difficulties with Master Tregonwell. I told him about the Abbess and about Sir Thomas Arundell who read us the poem by Thomas's father.

'And when you all had to leave? Was that really so very terrible?'

Thomas would never grasp what it was like. I just said, 'Yes, it was very terrible.'

I told him about my peregrinations since then, and the places I saw and the people I met and left, and how I came to be living on Hay Hill.

He took my chin in his hand, turned my face to the moonlight, kissed me and said:

'You are picaresque.'

I did not know what that meant.

'In Spain they tell stories about a kind of rogue they call a *pícaro*. He is charming and sharp-witted and makes his way by attaching himself profitably to a person in a high position, and getting the better of his master, making a fool of him. He then moves on to batten on someone else. There is no conclusion, just episodes, one thing after another, with no moral – and no morals, either.'

I was cast down. Robert Parker maybe, but surely not me.

'You are picaresque, Agnes, but you are honest. With you, it is more a matter of...'

'Of just one thing after another?'

We left it at that and went to bed. Just one thing after another.

We were together for less than a year. When he paid secret visits to me at Hay Hill he came with an armed guard, a man from his home county of Kent. His name was Finch. He was short with a round face like a child's although he must have been twenty-five years old at least. Finch would remain on duty at the foot of my stairs until Thomas was ready to leave. I thought nothing of it. I grossly underestimated Thomas's perilous involvement in the kingdom's affairs.

He did attempt to explain the issues to me. Lady Jane Grey was a Protestant and a clever and well-educated young lady, a distant cousin to poor King Edward and his half-sisters, the Princesses Mary and Elizabeth. As a child Lady Jane lived with Edward's uncle Thomas Seymour, who married King Henry's widow, his sixth and last wife, Catherine Parr.

Princess Elizabeth was cared for by this Seymour couple as well, because her mother Anne Boleyn was executed when she was only two years old. My Thomas told me that Thomas Seymour, old enough to be Elizabeth's grandfather, treated the little girl as a love-toy.

I think that is right. It still makes my mind reel. The nearer you get to the hub of the wheel, the more convoluted and toxic are the relationships. And all these people, ready now to slaughter one another, have been on familial terms since they were children. Some of them still *are* children.

Keep up, Agnes.

9

THE GREAT WORLD

I need to piece together the year 1553, the year in which Thomas Wyatt and I were together. If I do not record it I will forget, and even now I will make mistakes.

Lady Jane Grey was married that May to the son of the Duke of Northumberland, the most powerful man in the kingdom according to Thomas and, reluctantly, proclaimed Queen in July by her father-in-law and his cronies.

She was Queen for only ten days. The government changed sides and proclaimed the Princess Mary as Queen. I forget what caused them to change their minds about Lady Jane. It could be they mistrusted her ambitious father-in-law.

Princess Mary passionately wished to be Queen. In August she rode into London with an armed force to the applause of the common people who poured out on to the streets to see the parade. Her young half-sister the Princess Elizabeth rode at her side. A couple of weeks later Lady Jane's father-in-law, no longer the most powerful man in the kingdom, was executed for treason.

At the beginning of October Mary was crowned in Westminster Abbey. Protestants were out, and adherents to the Old Religion were in. The ageing Duke of Norfolk was released from imprisonment. Lady Jane Grey was sent to the Tower, charged with high treason.

That never seemed just to me. Lady Jane Grey never wanted to be Queen and she was not yet seventeen years old.

*

Thomas favoured Queen Mary because she is the next in line, although she is not ideal. She had a wretched girlhood, he said, kept away from her mother, King Henry's first Queen. She has a troubled and a troublesome temperament. Her female cycles are known to be disordered. Her father the late King tried without success to find a husband for her. She is in her late thirties – and still unmarried.

If her half-sister Elizabeth were to marry and have a son, that son would be the rightful heir to the throne because males take priority over females.

'I do not know the Princess Elizabeth, but she is young, and cleverer and more sprightly than Queen Mary. She is a Protestant as King Edward was. Her bloodline would make for better continuity. I really do not know what to think.'

He did know what to think when it became known that a marriage was planned between Queen Mary and Prince Philip of Spain. Philip was the son of the King of Spain, and it was the King of Spain who proposed the match. Few English people liked this idea. England should never submit to being a dependency of Spain and the Holy Roman Empire. England's sovereignty would be compromised. Everything would be turned upside down all over again. The Old Religion and its rites and practices would be brought back. That would of course be a comfort to many.

Maybe to me? I did not know. In Spain, Thomas said, non-Catholics were persecuted, tortured and burned alive.

'Not that there are many Protestants in Spain. It is a matter of Jews and Mohammedans.'

I understood, and it was like a shock of cold water that Christianity was just one religion among others. This was a door opening on a void.

'Across the sea, you mean? They have a different God?'

'It's the same God, but they slaughter each other for the small differences. And in India, in Africa, they have many gods and not our God at all. And yes, across the sea, of course.'

'I have never seen the sea. Tell me about the sea.'

He bade me recall how it was when one stood on a high place and looked over to where the land stopped and the sky began. I pictured to myself the view over the Abbey Park at Shaftesbury, and the line of forest far away.

'Now imagine if there were nothing but water up to the line where the sky begins, not just in front of you but all around you, with no land in sight in any direction.'

Seamen, he said, have a name for that line where the sea meets the sky — something like 'orisoun', a French-Latin word, he said. There was, he said, great delight in being at sea:

'The blue-green of the ocean and a lively breeze on a fine day. The millions of stars above you in the night. On my last voyage from Spain I lay on the deck and knew myself to be swinging between the ultimate of tranquillity and the ultimate of mortal danger.'

For there you were, he said, cooped up for months with your companions in a fragile oaken vessel, at the mercy of the winds. And there were storms, and the ship battered by waves as high as castles. Or there was no wind at all and the ship drifted, and men fell sick or lost their wits or died of thirst.

'Always we are waiting for the boy in the crow's nest at the top of the mast to shout out that he sees land, pointing his finger and hallooing, and the crew running to the side hoping to see what he sees. You can smell land from many sea-miles away. But you are never safe. There are underwater rocks as you near the land which can pierce the hull and send you down to death.'

I never heard him so eloquent.

'The sea is not like a river or a lake. The sea is a salt-water world – full of strange creatures and tormented by whirlpools and currents to drag a vessel off course.'

I want to see the sea.

If the Spanish marriage were to go ahead, there could be torturings and burnings of fellow-Christians, Protestants, here in England. 'Quite right too,' said some. 'Bring back the old values.' As the evenings drew in, the night-time talk at Hay Hill became confrontational.

'Scaremongering apart, it is a simple question of patriotism,' said Thomas privately to me. 'This marriage is an insult. Why cannot Queen Mary marry a decent Englishman?'

Thomas began conspiring with others who were already determined to stop at any cost, by force, the Spanish marriage. Lady Jane Grey's father the Duke of Suffolk, and Edmund Warner, Thomas's step-father, were among them.

If Queen Mary were not to marry Prince Philip of Spain there had to be another candidate.

'Edward Courtenay fits the bill,' said Thomas, 'he is Earl of Devon.'

'A decent Englishman, then?'

'He is a nonentity, a shallow popinjay. A more forceful man might have ideas of his own. All that Courtenay will be required to do is marry the Queen and if possible impregnate her, and please God he is capable of that.'

By November he was meeting regularly with his fellow-conspirators. I never saw Thomas in the light of day from then on. He was so occupied that he could only come through the back door and up the stair to my chamber after dark. Though we did not need light when we were together. He was excited, like a boy included in the plots and plans of bigger boys. The

French too wanted to curb the power of Spain, and Tom was in personal contact with the French ambassador who wrote most flatteringly, promising French equipment, troops, perhaps even an invasion.

At some point the purpose of it all escalated from stopping the Spanish marriage to deposing the Queen altogether. I suspect half the conspirators had no very clear idea of what they were doing, or why. They plunged on regardless and made a date for the armed rebellion. It was to take place on March 18 of the following year.

It did not happen like that at all. It happened much faster. There was far too much gossip, far too many people knew about it, and Edward Courtney was useless. His attempts to raise a force in Devon were half-hearted. He never even left London to drum up support, whingeing about the difficulties of travelling down to Devon in the bad weather. Most other leaders – distinguished gentlemen all – failed to muster much support in their own counties either, and with the plot becoming public knowledge, some were arrested.

So Thomas, a latecomer to the conspiracy, by force of circumstances found himself its leader. This terrified me.

'Drop it,' I said, as if he were a dog. 'Please drop it. This cannot succeed and you will come to harm.'

He would not drop it, not even after the government, desperate to avoid armed confrontation, promised pardons to all rebel militiamen who departed peacefully to their homes within twenty-four hours.

Thomas was exactly where he wanted to be, in the eye of the storm.

'You may not see me for a while,' he said, in the middle of the January of 1554.

*

I followed events by listening with all my ears to the gentlemen who came to Hay Hill. I dreaded being called away for some domestic purpose and missing something. There was little secrecy. Everyone seemed to know something.

Thomas apparently rode off to Allington after he left me to see his family and prepare his Kentish militia for action. He had a proclamation read out calling for all men to join up and march on London with him to unseat the Popish Queen. He mustered about one thousand five hundred, and marched them northwards towards the capital. He arranged for a store of arms and ordnance to be waiting for him and support was promised from within the city itself.

But the omens were not good. The contingent from the West Country never arrived. They never even set off. His letters were intercepted and the French ambassador's involvement was discovered. French support was hastily withdrawn. Thomas chose not to reveal this to his followers.

Next night we had better news. Better for me, that is, because there were many at Hay Hill who thought that Thomas Wyatt was wrong-headed. The Duke of Norfolk with a gaggle of Londoners attacked Thomas and his rebels on their way through Kent – and most of the Duke's followers deserted and came over to Thomas's side.

'The Duke has run away!' said our informant, 'and left behind his guns and his treasure and his baggage. It's good luck for Wyatt. He must press on now into London.'

But he didn't. It was a fatal mistake. He waited for a couple of days, expecting at any moment the arrival of reinforcements from the Midlands, under Lady Jane Grey's father. They never arrived, and those few days gave time for the Queen's government to make their preparations.

All this happened within just one week of his leaving Allington. He said to me, on that last visit before the rebellion:

'I may never see my old grey castle again.'

The next thing we heard was that he was leading his army into London through Southwark.

I could not forbear to ask: 'What is Southwark?'

The Hay Hill gentlemen told me that Southwark – they call it the Borough – is on the south bank of the Thames, over London Bridge, and outside the city's jurisdiction.

'Southwark is a naughty place, Mistress Agnes.'

Southwark means bear-baiting, and scurrilous theatricals, and Winchester Geese. The ladies laughed behind their hands. Winchester Geese are loose women.

'Not many of us here who haven't been over to Southwark. But now Wyatt cannot get away from there. Everyone tells him he can't cross the river. No one can. It is most inconvenient for the market-traders.'

The Queen's men had broken up a span of London Bridge to make it impossible for the rebels and all their ordnance and equipment to enter the city.

'Shall I tell you what Wyatt did then? I'll need another cup of wine first, Miss Agnes.'

It was like the little tailor in Sherborne all over again. If the speaker is a customer of the little tailor, this tale will soon be known all over the country.

'Well, friends, Sir Thomas Wyatt would not believe the crossing was impossible. Late that night he climbed up all alone on to the parapet of the gatehouse of the bridge, jumped down on to the roof, forced open a window, crept down a stair and ended up in the lodge where the gatekeeper and his family were sitting round their fire. Imagine their terror! He swore the family to silence if they valued their lives and walked out onto the bridge.'

It was as he was told. A complete span had been knocked down, and guns at the further end were trained on the space. Thomas went back by the same way he had come. This exploit was thought to be highly comical and probably untrue:

'A typical Wyatt story.'

Typical indeed. It sounds very like Thomas to me. I picture him climbing in like a burglar and erupting into the warm room, a devilish apparition. But so dangerous, he could have fallen to his death in the space where the bridge was broken.

In the morning, cannons from the Tower of London bombarded the Southwark shore.

'Men are deserting him, melting away into the dark. He had better leave Southwark, and fast. There's a government bounty — land to the value of a hundred pounds a year — for the capture of Sir Thomas Wyatt.'

Anyone but Thomas would have abandoned the rebellion. He did not. He retreated with his remaining men, straggling westwards upriver, still on the south bank, in driving rain. It was raining steadily on Hay Hill too. I left the company and stood at the door and thought how cold he must be, how wet and hungry. The roads everywhere were deep in mud. I went back into the warm.

Next day, before dark, Finch arrived, bursting into the house out of the rain, his leather coat black with dirt, his childish face crumpled. There were no clients at that hour. He was well known in the house as Sir Thomas Wyatt's man. I stood by, as tense as a wire, while he was plied with food and drink and pestered by Anne Cathcart for the latest news. Sir Thomas, he said, had determined to enter the city though Ludgate. He hoped on the way to capture Queen Mary herself, who was said to be lodged at St James's Palace.

It was only when Finch stepped outside to relieve himself and to see to his mare that I managed to snatch a private word. We stood under the eaves of the barn.

'How is Sir Thomas?' I asked. Such a light, slight question. I did not know what else to say.

'Madam, he is superb. He admits no talk of defeat. But it is hard. Very hard. We managed to cross the river a good many miles upstream. Then the carts carrying the guns overturned or became stuck in the mud. The men dragging them are exhausted. Many of them just abandoned us and peeled off. They are all volunteers, they did not bargain for this.'

Thomas I know was on horseback, but nevertheless I cannot bear to think of him on that nightmare journey.

He still did not give up. I could not see Finch's face in the darkness but his voice grew shakier.

'We lost guns when they fell off carts into ditches and hours were wasted striving in vain to haul them out. Government spies followed us and galloped back to the city to report what they saw.'

Even from the foot of Hay Hill, he said, you can hear the roll of drums. All fighting men in London are summoned to assemble overnight around Charing Cross. There might be as many as ten thousand. His voice shook.

'It does not look good, Madam. But my master will not be told.'

'How many men does he still have with him?'

'He says, three thousand. But I think there will not be more than one tenth of that by morning. He is leading them up here, to the ridge of the hill, to rest up until dawn. He charges me to say, Madam, that he will come to you if he is able.'

Thomas came to me in my chamber in the small hours of that night. It was black dark and still pouring with rain. I could make out by touch that he was wearing a velvet coat – I could not tell the colour – with stiff lace, and all soaked through. Under it he was wearing chain mail, so that I could not hold him close.

'Mind your feet and ankles,' he said. 'My spurs are knife-sharp.'

His troops and ordnance, he said, were up at the top of the hill.

He was tense, elated, overtired but with no desire for sleep, he was in his element. Finch, he said, would keep me informed. I might trust in Finch, he was a good Kentish fellow.

He kissed me and then he was gone, clattering down my stair, sideways because of the spurs, out of the back door and away up the hill to his troops. We had not heard their approach earlier because they came up from the other side.

That was the last time I saw Thomas Wyatt before I saw him die.

The capture of Queen Mary was a fantasy, it never happened. Of course it did not. There was something magnificently un-realistic about my Thomas. Puerile, his detractors said. If he had succeeded, he would have been hailed as a hero. To my mind, he was a hero.

Thomas and his troops, further depleted after skirmishes coming down Hay Hill, reached Charing Cross next morning and were attacked head-on by the Queen's cavalry. Incredibly, they broke through. Desperation makes men savage. After noon Thomas and his officers, with followers on foot struggling with the weaponry and damaged gun-carts, were riding up the Strand and along Fleet Street to Ludgate. The gate was closed and barred against them.

They told me that Sir Thomas Wyatt knocked on the gate and shouted out to his supporters within that he had kept his word. He arrived precisely when he said he would. But there was no response. There were no supporters within the gates awaiting him.

That was as much as I gleaned at Hay Hill. After this, few people who knew anything about anything came, and the hall room was half-empty. Our regular informants, the gentlemen normally so opinionated and loquacious, were considering their positions and keeping within doors. The roads out of London were barely passable because of the weather, and unsafe on account of vagrant soldiery.

My guts were gnawed as if by rats. Fortunately there was little demand for mutton pies. I was not wanted in the kitchen. I retreated into my chamber. I avoided Anne.

Mercifully Finch came again to see me, not the next evening but the one after. The news he brought might be terrible, but anything is better than waiting, waiting, waiting and not knowing. Waiting for news of the beloved takes all one's energy.

I could hardly ask Finch up into my chamber, and did not want to talk with him in the hall room. I led him to the pasture across the track from Anne's house. The cattle had been taken indoors and it was a dank and desolate expanse. We sat side by side in the dusk on the wet trunk of a fallen tree. Finch was in a state of agitation. I could not always follow what he said in his Kentish voice and had to ask him to repeat.

Finch said:

'When Ludgate was not opened to him, Sir Thomas went into the courtyard of that inn which lies up against the gatehouse – it's called La Belle Sauvage – and slumped down on a bench. I was there with him, and also young Edward – his son, or his half-brother, whatever, who had come with him from Allington.'

'How old is this Edward? And how did Sir Thomas look?'

'Madam, I cannot tell, perhaps twelve years old? And my master was weary, his face was grey.'

Poor boy Edward. Poor Thomas.

Finch said:

'Sir Thomas left the inn, collected up his troops – only about sixty or seventy of them remaining, Madam – and made to retreat to Charing Cross. Government troops had blocked off every side street and barricaded Fleet Street. Sir Thomas and his men managed to hack their way through the barricades as far as Temple Bar where they were faced with a more powerful force.'

They were so brave. They were so few, and their opposition so many, yet the fighting at Temple Bar went on for a whole murderous and bloody hour. Swords, daggers, pikes, clubs. There were calls from the government side for Sir Thomas to surrender to prevent further bloodshed.

The intention was to take Sir Thomas alive, Finch said. In the end one gentleman rode up to him alone and unarmed. Whatever he said, Sir Thomas gave up his sword and assented to be mounted behind him and removed from the scene.

'Who was this gentleman?'

'Sir Maurice Berkeley. He is reputed to have been for Lady Jane Grey, in the past. I know nothing of him.'

I did not know he had been knighted.

'Sir Maurice Berkeley owns most of the town in which I was born,' I told Finch.

'Indeed, is that so, Madam. I followed my master on foot, running, I saw my master put into a barge and rowed down river towards the Tower. They had taken his sword from him but he looked very fine in his velvet coat. He held his head high.'

'Of what colour is the coat?'

'Plum colour. But much stained and soiled.'

Finch said that those of his followers who survived tried to run away, but the ways were blocked and most were caught. Gallows are being erected all over London for the hangings.

'There are forty men from Kent among them, eight of them my cousins.'

'What will you do now?'

'I do not want to leave my master.'

'He is in the Tower. You cannot reach him. If you stay you will end up on the gallows like your cousins. Go now, go straight home to Kent. Are you married?'

'I have a sweetheart.'

'Go back to her and make your life. Cross the river by whatever means, and go home. Wait...'

I ran across the track to the house, up my stair, found a few coins, came back to Finch and put them in his hand.

'This is what your master would wish. I know it. Go now, saddle your mare and be gone.'

I hope to God he did escape.

I had a hope before we parted that Finch would at the last minute pass to me some gift, some token of love, entrusted to him by Thomas. There was nothing like that. No.

The customers returned to Hay Hill. The crisis – 'Wyatt's rebellion' they were calling it – was already history. Back came the gentlemen with their broadsheets and pamphlets and tales from the city and the Court. Back came the ladies.

I sat like a stone through tirades against Thomas. Because of his rebellion, the government decided that Lady Jane Grey and her associates must be eliminated in case of further manifestations of dissent. She was already in the Tower. A few days after Thomas's imprisonment, her young husband was executed on Tower Hill. She saw his headless corpse brought back on a cart. She herself went the same way straight afterwards.

'Sir Thomas witnessed all this,' said Master Piers Perceval. 'I have it on good authority that he would have seen the whole thing from his chamber in the White Tower. I only hope that he has a proper sense of his responsibility for this gratuitous tragedy.'

I felt it almost as my own guilt. Lady Jane Grey was used, abused and lost her life through no fault of her own. A pawn knocked off the board. Her father the Duke of Suffolk was beheaded too. Then, Thomas's cousin Thomas Cobham, and young Edward Wyatt – that poor little boy – were hung, drawn and quartered.

There were many, many more executions. A wholesale slaughter. Queen Mary was taking no chances.

They were keeping Thomas alive for a reason. The marriage of Queen Mary to Philip of Spain was imminent. The talk at Hay Hill was all about the Princess Elizabeth and the threat she might pose to the new regime. If it were proved that she had been party to the plot against her half-sister, she could be got rid of, eliminated.

Elizabeth was fetched from the country and shut up in the Tower. Under interrogation, she swore she had no part in any conspiracy against the Queen. She was lying, they said.

The Court was nervous, alive with rumours of further plots. So was Hay Hill, and Piers Perceval was relishing the drama.

'It is clear that Elizabeth conspired against her sister, and naturally Thomas Wyatt knew that. They have had Lady Wyatt – his *wife*, Mistress Agnes – brought up from Allington. She implores him to confess, to save his life and their children's future. He swears there is nothing to confess. Now he is being tortured, to force him to confess. Then Elizabeth can be accused. They must have evidence.'

Tortured? Tortured?

Master Perceval was looking straight at me across the table. He was very drunk.

'On the rack, Madam. Do you know what the rack is?'

'No, sir.'

'It is a matter of rollers and ropes and pulleys and levers. On a wooden frame like a bed. They stretch you, Madam. It is a matter of snapping sinews and cracking bones and shoulders torn from their moorings. While they pull out your toenails with pincers.'

Thomas's toenails.

Piers Perceval slumped over his wine goblet, one hand covering his face.

'The fool,' he mumbled. 'The fool. The fool...'

*

Thomas was sent to trial and sentenced to be hung, drawn and quartered. After that, he was put on the rack again in the hope of obtaining evidence of the Princess Elizabeth's guilt.

He could so easily have lied, to save himself. He did not, he could not, he would not. That is the measure of the man, that is the measure of my Thomas. They gave up, and fixed the date of his execution. I state all this flatly, so that it may all be known in years to come. When matters are as bad as they can possibly be one must either go mad, or take one's own life, or close down, becoming devoid of hope or will or desire. That is how it was for me. I made the paste for the crust of mutton pies. I could not eat. I will not speak of the nights. It is in the past now.

I was up on Tower Hill early on the eleventh day of April, wishing to be near to him at the end. I was not early enough. There were already hundreds of people milling around.

I had never witnessed an execution before. I looked at the block, and beside it a basket of sawdust. Black-clothed officials were muttering among themselves. And suddenly there was my Thomas and everything happened quickly.

He was limping when he stepped up on to the scaffold. He turned to the crowd, raised his head, and spoke in a loud clear voice. He had acted, he said, on his own responsibility.

'The Princess Elizabeth and her friends had no part in any of it, none whatsoever.' A clerical person leapt up on to the scaffold to contest what Thomas said. He was shouted down and dragged away. It is shameful, it is just not done, said the people pressing all around me, to challenge the last statement of a man about to meet his Maker.

I was pushed and shoved by men and women trying to get closer to the front. For a moment I thought I saw Eleanor Wilmer among them. It could not have been Eleanor, just someone who looked liked her. I scoured the crowd with my eyes and did not find her. There were so many people. I dreaded encountering her again, but – but what? Something unfinished, perhaps.

Thomas had not noticed me on the day of his father's funeral Mass and he did not see me now. I am not tall and his eyes did not search the crowd. Without aid he took off his black gown, laid it down, and unlaced his doublet. He shook hands with the officials, took out his own handkerchief and tied it over his eyes himself. The executioner picked up the axe. He was wearing a mask. Thomas knelt and laid his head upon the block.

He was brave. He behaved honourably. Everyone said so.

Thomas's head was severed in a single stroke. That was a mercy. The executioner picked up his head by the hair, pulled away the handkerchief and displayed Thomas's face. Then he threw his head into the basket. I do not forget the sounds the onlookers made. There was something animal, sexual, about those sounds. Shocking, disgusting. I turned my head away and vomited, spattering a man's hose and shoe. He swore at me. I pulled up my hood and slunk away. I did not stay to see Thomas's body being hacked into pieces.

He said to me once that execution was less degrading than hanging. Maybe. Maybe.

On my bad nights, I still after all these years see his head, and the bloody stub of his great neck, shreds of pipes and sinews trailing from it.

They took up Thomas's head and put it on a cart and drove it out of London and stuck it in a cage on the gibbet on top of Hay Hill, up the lane from Anne Cathcart's house. We heard shouts and the rumblings of wheels but did not chance to look out. It was Anne's man Luke who came running in to tell us, his blue eyes bulging.

I knew that place up on the ridge. I often walked up there in the early mornings, for the fresh air and the quietness. The gibbet is an old one, the timbers coming apart at the joints. I used to sit down on a fallen cross-beam at its foot, unthinking of the structure's function.

'But why?' said Anne. 'Why is he stuck up here?'

I knew. I began to tell Anne what Thomas had told me on that last night, before everything went so horribly wrong, when he collected his scattered troops together up on Hay Hill. They were attacked and some of them wounded on their approach. Hay Hill was the beginning of the end for him, emblematic of his failure. To expose his head in this obscure spot was a gesture of contempt.

Anne was not listening. I know her so well. She was wondering whether curiosity would draw more gentlemen out to Hay Hill to see this spectacle, and how she could best turn the occasion to profit by offering refreshment and comfort to the well-heeled and prurient. I clambered up to my room. I was in shock at that time and somewhat insane. This is the only explanation I can give for what I did.

A few days later the head of Sir Thomas Wyatt was gone from the gibbet on Hay Hill. Someone had stolen it. The world never knew who took it.

Because it was me. I walked up to the ridge in the light of half a moon and yanked it out of the iron cage and put it in a cloth bag. Thomas's head had been boiled. A head is nearly all bone, with pockets and cushions of flesh. My father used to make brawn from the heads of sheep and pigs, stewing them with onions and herbs until the meat fell away. When the liquor cooled, the meat was suspended in jelly. This was the brawn. It was popular with customers, though if the boiled head were not picked over carefully, chips of bone remained in the finished article on which one could break a tooth. My job, in those far-away days, was to pick out the chips of bone with my fingers before adding the meat to the liquor and putting it in a cold place to set.

I could have made brawn from Thomas's head, and ingested my beloved, so that I would be he and he would be me for ever. I imagined doing it.

A man's head is heavy. I kept transferring the bag from one hand to the other as I walked back down the hill and through the night all the way into London, keeping my hooded head down. I made my way to the Strand and to the river. The tide was beginning to run out fast eastwards, towards the sea that I had never seen.

The stones on the foreshore are always wet and slippery. Then there is mud, and the lapping waters. I stepped off the stones into the mud. I waded into the river up over my knees, the out-going tide nearly unbalancing me. I opened the bag and heaved out Tom's head. My sacred relic. The one and only sacred relic with any meaning.

I thought, he will float free. I was cradling him in farewell when I heard a woman's voice calling my name.

'Agnes Peppin!'

My heart thudding, my skin prickling, I turned and saw in the darkness the grinning face of Eleanor Wilmer. An illusion, surely.

Not an illusion. It was she, in the flesh, in the even more ample flesh. What happened next is so horrid that I can hardly write it down. It is hard to believe it happened. It did.

I shouted at her:

'Why ever are you here? What do you want?'

She shouted back:

'I know what you have done. I saw what you have done. I have been watching you, I have been following you.'

'You have been stalking me? That is disgusting. And why, in heaven's name?'

'I want you, Agnes, and I want your money. For us, for you and me together. You owe me. You are nothing without me.'

'I will give you money, if that is what you want. But now just go! Why are you not away with Jack?'

'Jack is useless, Jack was not the answer. I know what you hold in your arms. I will denounce you to the First Minister and you will be terribly punished for what you are doing.'

'And who pray is the First Minister now? Cromwell is long gone. You know nothing, you know no one.'

'I shall go to the Palace of Westminster and find someone important and denounce you.'

This was just the sort of know-all, know-nothing, idiotic altercation we used to have in Sherborne when we never had enough information between us. It was utterly ludicrous, with me standing in the river with my lover's severed head in my arms. So ludicrous that I began to laugh. Thomas was right after all. Eleanor was comical.

'Go away now, Eleanor, just go, go quietly, I want nothing to do with you, I have nothing to say to you.'

'You have no choice. I know all about you. You are a traitor's whore.'

Eleanor began to stumble heavily down the slope towards the river. I turned and threw Thomas's head as far as I could out into the stream, but could not stay to see whether it sank or whether it was carried away on the surface of the tide-waters. Because glancing back I saw Eleanor balancing between stones and mud, stretching out her arms to me. I waded back out of the river, stepped into Eleanor's embrace, spun around, and pushed her with all my strength into the river.

I heard her scream and I turned away, scrambling as fast as I could back up the slope towards the highway. There I ran and ran, hardly stopping until I reached the ascent of Hay Hill, where I crouched in a hedgerow, getting my breath. I staggered like an old woman back to Anne Cathcart's house, where everyone was sleeping, up the ladder-stair, and collapsed on my mattress. In the morning, when they called out for me, I told them I was sick.

People die all the time. It doesn't matter. Men are killing men every day, every night, everywhere. Women, I think, kill not so much. Possibly I just imagine that I killed Eleanor.

No, I did it. Thomas's head, Eleanor's body, carried away in the dark stream. Thomas's head rolling along the bottom, dragged by the tide, until it became wedged in the timbers of some sunken hulk. Perhaps it rolled free, and was carried out to open sea. The salt water, and the creatures that live in salt water, will long ago have stripped it clean of flesh and hair. A white skull.

And Eleanor — a dead rat.

It's possible that Eleanor did not drown. She could have dragged herself from the water somewhere downstream, or been rescued by a ferryman.

All I can say is, I never ever saw Eleanor Wilmer again.

I think she did drown. And no one on this earth, from that day to this, ever knew what happened to the head of Thomas Wyatt, and no one ever will unless they read the words that I have written.

I think about him. Not a day passes without Thomas coming into my mind.

I am fortunate. What we had was not for ever, but for me it was all-consuming. What Sister Isobel knew, and what I know, may seem as different and chalk and cheese. The Church would say so. I am not so certain. I was inadequate for the religious life, but any inkling I have of its holy mystery does not seem to me so different in kind from what I knew with Thomas.

While Thomas and I were together, nothing I saw or felt, even when we were apart for days or weeks, was ordinary. The world was transformed. Never do I have to wonder what a great passion might be like, or wonder whether there is some marvellous secret pleasure that I have missed. I look at common couples on the streets and wonder if they too know. Appearance is no guide. The most beautiful and aristocratic men and women may never know.

I call him my Thomas, my Tom. But he was never mine, nor any woman's. On one of our last nights, my brain softened by love, I asked him whether I could not go to live quietly in some remote place, and he would come to me when he could, and we would make a good life together.

It was a terrible mistake. How little I understood him. He uttered a groan like a roar and unpicked my arms from around his neck as if they were ropes. He sat up on the edge of the bed with his back to me. He shook with wordless male rage. He turned to me, he swore, he struck me across the face. I leapt from the bed and stood naked at the low hatch which leads to the stairs. I might have to run from this man.

'I have a wife, Madam. I do not need a secondary one. Wife, wife, wife. That is a burden I do not want. I could never be with you in that way, in some quiet place. I am not as the common people are. Do you not know who I am? What do you think that I am?'

'I belong to the common people and I want to be with you all the time.'

'No one must be with anyone all the time. Have you understood nothing? What matters is what is happening in the country and at Court. My head is filled with the names and faces of men — who is for this and who for that, those whom I can trust and those who would be happy to see me dead.'

'All of them known to you since childhood, I suppose,' I said, 'and most of them related to you one way or another.'

'What has that to do with anything?'

I asked this harsh stranger what it was that he most wanted.

'Reputation. Riches. Victory in battle.'

He was quiet for a moment and then said no, that was not all. Because all success, all wealth is provisional. Look at Cardinal Wolsey, he said, look at Sir Thomas More, look at Thomas Cromwell.

'I will have my time in the sun before the dark comes down upon me. And I will be in the eye of the storm when that time comes. Nothing is for ever except my high name and my reputation.'

I thought he would leave. But he turned towards me, weary, more like the Thomas that I knew.

'I need women too — dear Agnes, I need you, perhaps more than ever. Just do not expect me to be other than I am. Do not seek to shackle me. It would be the end of us.'

I wept. It was a weakness in me. I knew I was carrying his child and did not dare to tell him.

This particular storm was over. For him, that is. He lay back on my bed and called me to him, and I went to him.

I forgave but I did not forget. Thomas Wyatt was not without faults. I think they sprang from a vanity which the world might call womanish. He was the hero of his own story. He had a habit which grated on me. In the midst of noisy companions, all of them unbuttoned by wine, when one of them praised him for some triumph he would affect not to have heard:

'What was that you said?'

Thomas heard perfectly well. He wanted the praise to be repeated, in such a way that everyone else paid attention and heard it too. Then he would smile and demur. It is only those whom we love that we observe so closely. The observation of frailties does not occlude love. I would like to have been able to reassure and to protect Thomas Wyatt. That was not what he wanted at all.

*

One summer morning, the year before, I tried to convey to Anne Cathcart the wonder of my secret life with Thomas. Seated at her ease in her parlour, wearing a green silk dress with pearls sewn on the bodice, she said:

'Ah yes, yes indeed. Desire. Lust. Were it not for lust, I would not be where I am today. Were it not for lust, no children would be begotten. No one would think if it. Lust is nature's way of ensuring a supply of new men.'

'Have you read *The Canterbury Tales*?' I asked her. 'Do you know about the Wife of Bath?'

Because Anne reminds me of the Wife of Bath, as did Lady Agnes Perceval, which in the circumstances is ironic.

'I never heard of her. I do not always have my nose in a book.'

In retrospect I wish I had asked Anne what nature had in mind when creating girl children, though I know what her answer would be. The purpose of females, if they are the daughters of the rich, is to be vehicles for the transfer of wealth from one man to another, and to breed. The commonality of women, that is. I have no doubt that Anne placed herself in a special category. I might have said that what Thomas and I had together was nothing to do with begetting children. It was about us, ourselves.

She may be right about the hidden purpose of lust. To me, my condition was the unintended consequence of love.

10

SEEING THE SEA

I remained at Hay Hill into the late summer, by which time Queen Mary was married to Philip of Spain. She hardly knew him, neither spoke the other's language, but it was said that she doted upon him. There were rumours that she had conceived. Her belly swelled up. But there was no baby in there. There is something altogether peculiar about this Queen Mary.

I ceased to concern myself about these matters. When I sensed my own baby was soon to be born I went away from Hay Hill into proper London.

I did not ask Anne for help or advice. I spoke with one of the serving women, Tabitha, who I knew had children of her own. It was a fortunate impulse. Tabitha has a sister who lives in the Borough.

'Honor will surely take you in – she has lost her husband, she'll be glad of the money.'

Tabitha sent her a message to the Borough – that was Southwark. I would be treading where Thomas had trod and breathing the same air.

The carrier put me down at Temple Bar, where Thomas had surrendered. I walked on eastwards up Ludgate Hill, through the gate which was closed to him, and past St Paul's Cathedral. I took a wrong turning off Cheapside into a slum of alleys. People were swarming in and out filthy courts and yards, shouting and crying and fighting and selling and buying. Also pigs, fowls, packs of dogs and tribes of skinny cats. Sewage running in the gutter. It was a struggle just to move along. I kept bumping into people, I do not have the knack of weaving my way through a crowd as everyone else seemed able to do.

No one of whom I asked directions knew anything, and they did not understand what I said. Many people in London were not born or raised here, it seems to me. I know there are mansions in London where great families live in comfort, but not in the parts through which I passed that day. A shack in clean country air among green trees would be preferable to me. But a London child would find only stagnation in the countryside. There is vitality in these teeming alleys.

I came by a winding route to the river and to London Bridge, and stopped, seeing a chaos of traffic. Dozens of loaded carts and wagons were lined up, waiting, not daring to cross all together and at once. Just one or two wagons were on the bridge, moving slowly.

I could see a gap in the rows of high tenements on the bridge, like missing teeth. That must be where the Queen's men broke through it. There were tar-blackened heads stuck up on pikes at both ends of the bridge. Whose heads they were I do not know. I saw a man with a handcart coming towards me from the other side, but still I hesitated. He shouted out to me:

'You can cross over. They have laid down timbers across the space. Go carefully.'

I imagined waters swirling beneath unstable planks. I went down the steps on the near side of the bridge where a single ferry-man was waiting, and had myself rowed over to the other side. In midstream, I looked back and saw the Tower. Ahead, on the Southwark shore, more carts and wagons were halted, as far back as the eye could see. The ferryman said:

'It's bad for business, this carry-on. This Queen, that Queen, who cares. Not me. There's only the one bridge. Everyone's losing time and time is money. More work for me and my mates, though.'

And indeed the river was criss-crossed with loaded boats and barges. The tide was out. When I stepped out of the boat there were three little girls on the foreshore playing and singing:

> *'London Bridge is falling down,*
> *Falling down, falling down,*
> *London Bridge is falling down,*
> *My Fair Lady.'*

Life is sweeter on the Southwark side. There are boatyards and vegetable gardens and a big busy market and, on Borough High Street, more inns and taverns than I ever saw in one place. Anne Cathcart might have done better to establish herself here, rather than out in the fields on Hay Hill. Tabitha's sister Honor lives in a yard off the High Street. She showed me to a clean chamber up her stair – it was her son Daniel's room, but he has grown up and gone – and we arranged terms. She earns her living by sewing up silk linings for coats. The pieces are cut out by the tailor, and Honor crosses the river and collects them from his workshop.

'Is the tailor a very small man?' I asked. 'Does he have a taste for Court gossip?'

'He is a normal-sized person. He is an Italian. We speak only about the work,' replied Honor.

Of course there must be scores and scores of tailors in the city. What a country mouse I still am.

The coat-linings are lemon yellow, grey, lavender – all pale colours, and the silk is precious. Her hands must always be clean, and her floor too. Any smudge or stain ruins the work and she has to bear the cost.

I told her about the little girls singing 'London Bridge is falling down'.

'It is very quick, surely, for such a song already to be known to children?'

'No, no, it's not about what happened now. We knew it when I was their age.'

She hummed the melody, and it was the same. I suppose bridges have always collapsed or been broken, by floods and in wars.

I didn't ask her how it had been for her when the Borough was full of armed men and bombarded. I made myself useful. I helped her to sweep and dust and mop and wipe, and waited for the baby to be born.

I walked out one fine day and saw, in another yard off the High Street, the Tabard Inn where Chaucer's pilgrims met up at the start of their journey. I stood and gazed at its galleried façade, and watched women and men going in and out making a great din, and horsemen clattering through, and fowls scattering up screeching from the horses' hoofs. I pictured the pilgrims assembling in the yard with their servants and their baggage, all ready for the long ride to Canterbury, which is in Kent. I thought of Finch and said a prayer for him.

It was an easy birth. Honor was a kind nurse and helper. My daughter, whom I called Abigail, was healthy. Her name means, in Hebrew, 'Joy of the Father', as Dorothy Clausey of all people once told me. The choice of name was wishful thinking. Abigail had no father, only a mother to rely upon.

I lay with Abigail in my arms in the bed. I cleaned and fed her whenever she woke, but mostly we both slept. I searched her little face for a likeness to her father, and fancied I found a resemblance. But she was who she was and she was perfect.

I had four days of calm and hopefulness, resting and dreaming.

Abigail sickened, suddenly and overnight. She had difficulty breathing. She would not feed. She no longer cried. Over another four days she grew smaller and paler. I did not know what to do, there was nothing that I or Honor could do. She would not even take water from the tip of a spoon. It was like the time when Dorothy's baby was in the same case. But little Esther had been neglected and chilled to the bone. Abigail was warm and swaddled and held close. It made no difference.

She was so quiet and still that I could not tell the moment when her soul left her body. I baptised her with water from the ewer and made the sign of the Cross over her. Honor and I prayed over her little body as it became cold and then stiff. Honor would have given me an offcut from the coat linings, but I wrapped her in the piece of silk embroidered with gold birds which Sister Mary Amor bequeathed to me. I kissed her hands and face over and over again and laid her in a box. Honor knew whom to ask to take it away.

Abigail is buried with no marker in a corner of the churchyard of what was, before the troubles, Southwark Priory, on the river. Abigail is safe, she is with the angels in Heaven.

I hardly wept. I was numb and dumb. My heart was a block of ice.

And then, on the Borough High Street, I found myself walking behind a man, a common workman, carrying a fair-haired child in a sling on his back. She was perhaps eighteen months old, looking solemnly out on to the world with her clear blue eyes. She pumped her little legs up and down, and called out 'Dada!' Her father turned his head and spoke to her over his shoulder, and gave a little jump, which bounced her and made her laugh. Then they turned into an alleyway and I saw them no more.

Tears flooded my eyes, the ice in my heart melted, and I ran like a mad person to hide in the Priory church – dark, cold, empty, no one there. I squatted in a corner and wept and cried and howled like an animal for the loss of Abigail, for the scent of her downy head, for her tiny fingernails, for the tug at my womb when she sucked. And for Tom, my only love, not lost to me entirely because of her – until now. I cried until I could cry no more.

After that I carried grief like a bundle that I could never put down. Onslaughts of uncontrollable weeping continued to ambush me. Honor grew impatient with my sobbing. She remarked drily that it was all very sad, but infants do die so easily, it is only to be expected, it is commonplace. Few women raise every child that they bear.

'I kept my Daniel. But I lost three. Two boys and a girl. Well, my Clemency was never right but she lived for five years until her guts turned to water and she was gone within twenty-four hours. You are not the only pebble on the beach, Agnes Peppin.'

Tough but true. It was time to move along. I did not want to break the contact with Honor, who was so good, nor lose the memory of my short time with Abigail. So I left in Honor's safe keeping all my writings up until then, and my lion tile from Shaftesbury, and some of my money. I took my books with me. At the last minute I rolled up the blue cloak Thomas had given me and added it to my bundle. I watched as Honor stowed everything away in a cupboard in her kitchen. I was sad to say goodbye to her but knew I would come back.

When I returned to Hay Hill, Anne asked me nothing about my absence but I am sure she knew. Never have I known a woman so coarse and at the same time so delicate. Or was she just indifferent?

She had worries of her own. Master Piers Perceval was behaving strangely. Anne fretted that his wife had come to suspect his intimacy with the Hay Hill establishment, and with herself.

I could guess how that might be. Just suppose that Master Perceval, a braggart, spoke freely to Robert Parker, as man to man. Robert Parker, spending much time with Mistress Agnes Perceval and under a courtier's obligation to keep her entertained, may have regaled her with an amusing account of an unusual establishment presided over by a certain Mistress Arundell. He may even, under pressure, have admitted that he had visited the place with her husband – oh, they went only just the once of course, out of idle curiosity, and never again. No, certainly not, never again. I could imagine the two of them sitting in the garden, Mistress Agnes dressed in a fashionably shepherdess kind of way and Robert with a book of Latin verses on his knee. Nothing could be more decorous or more civilised.

Mistress Agnes Perceval is no fool. If she pressed Robert for further and better particulars about Mistress Arundell, and Robert revealed who she was, keen to impress her with his privileged knowledge, then Mistress Perceval would suspect where it was that her husband went after dark, returning so late to their bed. I did not tell Anne, for fear I should laugh in the telling.

I knew most of the regulars who came to Hay Hill. I had my favourites. One of these was a Captain Combe, an affable fellow with a familiar West Country way of speaking. He lived in Bridport. This endeared him to me if only because I knew of the place and it is where Dick and Weasel somehow found one another before they fetched up in Shaftesbury. I often sat and chatted with him. He knew where I was from and we always found much to talk about.

This Captain Combe is a boatbuilder, with an interest in a chandler's establishment upstream from London Bridge at Queenhythe. This brings him into London, as does his periodical mastership of what he calls cogs – merchant vessels – trading from the port of London up the east coast. He shows no interest in the easy ladies at Hay Hill, but drinks his ale and takes himself off at a reasonable hour. God only knows how he first found his way to Mistress Arundell's.

I was occupied with other customers when I heard Captain Combe's voice above the hubbub:

'Mistress Agnes! Be so good, when you are able, as to bring a jug of ale for myself and my good friend Master Mompesson!'

What? What? I looked round, and saw Captain Combe seated at one of the small tables. His companion was a thickset man with dark curly hair and beard turning grey. Peter Mompesson.

The sky did not fall. It was astonishing and yet natural. I fetched the ale, drew up a stool and sat with Captain Combe and Peter and we talked in a desultory way as if we had seen one another only yesterday. There was no need for dissimulation. Captain Combe knew our story and was a benign third party. He tactfully absented himself from our table for a while.

I learned in short order that Peterkin – 'My son,' said Peter; 'Our son,' said I; 'Yes, yes,' said Peter – did not want to be a farmer. He has been gripped by the story of the *Mary Rose*, the late King Henry's warship which sank to the bottom of the sea off Portsmouth for no apparent reason.

'He is obsessed, he is convinced there must have been a design fault. So he is studying the construction of vessels. He has taken himself off to Bridport to learn shipbuilding with Captain Combe. It is a fine thing to have such a strong desire, like a vocation.'

I agreed, and felt proud for our son. I dared to ask, afraid of the answer:

'Does he know that I am his mother?'

Peter was trying to find the right words, I could tell.

'He is familiar with your name and knows that it is the name of his mother. He knows that his mother is an honest woman who entered a convent. He knows the name of his grandfather, your father, and who he was. I would not, could not, leave him in ignorance.'

I felt the colour rising hot in my face. What he said was little but it was good enough. It was everything.

'One day he will have children of his own and will need to tell them who they are. There are no Peppins in Bruton any more, not since your parents died, but the name pleases him. He says it sounds like a little bird.'

'A French nun in the Abbey told me that it meant the pip in an apple, or the stone in a plum. And in Spanish a pepino is a cucumber.'

Thomas told me that.

'You Peppins surely grew in a garden then, one way or another. He said to me that when he has a son, his name will be Peppin Mompesson.'

My eyes brimmed over. Peter leaned over the table and laid a hand over mine.

'How have you fared, Agnes, since you left the Abbey? How have you fared?'

I would not have known where to begin, but at that moment Captain Combe took his place with us again.

'We were speaking just now of Peterkin,' said Peter.

'He is promising,' said Captain Combe. 'He is a fine lad, your boy, a hard worker, and a natural for the job. His mates call him Skipper. I have him working on lerrets at the moment. Flat-bottomed.'

I was out of my depth there. But why was Peter here?

'To meet with the Captain and finalise the terms and conditions of Peterkin's apprenticeship.'

Captain Combe was off in the morning on a long voyage on what he called a hulk, taking heavy cargo up the coast to the port of Hull, then on to Scotland.

'I'll be away for many weeks,' said the Captain, 'and everything must be shipshape before I leave.'

The two of them had completed their business and were taking their ease. I sat quietly with them as they talked, overwhelmed by such quantities of new information.

Suddenly Peter interrupted Captain Combe in mid-sentence, sniffed the air and said:

'Do you smell smoke?'

Yes, we did. And other guests were rising from their benches, knocking over trestles and trenchers, calling out that they smelt smoke.

The doors burst open and in rushed Luke, distraught, shouting:

'The barn is afire! The barn is afire!'

Everyone, guests and servants, rushed outside, pushing and shoving and stumbling over each other. I lost sight of my companions in the confusion. I was outside just in time to see flames from the barn licking the thatch of the main house. It flared up like a furnace. From the blazing barn came the frightful screams of horses.

The sober and able-bodied were throwing pails of water onto the house and onto the further wing. There is only one pump and there were not enough pails. It was hopeless. The heat was intense, the smoke made us cough and choke, and there was no possibility of salvaging anything from within. It is a miracle that no one was hurt. Except the horses in the barn.

My first thought was, where is Anne? I bumped into Luke, running wild-eyed, and caught him by the arm.

'What happened?'

I had to shout to be heard above the roar of the fire. Luke looked at me with utter hatred.

'Two of them,' he yelled, gasping through the smoke, 'two ruffians with torches came into the barn and set fire to the hay. They shouted at me that this was a gift from Mistress Agnes. What in Hell's name have you done?'

'Not me!' I screamed at him. 'Not me! The other Mistress Agnes!'

I caught hold of him. He pulled himself from my grasp but I ran after him.

'Where is Mistress Arundell?'

'She is gone, I dragged Minstrel out in time and led him round to the back field and she's well away by now. But you, Madam, for Christ's sake, what kind of a hellcat are you?'

He had not understood, how should he? He glared at me with his red-rimmed eyes, tore my hand from his sleeve and was away.

So Anne was all right. She will be, she would be. Good. Fine. I hope she had time to snatch up her diamond ring.

I escaped from the choking smoke into the field on the opposite side of the track where I had talked with Finch. I collapsed on the grass and watched the blaze. I saw everyone leaving, singly and in twos and threes, silhouetted against the flames, trailing on foot through the darkness down the hill towards the highway. I saw the flames subside. As dawn came grey into the sky all that remained was a red-smouldering black mass and clouds of smoke. The smell was horrible.

I began to think about what I had lost. All my clothes. A bag of small money.

And my books.

I sat on in the field, smuts and flakes of ash drifting over me, attempting to face up to the losses. The Hand of God lay heavy upon my shoulder. For what was God punishing me, what was my sin? Peterkin? Thomas? Eleanor? Abigail? I seemed damned all my life to lose everyone and everything, including now my reputation. Luke would be telling the tale of the arson for the rest of his life: 'A gift from Mistress Agnes.'

I steadied myself. No one has heard of Agnes Peppin. Anyone in the know will be aware who the vengeful Agnes was. Piers Perceval had not been at the house when the fire broke out. Probably his wife kept him at home on some pretext. She would not want the supplier of her life's luxuries to be burnt to death. Only, she would have hoped, Mistress Anne Cathcart, and she had been foiled in that.

I was cold and shivering and hallucinating. The Hand of God upon my shoulder was firm and warm.

It was the hand of Peter Mompesson.

'I have been searching for you everywhere. I feared you were caught in the fire.'

He drew me to my feet, wrapped some kind of a blanket around me, and led me away from that place.

He was as an angel to me. A sensible, capable angel. I was exhausted and in shock. I remember we travelled into the city on a farmer's cart loaded with beets. I remember walking with Peter over London Bridge into Southwark, he holding my hand over the unstable planking in the middle. I remember finding Honor's yard, and collecting my money and the precious belongings which I had left with her. I remember Peter leaving, and returning with a stout grey mare, saddled, which caused no end of commotion in the narrow yard.

'I'll take you home now,' he said. 'You will be with me now. I shall take care of you.'

'What home? Where is home?'

'The farm at Brewham.'

'I do not want to go back to Bruton. I cannot go through Bruton.'

It was all that seemed to matter at that moment. Stupid.

'We need not pass through Bruton. We can come into Pensel Wood and ride home through the forest.'

'There were battles in Pensel Wood in the long ago. There are bad spirits in the trees.'

'I have never seen them.'

He stowed my belongings in the saddlebags. Honor gave us bread, a couple of onions, a strip of dried fish. I wrapped myself in the blue cloak and pulled up the hood. Peter set me up behind him on the mare and off we went, keeping on the Southwark side of the river and bearing towards the south-west.

I know, only because Peter told me, that it was a journey of more than a hundred miles and took us more than four days. I clung with my arms round his waist, my cheek against his back, half-sleeping. We stopped only to eat, to water the mare and let her graze. At night we were so weary that we cared little where we lay.

This long ride together was a time out of time. We hardly spoke. By the time we reached Brewham I was almost myself again. And Pensel Wood is like any other wood apart from some inexplicable mounds and ditches.

A dog ran barking to greet us as we clopped into the farmyard.

'Her name is Nell. No need for fear, she's a good girl.'

It was late in the day. Peter caressed Nell and kicked her aside. Nell did not come into the house. Peter unlocked both halves of the door with heavy keys retrieved from the back of a woodpile.

'You will have your own keys.'

'Will I?'

The place looked well cared for. The house had a new stone-tiled roof.

'I must stable the mare and rub her down and feed her. And fetch us up some watercress for our supper. Make yourself at home. Look around.'

I went into the house. The hall room was like a parlour, with a flagged floor, a trestle, two chairs and some stools. Capes and cloaks on nails behind the doors, pairs of boots in a row. I did not care to penetrate further before Peter returned. I sat down and waited for him.

'Come now and see the kitchen. Look, I have made a fireplace, with a chimney to take the smoke up out of the roof. I brought that lintel stone above it from the Abbey, Sir Maurice Berkeley cannot have everything, and look, I built ovens at either side.'

'It is beautiful.'

The fireplace was in the new style, set in the wall, like the one I saw at Place Farm.

'I brought a pipe from the pump through the wall so that we have water in the kitchen. In this little tank.'

'You have thought of everything.'

Upstairs was just one long chamber with a darkened plank floor. The big bed stood in the middle. The bed-curtains were old and worn but they looked clean. The bed-coverings and pillows were piled high.

'It was my parents' bed. I was born in this bed and my parents died in it. It is a good old bed.'

'Where did the children sleep? You and your sister?'

'Through here.'

A half-room, a closet, with its own little window. A cell.

'Peterkin slept here. It can be yours, for your clothes and books and your own things.'

My books are burned. I have no books. I did not say it aloud. I stood for a moment in the closet. I breathed in air to the bottom of my lungs, inhaling particles of Peterkin.

Downstairs, Peter took a white sheep's cheese and two pewter platters from a cupboard. He set them on the trestle with his bunch of watercress and some dry biscuits. He drew ale from a barrel in the kitchen. We ate and drank. The food tasted good. But I found it hard to say anything. Time moved slowly.

He pointed out of the window at the back of the room, to where grass sloped downwards towards a line of trees.

'The Home Field. You could make a garden there. And an orchard.'

I looked out at the field, still sunlit at the far end.

'I see that one could.'

'The river runs along the bottom, the cresses come from there.'

Silence. I looked at the backs of my hands in my lap, I turned them over and looked at my palms. I knew what was coming.

'Well, Agnes? Will you live with me here and be my wife?'

'Thank you. Thank you. I will have to consider.'

'What is there to consider, now?'

'May I go outside, by myself?'

'Of course. It'll be getting dark soon. I'll feed Nell and close up the fowls and check the ewes. My man came in to see to them while I was away but you never know.'

He let me out through a back door opening on to the Home Field.

I walked down to the bottom, in and out of lengthening shadows. I looked back up at the farmhouse, solid and settled. I heard sheep bleating in the fields on the far side, and Nell's bark. I heard the river, sunken between deep banks, a few yards away. The river is small here, running fast down towards Bruton.

I was being offered something serious. The affection and protection of a good man. I did and do believe that Peter Mompesson is a good man, and he is the father of my son. I would sooner or later see my son. I was being given a home. The fact that I was still a Bride of Christ was irrelevant. I acknowledged that I no longer believed that at all, and felt no pang.

It was the fairy-tale ending. 'And they lived happily ever after.' So what was wrong with me? Why this dragging dread? I sat there on a fallen tree until the sun went down and the dusk crept about me.

When I returned to the house Peter had lit the rushlights. He looked at me as I came in the door, searching my face. It was sweet, pitiful. I went to him where he sat. I stood over him and put my arms around him and bent to kiss his cheek above the beard. His hands, around me, were trembling.

'I am tired,' I said. 'Can we talk in the morning?'

'I am tired too. And, I have to tell you, I am glad to go to the bed. I have some pain tonight. It is a pain in my gut that comes and goes. I'm sure it does not signify, but it depletes me. I am no longer a young man.'

He laid his cheek against mine, and we rocked one another. We went upstairs. We took off our clothes. We lay down side by side on our backs under the covers in the big bed. We held hands. He turned to me, kissed me on the forehead, then gently not forcibly on the mouth, and turned away from me.

'Sleep now,' he said.

'Sleep now,' I said. 'I hope you will be better in the morning.'

I rarely dream, but dreamed that night that I was trying to fit Peter's house on to the cart of beets which brought us into London. It was not quite his house, it was a wooden model such as I have seen somewhere of a church. It splintered and broke, but still would not fit on the cart.

When we woke in the morning, it was I, not he, who was unwell. I could not face climbing down from the bed. Peter brought me ale and a last year's apple, soft and crinkled. He drew back the bed-curtains and then the shutters and went out to the farm.

I lay in that bed all day watching clouds pass across the window. All my available strength was channelled into making the decision. That was why I felt ill. Peter knew nothing about Thomas Wyatt, nor about what he had been to me. He did not know the horrors that I had seen, he did not know anything of what I had done. He did not know about Eleanor Wilmer. He did not know about Abigail either. All of which meant he did not know who I was. He really did not know me at all. But the thought of telling him everything made me quail. More than that, the notion of telling him was distasteful to me. He would not understand any of it. It would bewilder him.

My mind kept wandering away. I preferred to think about the sea.

I asked Peter at day's end:

'I know we live on an island. Where is the sea, the ocean, nearest to us here?'

He smiled, surprised, and thought a bit.

'You could travel from here in any direction except eastwards and you would reach the sea. The best might be up through the Mendips and the Quantocks, but then it is not quite the sea, it is a wide tidal river running out west into the ocean. You can see land on the other side. That land is Wales.'

'What are Mendips and Quantocks?'

'They are hills, I'll take you that way one day.'

I sat up in the bed.

'But the open sea, the ocean?'

'One way would be to cross Exmoor. I am not sure that I could take so much time away from the farm.'

'I would not expect you to.'

'It is quicker the other way, to the south.' he said. 'To Bridport or Lyme and the long empty shore down there.'

I might catch a glimpse of Peterkin in Bridport.

If I stayed with Peter in this pleasant place, it would be like being in Shaftesbury Abbey, in a very small way, and I the Abbess, in a very small way, in an abbey without visible walls. What kept arising in my mind was the one word, 'Wife'. Even if we did not marry in church, I must commit myself, I must take as it were a Vow of Stability.

Wife. Wife. Wife. Why does that word make me flinch? Thomas had hated it too.

For the Wife of Bath, being a wife was a trade or a profession, it was about money and amusement and manipulating the lust of men. That would not be my way, nor most women's. I have seen women who are wives aged before their time, working until daylight end and beyond, keeping the man and the children fed and clothed. And sometimes washed. They are their family's servants. Like Martha in the story. No time for books. Most probably no books at all.

I did not know if Peter reads and writes. I was sure he could, like my dear father, calculate.

Good wives know what they are for. They have an unquestioned function, as does a hammer or a spoon. And then there is love, the sweetener. Love for a man – and ending up as his nurse. Love for children. If Abigail had lived, this would have been a good place for her. I still, however, would be the wife. Wife. Wife. Wife.

No.

My mother could not be a wife, not really. She withdrew and sickened, finding no other way to be. I am more like her than I knew.

I do not care to think of Eleanor Wilmer. But I do remember things she said to me, and in particular: 'From now on, for us, it will be just one thing after another.'

That may suit me. I shall have a dog again, a companion dog who will read my mind as I read hers. I'll easily find some farmstead at this time of year which has a litter. And she, the little bitch I choose, will see the sea with me. I may become one of those women seen as deranged, walking the roads from nowhere to nowhere. But there will be no walls around me.

By nightfall I was definite in my own mind. It was easy for me to let Peter make love to me when he came to the bed because I had a plan and because he was kind. I wanted to leave him with something good to remember.

Anne Cathcart, late one night in her parlour, had treated me to a disquisition on the varieties of the male member. The largest one she ever saw had given her no more pleasure than others. She did not

care either for thin, whippy ones. I have mercifully no recollection
of her conclusions, though she discoursed between one and two of
the clock on the subject. I do recall deciding not to enquire about
the endowment of the newt, Master Piers Perceval, because I did
not want to know.

This conversation only comes into my mind because Peter's was
short and thick and strong – reliable, like everything else about him.
Our coupling was easy and unremarkable, as I imagine practised
marital coupling might be. We did not speak afterwards. We just
went to sleep.

At dawn Peter rose and dressed and went out to check the sheep.
When I was sure he had gone, I left the bed and put together my
bundle.

I did not want to leave without a word. A door downstairs
opened into a windowless closet arranged as an office. In the light
from the hall room I made out ledgers, papers, bundles of quills,
ink-blocks, candlesticks. Peter was more lettered than I knew.
I found a scrap of paper and wrote:

'Thank you. I cannot be your wife. I have to go.'

I put down the quill then picked it up again and added:

'I have to see a man about a dog.'

I left the paper on the trestle in the hall room. I opened the door
and looked about me. No one to be seen. I ventured out, looked
round again, and set off across the farmyard and down the track.
I had left the half-door swinging wide at the top, and thought of
going back to secure it.

Was I a little disappointed, not to be discovered, embraced,
cajoled, brought back? Maybe I was. Maybe I still am.

It was a delicious morning, the sun coming up into a clear sky,
birds singing, the trees heavy with growth, berries reddening on the
hawthorn, sweet small yellow plums overhanging the track. They
were my breakfast. Anyone would feel her heart rise, walking the
lanes on such a morning.

What if there had been rain, and a biting wind? There well could have been, at that time of the year. I might then have thought, three days and nights like this and I shall be dead in a ditch. I might have turned around and crept back wet and shivering to Peter's house and remained there. It was the fine weather, not my fine thoughts, that allowed me to leave. Choice and chance.

I walked to Wincanton. I knew the way by now. Having all my remaining money about me, I hired an attic room at the Lamb Inn. I was learning to take care of myself in the interest of survival. Then began the all too familiar business of asking around, trying to find some wagoner who was going south, to the coast. This turned out to be a woman, a Mistress Rachel Dortch.

She was not young. Her face and the backs of her hands were sun-browned and wrinkled. She was born in Wincanton and retained some small family property in the town where she had rents to collect. She was on her way back to her family in Pucknole, Pucknowle, I do not know how to write it.

'It is a small village near the sea.'

'How near? How near to the sea?'

'You can walk it in less than an hour.'

'Is it close to Bridport?'

'Five or six miles.'

So I threw in my lot with Mistress Rachel Dortch for a small payment. We travelled south and south-west in her farm cart, drawn by a piebald pony. The wheels looked and sounded as if they might not last long on rocky ground. As we bumped along we talked about dogs easily, about marriage and children warily, about the weather, and divulged nothing of importance to one another. This suited us both.

I found my dog at one of several farms where we stopped on the off-chance. This one was just south of Sherborne. As we rattled through the town I did not tell Rachel Dortch that I had spent many years there, even though my eyes were out on stalks. We drove past the Abbey and very near to where Eleanor and I had lodged. It was not a market day, I saw no one that I recognised in the streets, and then in no time at all we were crossing the river and away. There is nothing for me in Sherborne now.

The farm where we found my dog was run down, the outbuildings neglected.

'Yes,' said the old man who came out to meet us in his yard. 'Yes, our Tilly is one too many for me. A crossbreed,' he said, 'six months old and skittish. She is named after my grandmother. She has a boss eye like my grandmother.'

'Like yourself too, sir,' I nearly said, but stopped my tongue in time.

'You can take our Tilly, if you have a mind to, and for nothing. She is no good to me.'

He whistled and three dogs came running up. Which one was Tilly?

She was medium-sized, mostly white with some black, lean and long-legged, with ears that flopped over, a clever questioning face and eyes that were not crossed like her master's, but looked outwards in opposite directions. I glanced at Rachel and she nodded.

Had Rachel frowned, I might have taken notice. But I already knew that Tilly was mine. The cross-eyed farmer gave me rope for a leash, and Tilly, Rachel and I left the farm, regained the main track and continued our journey.

It is interesting, travelling with a woman. We stopped and greeted whomsoever we met, we were friendly with men and dogs we would never see again. With Tilly quiet between my feet we spent two evenings in inns, talking of this and of that with whoever was there. Or at least I did. Rachel Dortch was more taciturn. She had got to that age when life has taken so many twists and turns that you cannot impart to casual acquaintances much of your hinterland. I feel this reticence coming upon myself also. You do not even wish to. You tell them what you choose or chance to tell – enough for them and enough for you. Rachel had a grasp of the limitations of occasions and encounters, including hers and mine, even though we shared a mattress.

Each morning, from my diminishing funds, I bought from where we stayed enough to eat to see all three of us through the day. We drank from the streams. Tilly caught a rabbit. Gradually we were coming closer to the sea coast. Gulls screamed above our heads.

Rachel left me and Tilly at the inn in her village towards daylight end. She handed down my bundle and pointed out the grass track up which I should walk to reach the sea. She said a place name which I did not grasp. She did not ask what my purpose was, nor where I would pass the night. Yet as I left her I was content. Many women crave protestations of continuing friendship. Rachel Dortch did not want anything of me. This is to my mind admirable. Sister Isobel was like that but then Sister Isobel walked with God. Rachel Dortch walks with God unknowingly. Or else she is of limited understanding and no curiosity. Possibly, two sides of the same coin. I do not know.

What do I know, about anybody? No one should wear a placard around her neck with just one word written upon it: Virgin. Saint. Servant. Mother. Wife. Nun. Or like those unfortunates who are put in the pillory: Witch. Slut. Pervert. Hag. Whore. The parable which preoccupied me so much in the past has lost its bite. I can be Martha and Mary both. Or neither. I do not have to choose. There is no point seeking an answer if the question is the wrong question in the first place. No one is the same all the way through like the transparent apple jelly we made in Shaftesbury Abbey. A good Christian woman may share her soul with a vixen or a she-wolf. Or a rabbit.

I took a deep breath, called Tilly, and began to walk.

Although not far it was hard going, uphill all the way. Then I came over a crest and saw a great stone.

A boulder, I suppose you would call it. Higher than myself, its base buried in long grass. The left side sloped down to a point, the other end was rounded. Like an egg. I touched its pitted surface. I put my cheek against it and it felt warm. I walked all around it and felt its weight and bulk.

Tilly ran on beyond the stone and I followed her, calling. A hundred yards beyond the stone the ground fell away.

I saw the sea, deep blue in the twilight, stretching to the curved line at the end of the world just as Thomas said. Headlands fingered the sea on either side. I could smell salt. Streaks of silver light fell upon the sea from the setting sun.

I sat on the grass and looked and looked. I saw a little ship with a rust-coloured sail, zig-zagging towards the land. Tilly came running back and sat panting beside me.

So we remained, my dog and I, as the light failed, the silvery streaks disappeared, and then a shifting darkness was all there was. All I heard was a rhythmic roar, rising and falling. It was the sound of waves breaking on the shore.

I go back to the rock and settle myself in my blue cloak in the lee of the round end. There is an overhang which will protect the dog and me from the chill of the night.

I have seen the sea. At long last I have seen the sea.

In the morning I will go down to the shore and watch the foam creeping up and I will bathe my feet and Tilly will bark at the waves.

Now that I have seen the sea, what else do I want? What next?

I shall walk to Bridport. I will see Peterkin, working on the boats. I will surely recognise him. I may announce myself to him or I may not. I gave him birth, I gave him life. He knows who I am. That may be enough in this world both for him and for me. I remember what the Abbess said, in the words of some long-ago sister: 'All shall be well and all shall be well and all manner of things shall be well.' What will happen will happen.

I think of those who touched and changed me, apart from my father and mother. Hugh Backwell and John Harrold. Dame Elizabeth Zouche. Dick and Weasel. Dorothy Clausey. Sister Mary Amor. Father Robert Parker. Sister Isobel whom I never knew. My Melancholy. Even the Winterbournes. Poor Colin from Sherborne Market, and Jacob the cheese-man. John Leland. Anne Cathcart, oh yes. Honor in Southwark, and just now Rachel Dortch. Eleanor Wilmer, whose name I cannot inscribe with serenity.

And the loves of my life – Thomas Wyatt and in another way, tinged with tenderness and regret, Peter Mompesson.

Even though in the eyes of the world I may seem a vagabond, picaresque as Thomas said, I am supremely fortunate.

I ask myself what it is that I now want, in these few hours before the darkness becomes total.

I shall have no more truck, ever, with the world into which Thomas was born. Silk and velvet are lovely. So are emeralds and pearls. A butcher's daughter may aspire to those things even though it is unlikely, the way things are, that they will come her way. But too much dross comes with all that gold.

I want to hear no more Court gossip, to hear no more about power-mongering or plots and betrayals and violent deaths, no more about jostling for place and favour and influence, or for riches and properties. Not that I ever played any part in all that, but I was a little intoxicated, infected, by my proximity to it. I want to find, before the End of Days, whether my own or the world's, a perfect refuge and retreat, so remote that no one will ever find me. I want to have books again and to read and to write.

It sounds like a return to the religious life. That is not what I mean at all. In this place of trees and grass and water and birdsong that I imagine, nothing and no one will restrict my liberty. I shall grow plants for food, and flowers. I shall raise animals. I shall know every inch of my small realm, every tree and rock, every rough place and every sweet spot, I shall know my whole fine world all the way up through my bare feet to my heart and through my careful hands.

Sometimes I will be apathetic and despairing and find no meaning in any of it, especially in winter. I will be like a dry-souled nun, like my Melancholy.

I shall always recover when the summer comes. There will be butterflies.

Will there be anyone with me in my retreat? In a shared solitude, and not all of the time. A companion who thinks as I do, whose work is important as mine is to me. Someone self-sufficient, contented and kind. Someone who prefers being with me, together but apart as we shall be, to all the splendours of the great world.

I do not yet know this person. But he – I think it is a he – is there somewhere waiting and when we meet we will both know at once.

I shall always read and I shall always write, but not any more about my own life. There is so much to do, and so much that is more interesting, outside myself.

And I may later want something else, something quite, quite different. Nothing is for ever.

Sleep now.

END NOTE

Agnes Peppin's accounts of contemporary events and public figures are necessarily limited by what she happened to see and hear, but she gets it mostly right. Some of her more surprising assertions are also true. It has proved impossible, for example, for me to discover where Elizabeth Zouche, the distinguished last Abbess of Shaftesbury, fits in to the Zouche family pedigree. And the head of Sir Thomas Wyatt really was stolen from the gibbet on Hay Hill, no one ever knew by whom. Since Agnes Peppin is fictional, her part in its disappearance is also fictional.

Agnes Peppin's vision in the last pages of a future life in a remote retreat, and of the companion who will share it with her, is a paraphrase of a poem by the Countess of Winchelsea, who lived more than a hundred years later.

VICTORIA GLENDINNING is a British biographer, critic, broadcaster and novelist. Born in Sheffield and educated at Oxford where she studied modern languages, she later worked for the *TLS*. She is an Honorary Vice-President of English PEN, winner of the James Tait Black Memorial Prize, was appointed a CBE in 1998, is the twice winner of the Whitbread Biography award and Vice-President of the Royal Society of Literature. A regular contributor of articles and reviews to various UK newspapers and magazines, she is also the author of three widely acclaimed novels: *The Grown-Ups*, *Electricity*, and *Flight*.